GAMES BETWEEN GODS

GAMES BETWEEN GODS

ELYSIUM'S MULTIVERSE | BOOK 5

Ranyhin1

Podium

Podium

GAMES BETWEEN GODS

CHAPTER 1

The world was changing, and new empires were rising from the ashes of dead civilizations as the merged worlds creating Panu began to come together. The tutorials were over, the initial shock of the integration now past. It was a time of new beginnings.

The terraforming of the inner lands of the Thane Necropolis had been a blessing to many of those drawing power from the Unholy Foundational Pillar and all associated pillars, especially the undead, who made up nearly half of the population under the Thane siblings' rule after the ongoing wars had added more bodies to the mix. The bone garden was working overtime converting more and more bodies to the cause, and thousands of people across the multiverse below combat level five who were unaffiliated with any major factions according to system standards were allowed their own pilgrimage to the newly integrated world as well—bringing tidbits of knowledge and expertise with them that helped the new nation progress over time.

After the battle for Mandon, capital of Dawn, as well as the subjugation of the elvish kingdom of Tereen and the absorption of Chicago's surrounding territories across the Riven's Eye Wormhole, the Thane Necropolis was one of the leading powerhouses in their respective areas on either side of the planet. Refugees were in abundance, coming from areas of wilderness where civilization still hadn't taken root due to monster nests or raging conflicts with other natives who wanted to carve out a piece of the planet for themselves. Local warlords vying for control along with roaming gangs and bandits were commonplace, but these were also prime targets for many of Allie's forces—specifically targeted for leveling opportunities as well as keeping the peace and maintaining a constant flow of new bodies for the bone garden in Brightsville. Thus the reputation of the Thane Necropolis had become something of a double-edged sword, a safe haven for some—and a treacherous calling to death for others. World forums often had starkly contrasting views on the faction as well, some praising them for wiping out the majority of an invading force while others called Riven and Allie evil for their blatant disrespect for life. The "Butcher of Carnis" title had stuck to Allie after her incredibly brutal treatment of her elves during the war against Tereen, and Riven was outright known as a genocidal maniac.

There'd even been three other top-ten rankers who'd spoken about the rise of Riven's presence on the world forums along with the country he represented. Judith Marcina—the number one powerhouse on the worldwide leaderboard, three spots ahead of Riven's own number-four spot—had issued a statement proclaiming the existence of an undead uprising as a concern, but she hadn't outright condemned them. She'd publicly stated that if their factions should meet, she would concern herself with the necropolis then—but it might be years before that were to happen, and until then she was focused on her own newly created empire's expansion. Meanwhile, Nithkik Brutishvase, the number-five Dark Elf ranker, and Sinthil Tuk'tuk, the rank-eight Lizardian had very opposing views on a vampire being in the top ten that lined up with their Charisma allegiances. Nithkik, being a Dark Elf, had a negative Charisma allegiance by race alone and praised Riven's ruthlessness and magical prowess—while the opposite could be said for Sinthil the Lizardian, who called Riven a madman after witnessing what he'd done to Daskus, city of canyons, to bring back what he called "an abomination from the hells that should never have been allowed onto this mortal plane" in reference to Athela.

Yet despite all the attention Riven had received from Elysium's showcasing of his exploits, he wasn't very invested in what people had to say about him. Mostly he ignored them entirely and was far more focused on the important things that were close to home.

Vampires from a local faction in the underdark had made contact in Deepnest concerning the world quest of the vampiric elder god. The dwarvish kingdom of Brya had fallen after their king had been slain by Riven, and it was being incorporated as another vassal state—but it would take time and some reeling in of their ratkin allies that still had a deep-seated hate for the conquered dwarves. Chalgathi's next quest was upcoming in less than three months from now, and the capital city of Dawn was still being rebuilt after the attack from Rippenvire. The Blood Moon Requiem was on the brink of an internal civil war after Jalel and Lord Barimont had been slain, resulting in multiple noble houses having their low-leveled elites enter into an all-out battle with one another on Panu, and Kathrine had even left to go back home for the time being to discuss family matters until her parents made sure things were settling down. The lesser lords and ladies of House Wraithtide were also scheduled for a meeting with Riven and Allie in upcoming days, and General Viku had stationed an entire garrison of House Wraithtide's own F-grade elites at level 90 apiece in the vampiric compound on Panu while simultaneously letting Riven know that there would be much talk on the matter of empire politics upon his projection's arrival.

All in all, given the recent events, Riven should have been rather busy.
Should have been.

The sunset cast brilliant orange-yellow hues on the horizon across a sprawling sea of grasslands, sending shimmering trails off the winding rivers etched into the landscape.

Fay squealed in excitement, reeling in the line on her fishing pole with wild abandon while sitting cross-legged on the shoreline. Her white Sunday dress matched her hair, which had been pulled back into a ponytail, and a wide, thatched hat shielded her eyes from the sun. "Oh! Oh, I think I finally got one!"

Riven laughed at her giddy display, sitting next to her a few feet away from his wheelchair that'd been parked on a grassy patch leading out to rolling hills and fields. "Good! Maybe that bait Azmoth got us is doing the trick after all."

Riven looked right to where Athela's growing pile of fish was being cooked and snacked on by the other campers here with them. His red eyes, cloaked by a black hood to block out the sun now that he wasn't wearing Messenger, shifted to meet Athela's own when she nuzzled up to him. "Athela, you damn cheater."

"Cheater?!" Athela repeated, aghast at the accusation and bringing up both pitch-black hands to pinch his cheeks like one would do to a cute puppy before smugly kissing him. "I would never cheat! My bloody strings are just more viable than your fishing poles!"

Athela wore an outfit nearly identical to Fay's own after the two demonic women had gone shopping for their trip together in Brightsville. Her bare feet dug into the sand and she mockingly grinned down at the fishing pole Riven held.

A large campfire crackled behind them by a couple yards where Luke Blissfallen, an old elf and one of Riven's thralls, was cooking some of the fish on sticks. He was deep in conversation with Genua, Riven's other thrall, who'd accompanied them on the journey with her daughter Len—the two older elves having a rather good time teaching the little blonde girl how to skin a fish and what spices to use in the soup they were making.

"You're making that face again," Fay said, finally pulling in the trout that she'd hooked with a knowing smile. "They chose to attack you first, Riven. Your decision was a sound one."

Riven grimaced with guilt, continuing to stare over to where Len was dangling her legs from a log and looking up to her mother with wide, wondering eyes and a bright smile. "I can't help but feel guilty. That little girl lost her big sister and her father because of me."

"She doesn't know it was you." Athela said from the other side, standing up and brushing herself off before turning around with her hands on her hips. "Genua never told her the truth about how they died."

"What did Genua tell her, then?"

Athela shrugged, then walked over to get Riven's wheelchair. "Perhaps you should ask. But come on! Don't be a downer—we're having fun tonight and all your friends are here!"

"She's right, you know," Fay stated, giving his hand a warm squeeze before standing up. "Cut loose tonight. You deserve it after everything you've been through."

"After everything we ALL have been through," Athela corrected the succubus, spanking the other young woman and getting a yelp before grinning to herself and bringing the wheelchair over. "Let's go, big boy. Lahn and friends are back from their walk. It's time to gather around for the meal!"

Riven glanced back over his shoulder, smiling in the dying light of day at the assortment of people present. "Yes, I suppose you're right."

He took her hand, hoisted himself up, and took a seat as she wheeled him around to join the main group.

Aside from Luke, Genua, and Genua's daughter Len, there were quite a few other familiar faces sitting in folding chairs or on logs cut from the few trees that scattered themselves onto the rolling hills and flatlands around them. Gurth'Rok, the orc chieftain–turned–vampire, and an orc woman he was courting were present and off to the side. Dr. Brass was—as ever—wearing his old white coat, but he had ditched the glasses after his body had undergone vampiric changes to become a younger man with sleek silver hair. The doctor was laughing and joking alongside Mara, Nin, and Vin—the three black-clad necromancers seated highest in the tiers of Allie's underlings running the necropolis. Azmoth and Fimrindle were seeing who could skip stones along the water better, pelting the skeletal, undead drake Tyranus while he napped in the deeper waters farther in. Allie, Lahn, and Lahn's mother, Shovi, were just now rounding a bend in the river and wading through ankle-high grass, with Allie occasionally zapping mosquitoes with her death mana. Shovi was pushing her own son's wheelchair as the three talked and joked with one another rather loudly. Allie was obviously drunk but was having a grand time, while Lahn was still recovering physically from his temporary transition into an angelic being after fighting the vampire lord who'd tried to take Allie as his own— but it was doubtful Lahn's soul would ever fully recover in terms of being able to wield magic or martial arts again.

Though the young man still had hope—his eyes had been grown back and he was in better physical condition than he'd ever been before, despite the complete loss of his left arm in the fight at the vampire compound. The stump where his arm used to be still retained significant residue from the possession, however, and the residue of the angelic possession had been so etched into his body that it would take massive amounts of possibly dangerous surgical interventions to fully regrow it given the knowledge Riven and Allie—or even Gaia—had now.

Otherwise the parasite that'd been exorcised by Fay had left toxins and scar tissue that had been eradicated by the angelic possession, and his physical recovery had increased threefold. It wouldn't be long before he didn't need a wheelchair at all.

There was also the topic of miracles. Miracles and divinity worked differently than spells and mana, or martial arts and stamina, by essentially summoning the power of another entity or the pillars themselves rather than using a person's own innate strength as a power source. It was possible, according to Luke, that Lahn could potentially utilize miracle-type abilities in the future despite the absolute destruction of his core and pillars.

Although the act would still be far harder to do than it would have been before his pillars and core were traumatized—and no one they knew had access to holy miracles, either. Even among the entire military of Dawn, miracles were apparently quite rare.

"Feeling better, I see," Riven said, phrasing it as a statement rather than a question, when Lahn was rolled up to the fire next to him. "You're looking healthier."

Lahn waved Allie off after she gave him a peck on the cheek, grinning as she and his mother joined Fay, Genua, Luke, and Athela at a picnic table right behind Riven on the left.

"Yes, I feel amazing." Lahn smiled back, then gestured to the wheelchair Riven sat in while the flames of the fire cast shadows across his body. "Looks like you've joined my club."

Riven blinked, then snorted a laugh and clasped his hands together—enjoying the warmth of the orange glow. "I certainly did. Hopefully not for too long for either of us. Everything okay with your eyes?"

"Your healers did a wonderful job; there are no problems at all."

THUMP

The ground shuddered just slightly when Gaia's small figure slammed into the earth beside them, and the dryad-like demigoddess gave everyone she'd startled a wave before creating a chair out of earthen soil to lean back in lazily while taking up residence next to the two temporarily crippled men. "Hello, children. How is everything?"

Riven raised an eyebrow her way. "Good to see you made it, Gaia. Wasn't sure you were coming."

"I never miss an opportunity to gossip."

"Is that so?"

"It is. Try being cooped up for as long as I have, and you, too, would seek as much social activity as possible given the chance. Thank you for inviting me."

Riven gave the little dryad girl, or what **appeared** to look like a little girl, a nod with a warm smile. "I never did get to thank you face-to-face for how you helped Athela. Thanks again for what you did—it means more to me than you know."

"She helped Athela? How?" Lahn asked curiously, scratching the back of his head with his pointer finger.

"She donated a tiny piece of her soul to Athela when Athela was killed, which helped re-form her from a mere speck that my gluttonous miracle was able to acquire."

"Oh. That's intense. Is that a normal thing? For demigods to give out pieces of their soul?"

Gaia snorted a laugh at the young man Allie was so interested in. "It is certainly not a normal thing, but it was the right decision. My soul has already begun mending itself, and in time it will be like the piece taken from it was never gone to begin with. Also—here."

Gaia extended a hand over Riven's and then dropped an amulet into his palm. It was sleekly crafted from the wood of a tree, circular and akin to a thick quarter, with a tiny flower carved into the front face. "What you asked for. A replacement for the one you broke, and somewhat upgraded so that it can act with Fay's illusions more fluidly."

[Gaia's Heartwood Token (Epic): Wearing this token around your neck allows you to suppress any Charisma effects you may have, suppresses your vampiric qualities as well as the demonic qualities of your contracted familiars, and changes your status page information to represent a level-55 human. Those with identifier classes at a high enough level can circumvent this passive ability.]

The amulet she'd given him was spectacular, and a wide grin spread across his pale face as he thanked the demigoddess and stowed it away. "This will come in handy when I visit Hakim."

"And Julie!" Athela called pointedly, taking a ketchup bottle and slathering the stuff all over a hot dog and handing it to Riven. "Julie is my favorite. By the way, these hot dogs look nothing like actual dogs. I'd been expecting a flaming canine or something."

"Yes, I was wondering about that myself . . ." Shovi stated with a raised eyebrow—having already finished two of them and starting her third. The usually well-dressed lady of the court was wearing a pair of jeans and a T-shirt with an electric guitar on the front—some of Allie's old clothes—since Shovi had made it known that she didn't own any traveling gear. "It is rather good, though."

Allie hummed in amusement and popped the cork off another wine bottle, motioning for Genua to slit her wrist. Genua did so and let a good amount of her blood settle into the wine before Allie gave a heads-up that she could stop, and the soon-to-be elf thrall gave a nod before twisting her hand and sealing the wound shut.

"Can all thralls do that?" Shovi asked curiously.

Genua shrugged. "I can, and I'm only ready for the transition. I haven't taken the dive yet. Luke? Can you do that?"

"I can." The old man acknowledged her question with a grim frown. "However, not nearly as fast as you can. That was impressive, Genua. Perhaps it has something to do with your other features . . . ?"

He gestured to the woman's reddening eyes. "I don't recall ever having heard of thralls gaining vampiric traits."

"They're not supposed to." Allie confirmed with a nod and a drunken side-bob of her head. Then she hiccuped. "It's weird. You're weird, Genua!"

"How many has Allie had to drink?" Riven asked Lahn under his breath while the two men continued staring over their shoulders. "She's plastered."

"Too many to count," Lahn confirmed with a chuckle.

Riven's eyes shifted between his sister and the thrall-to-be, and he shook his head with a smirk before turning back to the campfire and biting into his own hot dog. Immediately the taste of a perfectly cooked bratwurst caused his mouth to nearly explode with saliva, and he let out a deep, content sigh while moaning loudly amid his slow chewing.

"Riven?! Was that you?!" Fay asked incredulously with raised eyebrows. "You must really be enjoying your food!"

Smacking his lips and nodding enthusiastically, he only chuckled through his nose while continuing to eat. It'd been way, way too long since he'd had some basic, bad-for-your-arteries Americanized food.

[Tear of the Blood God (Legendary F-Grade Dao Treasure): Must have a bonded, contractual partner to use. Reveals insights into the Dao of the Blood subpillar and drastically increases the resilience and size of both partners' Blood subpillars after use regardless of what your insights gain for you.]

Athela handled the large, glowing, tear-shaped red gemstone in her hands carefully, sitting cross-legged in front of where Riven was doing the same—albeit being supported by Azmoth due to his weakened state. Fay sat to the side, continuing to chomp and crunch on the s'mores Allie and Lahn had so enthusiastically begun making repeatedly after Lahn had joined her in getting drunk and getting the munchies.

"I hope this works!" Fay said, smiling widely, absolutely on top of the world ever since rejoining the group and after recognizing that there was no ill will held toward her for her abrupt leave of absence.

With her words came a wink from Athela, and the succubus blushed slightly—something that Riven did not miss due to his concern about how the two would interact after Fay returned. To his surprise, things were going well—very well, in fact.

The odd new twist to how she and Athela were acting toward one another over the past two days was somewhat odd to Riven, as they were a little handsy, which was certainly a surprise, but he didn't mind in the least and was just happy to have Fay back. He was getting suspicious concerning their behavior, but if he was right on the money of just what had happened when Athela had decided to try and have Fay come back—he couldn't say he was mad about it. If anything they were making it kind of obvious, and he was curious as to how that'd play into his relationships with both of them.

"All right, so how do we do this?" Riven asked curiously, appreciating Azmoth's supporting hand when the muscles in his lower back began to spasm and his shattered pillars twitched with electrical currents.

Athela frowned in concern at Riven's brief grimace of pain, but she placed the hand-size ruby-colored crystal in between them—continuing to grasp the object with her right hand. "We can try touching it at the same time. Probably our best bet."

A loud splash echoed from farther down the river, where some of the others had taken to swimming under the starlight. Riven only hesitated a moment due to the distraction before placing a steady hand over top of Athela's. When he wrapped his fingers around hers and let his skin touch the red crystal tear underneath, the red light inside the treasure began to build.

"See? Easy as pie." Athela winked at him fondly, only for her eyes to roll back alongside his own when a flood of power tore through their minds—and began to roar to life as the energy made contact with their Blood subpillars.

Or, in Riven's case, where his Blood subpillar should have been.

CHAPTER 2

Crimson threads tore out from the treasure and into Riven's soul, but he didn't scream—nor did he feel pain. The threads were soothing, caressing his damaged core and the obliterated Blood subpillar that'd been reduced to fragments.

He watched as they intertwined with each of them, collecting them up and pulling the shards together—only to frown in confusion when other, pitch-black threads flew forward from his fragmented Shadow subpillar and intertwined. He felt his Path of Red and Black radiate and synergize between the two pillars after that, a shudder going through his body and mind, harmonizing and . . .

And stitching the two pillars together?

Riven's eyes widened, and his hand instinctively tightened around Athela's while his mind's eye focused on his internal soul. Something like this had happened before when his Blood and Shadow subpillars had connected to one another—but this time it was far more than just connecting.

They were locking themselves together with crystallized bridges, one after the other. They were extending. They were becoming far, far larger than they'd been before—like a mixed tapestry painted between the two monoliths of black and red.

The two colors swirled and meshed, the fragments coming together to create something entirely new—aided by the power of the Dao treasure he and Athela were holding in unison. His Blood subpillar then began to grow, and then grow even more. It expanded upward off the base at the soul core it was attached to, surging forward until it slowed down and stopped at nearly twice the size of the previous one he'd had as shards continued to slam into it, filling the cracks and crevices with more and more pieces of its shattered remnants.

But then the swirling shards of his two meshing pillars all simultaneously twitched, and the fusion between black and red stopped right as his orbiting sin core—an ominous black and deep-purple orb—came to rest directly over the enlarged Blood subpillar and its subserviently bonded Shadow subpillar.

"Riven . . ."

The voice echoed in his mind as a sea of whispers, causing him to tense and shudder when a cold dread overcame him. A deep, demonic laugh of glee followed, and the voice continued to whisper into his ear.

"Ah . . . You can finally understand me . . . Can't you?"

The sin core pulsed, he felt his body tear at the seams when the voice called to him, and Riven's senses tingled when a maw opened up in the black and deep-purple sphere. Rows of teeth let out a low hiss, and he realized the voice was coming from here.

He nodded hesitantly, not sure if he was saying the words aloud—or if he was just thinking them. "I can. Hello, Gluttony . . . I'm surprised you're showing yourself in person to a little peon like me. To what do I owe the honor?"

The maw's laughter roared to life, and Riven felt blood begin trickling from his closed eyes, nose, ears, and mouth. Riven vaguely heard shocked yelps and cursing, but he held up a hand to let the others know he was all right—though his body certainly took a toll just by talking to the entity. And it wasn't just a piece of the entity, either—oh no, this was the brain, the main aspect, the collective consciousness. This was far different.

"What are you doing in my soul?" Riven asked, growing more curious than anything else. He sensed no malice from the sin, and he doubted there'd be any anyway, considering how it'd saved his life when Elysium's tribulation had tried to kill him. "Just sightseeing, perhaps?"

"Testing the waters is all . . ." the sin replied with a hiss, the soul aperture around him shuddering with every word. "Repairing and preparing you for what is to come . . . and it will come sooner than you think. I came to say hello so that you are not terrified of the bond when it solidifies in upcoming weeks."

At this, Riven's eyebrows raised. "Bond?"

Gluttony's mouth widened, and slowly it began to reveal a maze of tendrils coming out of the pit of its throat. They were dark, pulsing with deep-purple and black energies that connected and pulled at the rotating shards that hadn't already sunk into the somewhat-restored pillars. The tendrils then flashed away and were gone before Riven even knew what to make of them.

"It has already begun . . ." Gluttony said in satisfaction. "Your soul, my soul, and the symbiotic relationship that has helped you already not just once—but twice."

Riven belched blood just from being in the presence of the great sin, and his vampiric regeneration kicked into high gear, fighting off the cracks and crevices of sin energy now leaking out of his skin. He could hear the worry in the others' voices, but they were a distant call—and he yet again held up a hand to stop them from interfering with the process. He needed to know what Gluttony wanted with him. "Symbiosis entails a mutually beneficial relationship. I hope you're not using this in lieu of being a parasite."

"I am certainly not . . ." the sin retorted gleefully, shifting its many teeth along the sin core placatingly. "The alternative is impossible despite my wishes. I truly do wish to coexist . . . but you must let me in for the bond to fully connect. Otherwise talking to you as a mortal will forever cause a violent reaction such as the one you are experiencing now. As a harbinger of my blood, it is the greatest honor one can be given. The others . . . my worshippers . . . even the other holders of my shards . . . they don't understand what it is I truly am. Or what it is I desire. Nor do you . . . but that isn't important now. What is important is that I can help—as I have already begun to do. May I pose a question?"

Riven snorted a laugh, despite numerous arteries bursting when he did. "Sure. go ahead."

Gluttony paused. "Did you not find it odd that your Harbinger of Gluttony class, and your Harbinger Soul Clone, manifested itself as my visage—rather than your own?"

Riven's eyes narrowed at this. He'd been considering this exact thing for a while now, even back in Daskus, when he'd somehow been able to summon Gluttony's maw in the sky as he destroyed the city in a wrath unlike anything he'd ever experienced before—and that was before he'd acquired the soul clone on his status page. Then, very recently, he'd called Gluttony's visage from the sky and then the earth underneath him to battle against Elysium's will when it tried to strike him down for using Malignant Prophecy one too many times.

He pulled up an old notification to reread it in his mind's eye.

[Harbinger of Gluttony, Sin Class, Secondary Class, has finally finished its construction. Harbinger Soul Clone is now finished. +2 Sturdiness, +9 free points per level will now be distributed with each level-up.]

Harbinger of Gluttony (Sin Class Title)—the Harbinger of Gluttony is the most basic sin class specific to the Original Sin of Gluttony and creates a superimposed wraithlike soul clone, a symbiote created from sin inside your body, allowing it to strike out at close distances against any nearby enemy. +2 Sturdiness, +9 free points per level.

The suspicion had been there . . . but . . . he didn't know what to think.

"You've been planning the transition for a while now, haven't you?" Riven asked cautiously. "Summoning your visage isn't normal for a harbinger. Is it? The description of my soul clone states it should be a superimposed image of myself. Instead, I got you. I had you even before I knew what a soul clone was."

The sin laughed. "Envy may be the schemer of us sins, but that doesn't mean I can't concoct plans of my own. You are a unique vessel with an even more unique situation after your soul was shattered, and we sins that spawned the first of demonkind—just like the commandments that the angels hail from—cannot manifest into a true life without a symbiosis unless all shards have been collected from our shattered bodies."

Riven grimaced.

"That brings up a lot of questions. Can you tell me what exactly the commandments are? Did you have an actual body of your own in the past other than the great maw I usually see? Why me? And just what is it that you desire, if it isn't to simply consume everything, as I'd assumed?"

The maw seemed to smile, and the ocean of whispers endured. "Those are questions that can all be answered in time . . . but you must accept my bond to find out. When the time comes, it will appear as a contract much like those of your demonic familiars . . . accept it, and I will be reborn."

"Reborn? How?"

This time, it was the sin that hesitated. "Let us just say that I wish to experience life once more . . . not this . . . everlasting prison I find myself in. I wish to be free of the memories that chain me here. Meanwhile, you desire power, power that I can help you acquire. Accept the contract and find out. The time is coming rather quickly now . . . The terms will be in your favor. I'm excited to see what you'll do."

The visage of the maw on his sin core vanished, and a torrent of black, red, and deep-purple energy exploded to life—with searing agony accompanying it.

Riven didn't physically blink, but it certainly felt that way when he found himself standing beside Athela on a vast ocean of red. The blood moon was half buried on the horizon, encompassing nearly 40 percent of the sky above with a single figure outlined in black against the red backdrop—floating there nearly fifty feet above the ocean his feet rested on.

Ripples of liquid radiated from his position when he turned to look at Athela, but the demoness was in a trance of her own—somewhere far beyond her current state while lights flashed in her eyes and her mouth twitched. "Athela?"

Abruptly the area around him shifted again, and he found himself floating beside the figure in black—red eyes gleaming underneath a dark hood as orbs of blood hovered around him to match the crimson landscape and the bright-red moon behind them both. An aura bloomed from the figure before Riven as if the very skies around them were bending to the hooded man's will, and he gently lifted a hand to show the artifact Riven and Athela had used.

It was the Tear of the Blood God.

Riven's eyes narrowed, but he found himself unable to talk anymore, just as the hooded man shattered the crystallized tear with a chuckle, and the oceans around him tore apart and soared into the heavens like a reverse avalanche. A sea of skeletal bodies was revealed under the depths of the ocean when the blood finally cleared after hundreds of billions of gallons of the crimson fluid covered the sky to blot out the stars.

Wait . . . Riven had been here before. He'd seen visions of this place, hadn't he?

"Blood, Shadow, and Death. These are the three pillars the vampires were created from," the hooded figure said, turning his red gaze and with it forcing Riven's own toward the piles upon piles of dead far below them. "You have taken the first step by converging the paths of Shadow and Blood, but you lack the trio in its entirety. Descendant, you show promise . . . otherwise Gluttony would not involve itself so directly in you. But you need to broaden your horizons now, before you hit the E-grade, or you will fall short of what you could otherwise become. Death is a sister component to Blood in more ways than one. Why do you neglect it?"

Riven's eyes were allowed to drift upward into the dark hood that outlined the mysterious man in front of him, but he felt his jaw remain locked. Riven assumed it was a rhetorical question when the man in the vision turned his gaze back upon the mountains of bones underneath them, and then he held out one hand—summoning a humanoid skeleton from the depths to hover in front of them like a rag doll.

The unknown man stared Riven down for a long, long time after that. Longer than Riven was comfortable with, until a single red finger rose out of the black cloak flowing around him—and touched Riven on the forehead. "Descendant, I bestow upon you insight."

Red cracks flashed across Riven's forehead where the man's red finger was suddenly digging into his skull, and Riven screamed in agony as images flashed through his mind at the speed of light. A field of battle on a distant planet roared to the forefront, where men skewered one another with blade and spear. Their bodies leaked lifeblood onto the soil in oceans of red, and their corpses dropped to the ground by the thousands. He experienced one by one the sensations each of them suffered, the sensation of dying, of losing life that their blood had kept intact. He experienced the darkness, the shadow, that overcame their spirits as they transitioned into the afterlife.

Then he experienced a reversal of that cycle, never allowing the cycle into true death to be completed. Shadow turned to a pale imitation of light, and crimson fluid washed through rotted corpses as necromancers summoned the decaying souls of the dead back into their bodies. They weren't the same as they'd once been, but pieces and fragments of these souls came together to form new beings—once again embracing undeath as a new form of life. The crimson liquid that'd saturated the ground rose up and embraced these new, unholy abominations, and three symbols began to flash in Riven's mind over and over again on repeat.

A scythe, a red teardrop, and a black sun.

They flashed over and over, replaying without stopping, faster and faster—overlain on the images of the battle, the necromancers, the forward and reversed cycles that continued to slam themselves into his consciousness. He saw them rise up and roar to the sky above, saw their bodies begin to flicker with red mana, and then saw the blood moon flash before his eyes one final time.

He let out an internal scream, his soul core erupting and shattering on one end where a new subpillar tore into the soul aperture with a frenzy. Neon teal flecked with black illuminated the spot between and to the side of his Blood and Shadow subpillars, beginning to form bridging connections to these other two pillars when their shards began swirling to repair themselves yet again. The three were slowly beginning to become one.

Only for the symbol of the great maw to completely press itself against his Dao vision and overtake his mind entirely. All other visions faded, with the teeth of Gluttony snapping down on them and obliterating them from his mind.

[Your Blood subpillar has been repaired and has grown significantly.

Your Shadow subpillar has been partially repaired. Your soul core remains cracked and in ruins, and your sin core is beginning to fuse with your soul core in its damaged state. You are now oriented toward the Death subpillar.]

[New Spell Learned: Legionaries of the Blood God (Death/Blood) (Tier 2): This is a temporary summoning spell that does not require minion slots. You may summon eight Elite-class Bloodstricken Undead from the Blood God's realm, equal in combat level to your own, and may designate whether or not you wish to summon Blood Knights, Blood Sorcerers, Blood Assassins, or a combination of the three when you do so. Undead are nonsentient and last for five minutes before disappearing. One-day cooldown time. Very high mana cost.]

[Gluttony has incorporated all the following ability properties from Jackal and Messenger as Sin abilities that you can cast regardless of wearing these items or not: Devour, Identifier's Clause, Beastform.]

[Black Lightning (Shadow) has finished manifesting and can now be cast at will.]

[Your bond with Athela grows stronger. Mind Link has been established between yourself and this minion, allowing for telepathic communication.]

Riven slowly opened his eyes, realizing he was covered in his own blood, which had seeped from all the holes on his head. It stained the ground underneath him as he sat cross-legged, and he took in a deep breath. Fay was staring wide-eyed at him while Athela lay crumpled in a heap on Fay's lap. Azmoth sat beside Riven, still holding him up in a sitting position.

Starlight twinkled up above, and the sounds of laughter filled the air while the rest of the camp went on about their lives as if nothing had ever happened.

"I can feel it. Your mana . . . part of it is back, at least," Fay said with a hesitant smile. "Am I right? And don't worry about Athela, she's just tired from the insights she got. Said she made a lot of progress and learned two new abilities!"

"Ah, I was about to ask. Good to know, and yes—I was able to use the treasure to repair part of my soul after all. Just like I'd guessed, but in a rather roundabout and unexpected way." Riven smiled back at her, a warm and comforting one. His body was still very weak, and his soul wasn't completely repaired by any means, but it was certainly stronger. And just like Fay had said, he could now summon magic to him again.

A storm razor bloomed over his right palm when he held out his hand, the bloody, pronged, circular blade of magic shifting over his hand in the colors of black and red. It rapidly transitioned to a storm ball at a thought, the more explosive and less piercing variant of the magical attack, before it vanished entirely. Black Lightning sparked along his fingers, dancing around them at a whim, before he used his Devour ability on a nearby wildflower without much thought. A maw grew along Riven's outstretched palm and a cord of dark tendrils ripped the flower up, pulling it into the jaws that snapped shut and receded immediately.

Glancing over at Jackal, which had taken its canine form, Riven imitated the creature by abruptly shifting his own body into a flickering black jackal, too—complete with red eyes to imitate the weapon's secondary body.

The two dogs just stared at each other while Azmoth grunted in excitement and Fay gasped, though other than for subterfuge purposes Riven couldn't really see a reason to use the ability quite yet.

He shifted back into his vampire form without having lost any of the items he was wearing. "Neat, but not sure how it'll be used in the future. Wanna see my last new spell?"

Fay raised an eyebrow in amusement. "You have more?"

"Indeed!" Riven chuckled, then used the last spell he'd acquired from his Dao vision of the mountains of skeletons underneath a bloody sea—and the three sigils. "I have some theories about the Dao treasure we just used, and I don't think it was necessarily for a Dao insight itself. And it turns out that the Shadow and Death subpillars are related to Blood in a lot more intricate ways than I'd expected. The experience was very complicated . . . Anyways, let's take a look, shall we?"

Shifting his focus to the river's edge, he activated his temporary summoning spell.

Eight flashes of light illuminated the small beach, and eight hooded skulls etched with crimson runes on their foreheads stared with equally crimson orbs for eyes. Four were heavily armored with red claymores and thick red plate mail. Two held thin, wicked daggers dripping blood mana in each hand and were strapped in red leathers, while the last two wore crimson robes and held staves with ruby orbs that flickered blood mana in the same way his own arms did when he summoned Blood Lance.

Each of their status reads was that of an elite, with gold lettering outlining their titles.

[Summoned Blood Knight, Bloodstricken Undead, Level 133 Elite]
[Summoned Blood Knight, Bloodstricken Undead, Level 133 Elite]
[Summoned Blood Knight, Bloodstricken Undead, Level 133 Elite]
[Summoned Blood Knight, Bloodstricken Undead, Level 133 Elite]
[Summoned Blood Sorcerer, Bloodstricken Undead, Level 133 Elite]
[Summoned Blood Sorcerer, Bloodstricken Undead, Level 133 Elite]
[Summoned Blood Assassin, Bloodstricken Undead, Level 133 Elite]
[Summoned Blood Assassin, Bloodstricken Undead, Level 133 Elite]

CHAPTER 3

The undead legionnaires were something else. Riven had watched alongside many of the others under the stars as he commanded them to battle one another, and although it'd only lasted five minutes, the battle was a sight to behold.

They were classed as elites, each poised at his own level, which was far above the norm on this planet, and the fields erupted in a brutal free-for-all as they clashed. Storms of blood energies and shock waves of clashing weapons eradicated much of the plant life for a solid five hundred yards, and Riven wasn't entirely sure he'd come out unscathed if he'd been pitted against all eight at once.

Unfortunately the fun didn't last, and as the night crept on, it was time for him to say goodbye. At least for now.

"I'll be back for our meeting with the fam," Riven said, giving his sister a hug when she bent down to throw her arms around his chest. "Feel free to call me whenever you want to talk otherwise. The coms engineers have really improved their craft, given we don't have satellites anymore."

Allie chuckled, ruffling his hair and kissing him on the cheek before backing up and evaluating Riven alongside his three demons. "You going to get a fourth soon?"

"A fourth?" Riven shot Athela, Fay, and Azmoth a sidelong glance. "Before Chalgathi's quest, sure. Yattazi leaving like that left a bad taste in my mouth, though. I'll give it some time; there's no rush."

Allie nodded sagely, leaning against Fimrindle's thin metal body. "Gotcha. Well, I do feel better now that you've got some of your abilities back, but take it easy. No serious fights until you're fully recovered and can walk again without hobbling like an old hag."

Riven stuck out his tongue and laughed when she did it right back. "Fine. I'm treating this like a miniature vacation, anyways. Luke, Genua, Len, it's time to go. It should be noon on the other side of the planet and Hakim will be waiting for us."

Len grabbed her mother's skirt and followed the thrall-to-be to where the demons were gathered alongside Riven's wheelchair, smiling hesitantly up at him and hiding halfway behind her mother's legs. She still didn't know exactly what'd happened between Riven and her family all those months ago, but her mother had told her they'd had a falling-out, so she'd been rather shy ever since and kind of awkward.

Riven himself had been even more awkward, and guilt still gnawed at him every time he looked down at her. Nevertheless, he gave his kindest smile and tried to avoid the child's gaze afterward, nodding to Genua and then Luke after they'd gathered the supplies they'd need for the next week. "All ready?"

"We are, Master," Genua said with a slight bow.

Luke just nodded with a grin and gave a thumbs-up. "This is how you all do it, right?"

"The thumbs-up?"

"Yes?"

"It means yes, or good—a positive connotation."

"Then I've got it down!"

Riven chuckled and lifted his hand, summoning Jackal to his hand—the weapon flew forward and landed in the open palm while his fingers gripped the solid black metal streaming with small rivers of blood.

Allie, Gurth'Rok, Dr. Brass, Mara, and all the others waved their goodbyes while the campfire continued to crackle behind them.

"Have fun and get some relax time in!" Lahn called out when the portal erupted in front of Riven's spear-staff. "You always look like you're about to have a stroke!"

Riven blinked, then laughed heartily and flipped him off when he realized the young man was trying to make a joke. "Fuck off—just because you're my sister's boyfriend doesn't mean you get to talk shit!"

Smiling and waving at the now furiously blushing Lahn, who sat in his own wheelchair, Riven immediately wondered whether or not they'd made it an official thing yet.

Probably not, at least not in Allie's queen persona, given Allie was going to go back to the royal academy again on her time off. The vast majority of people in Dawn—more to the point, the people at the Imperial Academy—didn't know who and what she was outside of Lahn's family and that Gleetus guy they'd already killed.

Whatever floated her boat. Riven was just happy she was happy.

Putting on Gaia's token, the red in his eyes began to fade to blue. The same could be said for Genua, and his three demons all abruptly changed as well. Athela's black hair remained but her eyes and skin became more human, adopting the look of a raven-haired, young track star. Fay adopted the same tanned blonde look she'd had back in Mandon, when she'd gone on a date with him to meet with the king of Dawn, and Azmoth turned into a hulking, muscular, four-armed barbarian lacking a face.

[Gaia's Heartwood Token (Epic): Wearing this token around your neck allows you to suppress any Charisma effects you may have, suppresses your vampiric qualities as well as the demonic qualities of your contracted familiars, and changes your status page information

to represent a level-55 human. Those with identifier classes at a high enough level can circumvent this passive ability.]

Riven raised an eyebrow Gaia's way with a small grin, hiking a thumb at Azmoth. "That supposed to happen?"

The demigoddess chuckled dryly. "I may have not tweaked it appropriately. Fay? Would you be a dear and fix it?"

The succubus tipped her flat-brimmed straw hat with a curtsy. "Of course!"

Her hallucinations kicked in, and a firm jawline along with deep-brown eyes and a nose all appeared—along with the disappearance of Azmoth's extra set of arms. "There we go!"

Azmoth looked down at his body, feeling his extra limbs and the eellike maws along his back—but not seeing them. "Looks good. Thanks, Fay, good to have back."

Riven's face softened, and he nodded in turn. "Agreed."

Fay paused, then blushed a deep red and kicked at the ground when Athela nudged her out of her stupor. "Thanks."

Hakim leaned against the wreckage of what had once been the Red Hand's home. Few in their reclusive part of the world cared that the gang was all dead now. If anything, it'd been cause for celebration. Hakim wasn't the only one they'd tried to shake down, and things had been a hell of a lot more peaceful with them gone.

Though there'd certainly been others trying to fill in that power gap in the meantime. But they were too busy dealing with other groups to worry about small fry like him.

"This was the day, right?" Julie asked from where she sat against a tree, dressed in a healer's robe that gave her a slight boost to Holy healing miracles and with her red hair pulled into a ponytail. "I don't like being here more than I have to be. Not after what happened to Caleb."

Tim, her brother, nodded in agreement. "I don't blame you. But yes, this is the right time. They'll be here soon. Riven wouldn't stand us up—especially not after Mom told him she'd bring sandwiches!"

He winked at his mother, Tanya, who had huffed and puffed on the hike here while carrying a large basket of the damn things. An ice crystal bought from a mage in town kept the food cold and preserved. They were all ham and cheese, because those were a lot easier to come by than other things like peanut butter or jelly, and she'd already announced that they'd be headed to her favorite spot near the orchards after Riven, Athela, and their friends got here.

"Don't make fun of me. I see that look you're giving me." Tanya slapped her hands onto her hips and pouted at her teenage son fervently. "I brought you into this world and I can take you out of it, mister! Don't make me come over there!"

"Better listen to your mom or I'll hear all about it." Hakim grinned with a wink, only to startle when a portal lit up inside the wreckage of the cabin. He perked up, stood straight, and helped Julie to her feet before turning around in his fur-covered leathers to watch. "Looks like they're back!"

Athela came through first, though they took a moment to recognize her due to the sundress and flat-brimmed wicker hat she wore. In combination with her more human features and skin color, they could have mistaken her for someone else if she hadn't waved at them.

"Hey, guys!" Athela called, running over enthusiastically and throwing her arms around Julie—causing the redheaded young woman to laugh. "I missed you! What've you all been up to while I've been gone?! A lot's happened since we last talked—boy, do I have stories to tell!"

Azmoth came next, sizing Hakim up with a spout of flames from his mouth that briefly disrupted the illusion before walking beyond the portal's exit. Then came Genua, holding Len's hand, the two elves followed by Riven, who was pushed through by Fay, and then finally Luke came up in the rear.

The portal snapped closed behind them in an instant, and Tanya's eyes lit up at the sight of them all. "Oh wow! You brought more people than I'd expected. Good thing I made so many sandwiches! I was worried I'd had too many!"

The middle-aged woman slapped the side of her basket with a giggle. "Who're the rest of these people? I've only met Athela and Azmoth . . . and . . . Wait, is that the succubus you used to have? Didn't she leave? Where's the snake?"

"She came back—long and complicated story. And the snake is gone. Another long story," Athela cut in, putting an arm around Fay's shoulders to save her from having to explain. "As for the others . . ."

Riven motioned for them to introduce themselves.

"My name is Genua, and this is my daughter Len," the elf stated very properly, flattening out her maid outfit and clasping her hands in front of her while giving them a polite nod. "You can think of me as Riven's servant."

Len waved nervously from behind her mother's leg. "Hi."

"I am a servant as well," the older elf stated, his white hair pulled back into a ponytail to match Julie's—but he had the stature of a confident and happy man with wrinkles to match frequent smiles. "Occasionally I'm also a sparring partner."

Tanya's mouth quirked up with surprise and amusement. "Servants? Riven, I knew you were on the leaderboard, but I guess I just put it together—you're rich, too. Aren't you?"

Hakim and Tim were a little weirded out, however.

"What happened to you? Are you okay?" Hakim asked, motioning with his axe to the wheelchair Riven sat in. "Don't you have healing properties due to your vampirism? I saw your neck get snapped once and you were fine."

"Probably just an act to cover his identity, like the illusions he has on," Julie said with a gesture. "Makes sense to me. It's what I'd do."

Riven opened his mouth to disagree but thought better of it and shrugged with a gentle smile—then winked. He didn't want to burden them with unnecessary worry, because it was very likely he'd be 100 percent soon enough. "Caught me. It's just part of the act."

His demonic minions and thralls didn't even blink at the white lie.

Riven's gaze turned to the town in the distance, settled in between large hills near a glistening lake. This entire area was temperate forest, pines, oaks, and elms in abundance, and it made him think back to the days where he'd visited various parts of Utah in the Rocky Mountains. "Is that the one?"

They all turned to look with him.

"That's the one," Tim confirmed with a nod, hands resting on his belt. "Not sure what it used to be called, but now that a bunch of new people moved in post-integration—we all call it Jerbyville."

Riven raised an eyebrow in amusement, crossing his fingers wordlessly while his hood shielded his eyes from the rays of the sun. "Jerbyville? Really?"

"You can't judge us when your capital is named Brightsville," Hakim muttered with a grin.

"Fair enough. I definitely can't argue that one." Riven chuckled under his breath. "To be fair, I was going to change the name but never got around to it. Now that it's become a known entity, though, I don't think we're going to change it, as lame as the name actually is."

The closer they came to the town, the more outliers they saw in terms of cabins, huts, or tiny fenced-off communities. There weren't many of them, but the whole mountain-man theme was certainly present and many people originating from Earth had gathered here. Some sported beards, others cutoff plaid shirts with hiking boots, and then there were still more that had adopted a more medieval-style outfitting after interacting with the system. The dungeons in the surrounding wilderness nearby apparently dropped a lot of low to midgrade gear for people around levels 10 to 40, with prizes often being things like Hakim's axe or the stat-imbued robe Julie wore. There were also two blacksmiths in town, both of whom had gained the Ascended Blacksmith class that allowed them to actually imbue their personal signatures into various items they made for additional stat boosts.

"Hey, Sara!" Julie waved to another of the brunette townspeople her age, a very pregnant one, who was walking alongside her husband on the dirt road leading into town. "How far along are you now?!"

"Thirty-one weeks and three days since I found out!" Sara called back, holding her belly and tripping slightly when a strong and warm breeze whipped at her hoodie. Her husband leaned over to prevent her from falling in the gust. "Oof! That was close!"

"Be careful, and good luck!" Julie called back while they passed, giggling when the husband started chiding Sara about being more careful. "Those two are a cute couple."

Athela nodded absentmindedly at Julie's words, looking deep into the forest and squinting with a frown. Then she turned back and stopped dead in the road, staring at the couple who'd just passed by. When the couple turned back a second later to look at her, their eyes met—and Athela let out a snort. "Uh . . . Yeah . . . Julie, how long have they been here?"

"Hmm?" Julie cocked her head to the side with a smile, then made the connection. "Oh! Sara and her husband, John? They've been here since before we were here. Why?"

The couple hurried down the dirt road and out of sight, not turning back around while Athela and Fay shared a look.

"Don't worry about it. I was just curious. Hey, Riven? Mind if I go for a quick jog? I could use a stretch."

Riven's eyes flicked left toward the spot where the couple had disappeared, and he let out a sigh while rubbing his temple with two fingers. "Sure. Make it fast."

Athela nodded, ruffled the hood he wore, and then flashed away—leaving the rest of them to continue into the settlement.

Speaking of which, the town was a lot more lively than Riven had anticipated given the size.

Dirt roads, log cabins, and poorly painted storefronts were in abundance. There were also a couple of people doing various crafts in open-air workshops, such as carpentry and mapmaking. Men and women laughed and bustled about, with a few patrolling groups of militia making rounds on the perimeter from time to time.

"Is there a mayor here, or something like it?" Riven asked curiously, watching a couple of rifle- and axe-wielding men trudge along while giving Riven's group sidelong glances. Some of them outright stared at the elves, many even rubbing their eyes to gawk, and it occurred to Riven that they might never have seen elves before.

Tanya shook her head, waving to one of the blacksmiths, who was hammering at a chunk of metal near a furnace. "No, there isn't. It's everyone for themselves, which is why groups like the Red Hand were able to pop up. There are a couple of guilds, gangs, and militias like the ones you just saw—but mostly we all get along unless you get in someone's way. It's overall safe, I'd say. What happened with Caleb the last time you arrived was . . . an outlier."

Tim gave Riven a flat look as if to disagree but kept his mouth shut.

"A little over twenty thousand people live here, including the surrounding homes a few miles out. Including even our own home that you saw last time," Tanya said without missing a beat, continuing to almost skip along happily toward a park in the center of town. "It means that everyone has a place in the community! Even a small-business woman like me! I make clothes for the people here, you know!"

The men and women on the streets coming in and out of trading shops, homes, and pubs all gave Riven and his friends sidelong looks or outright stares. He got a few pointed fingers as well, but he was pretty sure they were all looking at Genua, Len, and Luke rather than anyone else.

"Most haven't seen elves yet, if that's what you're thinking," Hakim confirmed a moment later, stepping into the circular grassy park and off the dirt streets—heading toward a set of picnic tables underneath some elm trees. "It won't be a big deal, but you'll probably get some finger-pointing and stares. There were actually some Lizardians that came through two weeks ago and that really stirred up a fuss, but even then, it was more curiosity than anything else. They came and went, and they'll likely be back—saying they were tradesmen looking to establish connections. They even brought over some cool trinkets for many of the people here, like enchanted amulets. A very nice bunch if you ask me, even if they did look similar to those lizard people you killed in the dungeon that first time I used Heroic Intervention. So if they can handle Lizardians, they'll be able to handle some elves who look far more similar to humans than those creatures did."

"Sandwich time!" Tanya called out, setting her basket on a table. "Who wants some!"

"Azmoth wants some!" Azmoth raised both hands.

Fay rolled Riven up to the table, sitting down on the bench beside his wheelchair, and leaned her head onto the table while he pulled out some pitchers of water from his spatial sack. Looking up at the sunny sky above them, she let her shoulders relax as laughter began to fill the air around them when Len hopped up onto the wood and savagely demanded that she be allowed to eat the first sandwich.

"Len! That's rude!" Genua chided her daughter, swatting her hand very softly but with a meaningful glare as the others laughed. "Apologize!"

Fay smirked when the mother-daughter duo started arguing, then shifted her attention back to Riven with a whisper. "They didn't know. They hadn't even a clue."

Riven didn't even grimace. Instead, he just allowed himself to take in the happy scene in front of him. Letting out a content exhale, he shrugged his shoulders and let himself slouch—putting a hand on Fay's own after accepting a sandwich with a nod of thanks. "Athela will take care of it. I have no doubt that she'll be more than enough to handle the situation."

Athela's black figure blurred through the trees, the landscape flying by at insane speed as her legs carried her forward without a single sound. The wind failed to whistle, the leaves she stepped on failed to crackle, and her shallow breaths might as well have been nothing but a butterfly beating its wings for all the sound it made while she raced forward.

And her prey had caught her scent.

The two figures in front of her were fast, very fast, especially for their level. What were skinwalkers doing here of all places? Were they contracted familiars, or were they ferals that'd escaped the lower realms on their own somehow due to sheer dumb luck?

[Level 99 Skinwalker, Demon]
[Level 86 Skinwalker, Demon]

They were also far stronger than anything that should be living in this area. Was anyone around here even close to level 80 or 90 yet?

Hakim's group certainly wasn't.

In front of her, two gray figures—humanoid with long, lanky limbs and alien-like heads—rushed forward at a frantic gallop. They moved almost like cats, on all fours, lacking faces with the exception of round mouths lined with teeth. Occasionally they'd glance over their shoulders and shriek to one another, becoming panicked while Athela closed in.

She grinned upon seeing their fear. She certainly had some questions for them, questions that they'd answer one way or another—and if they didn't . . .

Well, she had two new abilities to test out on them if they didn't. Ones she'd been absolutely dying to use.

CHAPTER 4

Sara and John, which were the names they'd adopted over the past couple months, were absolutely terrified. Their real names were Selzi and Ak'ra. They'd escaped the hells with their clan and moved to this desolate wilderness, away from the rest of the world to avoid abominations like the very creature rushing toward them at breakneck speed.

"Selzi!" Ak'ra, or John, yelled back over his shoulder—pausing only for a brief half second to pick Selzi up from the ground where she'd skidded to a halt after tripping over a fallen log. His pale, eyeless head whipped around—and his body began to shiver in fright when he saw the sleek black form of the Arshakai demon tearing through the forest like a speeding bullet. "SELZI, WE NEED TO MOVE!"

He picked his mate up when he realized she'd sprained one of her legs, badly, and he rushed ahead toward the clan nest with frantic abandon. His heart beat wildly in his chest and the pores along his skin began to weep. "This can't be it . . . This can't be the end, not here, not now . . . We only just got here!"

But the life of a demon was unforgiving. He knew what this creature would do if she caught them before they reached the relative safety of the brood. But even then . . . Was he being selfish?

His long, gangly, clawed limbs scrambled over a large boulder and he launched his body at high speed toward the hills. He only dared look back once, to where the demoness had gained ground. Long spiderlike blades were carrying her forward through the trees now, the demon having abandoned the ground for an aerial attack—and he managed to identify her after three quick attempts only for his round mouth to exhale sharply in horror while he sprinted to lose her.

[Athela, Level 127 Archdemon: Unique, three forms. Cute Wittle Blood Weaver/Gluttonous Arshakai/Gluttonous Fae Drider. LEGENDARY. PANU WORLD BOSS.]

By the hells.
He was going to be eaten today.

The realization hit him like a freight train, and his mind blanked. He had a decision to make, and with one final look at his mate, he threw her forward and turned to meet the beast pursuing them. It was an act of love, one final sacrifice to save Selzi so that she might have a chance to finally find that happiness they'd been searching for all these years. "SELZI, RUN! I WILL HOLD THIS MONSTER OFF!"

CRACK
SNAP
CRASH

Athela launched herself from the treetops like a torpedo and smashed into the higher-leveled skinwalker with absolute accuracy, despite having jumped a gap of over fifty yards to do it. She cleared the jump in less than a second, and her six blades slammed into the monster in numerous spots like pistons all along its four limbs.

The resounding sound of her impact intertwined with the snapping of trees when they barreled into two of them and slid to a stop, the demon underneath her screaming and squealing while trying to get loose.

The other skinwalker had been thrown and was scrambling to her feet, wailing and limping forward. The red strings extended from Athela's hand, spinning out in a net that snapped shut around the other female demon and pulling her to the ground in an instant.

"Well, hello, chaps!" Athela said with a proud smile, pretending to dust off her hands and looking around to see nothing and no one else present. "Mighty fine day today, isn't it?!"

"Curse you to the abyss!" The skinwalker she was currently standing on and impaling to the ground spat viciously. "Our clan will find you and gut you for this! You will not get away with taking our lives so easily!"

Athela snickered, then began yanking the squirming ball of bloody threads closer and closer—pulling it in until the two skinwalkers were beside one another while they continued to thrash.

"Just get it over with!" the female skinwalker said, shuddering, her skin weeping like so many of her kind did when they were seriously upset. It was the equivalent to humans crying, and Athela momentarily took pity.

"I have questions first before ripping off both of your heads," Athela said, putting a foot on the male's neck and causing him to gasp. She put on a little pressure for emphasis and glared down at them. "What are the two of you doing here? Are you contracted familiars? Or are you escapees?"

"Why do you care?!" the skinwalker underneath her screeched in a raspy voice, even snarling her way with pinned claws extended. She tried to activate an ability, but Athela's stamina and aura snapped down on the both of them so fast that whatever it'd been, the ability shut off without even having a chance to start.

The creature underneath her began to wail loudly, high-pitched grunts and squeals echoing through the forest, while the female began to do the same.

Ugh.

Athela promptly slapped both of them across the face, one after the other, and then yanked the male up by his neck to stare down at his featureless gray head. "You have one chance. Answer me, tell me what you're doing here, and you might live depending on what you say."

They slowly calmed down, though the male was still in a lot of pain. Athela remedied that by slapping a web onto his front and yanking out her bladed arachnid legs. One by one the skinwalker's wounds began to heal—not quite as fast as Riven's healing, but still able to be seen with the naked eye.

"Now . . ." Athela muttered, her limbs twisting and snapping in an abrupt and violent lurch. Her body morphed, quick and fast, forming the house-size drider form. Her body turned bright white, she grew an extra set of red eyes, and her upper torso was that of a beautiful young woman while she had the body of an arachnid so large that each ice-covered leg could crush the two demons beneath her shadow with a mere flick. "How many of you are there?"

The demons squealed in horror when her large hands reached down and plucked them up off the forest floor, taking piles of leaves and dirt with them when her fingers wrapped around their bodies.

"Squealing isn't an answer, you little pests," Athela sneered—showing rows of jagged, sparkling white teeth. Crystal roses bloomed along her body, and a fine mist of frost began to spread. "What are your names? How many of you are there? How many people have you killed, and what were your plans for this town nearby?"

The larger male spat blood when Athela's grip tightened on his rib cage and a bone snapped. "I am Ak'ra. I have killed and eaten three people. The town is an excellent hunting ground for us, low-leveled, unsuspecting humans. There are over twenty others aside from us that will come for you if we die. We are not bound to any summoner. We've been here since the beginning of the integration. What is it to you?"

"My name is Selzi. Five humans I have eaten; my appetite is stronger than my mate's. One corpse may last him for months, but it is less so for me." The female hissed in pain, arching her back when her words faltered and she hesitated. "Ugh! There are indeed many more of us! Please release your grip . . . thank you. It is as Ak'ra said: This place is an easy hunting ground for our kind. We merely wish to live in peace. Please . . . let us go. We can pay you, or even serve you if you wish! We can offer you more than just a meal if you let us leave alive! Achieving the rank of archdemon at such a relatively low level speaks volumes of your power and majesty! We would gladly serve someone who is so quick to rise, one who is no doubt destined for glory!"

Athela raised an eyebrow, but it was amusement that colored her features rather than anything else. "Glory, huh? Go on."

If Selzi could have blinked in surprise, she would have. "Y-yes! You are a majestic creature if we have ever seen one! Your power is obviously far beyond our own; it is only natural that we compliment you so!"

Quickly getting on board with Athela's mood change, Ak'ra nodded fervently. "Of course, it is natural! Yes, absolutely natural! I'm sure that one such as yourself no doubt has an entire nest of loyal followers! After all, you are not only archdemon— but you are of the Legendary tier! Elysium has judged you as grandiose indeed!"

Both skinwalkers rapidly nodded their heads three times in unison.

Athela's narrowed red eyes flicked back and forth from one to the other. She let out an amused and content humming sound, then gently placed both creatures on the ground in front of her. "Do not run, or I will kill you. Do you understand, maggots?"

The jittery demons were obviously shocked, and they glanced at one another in disbelief before prostrating themselves before Athela's massive arachnid limbs.

"Oh great one! We thank you for your supreme generosity!"

"One as strong and powerful and beautiful as you honors us measly worms by allowing us to live!"

"Let us show you to our nest so that the others may worship you with us!"

"Praise be to the great spider queen!"

"Praise be!"

"Praise beee!!!"

Athela waved a hand in the air as if fanning herself. They'd no doubt killed the young married couple they were impersonating, and the two skinwalkers had admitted to eating more people, but at the same time—wasn't that what demons usually did, just out of instinct? Humans were no different to most demons than what pigs were to humans. Could she really blame them?

And if she used this opportunity to better suit her own needs, and Riven's needs . . .

She nodded in satisfaction. "Yes, yes. This is how it should be, no doubt! I'll have to teach Riven a thing or two about how he treats me after showing you lot to him. You're going to be my pets from now on. If I say bark, you bark. If I say jump, you ask how high. If I say go fetch me some wine, you're going to fetch me some wine and then rub my back for fifteen minutes before you get to leave. Got it?"

"We will serve if you protect!" Ak'ra said, slamming his head hard and fast into the dirt floor of the forest. "You have shown us mercy when you could have killed us—we will pledge!"

"A pledge!" repeated Selzi with glowing admiration, looking up in awe at the archdemon that—unknown to Athela—Selzi had only heard stories of as a child. To this particular skinwalker, and probably to many other lesser demons, standing in the presence of an archdemon was truly an honor and awe-inspiring. "We will serve our better!"

Athela humphed, puffing out her chest and raising her nose to the sky. "Yes, my plebeian peons! Take me to your previous leader. I will have words with him, I daresay! Oh, and one more thing."

Athela glowered at the two, suddenly slamming the presence of her aura down on them both as a suppressive weight that caused them both to gasp. The air cracked with elemental lightning, sin energy began to ripple and tear at space, and their skin began to freeze over while she flexed. "No more eating humans until I say you can. Only animals. My master would not deem it okay if you did eat people and I'd be forced to kill you, even if he is a vampire. Odd situation, I know, but rules are rules."

Both of the skinwalkers dropped their jaws in shock, gasping for air when her aura vanished from their presence. But the look of shock remained when they raised their heads to meet her gaze.

"You . . . YOU have a master?! YOU?! How is that possible??!" Ak'ra asked, bewildered. "HERE?! On THIS frontier planet?! Is there anyone who even remotely comes close to your power?"

Selzi shuddered outwardly. "He must be a very intimidating figure to hold sway over someone as amazing as you, my spider queen!"

Athela's lips twitched upward in satisfaction, and she let out another loud "HUMPH!"

She could get used to this.

Riven was sitting in his wheelchair eating another sandwich when he got his first-ever telepathic message from Athela, whose voice blasted into his head like a megaphone.

"RIVEN, GUESS WHAT?!"

He flinched outwardly, cringing and holding the side of his head to stop her voice from echoing around in his skull. It was an odd sensation, hearing her voice channel directly into his head, but he knew what it was as soon as it happened just by concentrating on the connection. "Jesus Christ . . ."

Fay was the only one who noticed while the others were laughing, talking, and joking around with one another while continuing to get stares for being in the company of elves. "Are you okay? What's wrong? Is it your soul again?"

"No . . . No, I'm fine." Riven gave her a warm smile and put his hand on her own, fingers intertwining under the table where she'd rested it on his knee. "Just Athela using that new telepathy thing we've got going—"

"RIVEN, CAN YOU HEAR ME? RIVEN?!"

He winced again, then internally scowled and thought back another message in reply. *"Athela, I swear to god if you scream into my head one more time, I'm going to put you in spider time-out for SO long."*

There was a pause.

"Fine. I was just so excited! Do you want to know why?"

"Why?"

"I've subjugated a nest of skinwalkers is why! They're calling me the SPIDER QUEEEN AHAHAHAHAHAHAHAhahahahaha! I AM GLORIOUS! I AM SUPREME! I WAS BORN FOR GREATNESS, RIVEN! BORN FOR IT!"

"Dear god in heaven. All right, well, you can tell me the details when you come back. Are you coming back soon?"

"On my way now, my sexy potato man!"

"What in the world prompted you to call me a potato man?"

"I don't know. I'm just excited! I have my very own minions now!"

He let out a long exhale. *"Right. Just travel back safe. Okay?"*

"Ah, you're worried about me! Aren't you?"

"I just want you to be careful is all. Especially if you're over there subjugating demon nests."

"You love me, don't you?!" There was a hint of amusement there, but also a genuine fondness.

He rolled his eyes. *"Yes. You already know I love you. Now shut up and get back here if you're done doing what you need to do."*

"Got it, babes!"

Athela's presence faded from his mind, and he rubbed his fingers into the bridge of his nose again before sighing in relief. He turned to Fay. "If we ever get a telepathy thing of our own going on, please don't scream obnoxiously loud stuff into my head just for the fun of it."

Fay blinked, then snickered and leaned over to give him a quick kiss. "Of course I wouldn't. Athela is just being Athela—it's part of her charm."

He let on a suspicious look after that but began to smile while Len and Julie were playing nothing less than Monopoly, of all things, with Hakim and Azmoth. Azmoth already had Park Place and was going for Boardwalk, while all the light blues and purples on the bottom side of the board were taken up by Julie, who had formed a hesitant alliance with the little elf girl—as if Monopoly alliances were even a thing. Len, on the other hand, had all the greens and was working on the oranges even now.

Hakim was shit out of luck.

"Don't forget to collect when you pass GO, Len!" Fay yelled out an exclamation of horror when the little girl landed on one of Azmoth's railroads. She then laughed and gripped Riven's hand more firmly, leaning into him with a deep sigh. "Why are you looking at me like that?"

He didn't blink, still hooded from the bright midday light. "Part of her charm? What exactly did you and Athela talk about when she went to get you back?"

"It wasn't like she just CAME to get me back. I invited her to talk first," Fay protested, putting an arm around his neck and nuzzling her nose against his with a playful grin. "And that's girl talk."

He simply raised both eyebrows.

"Okay, fine. I'll talk," Fay said, throwing up her hands in defeat. "But ONLY when Athela gets back, and when we go to sleep tonight. It needs to be a talk between the three of us."

Riven's frown deepened. "Is it bad?"

"No! Not at all. It actually went very well, as long as . . . you're okay with it." Fay looked around, making sure no one else was listening, then huffed. "Yeah, okay, I'm not going to be able to hold this in. Athela said that if I were to come back, that we'd need to work on our own relationship, too, so there wouldn't be any jealousy issues sharing you. And we might have slept together. There."

"Knew it," Riven said flatly. He hesitated when she looked back at him with concern etched into her face, then held up a hand to stop her from speaking. "I'm not mad, if that's what you're thinking. I'd originally been the one to throw that idea out when you were about to leave, and I'm glad it worked out that way."

Fay's features softened. "All right. I knew that was probably the case, but Athela didn't ask you first and I wanted to make sure . . ."

"I'd much rather pursue a relationship with both of you than a relationship with just one of you if it means that neither of you leave," Riven confirmed with a brief glance. "I know I'd said I was looking for 'the one,' and a soul mate, but you leaving made me realize that it's possible to care deeply about two people at once. As cliché and shallow as that sounds. I'm glad you're back, Fay."

The succubus went from shocked one moment to a furiously red blush—and she averted her eyes but tightened her grip on his hand with a poorly hidden and embarrassed smile. She nodded. "I'm glad I'm back, too. I thought about you the entire time I was gone."

There was a pause.

"As did I for you. It was hard, seeing you go."

From across the park and coming in from the street, a group of three men began to approach the table. One of them had a large rifle on his back, while the other two were completely unarmed—or at least at first glance they were. They all looked rather gruff and one had a jagged scar running down his thick neck, all of them sporting shaggy beards.

Riven watched them come in silence, watched them evaluate him and the rest of the group in turn until one of the men came to a stop behind Hakim—waiting for all of them to give him their undivided attention as the board game playing, laughing, and joking all subsided within twenty seconds.

"Hello, friends," the man said in a thick Southern accent. He wore denim overalls and was spitting tobacco out to the side and gesturing to Genua with an upturned chin. "Don't mean to be rude, so please don't take no offense, but is that there really an elf? Or is ya fake?"

Genua blinked, then exchanged looks with Luke, and then Riven, before answering. "I am an elf, yes. Why?"

"I bet my friends here five silver coins you was the real deal, so I was hopin' you could pull on your pointy ears there a bit to show these fine gentlemen they're actually attached to your pretty blond head," the man said with a genuine smile. "If it ain't too much of a burden, that is. Also, ya see . . . my boss here has been looking for one of your type. He'd pay handsome dollar bills, if ya get what I'm sayin', if you were to visit him for a bit so he could . . . have a chat. If ya get what I'm sayin'."

Riven's eyes darted left to the place where the three men had come, and standing there in the dirt road watching the exchange was a man in a fancy top hat, wearing a monocle of all goddamn things, and using a cane to support himself. He was surrounded by bulky, gruff-looking men like the three who'd approached the table Riven now sat at, and he looked to be waiting expectantly.

"I'm afraid I'll have to refuse," Genua said politely, giving a smile that didn't reach her eyes. "I'm on holiday duty attending to my lord. I am his servant and cannot be bothered to leave at this time."

The gruff man in the center of the three raised an eyebrow quizzically, giving the group a once-over. "Servant? Did I hears ya right? To what man or lord is it you speak of?"

"That'd be me," Riven said without missing a beat, meeting the gazes of the three men unflinchingly and with a polite but simple smile. "I'm afraid that Genua is preoccupied. I'm sorry, he'll have to find another elf to bother."

A bag as thick as Riven's fist slapped onto the table a second later, spilling coins of gold, silver, and copper onto the thick wood and startling Tanya.

"You can't just come over here and ask for someone to play your whore, thinking you're the new dogs in town now that the Red Hand is gone," Tim said with a scowl. "That's absolutely insulting. Get lost."

Tanya's objecting frown seemed to agree with her son, while Hakim and Julie just stared blankly—unconcerned in the least but with a slightly annoyed look on Julie.

"That's a lotta money, 'Lord.' I'd take it if I was you," the middle bearded man said with his hands coming up to rest on his overalls—ignoring the protests of the others. "But if you don't want it, we can just give it to the lady here directly if need be."

CHAPTER 5

Riven frowned down at the bag of Elysium coins glinting in the sunlight, ignoring the challenging tone of the rough-looking man in front of him. "Genua?"

The elf immediately straightened in her seat. "Yes, Riv?"

He snorted in amusement at the reduced name they were using for him in public. It wasn't like his features were all that different, and in time people would likely put two and two together, but still. "Would you like to go?"

His head turned and he clasped his hands with a polite smile. "I won't stop you if you do want to. You can always come back if it's me who's holding you here. I can watch Len for you and have Azmoth even escort you back and forth if you'd like. Is that something you'd want?"

Genua's face twisted in disgust, and she gave the three bearded men a once-over before leaning forward to get a better look at the man in the top hat. "No. No, it is most certainly not."

"Are you sure?" Riven said, scooting the bag of coins over for her to get a better look. "They're willing to pay."

"I said no, Riv. Please don't ask me again." She stiffened and one of the men standing nearby scoffed audibly, picking up the bag of coins and pocketing it.

Riven shrugged their way. "There. I asked, and she didn't want to go, even given leave of her duties. Please, go away."

Azmoth took the liberty to stand up, getting some wide-eyed looks of astonishment when they realized just how tall he actually was. Even in "human" form, he was absolutely huge and towered over even Hakim, who was already a beast of a man.

The middle of the three men, the one wearing overalls and fidgeting with one of his pockets, glanced over his shoulder to shake his head at his boss before shrugging and sighing. "All right, that be fine. If ya change your mind, lady, let us know—my employer is mighty rich and treats his women well."

With that, much to Riven's surprise, the three newcomers turned around and simply walked off without a care in the world. There were no attempts to intimidate anyone, no threats, no angry yelling or pointing fingers. They just left, and the man wearing the top hat and monocle sighed reluctantly before turning around with all his hired thugs and walking away down the street.

Azmoth sat back down, causing the bench underneath him to creak.

"That actually went rather well," Riven said with surprise. "Usually I end up killing a bunch of people when things like that start."

Hakim chuckled under his breath, shaking his head and resuming the Monopoly game. "You say that so casually! I hope I don't become like that. Do you ever have questions about your morality? Not trying to be offensive, I'm just seriously curious."

Riven considered the question, drumming his fingers on the table and staring out into the forest beyond town where Athela was likely still running his way.

"It isn't so bad." Riven shrugged, taking another bite of a ham and cheese sandwich and chewing slowly before swallowing. "I've given up trying to determine what is good and what is not, what is evil and what is not. I just do what I want and hope for the best. Now, tell me, is there a shop around here that would sell anything on this list?"

Riven pulled out a sheet of paper and shoved it across the table for Hakim, Tim, Julie, and Tanya to look at. Over thirty items were listed on the sheet, with various notes and starred items written in black ink.

"It's stuff I could use for totem making based on the few beginner's manuals I got back in Brightsville," Riven said with a toothy grin. "I'm really looking forward to starting. I have enough to start out and make a few really basic totems, but by the time I go back, my goal is to have finally acquired an ascended craft. One of my previous familiars, Yattazi, had a cooking skill I never got to see, even though she didn't have a cooking class—so I know it's possible."

"Might not be as good as those with a class, but yes, it's definitely possible. I personally have a crafting class regarding the clothes-making profession, but there are others here that have only the ascended craft," Tanya muttered under her breath, flipping the page over to read the back and brushing her fingers through her shoulder-length red hair. Her face scrunched up and her freckles became more pronounced when she handed the paper back. "There are two shops you might want to check out."

"Glee's General Goods Store and Odds & Ends." Tim nodded in agreement, standing up and beginning to stretch. "Want me to show you while the others finish their game and wait for Athela?"

"I still hungry. Stay and eat," Azmoth confirmed in his hulking, bald barbarian form—but it looked more like he was just invested in the Monopoly game and didn't want to get up.

Riven chuckled, wheeling himself back and then around the table while Fay gave a polite nod to the others and stood up with him. "Absolutely. Let's go—I want to start building things today!"

Glee's General Goods Store already had a pack of men and women of various levels carrying backpacks or pushing carts right outside, talking about nearby dungeon runs or trading opportunities with other towns that were somewhat out of the way, according to Tim. The building was a boxy two-story log cabin with the bottom floor being a general goods store and the top floor being where Glee—the owner of the establishment—lived with her two sons.

"'Scuse us," Tim called out, getting a few head turns but also allowing Riven, Fay, and himself to pass through when the other people crowding the area made way.

"New to town, eh?" a stick-thin woman wearing hiking gear asked with a puzzled but warm smile. "Not often we see people coming through here besides the regulars. They with you for a while, Tim? Or just acquaintances?"

"Hey, Jarla, and they're going to be here for at least a few weeks, I think." Tim gestured to the two behind him. "This is Riv, and that's Fay pushing his wheelchair."

"Can't walk?" another short, bald man wearing a backpack asked—only to be chided by the woman named Jarla.

"'Course he can't walk, idiot!" Jarla smacked the bald guy with the back of her hand across his shoulder, causing him to wince. "What do ya think he's in the chair for?! You got two brain cells up there in that tiny skull of yours and only one of them is working! Riv, ignore this moron."

Riven smirked at the man's expression—he'd thoroughly tucked his tail between his legs—but held up a hand to dismiss the question. "Not a problem at all. To be fair, I can walk, but it takes a lot out of me and it isn't for very long. Hopefully I'll recover soon."

"See! It was a valid question!" The bald man humphed, getting a laugh from his friends when Jarla scowled ferociously his way—but Tim was kind enough to hold the door.

Riven waved to his brief acquaintances and let Fay push him inside, the succubus getting more than a few stares on the way in.

A bell jingled when the wooden door shut, and they found a well-lit interior with a couple barred windows as well as a few light bulbs powered by a generator in the corner of the store. Glass cases stood against the walls, with a few shelves and tables all displaying various goods and attached price tags. It was obvious this had once been an outdoors and hunting store by the layout—and all the stuffed deer heads.

"Hold on! I'll be right there!" a feminine voice called out from the back. The gruff laughter of more masculine voices was audible from around a corner and into an office area near the generator. Opening the office and saying something to the occupants inside, a tall, overweight woman with happy features and wrinkles indicating she smiled a lot said something sassy—getting a laugh from the men inside before she let the door click shut behind her.

She turned, frazzled brown hair completely unkempt and a smudge mark of grease on her face. "Oh hello, Tim! You brought some new ones with ya today? My name's Glee, and this is my store!"

"Hey, Glee!" Tim replied happily, bouncing over to the counter and introducing "Riv" and Fay one by one. "They're here for the next couple weeks and he's looking for some supplies. I know that a lot of people come through here and drop off their finds from monster kills or dungeon runs, so we decided to come here to take a look."

"What kind of supplies?" Glee asked with a raised eyebrow, coming behind one of the glass counters and leaning her weight onto the top while giving Riv and Fay a once-over. "Kinda odd you came all the way out here to Jerbyville with a chair like that. I don't know how you made it through the wilderness, frankly."

"He had help," Fay said kindly, brushing her long, silky blond hair out of her face and blowing at it with a puff of air when it came right back over her right eye. "I babysit him. Basically he's my pet."

"You what?!" Riven said aghast, dropping his jaw in fake protest and whirling around to get a laugh from the young woman. "That's just plain rude!"

Glee grunted her acknowledgment while her eyes traced Fay's figure in the sundress. "Yes, I think many a man wouldn't mind being your pet, missy. So what is it you both need? A comb, maybe?"

Fay snorted with a smirk. "Yes, that. But mostly we came for Rive—Riv's new hobby. He's trying to become a totem maker."

Riven playfully stuck his tongue out at the girl behind him and then took out his list, handing it to Glee across the countertop and waiting for her to read.

The store owner frowned slightly upon getting the list, then took out a pen and paper of her own before writing three things down. "I have a few of them, but not much of each. Werebear fangs, icewind roots, and glowstones I have in stock. You said you were into totem making? I heard that was a rare one. Only Fae users can make and utilize totems, right?"

"Unholy as well," Riven corrected with a nod.

The woman paused, raising her eyes to meet Riv's and blinking twice. "You an Unholy user?"

"What if I am?"

"Then I'd say your type is very rare around here. We only have two people with the Unholy Foundational Pillar in town, and neither of them are very talented." She finished writing on her own sheet and handed Riven's list back to him. "Might want to try Odds & Ends after my place—they probably have some of those soulstones you're looking for. I used to have 'em, too, but I sold all of them for a discount because they were wailing so damn much. Made an absolute ruckus."

Her frazzled head bobbed up and down while she fumbled with a key and turned a lock down the row. She collected a couple of bear fangs from the glass cases, went around to a shelf to collect a couple of white roots, and then bent down to snatch a few small round stones. Coming back to the counter and laying them all out for Riven to see, she gestured to the items with a flick of her wrist. "These what you're looking for?"

[Werebear Fang: These fangs are often used as crafting ingredients for jewelry. They contain a faint pulse of nature-attuned power.]

**[Icewind Root: Alchemy ingredient. This root is often found in cold
climates, thriving in harsh tundras, but it can also be found in cave
systems underground.]**
**[Glowstone: These stones are most often made through mana polish-
ing. Occurring in nature most often in rivers with creatures possessing
a high water affinity, these stones can collect ambient energy over time
that causes them to glow when they hit maximum storage. After release,
they turn back into dormant stones until the cycle is repeated.]**

Three of the fangs, two roots, and five small round glowstones. The stones
weren't glowing now, at least not until they had enough mana infused into them,
but they were the real deal, according to his identification skill. He didn't even have
to wear Messenger anymore to thoroughly identify things, though it also wasn't
anywhere close to what a real identification class at high levels would get you.

"Price?" Riven asked, noticing that the tags had been stripped off these items
before Glee placed them on the countertop.

The storekeeper grinned mischievously. "What're they worth to ya? Seems
mighty interesting you have an entire list to collect. You must have enough coin to
buy it all, or I'd assume so, anyways. Is that right?"

Riven's expression flattened, and he tsked in irritation. It wasn't that he didn't
have the money—he had more money than he knew what to do with. In fact, he had
so much money that he barely had time to spend any of it, but that didn't mean he
liked being taken advantage of. "Come on, don't do that. That's just mean."

Glee laughed heartily, slapping her hands onto her hips with a shake of her
head. "No, no! It's business. We all have to make a living, young man! Now, how
about we price these at . . . I don't know . . . fifty gold apiece?"

Riven didn't even blink, flat stare boring into the woman while Tim let out a
loud huff of surprise.

"Fifty gold APIECE?!" Tim gasped. "That's robbery?!"

Glee kept eye contact with Riven for a solid five seconds before deflating when
he didn't make a move for the items. "Ah, fine, I just wanted to see if you'd do it.
I'll be real with ya, lad. They're more worth twelve silvers apiece. How about it?"

Riven still felt like he was being ripped off, and he slowly tilted his head to
the side in consideration of her offer. "Do you people even have an Elysium altar
around these parts?"

"You people?" Glee repeated with a chuckle. "Hardly. But Elysium coins are
the new currency and there is an altar far to the south of here down Pig's River. We
have traders come up from there once in a while but not too often, the trek is well
over two weeks on foot and there aren't any roads—making it a bit unsafe."

"How about seven silver pieces for each?"

"Ten."

"Seven."

"Won't do less than ten. Final offer."

Riven huffed. "All right, ten apiece it is. Three of the fangs, two roots, and five small round glowstones. That's one hundred silver pieces straight . . . Fay, could you get it for me, please?"

Fay happily obliged, pulling at his spatial sack that they'd tucked into the back of the wheelchair. Digging around in it, she pulled out the one hundred silver coins in neat stacks and slid them over. "You can count if you wish."

But Glee was already struck dumb at the sight of the bag.

"IS THAT A SPATIAL SACK?!" She nearly tripped on her way around the glass bar, peering close at the emblem in Fay's hand bearing the eye sigil of Negrada. "I KNEW IT! You lot ARE rich! Damn it to hell, I should have swindled ya more!"

"Take it or leave it," Fay muttered, only faintly amused while the ticking clock in Glee's brain seemed to work overtime. "You already agreed, so don't go changing the price now."

"Bah!" Glee silently cursed again and took the coins, taking her time to make sure it was all there before nodding and putting the ten crafting pieces into the sack Fay held out. "Fine, fine, fine. Just remember to come find me if you think of anything else ya need—I'll be sure to up the prices when you do, too."

Riven rolled his eyes, then waved back at the clerk. "Thanks anyways. Come on, Tim, let's go to this other store to check it out. What was it again?"

"Odds & Ends," Tim stated dryly. "Hopefully they won't try to rip you off there, too."

"I heard that, Tim! Don't talk bad about me or you'll have it comin'!"

"Bye, Glee! And I would never dream of it!"

The bell jingled, and the group of three left to explore more of the town on the way to their next destination.

The Blood Moon Requiem was almost at a standstill as a society with all the turmoil going on, and tension was sky-high between the ruling families of the courts. Maneuvering the political landscape was an absolute nightmare that General Viku had never enjoyed, but it was even worse due to the fact that Allie and Riven were at the very center of House Wraithtide's current predicament.

Not that he could blame them. He'd outwardly exclaimed with a roaring cheer when that lordling from House Barimont had been killed by Riven's minion Athela, and had doubly cheered along with half of the officers around him when Jalel—that prick of a prince—had been eaten by Riven's gluttonous maw. It'd all been live-streamed after the empire had paid an extraordinarily high price to Elysium itself for selective cut scenes or frequent theatrical streams for the population at large to watch.

But those two deaths had led to problems. Problems only exacerbated by the fact that Princess Kathrine Vonsilla Crushada the Ninth had almost been murdered by a political rival, Lady Muren of House Muren, before Lady Muren was killed, too. Captain Rusof, a favorite great-grandson of one of the greatest generals their empire had ever seen, was killed by Jalel himself, and there were more than a few daggers in the night searching for retribution and revenge behind the scenes in all directions. Already, scuffles on the bordering territories between House Crushada and House Muren were in abundance and on the brink of an outright genocidal fervor, and that was only the least of it. House Wraithtide's spies reported numerous military movements concerning House Barimont forces on the outskirts of Wraithtide territory, while the High Queen Nephridi and Elder Thune had publicly criticized one another before going into seclusion.

No doubt the elder council was trying to wrap this up out of the public eye so that people didn't get ideas about the empire's leadership not seeing eye to eye, but that image was already shattered. The damage had already been done, and General Viku couldn't help but wonder if this had been a calculated move by the high queen. Whispers in the courts claimed that the queen had warned both of the Wraithtide siblings, but yet other rumors described her as the one who initially warned the late Lord Barimont about Allie's potential reaction—even if it had been Elder Thune to actually send him to Panu in the first place.

But just what reason would she have to pit Lord Barimont and Jalel against Riven and Allie? Surely it couldn't just be a great-grandmother's love for her descendants—she barely knew the siblings and there were many easier ways of disposing of a young lord such as Justo Barimont than what had actually happened.

No, there was more to this picture—and if General Viku of House Wraithtide's forces had any guess, it was likely very much woven into events revolving around Elder Thune.

The doors of the supercarrier's great hall swung open, revealing servants and soldiers in uniform lining the walls and standing at attention. His eyes fell to the large rectangular table where a dozen of the highest-ranking family members of House Wraithtide sat, all of them either glaring at one another or shooting him worried and angry looks.

One man in particular stood up before all the others did, however. It was none other than Baron Orimus Wraithtide, a very outspoken antagonist to Riven's policies and a man who was obviously disgruntled by the way things were going. Not only in the empire, but on their home planet, Luteski. Slave uprisings had been the prominent reason the baron had given people concerning Riven's inadequacies as a long-distance ruler of the house, but upon Riven's overruling orders concerning General Viku's intervention that had previously been halted by other nobles of this house, those uprisings were quickly quelled.

It now meant that Baron Orimus Wraithtide was very grumpy and that he was looking for other reasons to pin blame on Riven for the problems this house and the empire at large were having. The most recent of those reasons, and a valid one, was the recent murder of Lord Barimont and Prince Jalel on a small, insignificant world of the newly integrating frontier.

"It's about time you arrived, General Viku. I and the rest of our esteemed house are growing impatient," Baron Orimus Wraithtide grumbled, his wiry posture shifting while he combed his slicked-back chestnut hair. "Please tell me this meeting won't take long. We already have an abundance of problems to fix with House Barimont at our doorstep creating what is probably going to become a blockade on all trade, if not an outright attack."

"Not to mention that we still need to go over taxes!" Lady Riska Wraithtide commented, the old woman's silver-gray locks pulled to one side while she waved a fan as if to cool herself. "Taxes are the most important part of running a planet, and we haven't been able to bring in revenue with all our tax collectors boycotting the job without proper escorts. Preposterous if you ask me! The slave uprisings are dealt with and there's no reason we need to supply those idiots with bodyguards just to do their damn jobs!"

"Enough," General Viku said, quieting the nobles who'd once been the ones giving him orders, and his red eyes tightened with delight when he saw the baron and many of the others stiffen at the lack of respect.

Viku clasped his hands behind his back, his domed head reflecting the light of the chandelier above them. "Prince Riven Wraithtide and his sister, Princess Allie Wraithtide, will be here within the hour. I ask that all of you please refrain from doing or saying anything stupid, as many of you are apt to do, because Allie in particular is very easily set off."

"As we are all very aware . . ." Lady Riska Wraithtide muttered, getting chuckles from some and scowls from others. "Hasn't even been to the empire yet and already has a name for her maliciousness and temper."

General Viku ignored her comment, speaking over the mutterings without hesitation. "The formations are already set and we'll let you know as soon as they arrive. Again, I very much stress that you should try not to antagonize them. Remember that they are the heirs to this house, Riven in particular being the one who—at a word—can dismiss you from the family. I only say this as a warning, and mean nothing by it other than letting you all know that he is likely not going to be happy with my report concerning what I found in regard to what started the slave rebellions. It is my duty to report all findings to the head of house, and I will do as my job requires."

Immediately the room fell silent, and many of the nobles went even paler than normal, shifting in their chairs uncomfortably.

"You wouldn't," Baron Orimus Wraithtide uttered with clenched fists. "General Viku . . . are you threatening us?"

The general raised one eyebrow the other man's way and shifted one pauldron with a roll of his shoulder. "Threatening? No. Just what reason would I have to do that, concerning such outstanding citizens of the empire such as yourselves? Surely there's nothing for you to hide, Baron. I am merely stating facts, and sometimes facts can lead to more questions that—in the wrong circumstances—can lead to heads being detached from bodies."

CHAPTER 6

Skinwalkers.

They were . . . fawning? Over Athela?

If that was even the right word.

Prostrating themselves or attending to her with different odds, ends, gifts, and food they had on hand. Riven watched the strange, pale creatures deliver her trays of refreshments while she sunbathed in their newly built temporary lair next to Tanya's family cabin.

Hakim's cabin?

Who knew. They all shared it, so who cared.

"Athela . . ." Riven said with a dumbfounded look on his face, equivalent to those the others wore when they'd returned to the woodland home to find this amalgamation of demonic entities. "One more time, just how did you convert them into servants?"

"We wish to serve the great one!" a pale, faceless humanoid creature with abnormally long and wiry clawed limbs said fervently. It bowed and prostrated itself before Riven next. "We did not know an archdemon existed on this planet! We are indebted for her gracious act of sparing us and wish to grow in her shadow so that we, too, may one day find glory!"

Athela smugly smirked Riven's way, gesturing to the nest she'd created. Bloodsilk now formed layers upon layers of walls, webs, and cocooned carcasses of animals—creating a multilayered structure between the large trees with only a single central tunnel shaped like a funnel that allowed the sunlight onto her sunbathing spot. "It was my charm! I am a princess, after all!"

She gave him a wink from the web hammock she'd created, then closed her eyes and enjoyed the deep-tissue massage one of the other demons was giving her. "You should do this more often, you know. I'd like it more if it was coming from you. Or Fay . . ."

Fay blushed, and Riven outwardly laughed and shook his head in amazement.

Julie was less enthused by it, and her voice quivered when she spoke next to Hakim. "Didn't these creatures eat John and Sara? Sara . . . she was pregnant . . . She was so nice . . ."

"We ate them long before you knew her," one of the skinwalkers said, cocking its head to the side from a perch up above in the webbing. "The person you always talked to was actually me. I am the Sara you've known all along. My real name is Selzi, and yes—I am actually pregnant with child. That is not false."

This admission was something of a shock to Julie, who didn't know how to handle the information at all. She stuttered twice, a series of conflicting emotions crossed her face, and then she simply turned to leave—walking out the hole used as a door with Hakim quickly following.

"Interesting. As long as they're not hostile, I don't mind," Tim stated with a shrug. "Going to start on your crafting gig today?"

"In a few hours, yes." Riven nodded, letting Fay help him up and feeling his soul jolt when a strand of Gluttony yanked a little too hard on one of his shattered fragments. "Um, I'm going to need to rest for a while, though. I have an off-world meeting later today with the Blood Moon Requiem, so I'll probably be out of commission for a while. If you need me, just talk to my demons—they'll be staying here while I'm gone, excluding Fay. She'll be escorting me to the vampire compound. Latest, we'll be gone until tomorrow morning."

Tim frowned, and Len's laughter was heard alongside Tanya and Genua outside. "Just what exactly is the Blood Moon Requiem, anyway? Not a lot is available about it on the forums—all the Panu forum community knows is you're registered as a lost prince of that place and it has to do with off-world vampires."

"That's basically all there is to it. Space vampires."

Tim snorted a laugh at Riven's deadpan expression. "All right, fine. Keep your secrets!"

They exchanged smiles and a handshake—Riven already feeling weak from standing for more than a dozen seconds. "All right, man, I'll see you when I get back. Athela? Mind making that thing bigger for Fay and me to join?"

"YOU'RE JOINING?!" Athela exclaimed in a squeal of delight, immediately opening her eyes and getting to work in a blur of motion that sent strands of blood webbing in numerous directions. "Ooooh, a midday nap! I'm so excited to cuddle with the two of you! Skinwalkers, take a hike. I need private time with my man and my succubus friend."

"Yes, my lady!" Ak'ra, Selzi's husband, grabbed the other skinwalker and abruptly shifted, turning into their Sara and John figures before exiting the bloodsilk nest with over twenty other skinwalkers in tow. They all bowed or gave respectful well wishes, and one of them even offered to help Tim train up his thieving class.

"You're willing to help level my pickpocket ability?" Tim asked, repeating the offer this unknown demon had just laid out. His freckled face twisted into a confused half smile. "Why? I would certainly appreciate it but . . . why me?"

The skinwalker's bald head bowed low. "You are friends of the great one. It would be an honor to help you along with your class evolutions! I have a very similar class involving subterfuge as well, and I, too, have the pickpocket skill.

When I overheard your mother, Tanya, talking about it, I told myself that I should ask. Not to brag, but I am rather good at it."

"Sounds like a good deal to me," Riven said encouragingly, smiling at the continued look of surprise on Tim's face.

Tim, for his part, slowly nodded and then gave Riven and the two women a wave. "I'll see you later tonight or tomorrow! Good luck with your meeting!"

"Thanks, man. Adios for now."

The last of them left, leaving Riven standing with an arm over Fay's blue shoulders to support himself and staring at the nest's entrance.

"You two just going to stand there looking sexy or am I going to have to drag the both of you down with me?" Athela said lazily from the back, getting a sharp inhale from Fay when she and Riven turned around to look at the other demoness.

Athela was missing her chitin now; the outer layer she usually wore was gone and in its place was softer black skin—emphasizing her now completely bare feminine qualities. She was seductively laid out with her head propped up on one hand, and grinning at the two of them like a predator about to pounce. Hiking up a pointer finger, she clawed the air, signaling them to come to her. "I'm waiting . . ."

"Didn't realize it was going to be that kind of nap!" Riven laughed, sitting down on the bloodsilk that'd very rapidly transitioned from hammock into a pseudo-bed. He winced when he put his entire weight down, his lumbar spine screaming at him with the act, and jolts of his injured soul painfully lit up when his mana channels that connected his physical body to his soul realm twitched. "I may not be able to be as active as I usually am."

Fay laughed, gently pushing him forward into Athela's grip and helping him up onto the bed. "We can do the work, don't worry. Just relax, enjoy the sunshine, and let us put on a show that I'm sure you'll enjoy."

"Did you tell him yet?" Athela asked curiously, pushing her warm body up against his with a gleeful grin.

"Of course I did!" Fay promptly replied—kicking off her knee-high boots and laughing at the smug look on Riven's face when Athela started taking off his belt. "I couldn't keep that a secret for long! You know that. He approves, just like you'd said he would."

Athela giggled evilly. "Yeah, I kind of counted on it, let me avoid the discussion myself. All right, cat's out of the bag—now let's have some fun!"

Helicopter blades whirred about them, beating against the air and delivering Riven, Fay, and Allie to the Blood Moon Requiem's compound, where dozens of vampire soldiers bearing Wraithtide's sigil of an orb wreathed in deathly black-teal flames stood at attention.

Allie gave the necropolis pilot a thumbs-up. "Thanks, Jack, we've got it from here!"

"No problem, my queen. Always a pleasure to escort you from place to place." The military man in the cockpit gave her a thumbs-up in return, and when the three others were off, he began lifting up off the landing spot before heading toward the airfields their military was using.

Riven and Allie watched the helicopter go as Fay adjusted Riven's legs on the wheelchair.

"Remind me to ask General Viku about getting some modification specs for our own fleet on Panu," Allie muttered under her breath when the sound of the beating blades keeping the machine aloft was no longer heard. "If what you say about Wraithtide's fleet is correct, they're thousands of years ahead of us. Maybe more."

"Probably more." Riven nodded in agreement. "But I doubt it would work. Already asked Kathrine about this, and she said the system would either tax the everlasting hell out of that kind of knowledge, or in the more likely scenario, it'd completely stop it from coming at all through numerous means including and not limited to smiting people dead. That kind of knowledge would be something that could shift the balance of these world trials and the political landscape so fast and so drastically that Elysium likely just wouldn't allow it."

Allie's shoulders sagged. "Damn. And speak of the devil . . ."

Out of the inner compound where the main body of the fortress was located came Kathrine. Her long brown hair was swept to one side and she wore her usual style: a formfitting black dress with red flowers of her house on it. She had six of her own personal house guards with her.

She took about twenty seconds to reach them, then nodded in greeting to both Fay and Allie, getting polite smiles in return, before giving a genuine grin Riven's way. She then bowed low at the waist. "Riven . . . I never got to say thank you for saving my life. What you did, using your Malignant Prophecy to make sure that I didn't die, has both me and my parents flustered in a good way. None of us are sure how we will ever repay your kindness."

Riven waved a hand dismissively. "Don't worry about it. You've had a rough time now, with two attempts on your life since getting here, and you've never done me wrong."

She raised her head and straightened her posture, a soft gaze lingering on him before she turned heel and gestured them to follow. "Suitable words from my future husband, I suppose. Come now, your family is waiting for you on the other side."

Allie and Fay shared a look, each of them rolling their eyes while Fay pushed Riven ahead—letting the vampiric guards fall in line around them while they marched into the inner compound.

Repairs were still underway, and there were many corridors and rooms still marked with bloodstains. The bodies had been cleaned out and servants were putting the walls back in place with various kinds of crafting magic, but they all stopped to prostrate themselves when the three royals passed.

"Anything I should know about this meeting?" Riven asked curiously, turning a corner in the inner sanctum of the fortress and eventually coming to a stop inside the ritual room he'd used last time.

Kathrine cleared her throat and nodded to the wizards, sorcerers, and ritualists lining the area, signaling them to start the process when the runes and crystals began lighting up. "Not necessarily concerning your family, no. General Viku no doubt knows more about the inner squabbling than I do, and he is a trustworthy man who served your mother well. I have no doubt he has your best interest in mind, so if in doubt, ask him for any advice you might want. As for the rest of what recently transpired . . ."

Her voice trailed off and her face fell, red eyes casting themselves to the floor and porcelain features contorting with worry. "The empire is not in a good place right now. There will be political upheavals at worst—assassinations are being carried out daily in one sector of the empire or another, and the elder council has congregated to enter seclusion indefinitely. Elder Thune and High Queen Nephridi have always been at odds, but it's never been this bad before."

"No point in worrying about things we can't fix, but sending that little bitch Lord Barimont to force Allie's hand like that was an absolute no-go." Riven shrugged. "Neither of us has regrets."

"You got that right . . . He tried killing Lahn," Allie muttered venomously. "Good riddance."

Kathrine laughed, shaking her head while Fay remained still and silent. "Good gods . . . Are the two of you ready to enter the ritual? I believe it is ready to activate."

Riven's hologram form materialized onboard the supercarrier right on time, and General Viku's spirits rose when—for the very first time—he laid eyes on Allie's figure alongside the prince. There was also Kathrine Vonsilla Crushada, but she was less important to General Viku than the two heirs of his house.

"My prince, princesses!" General Viku bowed low and took a knee, the glow of light from above reflecting off his perfectly shaved head and polished plate armor. "Your Highnesses! Thank you for coming. I sincerely appreciate the time you're taking out of your doubtlessly busy schedules in order to attend to the inheritance your parents left behind! Much needs to be done."

The walk through the flagship was just as awe-inspiring to Allie as it'd been to Riven. She, too, stopped at the bay doors shielded by some kind of force field—a replica of how her brother had been taken so aback by seeing the nebula and starship fleet of sleek, daggerlike black and red vessels outside in planetary orbit.

"Wow . . ." Allie said, staring wide-eyed at the thousands of crafts floating with the backdrop of a beautiful starry display. "This is incredible . . . Riven! Why didn't you tell me about this?!"

She whirled and glared at him accusingly, getting a laugh from his spectral image.

"I did tell you about it! You just chose to ignore it."

"Did not! This is WAY cooler than you made the previous trip out to be!"

Fay was equally stunned and came up to the force field's edge while gawking into the abyss beyond. "This is incredible . . ."

"Right?!" Allie agreed with a huge smile, joining Fay at the lip of the drop-off while lights blinked randomly throughout the fleet beyond.

Kathrine cleared her throat, getting Riven's attention while General Viku grinned in satisfaction at Allie's reaction.

"Yes, Kathrine?" Riven asked, glancing left to where her own spectral visage stood beside him.

Kathrine beamed. "I think you two should come visit my own place sometime, now that General Viku was kind enough to create such a message delivery system. My parents have been wanting to meet you, and Allie as well, to discuss potential trade negotiations and upcoming wedding ceremonies scheduled for next year. Would that be all right?"

"Next year?" Riven repeated—suddenly struck dumb. "That's . . . awfully close."

Kathrine's face fell into a concerned frown. "Is something the matter? I'd already talked to Athela about things like you'd said, and she understood the situation . . . I hope there aren't second thoughts on the matter. I realize that our relationship will never be real and is more of a political ploy for both our houses as well as a means to acquire more of the gift for the empire—but . . ."

Riven shook his head, giving her an encouraging smile. "No, you're fine. It's just hitting me a bit harder now that you're giving me a timeline. Sorry if I seemed shocked."

Her eyes searched him for a bit, and she took in a deep breath before steeling herself. "Very well. I'll tell my parents you need some more time, and if we need to put a hold on the wedding, we can. Whatever makes things most comfortable for you."

They stared at each other in silence for a solid ten seconds after that, while Fay and Allie continued to point out things to one another at the edge of the pilot's bay like little schoolchildren at the zoo.

"Thank you, Kathrine," Riven eventually replied, and he gave a nod. "That would be appreciated. I'll meet your parents in time, just . . . give me a bit. With everything that's happening, I'm beginning to feel overwhelmed."

"Of course." She politely smiled back, though the smile no longer reached the corners of her eyes. "I'm sorry if politics have corrupted your view of our empire. It really isn't that bad a place most of the time."

"Questionable," General Viku muttered with a sideways glance, getting the attention of both Kathrine and Riven simultaneously. His red eyes narrowed. "It's a cesspool. One that the queen has been trying to clean up for some time, but the corruption is rampant and the other elders make things hard for the rest of us. At least, that is my opinion. I am, however, far older than you, Princess—I am sure you'll probably come to the same conclusion as I, given time. Your parents are good people, though, so at least you have that going for you."

Princess Kathrine Vonsilla Crushada was somewhat taken aback by this statement, but she shook herself out of her momentary shock at being addressed by this high-ranking military official with a curtsy. "Thank you for your kind words concerning my parents, and for the insight you have granted me. I will meditate upon your wisdom and seek answers, I assure you."

General Viku scoffed with an eye roll, then quickly corrected himself and shook his head like a wet dog. "Sorry, Princess! I did not mean that as a rude thing. I just don't need to be addressed as formally or placated with such aggrandizing words. I am merely the head of House Wraithtide's military. A privatized general of the empire. Nothing more."

The rest of the tour was much the same as last time: The central deck showed the large constructed stargate with merchant fleets coming in and out, as well as the large space station they were docking in and the planet Luteski far below.

"Fifty-one million, two hundred and thirty thousand vampire citizens, and over six billion slaves," General Viku stated to shocked stares from the two women who hadn't been here before. He turned his bald head to meet Allie's respondent gaze. "That is what your family controls. It is your inheritance, where your brother—and you, to a lesser extent, as second in line to the house name after your parents left—is able to make and change laws that determine the way people live. To most if not all of those slaves, your word is law. You are gods to them, so far out of their reach that they can't even comprehend it."

Allie blinked. "Why are you telling me this like you're trying to make a point?"

General Viku gave a sad smile. "Because, Princess Allie Wraithtide, though it is Riven's name that holds the most dominant power of this house—you hold the true power behind it. After speaking with Riven previously and after watching the two of you on Panu, it is very apparent to me that Riven is a weapon. A sword that he begrudgingly shapes himself into in order to make his own version of the world. He is a threat, a hidden dagger you use to spearhead the advancement of the civilization you are building on the frontier—and he allows you to do this because he loves you. Would I be wrong in assuming that it will likely be a shared venture between the two of you when running Luteski?"

Allie slowly began to blush at the mention of Riven's brotherly affection toward her, but Riven gave her a warm smile and calmed her down—allowing her to nod. "You're probably right. What about it?"

General Viku chuckled and folded his arms while his gaze shot back to the planet and merchant fleets beyond the window. "Because though you haven't yet been to the empire up until now, you are already known far and wide as being absolutely ruthless. It is a quality many of our kind are proud of—proud of FOR you! It is needed in your line of work in order to get things done properly. To crush your enemies into dust so that order may remain."

The man sighed, then fully faced the young woman with determination set in his hardened jawline. "Those enemies I speak of live within your own house, Princess. Before you enter into the room where your extended family is now gathered here on this ship, know this: They are not your friends. They are vultures, maggots trying to eat away at the diseased corpse of the dying animal that was your house so that they could squeeze the last of life and prosperity from it before its end. They are corrupt beyond measure, and they think only of themselves. Granted, there are a few of them who aren't like this, but that's how most of them are—and I want you to be very aware of this before speaking to them. They have the smiles of snakes and the venom to go along with it. The reports I give you when we meet the rest of your family will show some of these things in an obvious light, while other things are not as well-defined—but Kathrine will be there to guide you if she sees things amiss. Things that I myself have seen, where you can make jumps of logic despite not having true proof. Now, are you ready to go in there? Are you ready to pull out that cloak of ruthlessness that you so readily wear back on Panu? Are you willing to do what needs to be done in order to better the lives of your citizens? Because if not, if you are not ready to face the family branches, we may perhaps want to postpone this meeting to another date."

CHAPTER 7

"May I present Prince Riven Wraithtide, presiding master of this house—along with his sister, Princess Allie Wraithtide, his fiancée, Princess Kathrine Vonsilla Crushada the Ninth, and his attendant demon, the succubus Fay."

The doors to the great hall swung open, revealing an elongated room with a crystal chandelier overhead. Paintings and sculptures of vampires performing great feats lined the walls where servants and soldiers stood at attention. Twelve very attractive men and women were sitting at a long rectangular table, all dressed in fancy attire consisting of either elegant robes, dresses, or Victorian-style suits, and all of them immediately stood upon the approach of the two royal siblings.

They all bowed their heads in greeting, with General Viku coming to a stop at the head of the table where four vacant chairs were already placed. Servants held them out expectantly for the newcomers to sit.

"Please, have a seat." General Viku motioned to the four chairs, which was somewhat odd to Riven, considering the four of them had spectral bodies.

Then again, he HAD been walking around the ship like this, and he couldn't really interact much with his environment—but he COULD just barely feel it. "Thank you, General."

Riven's eyes shifted over the gathered vampiric nobles, all of them out of xianxia cultivation novels, medieval fantasy, or Victorian-era fiction. It was certainly an odd combination in his opinion, but it seemed to be the norm here. Six figures on each side of the table gave him fixed, polite smiles—all their eyes glowing the same bright crimson as his own. All of them fanged, all of them pale, all of them with extraordinarily perfect facial features.

"Riven, I believe they're waiting for you to sit first," Allie said with a raised eyebrow, her own chair already having been pushed in and her spectral body leaning onto the wood.

Riven wordlessly shifted, faintly feeling the wood under his apparition when the servant pushed his chair in.

The others of House Wraithtide all took their own seats when he did, elegantly flowing in one synchronous motion to join him at the table again.

General Viku cleared his throat, then took the equivalent of a tablet from a nearby soldier with a muttered word of thanks before stepping to stand at Riven's side. "We have with us the minor branch families and nobility of House Wraithtide in attendance, my prince. They represent the families that control various aspects of production, security, management, and trade with your house resources. They are what makes the machine of your trading hub here on Luteski run. I will introduce them one by one, and because you are so new to the empire, please feel free to ask any questions—no matter how trivial. I will try my best to fill in the gaps."

The vampire general started on the right-hand side of the table, where an older but very fit and slender woman with silver-gray locks of hair down to her bare shoulders sat unblinkingly staring. "This is Lady Riska Wraithtide, head of taxation and treasury, and in my opinion the most competent person at this table."

This got poorly concealed frowns and huffs from many of the other nobles present, but the old woman absolutely beamed at the praise—displaying her fangs with the first sign of genuine emotion Riven had seen since entering the room. "General Viku honors me. I am merely a humble servant of your estate—Prince and Princess Wraithtide."

The corners of Riven's lips quirked upward a bit, and he nodded but otherwise remained silent and waited for Viku to continue introductions.

"Then there are Lord Ruim Wraithtide and Lady Nulasta Wraithtide, husband and wife who oversee infrastructure and education." General Viku gestured to a man and woman who both had eccentric pink hair, hers in dreadlocks and his in a mohawk that made them stand out like a sore thumb.

Both husband and wife smiled politely but did not say anything.

"Count Amestrius Wraithtide oversees our judicial branches here on Luteski. Viscount Adian Wraithtide, Baroness Julasi Wraithtide, and Baron Eethinsa Wraithtide deal in any major trade negotiations with *other parts of the empire*. Duke Hazith Wraithtide and his wife, Duchess Ova Wraithtide, deal in any major trade negotiations with *factions outside the empire*. Lord Wyvern Wraithtide deals in maintaining food supplies and slaves."

Coming to the last two men on the table's left side, General Viku paused and took in a brief breath of air. "Lastly, these two are Baron Orimus Wraithtide, overseer of mining operations in the northern hemisphere—along with his cousin Count Jaricock Wraithtide, who oversees mining operations in the southern hemisphere. Our mining and vast crystal farms on Luteski are some of the most profitable resources House Wraithtide possesses. Alongside our strategic location in the empire's borderlands with a natural wormhole that we were able to turn into a warp gate, it creates a unique opportunity that has allowed our homeworld to become a centerpiece of galactic trade in this sector."

Baron Orimus Wraithtide was a very thin man with slightly sharper features than the others, with slicked-back brown hair and slightly hunched posture. Meanwhile his cousin Count Jaricock Wraithtide was quite the opposite—a very well-built, thick mountain of a man with knotted muscles that bulged through his vest.

No one moved or said anything after that, with only Lady Riska Wraithtide having spoken at all since the arrival of the royal siblings. The silence grew heavy after that, everyone in the room looking to Riven expectantly as if he should make the next move.

"That's a lot of names to remember, but I'll do my best. It's nice to finally see my extended family. I'm just sad that my mother and father aren't here to be with us, too," Riven eventually said with a polite smile, acknowledging each of them in turn. "I appreciate all of you coming. I'm sure you're all very busy. Unfortunately, this meeting had to be called due to what I believe to be discontent among house members, and though I'm quite a far ways away, it still falls to me to make sure Luteski is properly run. Apparently, there have been not only minor thefts . . . but rather treacherous acts as well. Even as far as some people trying to sell major components of our inheritance, such as continents on the planet or large caverns of crystal farms, to private buyers."

He glanced up at Viku. "At least that's what the general tells me."

Nervous laughter echoed throughout the hall, and Count Jaricock Wraithtide leaned forward onto the table with hands clasped in front of him, muscular arms bulging through his sleeves. "May I be the first to say that it is an honor to finally have Lady Sheline's children home, in your rightful places in the cosmos. Even if it is just through a communication array."

"I second this!" Lady Riska said with a more genuine smile than any of the others had. "Sheline was my best friend. I'm sure she'll return to us one day if the queen has anything to say about it. I'm glad you called this meeting—there have been many questionable things going on regarding how this house has been run in Sheline's absence, and frankly it has grown tiresome."

"Rich, coming from a penny-pinching nymphomaniac who doesn't have the foresight of a gnat," Lord Wyvern Wraithtide, a younger man with sandy blond hair, muttered loud enough for everyone to hear. "If you'd just allow us to spend more of the treasury on slave acquisition by even ten billion A-grade coins for the next year, we'd easily increase revenue by 20 percent and make up the difference in no time. Just ask Baron Orimus and Count Jaricock—they've been badgering me about slave acquisition in the mines for a decade, and all I get from you is the same whining complaints about how the numbers don't add up."

This immediately sent Lady Riska to her feet. "You watch your tongue, little man! There ARE discrepancies in the vaults. Someone is stealing from our house coffers, and I have a pretty good idea of who that is!"

The room went into an uproar, with Lady Riska pointing accusatory fingers at numerous people while Count Jaricock, Baron Orimus, Duke Hazith, and Duchess Ova got to their feet, flinging insults at the old woman while Lord Wyvern put on a sly, amused smile and leaned back to watch the fireworks go off.

"It is not STEALING if it is for the betterment of our house, Lady Riska!" Count Jaricock hissed angrily with clenched teeth. "We need more manpower to make more money and you're not willing to invest! It's that simple! Do you even know WHEN was the last time that we bought slaves in bulk?! It's been twenty years! TWENTY GODS DAMNED YEARS, YOU OLD HAG!"

"With six billion slaves, you should be able to repopulate your losses easily enough!" Lady Riska snapped back with a snarl. "Your operations in the mines are just as careless as Orimus over there! Zero safety measures and cattle dying off like flies whenever a tunnel collapses or a smelting chamber blows up! Completely careless and unacceptable! If you want money to reorganize the mines and set out new safety measures, then I'd gladly hand you money to do so—but I will NOT give you more money to buy more slaves just to kill them by the hundreds of thousands with your careless laziness! Not to mention the amount of food it'd take to FEED another influx of slaves—food that Lord Wyvern here knows VERY well we'd have to import because our farmlands were RUINED in the slave uprisings that mysteriously started popping up as soon as Riven and Allie were found. How odd is that, hmm?! DOES ANYONE ELSE THINK THAT'S RATHER ODD?!"

Next to her, the couple Lord Ruim and Lady Nulasta nodded sagely in agreement.

"It is certainly odd," Lord Ruim allowed, eyelids half lowered like he was bored.

Duke Hazith tsked in irritation. "Oh, shut up, you pink-haired fucking fairy twat! I don't even know why you and your wife are on this council, for all the good you do! Infrastructure and education are peasant work if you ask me!"

Lord Ruim only rolled his eyes, not bothering to reply.

Riven's one raised eyebrow stayed aloft, and beside him Allie began to giggle and snort underneath a hand raised to cover her amusement.

"This is like a *Jerry Springer* episode—family feud edition!" Allie said with another snorting laugh, and Riven had to chuckle with a shake of his head while just taking in the absolute madness that Lord Wyvern had obviously intentionally provoked.

Even now the man was sitting back with that amused grin, silently sipping on a drink while the other nobles of House Wraithtide raged at one another.

General Viku, on the other hand, was unamused. "Prince Riven, Princess Allie, should I shut them up?"

"Absolutely not. At least not yet," Allie replied with a dismissive wave of her hand, leaning forward and taking in all that was being said with a keen eye. "Let them talk for as long as they can. I'm finding all this information very interesting. Oh, and please—bring up that slave you talked about right before we entered the room . . . I want to confirm a few things with him before really making any decisions on what to do here."

Jeltuna was a Sarak, a native species to Luteski that'd been enslaved hundreds or possibly even thousands of years ago by the vampires—though he'd not lived long enough to know the exact timeline. He'd been born into slavery along with all the others now kept in the mines, on the farms, or in homes as servants and sex workers for the vampiric population. He'd dreamed of freedom his entire life, dreamed that a savior would one day come to free his people from this hellish life they and their children now lived. It was all he'd ever known, and it had caused a burning hatred for the vampiric kind.

Yet he'd also been afraid. Too afraid to act on his own . . . until something akin to a miracle was found in the form of a small note on his rotting wooden desk in the slave barracks. It was a location with a key code to a vault, as well as a threat—and a set of instructions.

His moment to take back the lives of his people had finally come. The threat had been unnecessary—he would do it regardless.

Jeltuna's drifting thoughts were interrupted by the sliding clang of his cell door, and his pale eyes lifted up to see two vampiric soldiers come in. His purple skin was a stark contrast to theirs, as was his white hair and two smooth antennae that were soft and fleshy as opposed to insectoid.

"You've come to kill me, I hope?" Jeltuna said in ragged gasps, the shackles around his wrists and ankles pulling against the chains that tethered him to the wall. He spat blood from bruised, cracked lips. Still, he managed to let out a chuckle. "I have no regrets. I took my vengeance, and I will never apologize for what I have done. Not after the horrors your kind has inflicted on my people for generations! You all sicken me!"

One of the two vampire soldiers shrugged, walking over to where Jeltuna was still tethered to the wall. "I don't care if you apologize or not, cattle. Personally, I'd rather just throw you out an airlock now to be done with it, but apparently the prince and princess want to see you."

Jeltuna was about to snarl something back, when the realization of what the soldier had said hit him. He abruptly stopped. "Prince? Princess?"

"House Wraithtide's main branch has finally returned. They're here now in spectral form and want to talk to you, hopefully before they let us gut you. Come on, cattle—let's get going, fast. If you slow us down, I'll start taking fingers."

Jeltuna was shoved out of the prison cell and into a long lane that stretched far into the dark. His kind were adept at seeing in the dark, however, just like the vampires, which made them good slaves to have in the dark mines beneath Luteski.

"Any disrespect to the royals will be an immediate beheading." His red eyes turned to glare down at the slave the other soldier was yanking along. "After that we'll kill your family, too. I know you have kids and a wife back on surface, so don't make us do that. Understand? These royals have the say-so to completely wipe out your entire pathetic race with a simple command, so don't test them. You creatures are already on thin ice and just begging for a purging after the shit you pulled in those rebellions."

Negrada's flaming eye shifted to gaze upon his breached body, where thousands of enemy undead poured over his demon and Azag warriors in the pits of hell to try and stave off the invasion of their home. Pillars of fire boiled and pulsed out of volcanic pits, the skies were filled with ash, and the raging hordes collided along a bridge connecting his fortress to an exit.

He was losing. His allies had already been overrun, and soon even his own dungeon core would be shattered and consumed by the enemy dungeons now finishing their ransacking of the last of his friends. If Riven hadn't given him the Azag relic, Negrada would have been long dead already. It'd been his greatest boon since the war had begun.

[Cursed Azag Sanctuary Stone: This sanctuary stone enables the bearer to create an Azag Hive Cluster Sanctuary and will list the creator of this sanctuary as this hive's Overmind. This sanctuary will seclude an area of the planet in a protective layer that has permanence for one year and can only be passed through by the Overmind, Azag, and whomever the Overmind deems allies. Becoming the Hive Overmind will enable the creator of this sanctuary to create a hatchery immediately upon creation and will open up the queen and drone pathways to breed units with. More units will be available upon creation of the necessary biological modification facilities. Warning: This item is cursed; it afflicts the owner with compulsions that are in the best interest of the Azag Hive Clusters and links the owner to the galactic hive minds for communication purposes.]

The great eye, wreathed in hellfire, flashed away and appeared back in his altar room where the dungeon boss he'd created now slept soundly. He didn't bother waking the creature just yet, no—his guardian needed as much rest as possible after slaughtering the last invading army. Instead, Negrada turned his sight to a crystal ball that depicted a frontier planet on the edge of integrated space. Negrada was in a very weak area of hell that was full of F- and E-grade enemies, with no one here higher than late E-grade. Low amounts of ambient mana meant less dangerous enemies, and it'd allowed an upstart dungeon like himself to remain viable for as long as he had.

Those days were quickly closing, however.

Perhaps . . . perhaps he could hire some mercenaries to help him.

Yes. That was what he would do. Riven still had the ability to portal back, and with him he could bring others . . . Or perhaps he could even use the mercenary guild system instead. Hadn't guild functions just arrived on Panu anyways? Elysium would be angry about it, but it technically wasn't against the rules. Taxes would be high, and that would be the end of it. He was desperate enough to pay the taxes even if it bankrupted him now, because if he was dead, what use would he have for treasures and wealth?

Sending a message to his demonic servants at the trading commune in Brightsville, he prepared a tribute to the vampire who'd started as a mere whelp in the depths of his first dungeon level. He was interested in Riven's response.

CHAPTER 8

"Prince Riven Wraithtide, Princess Allie Wraithtide, and Princess Kathrine Vonsilla Crushada the Ninth, we have brought the requested prisoner."

Jeltuna the Sarak was led, bound and chained, into a large and elegant hall, filled with some of the most prominent faces on the planet. Despite having led insurrections in protest of his people's treatment, enslavement, butchering, and worse, he couldn't help but go slightly pale at the sight of the vampiric nobles who were glaring at one another before sending smoldering looks his way. Immediately upon coming into their presence, he began to feel their auras slowly and passively bearing down on him.

Lady Riska, Count Amestrius, General Viku, Count Jaricock, and Baron Orimus were all immediately recognizable from pamphlets and propaganda campaigns in the Luteski forums and on display crystals in the mines. The others were less so, but each of these Wraithtide nobles was far, far beyond anything Jeltuna had come to face in his rebellion's battles against relatively weaker vampires.

The soldiers and civilians he'd fought and killed were middle E-grade at best, and those skilled enough to even reach E-grade at all were some of the most feared opponents Jeltuna had ever come across. They were machines of war, slaughtering hundreds of Sarak slaves who'd in turn been quarantined all their lives and restricted in their leveling. The best of the Sarak, including Jeltuna himself, had needed to pile their enormous number advantage onto these opponents just to bring a single one of them down. But here?

Here he couldn't even recognize what grade of cultivation any of them were at. Just a single one of them could have crushed entire armies of Sarak, which led to the question—why hadn't they done so? Were his attempts to buy freedom for his people truly pathetic enough that they would not even bother metaphorically glancing his way?

Unfortunately, he didn't last long before the effects of their cultivation differences broke the tension resonating around his soul aperture with a thunderous internal crash. The mere presence of EACH of these vampires was astronomically high, excluding the four ghostly apparitions at the end of the table, which gave off no signature at all. But the presence of the vampiric nobles weighed down on him like the weight of a world—crushing him abruptly as he gasped and fell to his knees. His eyes boggled, his heart frantically beat and felt like it'd explode, and his entire body began to quiver and spasm when a seizure began to take him.

"Please nullify your passive auras," General Viku called to the other leaders of House Wraithtide in a stern voice that allowed no objection. "You're going to kill the slave before he even gets to speak. As much as I'm sure some of you would prefer that, you will do as you're told or I will suppress your auras for you."

Baron Orimus glared daggers at the military man but did as he asked, and soon all the others had done so as well.

Jeltuna stopped seizing, but the bruising along his body had increased with small tears in his skin opening up at random. Coughing and gasping for air again, he was yanked up by his metal collar back into a kneeling position. Head spinning and gaze shifting from face to face, his hatred for these vampires began to bubble up to the surface as a sneer took hold of him.

"Get that disgusting look off your face, maggot." One of the two guards glared angrily, drawing his broadsword and putting it up to Jeltuna's neck. The weapon flickered with Unholy energy, and runes began lighting up the base of the blade with a hiss. "You are in the presence of royalty, and you will show proper respect."

"Do not harm him," a man's voice called from the very end of the table, from one of the ghostly apparitions that sat in a chair with hands clasped on the wood.

The soldier immediately straightened and bowed. "Yes, sire. My apologies."

The soldier stepped back, sheathing his blade and straightening to face forward.

Silence engulfed them, and Jeltuna used the ticking second to better get ahold of his breathing again. "Is this some kind of sick execution? Or are you playing mind games before you torture me to death like you do so many of my people?"

The Sarak man spat in the table's direction, but he was so weak from lack of food and beatings that it barely went a few inches and onto the floor, where a nearby servant quickly came over to wipe it off the polished metal with a handker-chief before returning to the wall.

"You would be wise to keep your tongue in check, slave," Baron Orimus said with a click of his tongue. "Know your place, and perhaps your coming death will be less brutal than I'd originally intended it to be—"

"His death is not your decision to make, Baron Orimus," the ghostly appa-rition at the end of the table announced, cutting the noble off with a wave of his hand.

The noble looked both cowed and irritated, but he shut up a moment later with a submissive bow to the apparition. "As you say, Your Highness."

Ah. So this must be the prince. Jeltuna silently eyed the apparition with a wary gaze. "Is it you who called for me? The so-called prince? Why? What words could you possibly want with a man you value so little—a man of a race that you use as a commodity rather than valuing us as real people?"

The apparition smiled sadly. "Yes, I am a prince of the empire. My name is Riven, and you can call me as such. Though I never said that I viewed you or your race that way."

The comment threw Jeltuna off slightly. Call the prince by his first name? He blinked rapidly, but then caught the glances shared between other vampiric nobility. They, too, wore looks of surprise and even anger. "Yet you enslave billions of us to work in your mines, on your farms, for blood sport entertainment, and as sex objects to be traded like collectibles in breeding programs."

"An unfortunate aspect of my heritage, yes," Riven said with a shrug. "I will admit, I even took part in enslaving an enemy force on the world I currently live on—but I also say that I let most of them go shortly thereafter. Now the only people who live as slaves from that particular group are the ones who can't behave and the ones who committed crimes too sinister to be forgiven. Now, most of those elves are living lives as second-class citizens . . . but citizens nonetheless. I'm here to tell you now that if you cooperate with me here and make this as easy as possible for me by answering all my questions, the same will be true of your own people."

There was dead silence for mere seconds after that while Jeltuna's mind tried to comprehend what the prince had just said. His blank expression only twitched, until none other than Baron Orimus Wraithtide launched himself to his feet with a scathing snarl.

"This is an OUTRAGE! Did I just hear this right?! That you intend to elevate these CATTLE to the position of second-class citizens in the empire?! THAT'S OUTRIGHT ABSURD!" The baron slammed a fist onto the wood. His sleek brown hair shimmered in the light of the chandelier, and though he raised his voice, he did not meet Riven's gaze directly. "My prince, PLEASE rethink what you are doing here! You do not understand the ramifications of what you are saying because you did not grow up inside the empire's borders. I understand this and will happily educate you in areas where you are lacking, but giving citizenship of ANY kind to these creatures is equivalent to madness!"

"I . . . I have to agree," Lady Riska muttered dubiously, for the first time in accord with what the baron was saying. "I admit that improvements to their lives and safety are needed in order to maintain our slave population, but giving them rights as any kind of citizen goes entirely against the dogma and core values of the Blood Moon Requiem. We do not have any citizen who is not a vampire, in any house, on any planet."

Riven raised an eyebrow at this, then glanced up to General Viku, who stood as still as a statue. "Is that true?"

"It is," Kathrine stated for the general, and Viku nodded shortly to confirm.

Riven sighed, then shot Allie a look. "What do you think?"

"Fuck the dogma." Allie smiled with a shrug. "Kathrine, is it against the law to consider them secondary citizens?"

"I am not sure—it has never been attempted before. I doubt, however, that the queen would allow it," Kathrine replied uncomfortably.

"Then there's a simple work-around," Riven replied indifferently. "They're all my property, correct?"

"That is correct."

"And I can treat them however I want to, correct?"

"Correct."

"Then as long as they stay on this planet, a planet that I own, and are themselves property that I own, I can treat them the same way I would treat citizens of the empire. They just wouldn't be officially recognized as such off-world in different parts of the empire I don't directly control. Correct?"

Kathrine hesitated, but nodded yet again. "That is correct."

"Good." Riven smiled smugly, leaning back and folding his arms. "Problem solved. Now, that doesn't mean that I'm just going to bankrupt the entire house by giving freedom to all the slaves at once, mind you—we'll keep the mines running, but the quality of life for these people is going to be up to standards with any other citizen on the planet starting this week."

Lady Riska slumped her tensed shoulders in relief, but the baron was not as easily swayed from his anger.

"Treat the Sarak cattle like vampiric citizens?" Baron Orimus let his jaw drop, only to pick it up with a spluttering snort and throw out his arms to the others at the table. "Are the rest of you hearing this?! Are the other elders of our house hearing this lunacy? He's ALREADY implemented child labor laws, has stopped butchering cattle in favor of regular blood drains, has built schools and established free health care for any slave that needs it! These two siblings have angered the other noble houses in ABUNDANCE. We have House Barimont on the verge of forming a trading blockade on the edge of Wraithtide space, the siblings have NO experience in running a planet, and all of a sudden they make massive changes to our way of life after having lived less than a century?! THEY ARE MERE BABES! This is utterly absurd! This will be the downfall of our house and lineage if we let it slide!"

Mutters of agreement spread among some of the house elders, while others remained stoic and silent. Riven and Allie merely watched, too, waiting for the baron to continue—and when Orimus finally looked in the direction of the prince, Riven waved him on.

"You obviously have a lot to say on the matter, Baron Orimus. Please, go on. I'll listen."

Seeming encouraged, the baron straightened slightly and huffed loudly. "Not to mention that for all the good you have shown these animals, how do they repay you—my prince?"

He swiftly shoved an accusing finger in Jeltuna's direction. "This man and many others spearheaded rebellions all across the planet, ending in the deaths of not only hundreds of thousands of slaves—but just as many vampires! Your loyal citizens—TRUE citizens of the empire like you and me! You cannot think of giving those barbaric animals that would so carelessly slaughter your innocent citizens another free ride?! If anything, you should retract the gifts you have already given them for their lack of gratitude!"

"Do true citizens of the empire plot against the royal family? Or is that just you?" Allie spoke out, a crisp edge to her words. "I'm curious. Enlighten me, oh esteemed elder of mine. General Viku—if you would?"

Once again the room became dead silent, and General Viku set a solid black cube on the table. He pressed a couple buttons and a recording of his talk with Baron Orimus Wraithtide from the command deck of the supercarrier went on display.

Recording of Past Events (Concerning the reader, feel free to skip if you wish to do so):
The cube in his hand gave off a steady vibration again and then began to blink. It drew his red eyes down to stare at it, and from underneath his helmet, a small smile crept over his lips to display his fangs.

Finally.

"General Viku!" one of the house elders, a man by the name of Baron Orimus Wraithtide, called out while walking onto the elevated platform of the command deck. His wiry posture moved like a practiced snake in burgundy robes, and his eyes glinted mischievously under slicked-back chestnut hair while glaring at the screens on the general's sides. "I see the rebellions are going well. The agents we planted are supplying as necessary—not too much but enough to cause trouble. Are the damages being quarantined to the designated areas?"

General Viku nodded gravely. "Yes. The production facilities and mining operations are all still under our protection. We're letting the slaves sack the Bezin and Norcof districts, where our poorer citizens reside. It'll be enough vampiric blood to get quite a reaction out of the rest of the empire—they'll be calling for a culling."

His eyes shifted to the well-groomed other vampire as Baron Orimus Wraithtide nodded in approval. "Do you really think it wise to go against a high-ranking prince like this? Sheline's son, of all people?"

The baron scoffed indifferently, watching as cargo ships from other sectors in the galaxy warped in through a spatial gate before changing course to dock at the space station nearby for check-in. "Sheline is dead, and her son made it very clear to the rest of us that he can't be trusted to lead the family when he gave those Sarak cattle rights. Can you believe this list of changes to the laws that we have to abide by? Just listen to this!"

General Viku rolled his eyes, turning his head so the baron wouldn't see. He knew very well what the changes were, and to him they weren't all that big of a deal—but to an old-timer like Baron Orimus Wraithtide, it appeared to be the end of the gods damned multiverse.

The old vampire pulled out a list, then put on a pair of reading glasses while loudly clearing his throat and staring down the bridge of his nose at the hastily scribbled-on parchment. "Ahem! Where is it . . . Ah yes. Just to BEGIN the list, we have protection for the cattle children!"

Baron Orimus Wraithtide raised an eyebrow and scoffed again in disbelief, glancing at the general, who continued to stare down at the planet from their perch on the flagship's deck. "Do you realize what that means, Viku? It means no child labor, which cuts down production by an entire 9 percent worldwide. No delicacies at the Rouge Café that I so frequently visit or ANY OTHER high-end establishment on the planet. No training them for unique positions such as concubines or slave warriors. No pets for our own vampiric children. It's absurd! Utterly absurd! And that's just the CHILDREN of these cattle!"

The baron smacked the paper again with mouth agape, shaking his head violently and huffing loudly. "No gladiator battles between slaves, no torture without reason, oh—here is one of my favorites—NO BUTCHERING CATTLE IN FAVOR OF REGULAR BLOOD DRAINS?! IS THIS MAN SERIOUS?! I nearly got up and left THAT VERY DAY after reading this ridiculous list! We literally BREED SARAK in some specialty lineages to become fatter so we can EAT THEM! WE HAVE TO SPARE THEIR LIVES AND JUST USE THEM AS RENEWABLE BLOOD BALLOONS? THIS IS RIDICULOUS!"

General Viku stared straight ahead, trying to give off apathy, but inside he was struggling very hard not to smirk. He'd never liked Baron Orimus Wraithtide very much, but since the ruling lady of the house left many years ago, never to return, the baron was one of three house nobles who were in contention for patriarch or matriarch due to Lady Sheline's absence. It was Viku's great misfortune that he had to listen to this idiot babble, otherwise he would have hung him from a tree many months ago when Riven and Allie had first appeared.

The baron continued to rant, jabbing a wiry old finger into the paper with each thing he listed. "We have improved slave housing, which has cost us trillions: compensation built into our tax system for slaves who donate more blood over the course of a year than others, ability to attend NEWLY BUILT CRAFTING SCHOOLS that also cost us a fortune, FREE HEALTH CARE, and a clause that allows slaves to own basic property? HE MIGHT AS WELL MAKE THEM HONORARY CITIZENS! And that doesn't even BEGIN to touch upon the fact that he and his sister are being auctioned off to the highest bidder AS WE SPEAK, with the conclusion of the bids in coming months allowing a FOREIGN vampiric noble house the rights to be WED to them?! We might as well just hand away the keys and pack up all our belongings now! I hear that House Crushada is especially invested in obtaining Riven and has even managed to get their daughter to seduce him on that integrating planet! This is the end for our lineage if we don't do something about it now, Viku! And I'll be damned if it happens while I'm still alive! It may take a couple underhanded schemes and maybe a couple years, but eventually if we're able to prove incompetence, we can petition the crown and have him removed. If it were anyone else without the bloodline, I'd just have him assassinated, but the queen would have my head faster than you could say 'Sarak cattle shit' if I even tried. So though I do not want to go up against a prince of our own house, I do not believe I have a choice in order to maintain our way of life. Sometimes, dark deeds must be done for the greater good of the family."

The baron reached out and put a hand on General Viku's shoulder pauldron, patting him twice. "I know I can count on you to do the right thing, Viku. Just remember what we're fighting for, and why we're letting this happen. I expect your full cooperation in this matter, and in future ones. We cannot let outside forces like House Crushada interfere in our internal affairs unless we want to be absorbed by them. I know they've been in contact with you, and I hope you see past their lies. Do you understand?"

General Viku spared the old man a glance, keeping eye contact and clicking his tongue before turning heel and beginning to head down the bridge. The cube in his hand was vibrating again, and he had an appointment to keep.

"General Viku!" Baron Orimus Wraithtide called out, a little more harshly than usual, and he rushed to catch up to the larger man while scowling deeply. "I expect an answer! Let me hear you say it!"

"Say what, exactly?" Viku asked with an exasperated sigh, turning to face the smaller, thinner man as officers from along the command bridge shot curious glances their way. Viku brushed off the hand Baron Orimus Wraithtide put on his shoulder again, and he gave an irritated grunt. "If you're looking for me to turn my back on the head of this house, you have me mistaken for a blood traitor—Baron."

The baron's eyes went wide, and his pale face reddened deeply while he took a step forward. "I would watch your words, General. You are essentially calling me a blood traitor by association, and I do not take such offense lightly."

"Are you threatening me?" General Viku's figure stepped forward to meet the shorter man, towering over him as his hand drifted to the broadsword at his hip.

He stood there glaring down at the baron, and the older man's eye twitched when he saw the general's hand on his weapon. Other soldiers in the room were now dead silent, watching to see whether or not the baron would keep his head on his shoulders. Viku was an A-grade warrior, nothing to be scoffed at by anyone, and if he wanted the baron dead, the baron would no doubt be dead very soon.

"Let me make something very clear to you," General Viku said with a sneer. "It was not you who elevated me to this position. Nor was it any of the still-living elders of this house. This house is a shadow of what it once was, thanks to you and people like you. Now that the main bloodline has finally returned, I no longer have to answer to you. My position is due to Riven's mother, a true leader, and I owe her everything. Everything that I have is due to her, and here you come years after she disappears to threaten what is rightfully her children's inheritance? In what world did you think I would agree to such schemes? Ask yourself one more time, Baron Orimus Wraithtide: Is what you are doing wise?"

When the recording ended, Baron Orimus was as pale as a sheet. His fists were clenching and unclenching, and a sincere look of fearful rage had overcome him when his eyes landed on General Viku only a table's length away. "You . . . you recorded our conversation?"

The baron's fists began to tremble, and like a caged animal he leaped back— whirling around to stare at soldiers who'd placed hands on swords while looking to the general and the royals for confirmation. Power in the form of blood mana began swirling around him—and his chest began to rapidly rise and fall with eyes going wide.

"Sit down, Baron. You are not going to be killed today," Allie called out, getting a confused and scared stare from the baron while other nobles and elders of House Wraithtide sat in rigid positions along their own seats. "I said sit, and I will not say it again. Unless you truly do want to have your head removed—which could be arranged. Riven has given me full leeway to decide your fate, along with the fates of other traitors currently sitting at this table with us. There are more than just you. The reports—which were going to be entirely unfolded here for everyone to witness in the open—have for the most part been put aside after my brief review prior to entering this room. Instead of wasting time, I'll just summarize."

Allie shifted her gaze to the other nobles, one by one. "Lady Riska has been skimming off the coffers for her own gambling problems, an addiction if I've ever seen one, by astronomical amounts. Lord Wyvern has bought his own moon with Wraithtide funds. Count Jaricock has an entire sheet of well-hidden schemes that range from smuggling drugs that the high queen herself has outlawed to attempting to sell pieces of the planet off to other noble houses. Duke Hazith and Duchess Ova take a slice of every trade negotiation they make—depositing 6 percent or more directly into their own coffers and telling all the rest of you it never existed. Viscount Adian blackmails lesser officials regularly to sleep with their daughters. Baroness Julasi also participates in smuggling and is even a part of an illegal syndicate, most often dealing in the movement of exotic treasures stolen from other murdered or kidnapped nobles of the empire. Baron Eethinsa has a bad habit of killing random people for fun and then covering it up. Count Amestrius takes bribes from almost all of you in order to look the other way, and he is currently holding General Viku's own daughter as a hostage to make sure Viku does what he wants—with the threat of removing Viku from power should he attempt to subvert the 'will' of our house. The ONLY ones who do not have any dirt on their names are Lord Ruim and Lady Nulasta Wraithtide. Did I miss anything, General Viku?"

"Many things," General Viku said, staring ice-cold hate in Count Amestrius's direction as the other vampire's fingers went rigid gripping the wood of the table. "Give me the word and I will execute as many of them as you'd like."

Lord Ruim and Lady Nulasta, for their part, both looked rather smug, snickering at the other house elders who'd begun looking sick to their stomachs.

Allie chuckled bitterly. "I see. Lord Ruim and Lady Nulasta will be rewarded for their loyalty and will be promoted to a position ahead of all the rest of you, to run the planet with General Viku when we are not here. An order to the military forces under our control has already been sent out to inform them, should any of you try to undermine them, but we'll get to that later. The first order of business in the present, Baron Orimus, is sitting down. Then we can discuss just what we are going to do with my dear distant relatives—but no, I do not intend to kill you, even if it is what the general here would like."

Baron Orimus was outright shocked, just as many of the others were, and he hesitantly let the power building at his fingertips fade before walking to the table and sitting down with a dumbstruck expression.

"Count Amestrius, you will immediately release General Viku's daughter," Riven announced for the room to hear. "She will be put on a ship and within General Viku's possession before you leave this supercarrier. If you do not comply, you and your entire branch will be executed for treason—and your estate will be burned to the ground. You will also be forced to pay compensation for the harm you have done to him and his family until General Viku is satisfied. Try anything like that again, and I give General Viku permission to kill you on a whim without my say-so, and if you try to escape you will be labeled an outlaw with a bounty put on your head."

The count gave a sharp nod, then pulled out a tablet and began to transcribe a message—hands shaking slightly under the rage-filled gaze of the military officers surrounding him.

"My prince! My princess! I would like to explain . . ." Lady Riska began with a sheepish smile.

Allie shook her head. "No need to explain. Let me be frank: despite the things you've all done here—it has been made clear to us by not only General Viku, but also by Princess Kathrine, what roles you all play in running the planet. Most of you have major problems and are very corrupt, but you—Lady Riska—are probably on the lower end of offenses. Mere gambling with house money is problematic considering how much it was, but it is reported that you otherwise did a fine job. Please be at ease."

Riska visibly relaxed, letting out a sigh of relief.

"For the rest of you . . . you'll be able to keep your positions, but needless to say, this all ends now. You'll be given a onetime pass for the crimes you committed in our absence—with two exceptions." Allie's words struck home, gathering all the attention of the surrounding nobles, who looked both very surprised and just as relieved as Lady Riska had been moments before. "Viscount Adian, you will immediately stop blackmailing lesser officials and will be spending some amount of time in prison for what you did. You will also be paying the families a solid chunk of change for the emotional damage you likely did to them. Baron Eethinsa, your murder-spree hobby is going to stop. Immediately. You, too, will be spending a solid amount of time in prison, but you will be let out on good behavior if you agree to the terms I set out. I'd rather not have an internal family struggle, but if you have a problem with our terms, you're free to try to run or fight. General Viku assures me that he'll easily put either of you down like a dog if push comes to shove, despite the private soldiers you two keep in your family estates."

"I willingly comply with your decree, Princess," Baron Eethinsa, the murderer, stated with a tight-lipped bow. "Your judgment is more than I could ask for in any normal circumstances, far more lenient than I would have thought possible. May I ask why? Your reputation on Panu is one of malice and brutality, if I may be frank."

Viscount Adian nodded in agreement. "I, too, accept your terms and will spend my time in prison as you suggest. Thank you for your mercy."

Allie merely gave a sly smile. "I intend to use each of you instead. I will give you a single chance to prove yourselves starting now. It is true that nearly all of you are, simply put, ready for the noose . . . but each of you has a vast amount of experience in politics and knowledge on how to run businesses, a planet, and our house that I simply don't have. Think of this as an olive branch, the only one you will ever get."

"In other words, your actions will be closely monitored and most of you are one step away from losing everything," Riven cut in with a raised finger, then he pointed at Jeltuna kneeling on the floor. "And I'll hear no more bullshit about how I treat my own slaves, either. Not from you people."

Sufficiently cowed, the nobles' muttering quickly silenced.

Baroness Julasi, a platinum-blonde woman wearing a black and yellow dress, cleared her throat nervously and tapped her fingers on the table before speaking out. "Your highnesses . . . May I ask what you are to do with me, specifically? Regarding the syndicate . . . if the high queen found out about smuggling, kidnapping, and murders of other nobles in different houses . . ."

Her voice trailed off, unsure of what else to say.

Lady Riska snorted in derision. "Here I thought my gambling problem was bad, and I'm sitting in the same room with a bunch of treacherous demons. No offense meant, Lady Fay."

Fay gave the vampiric woman a brief smile of acknowledgment. "None taken."

"You will continue as you have been, but your loyalty will be to this house—not to the syndicate. You will feed us information regarding syndicate activities around the empire. Acting otherwise will lead to a swift execution without warning," Allie stated matter-of-factly—getting more looks of surprise from not only the nobles, but from General Viku and the surrounding soldiers as well. "Let me be clear: I'm not sure who my allies are and who is truly my enemy. My great-grandmother the high queen does seemingly have good intentions for us in some ways, but in others I am questioning whether I am simply a pawn for her, as was seen in the most recent attempt to sell my hand in marriage. Was that her? Or was that Elder Thune? I don't know, and I don't pretend to know. Some of you might call this borderline treason, but that'd be rich coming from the lot of you. This room was also completely swept by General Viku and his men, so there won't be any recordings of what is said leaking to the public by any known means available. The soldiers and servants were personally picked by the general as well, and I have full faith in his abilities to maintain their well-being—to take action against those that might think disposing of them for knowing too much is a good idea. Should any of them mysteriously die off for knowing your secrets, I'll start ordering heads to be removed—starting with the lot of you. I want to avoid any political upheaval in this house, but don't think that I will shy away from it just for the sake of maintaining experience. Riven, did you want to add anything?"

Riven coughed, then nodded and leaned forward again. "Yes. Back to the topic of slaves and slave rights. I've written a draft of what I want changed and have already given it to the general here, who will enforce these laws. As stated earlier, General Viku will have absolute authority in our absence while Lord Ruim, along with Lady Nulasta, will be placed firmly at the top of the house hierarchy underneath General Viku starting immediately. House Crushada and House Wraithtide are to sign a mutual agreement of self-defense in case of an internal blood feud regarding recent events at the vampiric compound on Panu, and exclusive trade rights will be given to House Crushada as a way of thanks."

Kathrine's eyes rose in surprise and then delight as a wide smile exploded across her features. "This is news to me! I thought you'd not wanted to talk to my family about such things yet!"

"I'll tell you about it later." Riven grinned her way. "Long story, you can join us for dinner tonight at my manor for the details. Oh, and one more thing."

Riven gestured to Jeltuna, the Sarak man with purple skin, who had been completely forgotten by many of the nobles in the room. "Jeltuna is going to be promoted to a position called the Voice of the Sarak, starting immediately. I believe that he was hailed a hero by many of his kind, and I'd like him—despite your poor attempts to push the deaths of these rebellions upon his back alone—to be the man who thinks of ways to better the lives of the slave population. Congratulations, Jeltuna, your rebellions seem to have paid off—despite them originating from Baron Orimus for quite the opposite reasons."

CHAPTER 9

Mara's hooded figure walked under a dreary sky alongside two necromancers, Nin and Vin, and two vampires, Gurth'Rok and Dr. Brass. Together, the five of them ran most things on his side of the world, along with the efforts of General Bruner from Chicago, who was not present today.

Crowds parted before their heavily armed escort, and they made their way through the active streets of Brightsville while heading in the direction of Riven's guild hall manor—which was technically home to the three undead necromancers as well.

"Three audiences in one day . . . what a rarity," Mara muttered in irritation. "At least we're doing it all at once. I was hoping to finish my experiments rather than deal with more politics."

"Such is the life of a second-in-command," Nin, the skeletal skresh, stated promptly with a skip to his step. "I for one am rather eager to find out just what Negrada is trying to pitch us."

Negrada had recently stationed one of his people inside Riven's guild hall as a hire-on, very similar to what Kathrine herself had done whenever she was on-planet. This made direct access to the Thane siblings rather easy, as opposed to being stuck at the Elysium altar or their trading compounds like most. That particular person had very recently sent a messenger to collect Mara concerning matters of "importance," while almost simultaneously a separate messenger had been sent saying that vampires of the underdark had come up from passing through Deepnest for more direct contact after Riven had flat out ignored them in favor of other events, such as when the dwarves had been conquered and made into another vassal state.

Mara knew Riven wasn't intentionally doing so, but she could only facepalm and shake her head—although the importance of the matter was probably high if they really were here on business pertaining to the vampiric elder god world quest. He was just so busy that he barely had time to breathe, and she was hesitant to complain about his brief getaway across the planet with Hakim's group, either.

The third audience that'd come up was none other than representatives from Deepnest again. This time, though, things were more on edge with the ratkin, who

believed that it was their right to claim the dwarves as food and slaves for themselves. Of course Allie had flat out refused them this, saying that it was Riven who'd
broken the war, and telling Deepnest that if it wasn't for the necropolis—they'd all
be rat shish kebabs.

That hadn't gone over very well. But Allie simply couldn't find it in herself to
care, thinking Deepnest's queen to be quite selfish and simultaneously ungrateful
for the help they'd gotten. That was probably why Mara had been the one to repeatedly hear their gripes ever since the Thane Necropolis had claimed the dwarves as
vassal citizens and slaves—similar to how the elves were being treated in Tereen.
Citizens who behaved were left alone or given opportunities, and people who made
problems were enslaved and made to do hard labor until they learned their lesson.
People who made more serious problems and committed steep offenses, if not
outright killed, were enslaved for life.

The multistory stone manor came into view soon enough, with guards
patrolling the fence and Genua already standing out in front in a maid outfit.

"Genua," Mara called out, nodding in affirmation when they all approached
the front doors that'd swung open—elf servants on either side. Most of the people
who'd landed jobs at the manor had kept them due to the pay, even though they
weren't slaves anymore, and it'd even become something of a status symbol for the
young women and few men who'd successfully retained spots there.

The elf-turning-thrall smiled and nodded, respectfully bowing her head at
the approach of her superiors. "Hello, Mara. Nice to see the rest of you as well.
The diplomats from Deepnest, Negrada, and the vampire covens of Bernzee are
awaiting your arrival in the east wing."

"Who or what is Bernzee?"

"A vampiric city in the underdark, or so say the ratkin."

"I see. Where is Tupper, if I may ask?"

"He's taking the day off. I believe he's indulging in some frivolous activities with
one of the other elf maidens in his room. That, or they really are watching one of
those 'movies' the Earth people always talk about. I told him that while I'm temporarily back here in Brightsville awaiting Lord Riven's return from the Blood Moon
Requiem's estate, I could fulfill the duties he otherwise takes on. It won't be long until
I return to join my daughter Len anyways, and Tupper was always very kind to me."

"That was very nice of you. How is Len doing, if I may ask?"

"Quite well. She has decreed that she and Azmoth are getting married one day,
and the brutalisk has taken a liking to being her babysitter whenever he's around.
She talks about it quite often—I think it's rather cute and very innocent."

Mara snorted, pale eyes rolling with amusement, then gestured for the maid
to go ahead. "All right, show us the way."

Genua swept her long golden hair off to one side, then turned heel and with
perfect posture continued into the reception room before turning right. Passing a
couple of armored death knights and cyborgs posted at intervals on the first floor,
they made their way to the set of double doors at the end of a long hall.

The stone manor's eastern wing contained the largest room in the entire building. It was here that the large indoor pool was located, and just above it on an elevated floor overlooking the pool were the dining room and kitchen. A large crystal chandelier had been installed, and candles had been placed all around the perimeter of the room on shelves and other fixtures. Food was already set out along the rectangular redwood table set with fancy glass cutlery.

The three delegations had already segregated themselves to a point.

Deepnest had sent Rashtalia, the broodmother of Brood-Tarrow—the equivalent of a noble house in ratkin society. She'd been the go-between for the queen and the Thanes ever since Snagger, the oversized and muscular ratkin warrior Riven had first met in the tunnels underneath Brightsville, had introduced them. She was sitting now, but when standing measured seven feet tall, and she wore a platinum necklace that hung down over her chest. She was thin with brown fur and was dressed in a formfitting white robe. Her long, bare tail, clawed hands and feet, and mouselike ears and face were certainly ratkin in origin—but anyone could still tell she was very feminine for a rat person. She was accompanied by two armored soldiers, positioned on either side of where she sat alone eating berries and tarts off a plate.

Farther down the table sat a hunched, red-skinned Jabob demon with three green eyes and a long braided beard, with a gnarled staff laid against his chair. His skin was wrinkled, but he was familiar to Mara. His name was Fred, or at least that's what he preferred to be called, since so many of the mortal races butchered the pronunciation of his real name, and he was the trading commune's leader—temporarily having shifted over to become an enlisted hire via the guild hall functions just like Tupper and Kathrine had done. He wore a rather odd-looking, pointy, bright-purple, flat-brimmed wizard's hat that expanded a couple feet in all directions, and the demon was apparently deep in meditation upon the flavor of the sauces used by the manor's cooks regarding a steak he was halfway through eating.

Lastly, and just a couple seats down from the other two, was another group of three blond vampire men. The trio all had red eyes and pale skin, though their eyes didn't glow the same kind of bright crimson the purebloods had—being more comparable to Gurth'Rok and Dr. Brass.

Mara frowned. Greater vampires, perhaps?

[Lesser Vampire Assassin, Level 40]
[Lesser Vampire Scout, Level 35]
[Lesser Vampire Warlock, Level 42]

Nope. Lesser vampires. Their bloodlines must be quite diluted when compared to the two allies following behind her.

The vampiric diplomats were all dressed in purple and black silks with hoods shadowing their faces, and all of them wore extravagant rings. The three grew quiet upon Mara's approach, though they were the first ones to stand in respect when she took the steps up to the elevated platform overlooking the shimmering indoor pool.

Genua cleared her throat as the others stood, then made formal introductions with a steely gaze cast upon the vampiric entourage in particular. "Honored guests and diplomats, I present to you Chancellor Mara Tovane of the Thane Necropolis. With her are the four esteemed counselors, Gurth'Rok, previously known as war chief of the Yellow Skull Tribe, Dr. Brass, and the two brothers Nin Kal and Vin Kal, previously of the Great Dead Plains."

Dr. Brass sighed, pushing a hand through the silver hair he'd let grow out over his white lab coat. "I really need to get a better title."

Nin snickered, the blue-teal orbs of light in his skull sockets quivering in amusement. "Or a title at all! Perhaps just 'Counselor Brass' would be preferred?"

Nin and Dr. Brass shut up when they saw Mara's beautiful features set into a firm scowl directed their way.

"Sorry," they said simultaneously.

Sighing and rubbing her temple where two pieces of her skull had been stitched together, the ghoul woman shook her head, then gestured to Genua. "You may proceed, Genua."

The elf and soon-to-be thrall didn't skip a beat. "Our guests include Rashtalia, broodmother of Brood-Tarrow, Fred of Dungeon Negrada and the outer realms of hell, and Aksilias Bloodmare of the vampiric covens of Bernzee, alongside his two sons, Rufus Bloodmare and Jakromi Bloodmare."

"It is good-great to meet-see once again!" Rashtalia said cheerfully, clawed hands clasped in front of her. "I-we just wish-say it would be better-good under other circumstance-happenings. Queen of Deepnest sends regard-tidings."

The Jabob demon, Fred, waved a hand. "Agreed, good to see you all again! Thanks for making time for a crotchety old coot like myself. The food here is great, by the way! Far better than what I get in the hellscapes."

Mara chuckled while she and the counselors all took seats at the end of the table opposite the vampiric retinue. "I'm glad you find our food to your liking, Jabob demon. Please, all of you sit. If you need further refreshments, just let Genua or one of the other elf servants on the perimeter know."

The diplomats all took their own seats soon after, all except one—the warlock and the oldest vampire of the diplomatic expedition from Bernzee. His dull red eyes followed Genua to where she took a stance next to four other elves in similar maid attire, all of them rigidly still and awaiting requests along the wall.

"Aksilias Bloodmare, was it?" Mara commented, eyeing the older blond vampire and shaking him from his staring. "Is there a problem? You seem to be glaring at our servants with ill-hidden contempt."

The vampire quickly straightened. "Apologies, Chancellor. I did not mean insult by it. I am just unused to having thralls so blatantly ignore the orders of their superiors."

The man sat down, pulling his chair in and crossing his hands one over the other—his words directed primarily at Gurth'Rok and Dr. Brass. "Do you let all your thralls have such open autonomy? It is a rare thing in our own city, but I realize that with our worlds having been merged, there are certain customs that do not translate easily."

Gurth'Rok replied before Mara could, and his pale-green hand opened palm up over the table in a gesture. "Curious words. Was there an incident that we need to be made aware of?"

"Father asked her for fresh blood, and the woman refused." One of Aksilias's sons spoke out with a chuckle, making eye contact with both Dr. Brass and Gurth'Rok in turn and smiling pleasantly. "Nothing a good lashing won't cure to remind her of her place, if you ask me."

Gurth'Rok exchanged a look with Dr. Brass, and then Mara. "Do you happen to be Rufus, or Jakromi?"

"My name is Rufus Bloodmare," the young man said simply. "My brother is Jakromi."

The vampiric orc paused in thought, red eyes narrowing. "I see. Rufus it is, then. May I ask the three of you, is it normal to go about this city of . . . what was it? Bernzee? To go about Bernzee taking other people's thralls to feed on without asking permission first? Generally we keep to our own here."

Aksilias furrowed his brows in confusion. "It is simply good manners to supply your guests with the blood of your thralls and cattle, so I would say under these circumstances—yes. It would be normal. When your wench denied my advances to taste her, it could be seen by some as a serious blow to your reputation. I had thought the Thane Necropolis would have leaders who trained their thralls better."

The room fell into an awkward silence.

Then Mara blinked, and she leaned forward.

"Ah . . . that's what happened. Let it be known that Genua is not a thrall yet, despite being what your kind calls cattle," Mara corrected, regaining the attention of the vampiric retinue who'd been primarily focused on her two counselors of similar heritage. "It is true that she is a blood source for our king, Riven, and she is certainly far along on her transition into a thrall, but Riven does not play by other people's rules in any case. Not only did we not know of your customs, but I doubt he'd abide by them or have us abide by them in his stead even if he did know. He's not an **ordinary** vampire, and neither is his sister. He cares not for the opinions of others—power trumps the need to save face."

Aksilias flushed slightly at the way she emphasized the word *ordinary*. "No offense intended, Chancellor, but being a ghoul, it does not surprise me that you don't understand the basic norms of vampiric culture. Offending me is the same as an offense to the people who sent me, and we have already been ignored for—"

"I'm sure that's a tragedy." Mara cut him off, unfazed. "But I fail to see why we should care. You come here of your own accord to discuss things related to one of the world quests, am I right?"

The vampire's frown deepened underneath his hood, and he slowly crossed his arms. "That is correct. We've been trying to contact the king and queen of your necropolis for some time now—but every time we reach out, we are ignored. We have matters to discuss concerning the vampiric elder god in the underdark. It is of great importance."

"Then let's stick to discussing that," Mara snapped with a smile that didn't reach her eyes. "I realize that it may be of importance to you and us, and everyone else on this planet, but Riven is already caught up in two other world quests, one concerning the apocalypse beasts, and the other the invaders from beyond. Even now our scouts are finding the last rats of Rippenvire's invasion force, and we are either executing them or converting them to our own side. To come into our home and complain of asinine matters regarding why you can't suck the blood of my king's personal servant, especially after we just annihilated a vampiric army that is no doubt far more powerful than your own, speaks volumes about the pompous and shortsighted attitude you and the people you represent bring. It is not a good look—vampire of the so-called Bernzee covens."

Mara leaned back in her chair, letting the words sink in while the three hooded figures in black and deep purple glared back at her. She turned her head, then gestured to Rashtalia. "Broodmother of Deepnest, you may go first—as I think our friends from Bernzee need time to process just how they want to present themselves before speaking again."

Rashtalia shot the three glaring vampires a very brief look, shrugged, and took out a scroll that she rolled out on the table after motioning for one of the elf servants to come take her dishware away. "Thank-praise to you, Chancellor-friend! I come-walk bearing word-tidings of the bearded ones."

The scroll was pushed across the redwood table, and Mara took the parchment up in her hands, pale eyes shifting across the text before the necromancer looked back up at the taller ratkin woman. "These are number estimates regarding population, resources, buildings, and different crafters concerning the dwarves and the conquered cities of the kingdom previously known as Brya. Why am I looking at this?"

Rashtalia hesitated, then inclined her head again in respect. "My queen-mother wishes to change-steer how land-valuables are given among our kin-peoples. She believes-knows it to be unfair-sad that we of Deepnest never acquired-received any of the territory-lands of the dwarves when the war-battles were done."

Mara cocked her head to the side in confusion. "What are you talking about? All your lands were returned to you after they were taken back from the dwarves."

"Yes-yes! And it is appreciated-thanked for!" Rashtalia eagerly nodded her head, mouse ears bobbing. "But we think-say that our kin-warriors and brood died-sacrificed much, that we fought-killed and our blood spills the bearded-ones' halls-lands. My queen-mother wants the dwarflings' blood-bodies for food, and asks for Charathigog—one of two bearded city-nests that were taken-conquered at the end of battles-war."

Mara sighed audibly, feeling a killer headache coming on. "We've gone over this thrice already, Rashtalia. Your queen knows you would have lost the war, and your people would have been purged entirely if not for our help. We guarded our trade routes and supported your city, our warriors regularly fought on the front lines for experience and pay, and in the end, it was Riven who struck down the dwarf king and ended the turmoil your people had been enduring. We were more than fair in giving back the many farming villas and resource-rich caverns stolen from your people when the dwarves first arrived, but the two dwarf cities of Charathigog and Reathian are to remain under the Thane Necropolis's control as a vassal state and will eventually be integrated into our empire. Nor will we give dwarf civilians over to your people for eating—you don't need the food and simply want to kill them out of spite for what their king ordered. This is not a topic for debate."

Charathigog was the capital of the small dwarvish nation that'd recently been conquered, with a few smaller dwarvish settlements of little note surrounding it in other smaller caverns. Reathian was its sister city and, unlike Charathigog, had largely remained untouched by the war, as it was positioned deeper into the underdark with only a single and very defensible tunnel in or out. Both cities, however, were full of talent in various crafts, had thriving populations, and were built around natural treasures. Handing Charathigog over, even in its half-destroyed state, was an absolute no-go according to Allie—no matter what Deepnest did to try and convince her otherwise. It'd led to tension between the two allies, but in the end, Deepnest probably knew they were being overbearing and just wanted to get as much as they could from their sworn enemies before turning over and accepting the fact that many of the dwarvish civilians would end up living to tell the tale. It was a hard pill to swallow, considering many of the ratkin citizens had been butchered like animals in a failed attempt at genocide in the early days of the war.

Rashtalia shifted uncomfortably with the answer, then pulled out another, smaller scroll, laying it out on the table next to read off it. It ended up being the names of all the cities the Thane Necropolis now controlled, which made Mara wonder just where the diplomat of Deepnest was going with this.

Charathigog and Reathian, the dwarvish cities, were at the top of that list. Then came Brightsville, Chicago, Rockford, and Milwaukee. Dungeon Alibast was mentioned, too, given it was a strategic ally and resource that'd developed a budding town around it—with Gaia being the one presiding over that particular settlement. The kingdom of Dawn with its rebuilding capital city of Mandon, along with the northern town of Bradshire and the southern town of Belmington, were mentioned. The Earthborn city two hundred miles down the southern coast of the continent, which had turned out to be none other than Corpus Christi, was also mentioned as a very recently integrated part of the necropolis after their military might was wiped out in the battle against Rippenvire before Riven, Allie, and the Chicago air force got to saving them. The five conquered high-elf towns of Nicina, Elvirinci, Podash, Asalia, and Twinleaf were named next, along with the two conquered elvish cities of Alvadore and the previous Tereen capital, Ortalight. Bluefang, the single largest community of greenskins from various orc and goblin tribes in the area, was listed next, with two dozen villages listed at the very end. These villages included twelve elf villages from Tereen, six human villages from Dawn, and five mixed villages that'd just been created since integration that included many races of undead, humans, greenskins, and even the occasional elf who ventured outside the vassal state of Tereen.

When she finished reading off the list, Rashtalia cleared her throat to summarize. "Two dwarf city-nests. Five human city-nests. Two elf city-nests. One mixed undead-human city-nest. Five elf town-nests. One greenskin town-nest. Two human town-nests. Twelve elf village-nests. Six human village-nests. Five mixed, mostly undead, village-nests. One Dungeon Alibast town-nest, elf human dryads. Forty-two population-nests total."

Rashtalia put the list back down and crossed her arms. "Deepnest only have-own five village-nests outside Deepnest, and our kin-people are starved of space-places. We need room-growth, and caverns of beards-dwarves are good to take-nest in. Charathigog half-part destroyed, yes-yes? Even if pay, we want to expand-take city of Charathigog so we too become-get stronger and larger-big! Other caverns given-taken back to us-we are unsettled or destroy-buried, need repair-resources and time-effort. Not expandable-settleable yet, refugees-homeless need place from cramped-closed Deepnest after flee-flee in war!"

Mara slowly blinked, her jaw becoming rigid. "We rightfully took those cities from the dwarves, and your people had room to live prior to discovering the dwarvish threat. As I have said many times over now, the answer is still no. You need food? We've provided that. You need access to materials and manpower? We've provided that as well. Your people even come regularly with caravans to trade, our trading compounds from off-world have been opened to you, and even access to our Elysium altar has been provided without any additional taxation. Your queen is pushing her boundaries, Rashtalia. We like you, and we like your people, but the answer remains a firm no. This is a direct order from my own queen, the butcher of Carnis, so I am sorry. If there's anything else that you want to discuss I'm open to it, but we will not be giving up the dwarvish cities of Charathigog or Reathian."

"But what if we pay-give price?" Rashtalia retorted boldly. "All things have price-list—tell us what price and Deepnest ratkin pay-pay!"

Her gaze held firm until Mara started rubbing her temple again.

"Goddamn it, Rashtalia. Fine, I'll ask Allie if there's a price that can be set on the old dwarvish capital, but I do NOT think she's going to go for it." Mara shook her head helplessly, shoulders slumping. "I am getting so damned tired of talking about this subject."

"Can't we just help you rebuild the cavern towns that were destroyed in the war?" Dr. Brass suggested, frowning equally to Mara's own. "I feel like we're being awfully generous here."

Gurth'Rok cut in next. "At least give them the opportunity to barter. The worst that comes out of it is we say no again."

Mara's eyes shifted to her old friends, the two skresh necromancers next to her. "Nin? Vin? Thoughts?"

Per usual, neither skresh cared. If it didn't involve their experiments in necromancy or war efforts that added to their piles of bodies, they simply didn't care—which meant Mara had to deal with all the political bullshit while they got to enjoy the more relaxed way of life.

Rashtalia smiled eagerly when Mara let out a defeated groan, but was stopped before she could put forth an offer.

"Write it down—it's not my decision anyway, so no need to give me the offer personally." Mara tapped one of her pale fingers on a nearby scroll. "I'll pass it along to Allie to review and give you an answer later. Don't expect a yes. Fred? What've you got?"

While Rashtalia began scribbling on a new, blank parchment she pulled out of her robe for the third time, the Jabob demon with the pointy purple wizard's hat stretched and yawned.

Fred then yanked a spatial sack onto the table and began digging around, his white beard swaying from side to side while he fidgeted with the contents, until a pale-teal crystal appeared in his hand. He placed it on the table in front of him before scooting it over with one finger. Black lines began racing along its outer edge when he first touched it, but it didn't do anything otherwise. "The status information is already prelisted on inspection—I've taken the liberty. Go on, have a look before we get started on just what I'm doing here."

"All right . . ." Confused, Mara's brows furrowed and she attempted to examine the object. To her surprise, she got far more than what was normal for someone without an identification class or skill.

[Death's Eye Crystal (Death) (Artificial Soul Core) (Ancient F-Grade Relic): An artificial soul core formed over thousands of years by Dungeon Kravash on the outskirts between hell and the Sanctified Graveyard, this item can be used to add a new soul core to nonsentient undead—or can be used to add additional soul core components to an already sentient undead. Guarantees one Dao advancement upon integration.]

As soon as Mara read the description she nearly spat blood, and Nin to her left literally fell out of his chair with a flailing motion—only to yank himself back to his feet and scramble toward the item to peer at it more closely.

"Is this real?!" Nin gasped, skeletal head whipping around to stare at the Jabob demon with avid curiosity and greed. "Tell me it's real and tell me you can get more of them, you little red monkey! TELL ME!"

"I take offense to that. I am not a mere monkey," Fred replied with a scathing glare before huffing and turning his attention back to Mara. "I suppose that this item may interest you . . . Yes? Perhaps, it may even interest the Thanes?"

Mara slowly nodded, eyes not leaving the crystal for an instant. "I guarantee you it would for all parties involved. What makes you bring out a treasure like this? Did you intend to sell it to us? I'm not sure anyone here could afford it, but perhaps Allie could when she gets back . . . Or maybe Riven. What were the taxes you spent just getting it onto this planet? Surely it was worth more than what you can attempt to sell it for! Which brings up the question . . . Why? Actually, you don't intend to sell it to us at all, do you?"

Mara's eyebrows knitted together. "What is it you want?"

Fred's scheming grin widened, smirking at the gawking looks from the vampires at the other end of the table—who also wore glassy, greedy expressions regarding the item. "I did not intend to sell it to you . . . but I did intend to trade it, and I wanted to show you just what was on the line. If I told you that not just one or two of you could acquire such a thing, but perhaps dozens or even hundreds of your people could do so? What would you say to that?"

"I'd say you're crazy," Mara retorted immediately, glaring suspiciously at the smaller demon. "These don't just grow out of nowhere. What's the catch?"

Fred nodded sagely in agreement, then leaned forward and intertwined his fingers. "Fortunately for you, there ARE many dozens of these cores . . . just waiting for the taking. It was taken off an enemy dungeon's miniboss in the hellscapes. Dungeon Kravash is very heavily oriented toward undead, after all. Fortunately for you, I can tell you where to get them. Even more fortunately, Panu's guild system just went live . . . meaning that, even aside from using guild hall prices to enlist help, you can now be HIRED by off-world entities as mercenaries. And given our little arrangement concerning the trading compound, it opens up certain avenues that would usually be . . . off-limits for a start-up dungeon like my master, Negrada. What do you know about the wars Negrada is involved in, and what do you think Riven and Allie would say to . . . Oh, I don't know . . . letting your citizens participate in mercenary work—or perhaps even involving themselves in that mercenary work as well? I hope you're interested, because this could be a lifesaving thing for my people and even the Dungeon Negrada itself, while simultaneously being very lucrative and experience-heavy for all of you. As long as your people don't die, that is."

CHAPTER 10

Three days later, near Hakim's village, Jerbyville . . .

The details of the vampiric elder god quest had been left for Allie to deal with since Riven would be leaving in a couple months for Chalgathi's next trial. Allie had essentially dropped out of the Apocalypse Beast quest line entirely after giving him her own piece, but that didn't mean she couldn't deal with the underdark while he was gone. He had faith in her to do so, and they'd decided that while Riven was gone for the next year, she would do what she could.

As long as it wasn't overly dangerous, of course.

She'd rolled her eyes at him and given him a kiss on the forehead when he'd insisted on this, but nevertheless she'd promised. However, the only real details they'd been given hadn't triggered the quest prompt, with both of them thinking it would likely take physical action to go down into the underdark at a specified location to start the world quest at all.

The short version was that a labyrinth had been found in the deepest depths of the world, and anyone who entered this labyrinth acquired said quest update. That, and the vampires claimed someone of pure vampiric blood was needed to unlock many of the seals. In the entirety of the Bernzee covens, there were only two purebloods—both of them in the same coven, which made the others very, very upset.

Hence, Aksilias Bloodmare and his two sons had ventured to the surface to try and get one of the Thane siblings to spearhead their own house's expedition.

He blinked his eyes, staring at the ceiling of the nest Athela had constructed near Hakim's cabin. It was a lot to deal with, and these rambling thoughts often kept him up at night. What if he failed? What if ALLIE failed?

What then?

Athela's warm thigh rubbed up against his, and she started talking in her sleep about being a princess again, to his immense amusement. "I suppose I should really work on sleeping during the day, and staying up at night . . . that might be another reason why I don't get good sleep anymore."

Yawning, Riven managed to push Athela's sprawled, naked body off his while chuckling about her midsleep grumbles. He scooted to the edge of the bed she'd procured for the three of them, his strength starting to return now that Gluttony was in full swing mending his broken soul and mana pathways. He was able to push himself up off the bed, too, but wobbled and fell back down after a brief stroke of weakness overcame his lower back—an area where his mana channels were still fractured.

He inwardly cursed, starlight from the small openings in the bloodsilk nest filtering through the ceiling.

"Where are you going?" a small voice asked, and Riven felt a light touch on his hand. He looked right, seeing Fay curled up in a ball with the covers flung over her—one slender blue hand gently touching his. "Are you okay?"

Her wide, black eyes were full of concern, and he couldn't help but smile.

"I'm fine." He took her hand in his, squeezing it softly. "I just needed to pee."

"Can I come with you?" Fay asked hesitantly, almost nervously even.

Riven's eyebrows lifted. "To pee with me?"

"No, I just want to go with you."

"Oh. Of course you can come, Fay. I'd love to have you along . . ." He winked, getting a playfully sharp jab in the side when she swung her own bare legs out of the covers and planted her feet on the floor.

They exited the nest into the forest of pine trees and began walking toward one of the two outhouses his friends from the tutorial had made.

"I'm . . . glad you came back," Riven eventually said, using Fay to support himself when he felt a searing pain down his back.

The succubus bore his weight for him, then put her free hand around the front of his bare chest to look up at his face—making him stop in his tracks under the starlight. "Can I ask you something, Riven? It's been bothering me . . . since Athela came to meet me, to convince me to come back."

He blinked. "You can ask me anything, Fay. I'll be honest with you."

Nervously, she gulped, and the grip on his body tightened. "U-um . . . She said some things that I, I would . . . I would like clarification on. I think?"

Riven nodded patiently, waiting for her to continue.

Fay let out a deep breath, then steeled her nerves. "Riven . . . Athela said that she thinks that you chose her, back then, because she is family to you."

Riven frowned and closed his eyes. "I'd rather not relive those moments for long if I don't have to. Please, ask your questions."

She gulped. "S-sorry . . . um . . . she said that you talked about me in your sleep? Is that true?"

A sad smile played across his lips. "Yes. At least that's what she, Azmoth, and Genua tell me."

She began to blush. "And she said that she thought you missed me?"

His sad smile turned into another soft laugh. "Of course I did. Why are you even asking me? Fay, you were and are important to me."

Her blush grew darker, and her eyes dropped. In a whisper, she asked, "Do you think you'll ever think of me as family, too? That you'll love me like that one day?"

He paused, thinking of how to say what he wanted to portray to her—then a memory came to him. A fond, warm memory. "Do you remember the day that I brought you flowers, after I thought I'd messed everything up?"

Fay giggled. "Yes. You were so nervous."

"I was. I was beyond nervous." He placed a hand underneath Fay's chin, bringing her to meet him eye to eye. "I said it before and I'll say it again. You mean a lot to me. Yes, I do think I'll get there, that I'll feel that way about you—but don't think that it should be a comparison. I loved Athela as family back then, but not as a lover. I'd actually been more invested in you as a romantic partner than I was with her, and she knew this. I've told her as much, and I'm working on my relationship with her just as I am with you—because that's what she wants."

"Because that's what she wants?" Fay repeated, frowning. "You aren't attracted to her?"

"Of course I'm attracted to her, as I am you!" Riven laughed, this time more loudly. "But her proclamation to me back then blindsided me."

Fay's frown turned contemplative, and a bright smile lit up her face before she got up on her tiptoes and whispered into his ear. "So . . . You were actually more interested in me as a wife then?"

"Stop!" Riven playfully scolded her, booping her on the nose before drawing the succubus in close with a hug. "None of that—that isn't healthy if we're really going to try to make this relationship triangle work out."

"I know! I know . . . I'm just lacking confidence and wanted to hear it . . ." Fay replied, embarrassed and shifting her gaze. "Sorry. I won't ask questions like that again, but . . . you didn't deny it."

She shot him a look, then blushed furiously again when he remained silent—still refusing to deny it, but with a raised eyebrow. "Okay, that's seriously the last time I'll ask. It's just that you actually did choose her . . . and now knowing what you really thought about it all—it just makes me feel good. Validated, that I'm not just a second choice. I don't want to feel like a third wheel."

Riven glanced back over his shoulder to where Athela was still sleeping in her nest, sighed, and turned back to Fay with a gentle smile. "Fine. I was, at that point, more interested in you than her for wife material—but I hadn't developed feelings of love for you. Meanwhile, I did love her as a friend and family, so when you made me choose, I couldn't . . . Ugh. Wipe that silly smile off your face—I'm equally invested in both of you regarding any kind of wedding now. That was all in the past, and this is the present, so if you go and tell Athela that I—"

"I won't say a word." Fay giggled, for the first time since getting back having a true giddiness about her. She was still blushing and brought a hand up to Riven's cheek. "Thanks for saying it."

Her lips touched his, pressing softly against his face, and she held him there for a long, long time until pulling back. Tears were wet against her skin, and she sniffled, wiping them off her cheeks. "Thank you, Riven. It means a lot to me."

Nearby, the sound of retching was heard from one of the two outhouses. Both Riven and Fay shared a look before heading over to see just who it was.

Coming around the corner and seeing one of the outhouse doors open, they both laid eyes on Genua—who was on her knees in her nightgown, vomiting and dry heaving.

Riven scratched the back of his head, then knelt down beside her to put a hand on her bare back. "Oof . . . You don't look so good."

The elf dry heaved again, wiped spit off her lips, then turned her glowing red eyes to meet his. They were abnormally bright now, far brighter than they'd been even a couple days ago. Wasn't it abnormal for thralls or people becoming thralls to have red eyes at all? So why were hers brighter than even Gurth'Rok's?

"Hello, Master Riven. I did not mean to wake you. I thought I'd be quiet." Genua's arms shook from weakness, and she nearly collapsed before he caught her. She made a belching sound, puked onto the ground in front of him, and groaned. "I am sorry . . . I did not mean . . ."

"Don't worry a damn thing about it, and you didn't wake me," Riven said, concern in his voice while he propped the blonde woman up. "Fay, could you go grab a glass of water?"

"Absolutely, I'll be right back." The succubus turned around and scampered back to the nest where Athela and Len were still asleep.

There was a long pause in the conversation after that, the silence drawing out with the sound of crickets in the night.

Genua's fingers gripped Riven's wrist, getting his attention, and the middle-aged woman coughed to the side before clearing her throat. "Riven . . . did you want to kill them? Did you enjoy it?"

Riven's brows furrowed in confusion, until a prickling sting of guilt flooded him when he realized what she meant. Sincere sadness and regret overcame him in that moment, looking down at her, and his shoulders sagged as he propped himself up against the outhouse next to her. "Your family—Ethel in particular—were some of the first people I ever came across out of Negrada who showed me kindness."

He tsked, remembering Greenstalk village and the elves he'd thought would be his friends. "The short answer to that question is no. I did not enjoy it. Not at all. Your husband was an asshole through and through, but Ethel in particular was a hard pill to swallow. I liked her a lot."

He gave a half-hearted smile. "I even had a crush on her. Then she attempted to murder me, and thought she had, until I blew them up."

"That was certainly a nasty trick you pulled," Genua muttered under her breath, a slight hint of malice underlying her words, but that malice quickly faded. "For months I absolutely hated you for what you did. For taking my baby girl away from me, and my husband. I won't deny, though, I understand why you did it—even if I still wish it was you who'd died that day."

She abruptly turned her head and belched out more vomit, going into a coughing fit while her fingers dug into the dirt. She spat, then turned and—oddly enough—smiled at him. "But I do not hate you. I wanted you to know that. In some ways, I even consider you a good person despite the grudge I have against you for taking Ethel's life."

Riven, who'd never thought he'd ever get closure on the guilt he still battled with, was shocked. He nearly choked when he realized she was being genuine, and a lump started to form in his throat. "Oh my god, you're being serious . . . aren't you?"

Genua nodded, shadows of pine trees shifting in the moonlight while a breeze picked up around them. "You're a good kid. A good man, I mean. Or at least you try to be. There are certainly some questionable morals regarding your choice to destroy Daskus, and the way you butchered my family, but those were not choices you actually wanted to make—rather, you were forced to. I understand that."

She reached out a hand, placing it on his shoulder and squeezing when she saw tears beginning to trickle down his face. "I've seen you trying to give us a good life after your initial spurt of revenge was done, after you'd been hurt and felt betrayed. A betrayal that I participated in when we tried to kill you for not a single good reason. I've seen you battle with that guilt of retaliating for a long time now. You should stop; you have enough to deal with as it is, and battling the demons of your past—no pun intended—will only burden you more. Let it go; in many ways what happened was our own fault due to extreme prejudices, and if you can't and still really want to make it up to me . . . if you want to make it up to Len, then just make sure Len grows up cared for. She still doesn't understand why her older sister and father were killed, and one day I'm going to need to break it to her that it was you who did it. I hope that, when that time comes, she won't judge you as harshly as I did."

Riven was crying silently now, and his reply came out as a wavering whisper. "How can you even say that I've tried to make her life better? After what I did?"

Genua gave him a fond smile. "You don't think I know it was you? First, it started out as extra recess time for her and her friends at the camps. That was only the beginning. Then it was extra tutoring in subjects she loved . . . private tutors, who even went as far as to read her bedtime stories when I wasn't there. Then you allowed her to live with me in your manor, when I was supposed to be nothing more than a slave without rights. The real kicker was when you allowed me out of that silly cage Tupper came up with!"

Riven snorted a laugh, wiping the wet tears from his eyes. "That was a little bit too far, I agree."

Genua's weakly shaking hand slid off his shoulder, and she clasped her hands together with an amused eye roll. "He thought you'd be more into it than you were. He misjudged your character. Regardless, Tupper later told me that the maids who'd been giving Len extra attention at the manor had been instructed to do so. At first I thought they'd just been awfully nice, but no—it was you. You'd told them to do it, because you care. You are worried about her, aren't you?"

Riven didn't reply, choosing to stare at the ground between his legs instead.

Genua's hand again reached out, pushing her fingers across the back of his head through his hair with a groan and another hiccuping gag. She spat one more time, glancing up to see Fay walking their way with an entire pitcher of water, and gave an amused laugh. "Thank you, Riven. A piece of me may forever hate you for what you did, but know that I am working on it—and that I am sorry. Sorry that my decisions, and the decisions of my husband, ended up causing the nightmare that I later endured. It was more our fault than it was ever yours—please remember that. And know that I forgive you."

Riven, for all that he tried, couldn't even form a response. Instead, he just nodded and closed his eyes—focusing on the feeling of her comforting touch while he curled his head down into his knees in a sitting position.

Crickets continued to chirp, and those chirps were soon joined by the padding of bare feet on forest ground.

Fay huffed, coming out of a jog to a stop—and leaned down to hand Genua the pitcher. "Sorry! I couldn't find the cups, but the pitcher should do!"

The succubus sat down on the other side of the elf when Genua took the pitcher and started to drink, frowning when Genua set it down to vomit again shortly thereafter. "Did you eat something bad? Was it that mutated raccoon Athela caught and cooked? I told her those things weren't good to eat and still she insisted . . . She's a fuckin' glutton!"

Genua and Riven both sputtered laughter, getting Fay to smile in self-satisfaction that they'd thought her funny.

"No, dear, I don't think that's it." Genua shook her head, then kicked out her legs and pushed herself into a reclining position to look up at the stars. "I've been getting sick almost every day for the past two weeks now."

"Huh?" Riven furrowed his brows and crossed his arms. "Why haven't you told anyone? We could have gotten you a doctor. You should probably be seen by . . ."

His words trailed off, and a light bulb seemed to click inside his small pea brain at the same exact moment that Genua gave him a knowing look.

Fay gasped, then frowned and scratched her head. "Wait, no . . . that can't be right. It hasn't been nearly enough time for . . . for that. Right?"

She glanced between the other two, remembering a very particular night when Kathrine had visited the manor. Fay's face scrunched up in concern. "I'm pretty sure it's not even possible to, you know, with a vampire and an elf? IS it possible?!"

Genua merely shrugged, then pulled out a small handheld mirror from a pocket of her nightgown. Staring up at the twinkling red eyes reflecting back at her, she hiccuped one more time. "You tell me, Fay . . . You . . . tell . . . me . . ."

CHAPTER 11

All of them, they were all going.

Tanya, with her son, Tim, and daughter, Julie. Hakim. Genua, Len, and Luke. Riven, Athela, Azmoth, and Fay. The twenty-three skinwalkers in Athela's new fan club, including Ak'ra and Selzi—better known to the people of Jerbyville as John and Sara.

They were marching through the forest, many of them laughing jovially in the early morning light amid the chirping of birds and crunching of leaves and pine needles. Athela wore an assassin's outfit with her black, ruby-studded Tiara of Silent Killing, disguised as a human with glossy brown skin and white hair—something she'd recently modified to look almost like a drow elf given Gaia's Heartwood Token. Fay took on her usual blonde, tanned appearance—not even needing Gaia's token but wearing it nonetheless. Azmoth had the appearance of a hulking bald barbarian, and Riven only changed his eyes to not give away he was a vampire—otherwise keeping his appearance of a handsome young brunet man.

[Gaia's Heartwood Token (Epic): Wearing this token around your neck allows you to suppress any Charisma effects you may have, suppresses your vampiric qualities as well as the demonic qualities of your contracted familiars, and changes your status page information to represent a level-55 human. Those with identifier classes at a high enough level can circumvent this passive ability.]

"Are you feeling well?" Genua asked, holding Len's hand while she walked beside him—shooting Riven a very concerned frown and bringing her free hand up to her chest. "You don't look it . . ."

She'd been nervous ever since the reveal of what she thought to be a pregnancy. It wasn't a certainty, but the dots connected. Even if vampires weren't usually supposed to have babies with mortal races, it'd happened before—Riven had done some asking around. It was just incredibly unusual, according to some of the many pardoned Rippenvire vampires who'd joined the Thane Necropolis after a deal had been struck for their lives.

He grimaced when a twinge of pain flared in his lower back, but otherwise smiled at the elf with a shake of his head—blue eyes reflecting back at her underneath a black hood that shielded his skin from the sunlight. "I'm fine. It's just a lot to take in . . . I never thought I'd have one so soon."

"Have what?" Len asked curiously, peeking from around her mother's leg, blond pigtails bobbing while she walked at a brisk pace to keep up with the adults. "What are you two talking about?"

"We're talking about those poison cookies you used to make." Riven grinned. "Remember when you poisoned my sister?"

Len giggled, holding a hand up to her mouth. "Those cookies were supposed to be for my big sister, Ethel! Not Allie! I wish Ethel was still around. I miss her."

Riven tried not to cringe. "Yeah. Yeah, so do I. And Genua—if that is what's going on, you have nothing to worry about. You will be taken care of, I promise."

Genua's tense shoulders relaxed, and she stared at the forest floor amid the laughter of Athela, Tim, and Azmoth behind them when Fay tripped on a root to screech and faceplant. "Thank you, Riven. I was worried."

"It's the least I could do. We'll talk more about it later, I promise."

Casually turning and raising a hand to point past Genua on her left, Riven summoned a Blood Lance the size of his arm. Red wisps of silky blood magic flowed out of his body and began sparking with black energy before tearing into the forest with a flash of crimson—blowing a huge hole in a large tree's body.

The tree, in turn, screamed out an alien cry and flailed about—its entrails pouring onto the ground in layers as the disguised monster toppled over and died with a crash.

"Mimic. It was getting closer every time we weren't looking." Riven shrugged after seeing Genua's shocked expression. "Picked the wrong group this time. Hey, Hakim, are we almost there?"

The large African man at the front of the group, walking alongside Julie and Tanya, gave a thumbs-up after shaking himself from staring at the beast Riven had just killed. "Another ten minutes and we should be at the clearing!"

Riven gave a thumbs-up.

Then, ten minutes later, Hakim proved right.

Two dozen tents were already set up right outside a massive cave, one that opened into the side of a tree-covered hill. People with various weapons, classes, and other equipment were moving in full swing—trading with one another, cooking, eating, and joking around campfires. There were three clearly distinct groups already set apart from one another—one of them a well-outfitted bunch of hunters in camo with compound bows, long knives, and rifles. Another was the same group of mountain men with axes and shotguns who'd harassed Genua just days ago—with three well-dressed men in top hats holding caster staves. The third was a bunch of mismatched, nonuniformed people with various types of metal armor, swords, pistols, rifles, crossbows, hatchets, and wands.

They all were in between levels 14 and 56, but this third group also had someone Riven recognized in it.

Her name was Jarla. She was the stick-thin woman in hiking gear he'd met outside the shop in Jerbyville, and she wore the same equipment, along with a large backpack and a couple cans of bear mace strapped to her hips.

[Jarla. Level 16 Pack Mule, Human.]

It didn't take long for her to see Riven's group coming, and a wide smile spread across her face as she brushed her dark hair back and put it up into a ponytail. "Hi, Hakim and Julie! Tanya, you look better than ever—I can see where Julie gets her looks. Hey, Riv! Hey, Tim! I was just tellin' my friend here about the new guys in town! Come for a dungeon run? And what happened to your wheelchair?!"

The other two groups segregated to other areas of the camp shot confused or surprised looks over at Riven's band of misfits, and the mage in the top hat who'd propositioned Genua not long ago quickly avoided looking in their direction with a flush of embarrassment.

At least the guy hadn't been an asshole about it when Genua had said no.

Hakim clasped hands with the thin woman and patted Jarla on the back. "That's right! We're here to get some leveling in, and with our new friends I think we'll go far."

"You think you'll make it to the third dungeon floor this time?" Jarla asked curiously, looking their group over one by one and pooching her lips. Her gaze lingered on some of the skinwalkers—who were all wearing various human disguises, all of them looking something like a cult with identical brown cloaks, simple rags for masks, and hidden weapons underneath—but she shrugged it off a second later. "Your friends are all pretty high level. Riv here is level 55, and a warlock no less! That's impressive, I hadn't seen that before. Thela is a level-55 assassin . . . Fay is a level-48 illusionist. Wow, that's a class you don't see often. That big barbarian guy is level 66! Holy hell, that's high!"

Jarla shot Genua, Len, and Luke a quizzical stare. "And those weird cult people behind y'all are in the forties to fifties, too. What about the three elves, though? You really bringing a kid into a dungeon? She's level 1, and so is her mom. I guess the old guy is all right, though—level-17 Stormrazor Battle Priest doesn't sound too bad."

"I'm not old! I'm just wrinkled!" Luke protested with a humph, getting laughs from the surroundings.

Riven brought up a hand and patted Len's pigtails. "She'll gain passive experience, and I am confident in our ability to protect her. She asked to come. I'm more than certain it will be fine."

Jarla gave them a skeptical look, but she also didn't realize what she was actually looking at. She didn't realize that she was talking to the holder of the number-four spot on the power ladder on this planet, that a single one of his eight summoned bloodstricken undead could likely blaze through most or even all of the dungeon within the single five-minute summoning he had if only he knew the way. She didn't realize that the entirety of a small clan of level-50 to -98 skinwalker demons were on babysitting duty to make sure the weaker members of the party weren't killed. She wasn't aware that two world boss–class entities were here, or that the "barbarian" Azmoth by himself had fought toe to toe with one of those summoned bloodstricken paladins and had come out even—adding another person to the party who could wipe this dungeon out with little to no trouble all on his own.

Riven had come a long way from fighting that level 20–something satyr warlord miniboss in Negrada. How he had struggled back then; it was a night and day difference now from the army-killing disaster on wheels he'd developed into.

"All right, well, just know that the average monster level is 29 on the top two floors, and it gets progressively higher the farther you go down." Jarla gave Len a worried frown, pulling on the straps of her backpack. "Just be careful. On the fifth and last floor, you'll even see some monsters reaching into the sixties! The one group to actually finish this dungeon and send it into hibernation said the boss they fought was level 61! That ain't nothin' to scoff at, ya hear me?"

"I certainly do." Riven nodded with a polite smile, hands clasped behind his back. "Let me assure you that I am not worried."

Those kinds of levels were exactly what he was looking for. Hakim was in the low forties, along with his barbarian class, while Julie was now a level-27 healer and Tim was level-24 thief. Fay was still level 48, not having moved up at all since she'd left, while Luke was level 17—and it was a perfect training ground for all of them. Even Azmoth might get some experience if the boss was good enough, and Tanya, Genua, and Len would gain some passive experience from being in proximity to the fighting. He, Athela, the skinwalkers, and Azmoth would all be waiting on the periphery as guards to make sure things didn't go south—in which case he'd send in the four-armed brutalisk first. Azmoth was leaps ahead of most things on this planet, but he also trailed behind Riven and Athela by around thirty-five levels.

Regardless, it would all be a good precursor and warm-up for what lay in waiting for them in Negrada over the next two months—because he fully intended to transition most of them to a real battlefield soon enough, should power leveling go as expected.

Hakim jabbed Riven's side with a laugh. "I think he'll be more than enough to make sure the lot of us do okay. Thanks for the concern, Jarla."

One of the others from Jarla's group of eighteen people, a tall and lanky blond man with a ponytail, walked over and placed a wooden staff onto the forest floor butt-first. "Hey! I was kind of eavesdropping and heard you guys would be going into the dungeon soon. I already asked the other two groups, but they honestly think we're a little too weak to pair with. Five of our top classers didn't show up today, don't know why, but perhaps you'd all want to throw in with us?"

Many of the ragtag men and women from Jarla's team were watching more intently now, having overheard the conversation and looking hopeful. One guy in half-plate and half-studded leather called out as well. "We'd owe you, big-time! I have a wife to feed!"

Some people laughed, while others just nodded in agreement.

"Wife to feed?" Riven asked, somewhat amused. "Does this dungeon really give enough loot to make a living off it? Especially since only one team actually made it to the end."

"Every monster drops meat and Elysium coins, sometimes items, and there are more than enough monsters to go around," Jarla confirmed with a wide smile. "Any items we get, they give to one of us three pack mules and we divvy it up at the end of the trip. They even drop **magical** items once in a while! Got a dagger that did an additional sixty-eight lightning-based damage the other day—I haven't seen my husband's eyes boggle like that since the integration!"

A thinner, balding man in the background scoffed, probably because of the teasing grin his wife was giving him, then looked away after sticking his tongue out at her.

"Anyways, we might not be as strong as you all, but Jarla seems to trust you," the mage went on, raising an eyebrow when the team of hunters in camo started their way into the cave on their own. He watched with everyone else as the hunters disappeared, then turned around to shove his free hand into a pocket. "We'll even split it seventy-thirty in your favor due to power discrepancy, but at least we'll get something instead of nothing at all if we just up and leave. How about it?"

Riven shared a look with Hakim, then the others behind him. No one spoke up, leaving the decision to him. "Yeah, we can probably do that. But know that this actually isn't a normal dungeon run."

Jarla and the mage both looked confused, as did many of the others.

"What do you mean, Riv?" Jarla asked while puffing out her cheeks, hands on her skinny hips. "How would this not be a normal dungeon run? Were you only wanting to stay on the top floor or somethin'? We'd only been wanting to go to the second floor, so if that was the issue I suppose we could just take in the first if you're more comfortable with that."

Riven shook his head. "No, not that. The thing is, most of us are here to make sure the ones fighting don't get killed. I won't be fighting unless needed; same with those cultist-looking people in the back. Thela won't be, nor will that barbarian guy. This is a power-leveling trip, and for most of it I'll probably be sitting in the background working on totems. So if you guys come along, that's fine—just know that we'll do our best to help you lot out but you'll be less of a priority than the ones we already have with us."

"Oh! That—that's unexpected. Power leveling doesn't come cheap!" The mage laughed, then raised an eyebrow Hakim's way. "No wonder they're new to the area! I hadn't realized you and Julie had the money to hire power levelers like this! Explains a lot."

"He's a friend. They're doing it for free," Tanya stated from the side, pulling out a sandwich from her icebox and handing it to Len with a warm smile. "And I, for one, am excited! I haven't actually ever been in a dungeon and I've always wanted to see my son and daughter do their thing! They always tell me these bold, adventurous stories—so now with some more protection I finally feel ready to come, too!"

"We'll be in the back watching the show," Genua confirmed. "Hakim, Julie, Tim, Luke, and Fay are the only ones fighting from our group."

"More experience for us, then!" The mage laughed. "With nearly thirty high rankers watching over us C- and D-rankers, I feel better about this already!"

The cave opened up into a huge tunnel that eventually smoothed out into a perfectly polished brown hallway of neatly packed dirt and stone that spiraled down into the earth. When it eventually came to a stop in front of a set of large stone double doors that were already wide-open, the sounds of battle and screams could be heard from inside with torches lighting the interior.

[You have entered Dungeon Petrus. Other in-area participants: 195]

Apparently there were multiple groups already inside, more than just the one that'd gone before them.

"Don't bother helping, they'll just get angry about us trying to steal their dropped coins and loot," Hakim muttered under his breath, nodding to where the hunters in camo were firing projectiles or engaging in close combat with large, swarming purple rats in the low twenties.

Riven didn't pay them much attention, instead turning his head around to look at the various other hallways leading out into the rest of the dungeon. This was a lot different than Negrada had been, and was more similar to the other dungeon Hakim had visited with the drake. But even there, Riven hadn't started out at the top floor, but instead had been summoned to the boss room at the very end.

In Negrada's hellscapes, his trek had led him across its top floor. Even Gaia's dungeon hadn't been fully completed before the demigoddess had introduced herself. So this would, in fact, be the very first dungeon Riven went through from top to bottom.

The first ever. This would be new.

The thought made Riven chuckle, considering he was actually just babysitting. He gestured to the others behind him, everybody from the additional eighteen of Jarla's raiding party having gotten the heavy hint that he was the commander here. "Same plan as what we discussed earlier. Noncombatants, you're with me, the rest of you are on Hakim—he'll be your de facto leader. Combatants, if you need to drop back to safety, we'll be here—but Elysium rewards those who struggle to win with more XP. You'll get more out of it if you put yourself on the edge—just keep that in mind."

Jarla, two other people wearing backpacks, including her husband, and one other man in spectacles exited the original eighteen of their raiding party to mingle with most of Riven's batch. Fourteen stood beside Fay, Julie, Hakim, Luke, and

Tim for a total of nineteen combatants—healers in the back, archers and casters in the middle, tanks and fighters in the front, with two rogues and Tim being a forward scout to check for traps.

"Make sure the scouts don't run into anything too lethal," Riven told Athela in a voice loud enough for all of them to hear. "If it's a trap—leave it for them to find and disarm unless you think it'll outright kill them, but give the scouts an opportunity to try first. Try to stay hidden so you don't alert any of the monsters here to your presence."

"Roger-roger!" Athela saluted. "And you never asked about my two new blood abilities! Meanie. I've been dying to show you since we used that Dao treasure—so if we come across something strong can I show you then?!"

Riven facepalmed. "Sorry! I've just been so busy I completely forgot. Yes! Of course, show me when the next opportunity arises!"

She aggressively groped his ass with a brilliant and almost predatory grin. "Good boy! I'll be on the periphery. Oh, and good luck, Fay! Get some levels in for us!"

Then she blurred across the room to where Fay stood—so fast that most people couldn't even see the movement, causing them to shout out in alarm and stumble in shock. She took Fay's face in both hands, gave her a solid mouth-to-mouth kiss, and laughed before disappearing in a flash of black.

"Where did that assassin go?" the blond mage from earlier asked hesitantly, looking around with many of the others and avoiding eye contact with Fay while blushing furiously at the public display of affection. "Does she have a teleport spell?!"

"No. She just moves very fast and is very stealthy." Riven stepped back, motioning for Hakim to take charge. "Go on, then. We'll be here if you need us. Do you already know the way to the second floor?"

Hakim hesitantly shook his head—still ignoring the sounds of battle down one of the hallways on their right. "This dungeon, as most other dungeons I know about, changes from time to time. There'll always be a way down, per Elysium's rules, but that way down can shift. Let's go the opposite way Jared's group just went. I don't like the look of camo anyways. Scouts, run ahead and let us know if there's anything there. Let's get a move on so we can make the third level by tomorrow!"

An excited cheer of agreement went up, and they all started down the leftmost hallway in quite high spirits.

INTERLUDE

A Refresher from Chapter 21, Book 1:

Totem Making—The Blessings of Fae and The Curses of Devils:
Author Unknown.

Totem making has long been used as a basic means of creating decorative monuments, household apparel, and things to keep evil spirits out as a focus of old wives' tales, and it wasn't originally such a lucrative or useful craft in the beginning. This is likely due to the disgust many mainstream mages hold for shamanistic practices despite its usefulness, and it is often referred to by great scholars across this land as "barbaric" for its affiliation with forbidden nature magics and the dark arts.

The key to understanding the basics of totem making is essentially understanding that it is an alternate path of enchanting. Enchanting requires a lock-and-key mechanism via runecraft and mana distribution through a conduit—the conduit being the person who is creating the totem, who must have the proper affiliated type of magic. The runecrafting is very similar to how one casts a spell with hand motions in Tier 2 and above spells. But the key differences between totem making and enchanting are twofold. First, that totem making requires an imbuement of a soul or soul shard, and second, different lock-and-key sets are utilized. To create a true totem with one step beyond an enchantment, it requires either death magic or specialized Fae magic to do so. Fae's Foundational Pillar has multiple specialized subpillars that represent the embodiment of life magic, most specifically in the realm of its major subpillar—the Forest subpillar, but it is not limited to that alone. With Death the opposite of life, both the Death subpillar and multiple Fae subpillars deal in the realm of souls.

Not only that, but totems require certain amounts of Willpower in order to control and utilize properly. Shamans, druids, necromancers, and warlocks therefore tend to use them more often than anyone else. Those affiliated with the Holy Foundational Pillar, Harmony Foundational Pillar, and Archaic Foundational Pillar along with their subpillars have tried creating totems in similar fashion, as told by the history books, but they have all failed to my knowledge.

Regardless, those who consider themselves totem artisans are often nothing more than that—artists who come up with fancy designs meant to scare children for the holidays. The true craft comes into play when we imbue these materials to create what are called influence fields.

Totem making is often used in conjunction with various runes or symbols of power, wards, and enchantments to create stable and consistent magical effects that we term influence fields. These influence fields are essentially a type of interactive enchantment that the soul shard imbued into the totem can control. It incorporates runes but is different from normal runecrafting, as influence fields use a different subset of locks and keys including the shapes and materials of the totem makeup. Why might this be, you may ask? What purpose is there to having different lock-and-key mechanisms in the sigils? The reason is that enchanting is a static thing, unmoving and unbending, while influence fields are ever moving and even become alive. It is also why influence fields that totems use are able to be controlled by souls you imbue the totems with, whereas an enchantment is not inherently able to be controlled by such an attached entity.

Totem making is thus the step between normal enchantments and awakened items—which are an entirely different type of category altogether. The three categories of magically enhanced equipment are therefore defined by the following:

Enchantments or enchanted items are rigid and unbending, and they lack the ability to be controlled by anything other than the direct user. This category also includes cursed or blessed items.

Influence fields or totems are fluid and are able to fluctuate or change under the influence of a soul.

Awakened items are entities that have their true consciousness bound to a physical item without any actual soul.

All three have different lock-and-key sets, or different runes or rules, that are bound by the system. All three have their own unique downsides or perks. They are three different parallel pathways to creating items of power, even comparable to how mana, divinity, and stamina differ from one another in their own abilities. But now we are getting offtrack. Back to totems and influence fields:

Influence fields can be anything from a pleasant smell to seduce the opposite sex to an electrified floor to a defensive barrier—the commonality between them being that they are bendable, fluctuating spell alignments and are contained within a physical object that we call totems. Specific combinations of the right materials, right ingredients, right incantations, the right soul shard, and right runes or symbols in just the right way can create truly potent effects. The important part about this is that the one who makes the totem must have the correct attribute in order to imbue the totem with a spell. If the mage creating the totem gets the symbols, materials, and shape right but fails to have the specialized Forest attribute—they will fail to imbue the totem with any forest magic regardless of how perfect the totem otherwise is. The same goes for Water, Blood, or any of the subpillars of Fae and Unholy. As Forest is a subpillar of Fae and Death is a subpillar of Unholy, you will only ever find totems enchanted with categorical magics underneath the Fae and Unholy pillars. Fae, Volcano, Storm, Ocean, Glacial, Swamp, Forest, Unholy,

Blood, Shadow, Death, Infernal, Depravity, and Chaos will be the only types of totems you ever run across. Well, that and their more specialized pillar types that evolve from the major subpillars. Additionally, those affiliated with the Unholy pillar may never be able to wield totems affiliated with the Fae pillar and vice versa, as pillar orientation is needed to command the soul shards and totems after they're imbued properly.

With the right knowledge and attributes, you may place the right runes or paintings in the right patterns to provide a magical webbing of sorts. Creating the right shape of the totem is also very important, as they act as a key to a lock in conjunction with the runes you place upon them. If the runes, shape, pictures, or patterns of the vase are incorrect, the key won't fit the lock correctly, and the effect won't take hold. Sometimes even the coloring matters. Sometimes if you do a half-assed job, you'll get a half-assed effect. That'd still be better than no effect, though.

Moving on to examples of what such things I have seen as a master totem maker, you would likely be surprised. I have created vessels that burn with fae light, illuminating the darkest of places as beacons to the world. I have created vessels to seal away the greatest of demons, placing them in forbidden tombs to keep them at bay from the civilized world. I have created totems that poison enemies around them and heal those who are marked as friendly, totems that capture the sickness from those they touch and towering bastions that bless farmland for miles around them over decades to come.

Many once scoffed at me, laughed at me, told me I was a fool for pursuing this very abstract and often disregarded profession. In the end, though, it was I who laughed, and as I sit upon a mountain of treasure and bathe in the gifts that kings shower upon me, I often ask my many wives if they'd have another man, to which they of course say no.

CHAPTER 12

"This feels very much like a vacation."

The comment gained him some curiously amused looks from Jarla and her noncombatant fellows, but none of them said a word. What would they say, when everything had gone so smoothly so far? Battle after battle, time after time, not a single one of the forward group had been seriously wounded—with Athela and the strange cultist-looking people having intervened twice to save someone from any real harm.

Riven munched on one of Tanya's standard sandwiches, going through the dozens of different ingredients, notes, and diagrams sprawled out around him on a large disc of solidified crimson ice he was now sitting on. It floated down a hallway at a leisurely pace under the orange and yellow torches lighting the dungeon at intervals, keeping in range but not too close to the sounds and shouts of battle farther into the dungeon hall. His ability to see in the dark also helped, because if he'd been a normal human it would have only been every dozen or so feet that he'd actually be able to see clearly with all the patches of shadow.

"This one," Azmoth said, pointing to the tiny rodent skull Riven was looking for while maintaining a cross-legged position next to him on the disc.

"Oh! Thanks, man."

Riven picked it up and added it next to the square block of wood he was going to change into his first-ever fully fledged totem. The ones he'd made in the tutorial all that time ago hadn't actually been complete, lacking souls or soul shards to control them, but now that Riven had the Death subpillar he wouldn't have much of an issue getting said soul.

Genua and Tanya watched him curiously, sitting in their own spots on the floating disc while the skinwalkers kept a closer watch on the fighters in front.

"You said you've done this before?" Genua asked curiously, staring down at one of the diagrams before entering another patch of darkness. "You create runes and plant them into an object? Isn't that the same thing as runecrafting?"

"It is very similar, yes," Riven stated warmly, growing excited as the mysticism behind magic once again set in. It'd been a while since he'd been able to truly relax, and he was finding this setup of arts and crafts for adults rather enjoyable. "Last time I created two small cylindrical blood totems that shot out damaging blood magic! But I've been able to buy a bunch of crafting manuals from the Elysium altar at ridiculous prices—it isn't anything intricate, but it is enough to give me the basics on how to approach this given my lack of real experience."

He picked up the square piece of wood, then held up a finger while Tanya watched under furrowed brows as a thin wisp of blood mana lasered itself into the wood—cutting off the top of the cube and then hollowing it out entirely. Riven took another look at two diagrams set out before him, carved another sigil into the rodent skull, placed the rodent skull into the cube, and then slit his wrist—getting a gasp from Tanya when his own blood started pouring into the cube's interior.

"Riven! Why did you . . ." Tanya's voice trailed off, and she sighed in relief when Riven's skin quickly began repairing itself. "Don't do that! You're going to scare Len!"

"I'm not scared!" Len replied with a giggle, watching Riven put an odd-looking red herb into the wooden cube before sealing it shut again with crimson ice. "Riven didn't even cry! I would have cried, but he's big and strong. I don't think he ever cries. One of my friends from camp said boys don't cry or they're girly."

Riven nearly choked in amusement at the look Genua shot her daughter. "Everyone is allowed to cry sometimes, Len. Even boys. I cried just yesterday, actually."

"WHAT?!" Len gasped with an open mouth, hands raised up in shock. "Oh my goodness! What made you cry, though?! Did you get hurt?! Did someone hurt your feelings?"

Riven tilted his head to the side, pondering what he was going to say and then slowly turning his blue eyes to where Azmoth sat in his barbarian visage. "Azy beat me up."

"Really?! But Azy is so nice!"

"Really."

"Azy! How could you?!" Len gasped again, utterly shocked and making her mother chuckle while facepalming. Len pointed an accusing finger at the demon with a stern scowl. "You leave Riv alone! You don't want him to turn into a crybaby!"

"Too late for that," Azmoth grunted. "Sorry, Len. He big baby, but we work on it. His character develops slow, but growing up is hard."

"HEY?!" Riven protested, landing a hand on his chest. "That's hurtful! You goddamn jerk!"

Len held up her hands to hide a smile, giggling again and leaning into her mom to put her head on Genua's lap and looking down the hallway. "Thanks for letting me come Rive—Riv! This is exciting!"

"No problem, kiddo. No problem at all."

Turning the cube around, he started using his blood mana to cut into its faces one by one, carving sigils that matched some of the basic inscriptions on the papers, when he felt Gluttony's presence enter the area.

He glanced left, seeing his soul clone in the form of Gluttony's maw watching from where it'd appeared in the air above them and to the right—but it quickly vanished after only staying for a few seconds.

Huh.

Funny that. Riven wasn't even fazed by the presence of the sin anymore—something that'd cause other people and creatures to cower in absolute terror was now just a passing partner of his. He knew the ramifications of partnering with Gluttony would be tremendous, but in what ways or if it was to be a good thing or not were yet to be determined.

It would PROBABLY be good?

Bleh. Who knows. What he DID know was that Gluttony had already saved his life multiple times. The first time being in Negrada when he fell into that pit of blood and the tentacle monster tried to eat him, and the last time being when Elysium's tribulation tried to strike him down for using Malignant Prophecy one too many times. The least he could do was to give Gluttony a chance, as weird as that was to think about, considering it was supposed to be an evil entity of extreme proportions.

Finishing his inscriptions on each cube face, he took a vial of thick gray powder and dusted it into the crevices, receiving a flash of energy on each of the rather sinister, gothic runes.

Clicking his tongue and having some time for introspection, specifically concerning his Death subpillar, he then began to channel small amounts of mana into it—shifting his gaze into the void . . .

Into the void to look for a soul.

Or better yet, souls—plural.

Fuck it, even soul shards would do. He just needed to make these totems work, and without at least a shard, he wouldn't be able to complete his creations.

Even if they were rather basic copies of the *Totems for Dummies*-equivalent book he'd bought from the Elysium general store.

Fay was a curse specialist, though one wouldn't know it by the complete lack of expression every time she cast one of them. Curses often had a negative trade-off for casting them—in Fay's case this was pain and physical anguish the more and more she cast. She'd become rather good at hiding the self-inflicted agony through trial and practice, and in turn they were usually more powerful than their counterpart spells that only used mana. Back when she'd fought with the orcs of Gurth'Rok's tribe in attempting to save the elves of Greenstalk village, she'd blown through dozens of enemies with curse traps, confused them with illusions using Curse of the Dreamwalker, and melted away their flesh in black clouds using Curse of Rot. But she hadn't grown much since then, and it was painfully obvious by the way she was struggling here in the dungeon beside Hakim, Luke, and the other more capable people in this combatant group that she'd been left far, far behind Riven and his other two minions.

Sure, she had her Charm ability that infatuated enemies who were close by, and she had the Dark Pact curse, her newest acquisition, which healed all allies nearby while simultaneously slowing enemies. It was a Tier-3 curse, it was pretty potent, and it built up over time in both how much it healed as well as how much it slowed enemies. The problem was the self-inflicted harm mentioned in the description—which was supposed to be a given since the ability was actually a curse. If it specifically mentioned self-harm in the display window . . . that did not bode well for the caster.

But she'd never had the chance to use that last ability with a team, and she was determined to try and use it here after getting back into the swing of things concerning her more offensive spells first.

SPLAT

CRASH

Fay torpedoed past a series of heavily armored rats bearing down on their party with metal-tipped fangs, setting curse trap after curse trap in flashes of green runes in front and behind the huge rodents while they swarmed down the domed room.

Explosions of Unholy might lit up the dark interior of the dome, sending waves of green energy blasting through metal, bone, and flesh in sprays of shrapnel. Each explosion detonating gave Fay a sharp pain randomly across her body, but she kept pushing herself further and further—setting down more and more traps as fast as she could conjure them amid the roars of incoming enemies.

And behind those rats were hulking humanoid mutants with purple goo for flesh—spurring the rodents on while laughing at the massacre of their own pets. Bright-orange eyes, bulky muscles, no necks with heads connected straight to a torso of dripping slime.

Was it slime?

She couldn't tell—but utilizing Riven's armor through the master-minion bond, she was able to get basic details.

[Petrus Mutant, Level 31, Beast Tamer]
[Petrus Mutant, Level 19, Sludge Warrior]
[Petrus Mutant, Level 40, Sludge Warrior]

WHAM

Fay felt something hard impact her gut midflight, and she gasped before being slammed into the far wall with an audible crunch of bone when one wing gave out.

"Gods damn it!" She wheezed, coughing blood and staggering to her feet only to see Athela begin to move in to intercept the hulking sludge warrior sprinting her way. "DO NOT INTERFERE, ATHELA! I NEED THIS!"

The archdemon was hidden to most, and to people outside Riven's contracts, the arachnid woman was pretty much invisible. So the sludge warrior didn't see who or what Fay was yelling at, only giving a passive half-second glance at the dark ceiling above while continuing to barrel ahead with large, bulky fists raising above its head.

Still, Athela slowed—letting Fay handle this by herself.

Because Fay was tired of being the weak link here. She was going to push herself; even if it meant being banished over and over again in temporary death—she was going to rise.

Pushing herself forward with one broken wing, Fay's feathered boots propelled her forward to meet the charging brute twice her size.

She dodged left and flung up a dreamwalker zone, narrowly avoiding an incoming vertical swing of both its arms when it perceived her to go left when she really went right—and a black mist of Curse of Rot was blasted directly into the monster's face.

Its purple skin began to sizzle and necrose as the sludge-like creature screamed and hit the ground with its knees, clawing at its skin, only for a rune to flash green right in front of where it knelt.

Next thing it knew, Fay's boot crashed into the back of its head—sending the monster directly into the rune that'd just flickered out into invisibility. But that didn't mean it wasn't still there.

The monster's skull exploded upon impact with the invisible trap rune, and Fay was sent stumbling back—cursing that she couldn't just light up a rune inside a living creature, which would have made things so much easier. Withdrawing her wings entirely because they were now slowing her down, she turned back to the fight, where Julie was busy focus-healing two armored warriors and Hakim.

"You okay?!" Tim called out, huffing and tearing out of the shadows with his hands on his knees to catch his breath. "You took a real hit there!"

Fay gave him a polite smile, though internally she was furious at her own lack of performance. She was supposed to be better than this, and she mentally moved her dreamwalker zone to hover over the majority of her party—causing enemies to see the world at a slant, to see swings that weren't there, or to see new enemies that simply didn't exist. "I'm okay, thanks!"

She watched as Hakim's downward axe created craters in the dungeon floor, splitting open numerous armored rats in a single go when he followed up with a shock wave stomp similar if not identical to the one Azmoth had. She watched as the lightning mage in Jarla's group hurled sparks and chain lightnings, killing two or three rats at a time from the back lines while archers and men with rifles activated martial arts to empower their projectiles in flashes of green and blue.

Why couldn't she have offensive abilities like that?

Had she chosen the wrong path to power?

Fay felt so useless.

She watched as Luke, the lowest level of them all but quickly gaining ground to catch up to even her, wiped out two sludge monsters ten levels above his own paltry level 19 with muttered incantations—creating miracles that sent whirlwinds that ripped creatures asunder with a maddening howl of noise.

Even Julie, who'd been a level-22 Healer Priestess Initiate, had been able to gain three levels since arriving in Dungeon Petrus.

Yet despite all that she'd tried, Fay hadn't even grown a single level yet—and had only managed to kill the weaker creatures of the dungeon, even if it was a good number of them.

But she would not be left behind despite the sinking feeling in her chest. She would NOT allow herself to take up one of Riven's slots, only to be useless baggage when he could have someone better.

Determination filled her, raging against despair, and the sound of shuddering weight pounding against stone made her head shift right. Through the darkness and behind a slowly opening gate at the end of a tunnel, the solid black eyes of a bus-size beetle glittered back at her.

Just like the rats, this creature was covered in spiked metal plates. Huge pincers that could crush a man in a single go flared out to either side, and when it opened its maw, a swarm of smaller beetles just like it flew out toward them like a silver tide of carnivorous rage.

[Petrus Beetle Queen, Level 62]
[Petrus Beetle Drone, Level 12]
[Petrus Beetle Drone, Level 8]
[Petrus Beetle Drone, Level 16]

This was her chance to prove herself!

Immediately, she began setting up dozens upon dozens of flashing green runes through the end of the tunnel and into the mouth of the dome room where the rest of her party now fought. Each time she did, another prickling sting or ache assaulted her body and another jab at her conscience tried to sway her away from the cursed path she'd chosen. However, she kept pressing on.

"Shift! Shift, damn you!"

Her dreamwalker zone did just as she asked, shifting away from where the battle behind her raged across the room and into the other tunnels. It moved, placing itself directly in front of her where the swarm of drones and the larger beetle queen were racing down the hall toward the flashes of combat.

She closed her eyes, focusing on what she wanted them to see—and bought herself time when hallucinations took on the incoming swarm.

The cloud of beetles and the queen herself went into a rage, fighting invisible enemies and killing one another off before they'd even reached her magical land mines. One by one they splattered, buzzed, sent sparks of electricity at one another, and died.

Until the beetle queen let out an angry roar that shook the hall and reverberated off the stones with some kind of martial art—pulsing with gray waves of power that caused Fay to vomit immediately.

The hallucinations shattered.

The Unholy land mines all shattered.

And her entire party all crumpled together in a mass-effect attack of violent puking and hurling. Even some of the skinwalkers started looking queasy, with two of the disguised demons immediately gagging.

[You have been afflicted with the debuff Extreme Nausea.]

She retched, only to scream aloud when two beetles each the size of her fist clamped down onto her right leg and began to tear at her soft blue skin.

Fay immediately reeled backward and exploded with a black cloud of rot, showering the oncoming beetle swarm and rebuffing them from joining their counterparts in the rats and sludge men. Insects died by the dozens and then hundreds, smoldering in black pockets of necrosis that ate them away at a rapid pace. Snarling and stomping down onto one of the two beetles that'd been blown off and half eaten by the sheer force of her black cloud of rot, she puked a third time before getting dizzy.

"Ugh . . ."

CRACK

A giant insectoid limb clipped her shoulder through the black cloud and tore a huge bloody gash through her flesh, smashing into the ground in a spray of stone with a force that'd no doubt have killed her outright should she have been hit full-on.

Fay hit the ground, rolling in agony while trying desperately to get ahold of her senses. She blinked rapidly, using a pillar in the domed room for support—only to see Riven looking her way with a worried expression from the back line. And when she saw him move to help, she held up a threatening finger his way.

"DON'T YOU DARE! THIS IS MY FIGHT!"

She whirled around again, trying not to get upset with herself for the embarrassing display she was putting on—then almost took a face full of purple goop to the head from across the room. Thankfully she managed to dodge most of it, but little spots of acidic sludge she hadn't managed to duck began eating away at her skin while she let out a scream.

Then she felt a searing golden energy flood across her body—burning the purple acid away but simultaneously causing her entire body to shake in rigid pain like she was burning from the inside out. Then she vomited profusely as random wounds started to rip across her sky-blue skin with Holy light.

Fay stared down at Julie, who was on her knees in front of her in a praying posture—golden wisps and rays of brilliance shooting up from cracks in the ground that her miracle was tearing into. Julie had attempted to heal Fay, not realizing that Holy magics had an opposite effect on demons, and Fay quickly shook the other woman while tripping over her own feet and vomiting yet again. "UGH! JULIE! STOP HEALING ME!"

A ritual circle encircled Julie while her eyes glowed gold before she realized in horror what was happening, and another burst of radiance lit up the room—healing everyone EXCEPT the demons in their party before her eyes rolled back into her head and she passed out.

Fay let out a sigh of relief as the golden and white lights across her skin faded, but she was in very bad shape.

And the fight still wasn't done. Over half of their combat team had been taken out of commission by the stronger spectators of the supervising group. In other words, they would have died in a real, nonsupervised scenario. Julie was out for the count, Tim was out, Hakim was out, even Luke was out.

There were only eight of them left, including herself and a bunch of randoms from the local squad.

Taking a deep, calming breath, Fay spread her wounded patchwork wings and launched herself toward the ceiling. She turned, taking in the oncoming swarms of vermin and beetles—the latter all chittering and buzzing to rush her way. Two dozen Unholy sigils flashed and evaporated around her in a protective reverse dome, a black cloud swirled and roared about her body for a secondary layer of protection, and she began to chant the rites of Dark Pact for the very first time.

[Dark Pact (Unholy) (Tier 3): Create a cursed zone of healing for allies while simultaneously slowing the thoughts and movements of your enemies. The more mana used to create the zone, and the smaller the zone is, the higher the potency of the hallucination effects. The longer you use this zone and the higher potency you use it at, the more anguish you personally experience until it hits a threshold. When the threshold is reached, you begin to take rapidly escalating physical damage.]

Her hands blew through the motions, arcing up and around her—twisting and turning in the lock-and-key mechanisms needed to summon this particular curse. In her mind's eye, she identified who was enemy and who was ally in a single abrupt thought—while her mouth uttered the words needed to go along with the dance her body was performing.

"Bluvetsa rucnav etlespronumas krakemi thor!"

The room around her seemed to freeze as a pulse of black and green rippled across the air, or at least it did for all the dungeon monsters. It was like watching a movie in slow motion: The beetles flapped their wings more slowly, the downward swing of a mutant's club fell far slower, even a nearby rat fell to the earth in its dive at almost a third of the speed that it would have otherwise done. All this happened under a blazing pentagram of crimson light over Fay's head and near the ceiling above, Unholy sigils swirling around to create an ominous feel to the very air around them.

Meanwhile, the rest of her remaining party surged with vitality as the same spell poured healing mana into them, while Fay's mind went blank with torturous pain.

"AAAAAAAAAAAAAAHHHHH!!!!"

Blood poured from her eyes and it felt like hot irons were tearing into her brain. Her ears started to ring from the sensation while enemies below her died, and she felt more than heard the defensive runes she'd created underneath her hovering position go off with explosion after explosion while beetles attempted to get to her.

It was unlike any pain she'd ever experienced before, a curse on an entirely different level—and she absolutely hated it. But as her mind gave out and broke under the pressure of the torture, what she didn't hate were the brief notifications she saw filter across her vision when she finally released the cursed zone to the ether.

[You have gained one level. Congratulations! Be sure to visit your status page to apply points.]
[You have gained one level. Congratulations! Be sure to visit your status page to apply points.]
[You have gained one level. Congratulations! Be sure to visit your status page to apply points.]

Her body limply dropped through the air like a sack of potatoes, but despite her vision going dark, she smiled. Elysium had recognized her efforts despite her role as a support, and she had to remind herself that despite not having a lot of direct firepower, it was still possible to catch up to her friends.

Fay's body landed in a soft bed of flowing blood, where she was gently transferred into the arms of Riven, who smiled down at her.

"I'm not sure I like your skill set all that much, even if it is useful," Riven stated with a concerned grin, giving her a kiss on the forehead between her two small horns. "But I won't take away your moment of glory. Good job, Fay. I'm proud of you."

Ah.

Yes.

He had called her useful.

He still thought she was useful.

That was exactly what she'd been wanting to hear, even if she hadn't specifically admitted it aloud. Her body relaxed, and with a content hum, she let herself doze while the remaining combatant squad did their best to cull what was left of the oncoming swarms.

Unfortunately, she'd pushed herself to the point that she didn't even realize what she'd done. She'd pushed herself hard to prove to herself and to everyone else that she was still worthy. That she could still be something, mean something, and provide something to the group—when she'd let her personal hallucinations slip. When she'd used her demonic wings to fly. When she'd accidentally lost Gaia's amulet due to a sludge ball to the face and had gone all out. She was too exhausted to notice how many of the people were now looking at them. At how her body had changed from that of a blonde, tanned supermodel into a similar but also very different visage of a blue-skinned, white-haired, winged succubus.

A very famous succubus at that, at least on Panu.

She didn't see the dropped jaws, the unhinged stares, or the looks of shock and awe from Jarla or her companions before she let herself drift off into the very warm and cozy embrace of her lover and master. And honestly, even if she had seen it, she probably wouldn't have cared all that much.

Because Riven had said she was still useful.

She was in a good place.

CHAPTER 13

Flashing magics tore through the air on either side as black-hooded figures and screeching waves of undead intercepted enemies of the necropolis with overwhelming force.

Allie's foot blurred—smashing down into the neck of a dying ratkin rogue, snapping the creature's neck while sneering in contempt. With a lightning-fast backhand she tore half the face off another ratkin warrior who'd dared try to take her head-on.

The creature was sent spinning, dead before it even hit the cavern floor. Crossbow bolts flew through the air toward her and simply bounced off her armor or were swatted away with contempt.

"Pathetic."

Flaming skulls were born from the ether, and they began to scream before shattering the sound barrier and crashing into their targets in explosions of death.

Allie's hands rose out to either side of her path as she walked, and the dead began to rise with them. Flesh peeled from bone, while necromantic magics gave life to the skeletons of those who'd been alive not mere minutes before. Her echoing footsteps joined the groans and shrill screams of the dead over the din of battle, and as one they rushed the oncoming ratkin vagabonds who were now mostly squealing and running for their lives in a panic.

People didn't call her the Butcher of Carnis for nothing.

The ground groaned underneath her, and ghosts swarmed up from the depths to tear at her enemies and inject themselves into the soul realms of the fleeing humanoid rodents. They died by the dozens, and then by the hundreds, while she and a dozen of her fellow necromancers watched the bodies pile up against the backdrop of a burning dwarvish village.

"They will stop coming eventually, if I slaughter enough of them," Allie said from underneath her hood, red eyes flashing from behind a skull mask and body flickering with teal and black energy. "Or they will be converted to our cause the hard way."

Mara nodded with hands clasped behind her back while Nin and Vin chuckled beside them. "More bodies for the necropolis is never a bad thing. Ratkin from

Deepnest are still angry with the dwarves, but these dwarves are ours now. I agree, they will learn—or their bodies will join us in death. And I doubt their leadership will ever come out to publicly support these vagabonds, either—their relationship with Your Highness is too valuable a thing for them to lose over little squabbles like this."

"Either way, we win . . ." Vin said in a raspy voice, his body of bone quivering with excitement at all the dying raiders who'd sacked the dwarf village only an hour ago.

A dwarf village that was owned by none other than the Thane Necropolis.

He slammed his staff into the ground, bone fingers scraping against the wooden shaft, and shrieked to the cavern ceiling above to unleash a dark-green wave of plague, one that rushed overhead and dived into the battling combatants where the living quickly started to pick up nasty afflictions of disease.

Allie snorted in disgust, walking toward a tunnel descending farther into the underdark. She didn't glance back, and the other dozen necromancers followed with sweeping black cloaks billowing out behind them. "Have the patrols continue to run them down, and have our soldiers put the ratkin heads on spikes after we leave. We have business to attend to, otherwise I'd do it myself."

Mara nodded, beginning to pull out a phone inscribed with sigils from the mechanics in Chicago.

Allie continued, only waiting long enough for Mara to relay the first message. "Send a letter to the queen of Deepnest. A letter letting them know that our guard patrols have just tripled. If she isn't competent enough to get her people in check, I'll start doing it for her. Tell her that word for fucking word. Fimrindle, scout ahead. And tell Lahn that I'm going to be late on our return after this unexpected fiasco, but that I'll still be back in time for the ball in a couple weeks."

The iron scarecrow exited concealment and nodded, vanishing into the tunnel labyrinths of the underworld like a silent wraith. Descending into darkness, with a horde of undead and the most elite necromancers of the Thane Necropolis at her back, Allie took her first steps on the edge of unknown territory. Following a map supplied by the Bloodmare coven, they began their trek toward the underground vampiric city of Bernzee.

The dungeon was covered in viscera, organs, and blood—with Athela tearing through enemies in her large archdemon form, standing over the corpses as a huge white drider touched by one of the seven primal sins. When the forward group had almost been overwhelmed, and now that Fay had already given their identities away, there wasn't much more point to keeping hidden. She'd gone all out as soon as the last of their side was pulled by the skinwalkers, and the sheer amount of killing intent released from her aura had caused nearly half of the enemy dungeon monsters to cower, shriek, and run.

Or at least they'd attempted to run, but their remains now plastered the walls, ceiling, and floor of the domed room in all directions. The body blender she'd become just continued pumping out death, and the dungeon had to resort to using some kind of mass-frenzy ability that'd pulsed from its very structure in order to keep its minions fighting.

Dozens more armored rats and their mutant purple masters barreled down the hall in a crazed frenzy, roaring as their claws and metal boots scraped against the stone floor. The hall shook, and another multiton beetle crashed through one of the hallway walls to join the swarming monsters that were driving toward the dungeon divers in an absolute rage.

Riven gently set Gaia's necklace on Fay's sleeping form, then handed her to Azmoth. She'd fallen asleep so fast that he had to do a double take to make sure she really was out, but he'd pushed the hair out of her face with a warm smile and stepped back when he was certain. Ignoring the stares of awe and fear from the others, in particular that of a slack-jawed Jarla—who was standing next to her husband with his hand clasped tightly in her own—he turned to face the oncoming enemies.

"I'll be right back." Riven stepped toward the rushing swarm, and crimson frost began to cover the ground he walked on. The stone floor began to shudder with every step he took, and blood mana began to flare along his arms.

And then that mana turned black when he rerouted the energy into his Shadow subpillar.

Sparks of Shadow-infused lightning crackled along his body, and the stone underneath his feet began to tear apart. At the roar of energy that ripped through the tunnel entrance, hundreds of enemies bearing down on his position were in the direct line of fire.

Lifting one hand, he let loose a roaring tide of Black Lightning.

The hallway shattered instantaneously.

Blood, bodies, and gore exploded in all directions, the screams of the incoming monster tide lost in the abrupt rupturing of internal organs. Stone from all around the hallway, bottom and top, side to side, was torn off and flung forward in a violent cloud of supersonic shrapnel. The back end of the hallway exploded as well, and the dungeon itself seemed to scream in pain and rage as the underground complex shuddered at the might of the strike.

In an instant they were all dead, outside of the few that Athela was still toying with in an adjacent passage connected to the domed room. Dust and debris mixed with red mist as black sparks occasionally traced up the ruined remains of unrecognizable corpse pieces littering the dungeon hallway.

Turning around, eyes burning crimson, Riven settled his gaze on his friends and acquaintances. Julie, Hakim, and Tim weren't necessarily surprised—but they were still impressed. Julie was still recovering from the very recent miracle she'd performed, though, and the blast had woken her up with a start. Tanya, on the other hand, had never seen Riven fight up close and was holding a hand over her open mouth with wide eyes and a furrowed brow.

"Riven . . ." she muttered under her breath, just as a piece of the hallway behind his black silhouette collapsed. "Riven, I don't think you should eat any more of those ham and cheese sandwiches I made. I think they might accidentally have given you godlike powers."

Tim grunted a laugh and swatted his mother on the arm while Tanya grinned. "Stop attributing our good fortune to your cooking, Mom! You're so ridiculous—he was obviously powered up because of my stunning good looks. He was inspired to perform in my presence is all."

"Oh, is that so?!" Hakim bellowed a laugh of his own, continuing to hold Julie up with one of his arms wrapped around her waist. "I think Riven was doing just fine before he saw your ugly mug!"

Tim frowned. "Now, that's just mean!"

Riven rolled his eyes and grinned, then walked back over to sit next to Fay and some of the others on his floating disc of blood magic. "It appears that everyone is worn out from the fight."

Another cackling laugh from Athela, a crash, and a resultant monster's scream echoed through the room.

"Almost everyone," Riven corrected with a backward glance. "Is everyone okay with setting up camp here for a couple hours to rest? I feel like all of you could use it."

The four campfires sent flickering yellow lights across the pillars of the domed room and the people encamped there. The tunnels that weren't caved in had been sealed off by Athela, and those strange cultist people in masks continued to walk the perimeter in groups of two or three.

"You told me his name was Riv! Not Riven, as in THE Riven! Not the crazy, city-killing warlock ranker that took out an invading fleet of ships and destroyed an Azag hive nest in Chicago!" Jarla hissed under her breath, glaring at Tim menacingly while taking time to shoot a look Riven's way—where the vampire and his demons were laughing and talking around a campfire of their own with the elves. "This is crazy! How did you even make friends with someone like that?!"

Tim shrugged, peeling an apple with one of his knives in a cross-legged position. "We met him in the tutorial. He's a nice guy."

"Nice guy?!" Jarla repeated, dumbfounded, and she leaned closer to make sure no one else outside their little circle overheard. "Tim! We are in serious, SERIOUS danger here! Vampires feed on people like us! We're like . . . like little sacks of snack for him to gobble up if he gets hungry!"

Julie, who'd been grinning in amusement at the exchange, snorted a laugh and covered her mouth. But the others sitting at this particular campfire who also hailed from Jarla's group didn't look amused in the least. Instead, they were either very scared or awestruck. Or a combination of both.

But mostly awestruck.

"Riven does not have a reason to kill you, Jarla," Hakim said with a lowered voice and a calming smile, giving Julie a neck massage while the smaller woman continued to giggle amid pleasured groans. "If it came down to choosing between one of his minions and you, sure—he'd kill you, too. But he doesn't randomly kill people just because he's a vampire. He's a good person, at least to us."

The blond male lightning mage with a ponytail who'd spoken with Riven previously before coming into the dungeon also looked rather nervous, but for different reasons entirely. He put on a pair of spectacles, squinted Riven's way, and cleared his throat. "You all have known him that long, then? I've read on the forums and even seen videos about the Elysium altar in Brightsville. It is an oriented type that can recreate one's soul into that which channels the Unholy Foundational Pillar. Do you think that perhaps he'd be willing to take us back to Brightsville with him when he next leaves? You said he can portal back, right? Maybe he could even give me some tips on the dark arts if I'm lucky enough. Oh . . . Maybe he could tell me how he got that warlock class of his so that I could get some demonic familiars, too . . . Goddamn it, he has such a cool class!"

"I'm just happy we have that monster on our side!" One of the front line fighters chimed in, cleaning blood off a metal helmet with minor enchantments at the fire's side. "We're probably going to be escorted like this the entire way through! I've never completed a dungeon before!"

"Uhhh . . . Is he really a vampire prince?" a young, petite, raven-haired woman wearing a fur jacket asked. She was one of the healers of Jarla's group and kept stealing glances Riven's way. "Like, a real one?"

"He's taken," Julie stated flatly. "Give it up, butterflies."

Tapping his foot against the floor impatiently, the mage had had enough talking and stood up. He cleared his throat, closed his eyes to settle himself, and turned his body to set himself on a path. "I can't not at least ask him about it, after seeing that Black Lightning for myself. So here goes nothing."

Stepping over a large divot in the floor made from the battle not long ago, the man pushed off with his basic wooden staff and headed over to the other fire. He got more than a few looks from others of his group, but no one said a word until he cleared the distance between himself and the rather famous—or infamous— vampire warlock.

Sweat began to drip down his forehead, and he took in deep, calming breaths when Riven's laughter died out and the warlock's eyes shifted in his direction. The two demonic women, one on either side of him, stopped their laughing banter and also paused to stare expectantly his way. The only one on this side of the fire who didn't give him any attention was the hulking four-armed brutalisk drawing pictures with the little elf girl—using crayons on manila paper.

Seconds ticked by.

"Is there something I can help you with?" Riven eventually asked, a curious eyebrow raised while leaning forward. "Everything okay?"

The lightning mage gulped. "Ye . . . yes. Yes! I, um, was just hoping that I could, just maybe, get some p-pointers . . . Pointers! My name's Jared, and I, um, have been something of a fan."

"Oh? A fan? That's new. But yeah, I'm not sure what it is you mean by pointers—I don't have an orientation to the pillars you have, but we can talk. Go ahead and take a seat. Name's Riven, though you probably already knew that—nice to meet you."

They shook hands, and Jared fell flat on his butt next to Athela. Gratefully accepting a flask of what had to be vodka from the smell of it, Jared's face brightened slightly and he gave a knowing grin before taking a small chug. "Ah, that hits the spot!"

He could feel the stares of his comrades at his back, and it only made things worse for him, because he was downright nervous to be sitting next to THE Riven Thane and his familiars.

"So . . ." Jared began, handing the flask back to Athela, who took a swig of her own and began making gargling noises with the stuff after throwing her head back. "Pointers, yeah . . . How common is it that people in Brightsville swap their pillar orientations?"

"With the Elysium altar?" Riven clarified pointedly.

"Yes, that!"

"No idea. Athela? Fay? Genua? Any idea?"

They all shook their heads, but it was Luke who raised a hand. The old man put some cooked meat to the side before wiping his hands. "I know a thing or two about it, because I actually considered it myself after becoming a thrall. I have the Storm subpillar, subservient to the Fae pillar, just like you, Jared. Being a thrall also gives bonuses to any Unholy-oriented subpillars, and I was very curious about potentially throwing my weight around with the Blood type."

CHAPTER 14

All heads turned in Luke's direction, with Jared in particular being quite captivated.

"So I went around asking people who'd done it, and I even made a forum post about this exact topic to let other people know what my findings were. If you go look for yourself, should you ever visit the necropolis, I'm sure you'd see my post has been a very big hit," Luke continued with a wave of his hand. "Some of the people I talked to gathering information were private guilds; others were undead soldiers in the necropolis army. Others still were orcs, and believe me when I say that the orcs in particular have a very keen liking to the Unholy pillar despite naturally being oriented to the Fae pillar more often than not. I even talked to Princess Kathrine Vonsilla Crushada of the Blood Moon Requiem about it! Her part of the recorded interview was rewatched more than any other part of my video. She was very helpful, by the way—she was keen to answer my questions since I'm Riven's thrall. I can't say exactly how often it is that people do it by a percentage, but I can tell you that it is far more common than you think. I mean, just think about it! How many people are born with a low-quality orientation affinity? It's very high. Anything above 20 percent can generally use abilities with effort, and 30 percent affinity to a pillar is considered pretty good. Above a 50 percent affinity is extremely rare and they're all downright talented. But what about those who have affinities less than 15 percent? What about less than 10 percent? Those would include people who can barely muster up a single ability even when straining to do so. Gods help you if you have less than 6 percent affinity for your highest pillar. So do you have any guesses?"

The question was directed at Jared, and the man slowly shook his head.

Luke held up a finger and wagged it in the air. "The answer is that by Kathrine's estimates, an entire fifth of most populations has their highest affinity at less than 15 percent. This also matches up with estimates from my own world, Zazir, before the merger. What does this mean?"

There was a pause.

"It means that a fifth of any population won't be able to gain levels or use abilities without extreme effort," Jared eventually answered.

Luke nodded. "Precisely. A fifth of the population is, rather unfortunately for them, useless—in the grand scheme of cultivation and leveling. Especially those below 10 percent. Do you know how the resetting of Riven's modified Elysium altar works?"

"No, I do not."

"It rerolls those numbers," Luke replied. "Not only do the affinities change, but the affinity percentages also change. Most of the time, at least according to the people I've talked to, they even increase those affinities. Not always, but far more often than the other way around. So, theoretically, if you have a fifth of your total population that can't level or cultivate very well or at all . . ."

His voice trailed off, and he made a flourishing motion with his hands.

Jared rubbed at his chin thoughtfully. "They're all going to the Elysium altar to try and reroll their affinities."

"Precisely. The Unholy pillar is, at least on this planet, probably the least common pillar affiliation out there. This can be guessed at by the world forum posts, when you compare subsection forums and the number of active users in each forum. Here, take a look."

A hologram appeared in front of Luke, and he began scrolling through the cortex pages almost immediately.

[Welcome to the Panu Cortex!

Here you will find forum categories and branching categories; you can scroll through subjects, post your own topics, acquire or share video feeds, create enemies or alliances, and even bargain for goods like a marketplace. Be warned that each of these has strict sets of rules, and you will receive a notification if your content is prohibited. Most prohibited material involves key events in the world of Panu or even in your local area, secrets of Panu that the Elysium administrator wishes to be found rather than publicly exploited, information released too early regarding worlds outside Panu, and spam content. Video feeds can only be uploaded by request. You must ask the administrator directly to upload content, and your request may or may not be recognized. Sometimes the administrator may also post video content even without an express request. In order to request video uploading, just mentally think of the time and place you want to upload and wait for a response.

Please note that restrained or imprisoned personnel may not access the forums of Panu's cortex. Forums extend only to places you have visited and guilds you have joined, with the exceptions of the main page discussion boards and the World Quest message boards—both of which are world-spanning and more heavily moderated. No forums outside key areas visited and guilds can exist other than Global Forums.

Feel free to select from one of the already categorized subjects, or you may use the search function for more in-depth selections of guild forums. Your options are as follows:

- **Main Page and Announcements (Global)**
- **Power Ladders, Guild, and Individual (Global)**
- **World Quests and World Quest Ladders (Global)**
- **The Thane Necropolis (Empire-Wide)**
    - **Brightsville**
    - **Chicago**
    - **Rockford**
    - **Milwaukee**
    - **Dungeon Alibast Township**
    - **Mandon**
    - **Bradshire**
    - **Belmington**
    - **Corpus Christi**
    - **Nicina**
    - **(+32 more empire options to select from)**
- **Deepnest**
- **The Golden Bull Sect (Empire-Wide is currently unavailable)**
    - **Muvare**
    - **(+7 Unavailable Options)**

NOTE: Continental differences along Panu have been detected in optional selections. To acquire access to continent-wide forums or map-sharing specs, please visit more locations on the continents where you have traveled.]

Riven stopped him before he selected an option, pointing to the "Golden Bull Sect" option quizzically. "Who and what is that?"

Luke looked surprised at the question, then chuckled and shook his head. "You really need to follow up more on the politics of your own empire, Riven. Your sister hasn't talked to you about it? The Golden Bull Sect is another faction to the north of our own, relative to Brightsville—not the side of the world Chicago is on. I went to Muvare once at the invitation of Mara, when they were discussing geopolitical issues with our relative neighbors."

"Ah. I see. Are they close?"

"Not necessarily, but that is why I called them relative neighbors. They're the largest faction on our continent after ourselves. They seem friendly enough, or at least are cowed by the fact that they know they'd be crushed if they ever came into conflict with the necropolis. Your sister is rather intimidating when she negotiates, and she uses your name as a metaphorical stick to beat her rivals over the head with."

Riven nodded with a laughing grin. "Of course she does. What's the continent's name? Do we have a name for our continent yet?"

"We do not. I'm sure that will be figured out in time, though."

Luke turned back to the cortex screen, then began shuffling through the options again—getting back to his original points concerning pillar forums.

[You have selected: Main Page and Announcements (Global)
You have selected a major subforum: General Discussions (Global)
You have selected a minor subforum: Power and Cultivation (Global)
You have selected six specialized subforum options: Unholy, Holy, Fae, Archaic, Harmony, and Machine Pillar Discussion Subforums (Global)]
[Unholy Pillar Discussion Subforum: 604,822 Active Users]
[Holy Pillar Discussion Subforum: 3,429,112,317 Active Users]
[Fae Pillar Discussion Subforum: 2,829,808,773 Active Users]
[Archaic Pillar Discussion Subforum: 996,325,199 Active Users]
[Harmony Pillar Discussion Subforum: 893,111,225 Active Users]
[Machine Pillar Discussion Subforum: 2,665,343,586 Active Users]

Luke pointed out the active user counts for each of the global discussion forums. The numbers fluctuated by the second, but they usually stayed within a certain range for each subject category. "Do you see a trend, Jared?"

Jared scowled. "Yes. It's rather obvious."

"Which is?"

"The Unholy pillar has far, far fewer active users than any other group, with not even a million total at all times. The Holy and Fae pillars hover around three billion active users at a given time, with the Machine pillar category right below them. Harmony and Archaic pillar categories are each hovering at a little less than a billion active members—staying in the hundreds of millions."

"Exactly," Luke agreed with a smile. "Which very likely means, based on these numbers alone, which very rarely fluctuate off the norm, that the Unholy pillar on this planet is by far the least acquired of all six major pillars. Now, I know I'm going off on a rant here—but why would I make this a big deal since we're talking about Riven's Elysium altar being able to switch people over into an Unholy alignment? Let's find out!"

Without waiting for an answer, Luke clicked on the Unholy pillar discussion forum. And when it appeared, the first three topics were related to the Thane Necropolis. Some of the top on the list were as follows:

[Where is the Thane Necropolis located, and do they accept new recruits? Am hoping to acquire the Unholy Foundational Pillar for myself, my friends, and my family from their altar.]
[Fellow undead and necromancers of the Thane Necropolis: a question on skeleton body part integrations for skresh.]
[In need of help acquiring a demonic familiar, am hoping to acquire a succubus like Riven Thane did. Any advice on how to go about attracting one? #NotAPerv]

[Casting advice needed concerning Tier-2 Chaos spells]
[Blood Rituals and Blood Miracles—a Healer Priest's Guide to the Profane]
[An in-depth analysis of high-level combat concerning Unholy-aligned abilities, with video footage including Paragon and Apex rankers such as Riven Thane and his familiars, Allie Thane, Retesh Vorath, Krush Rinnil, Chitter Teh-Sneaker, and Lucas Von Calimont.]

Luke let out a low chuckle. "As you can see, the most popular topic in this forum is talk about whether or not Riven and Allie allow others to acquire the Unholy pillar for themselves—and Chancellor Mara Tovane herself answered yes, with Allie's permission, given they pledge loyalty to the necropolis. Since her reply, she has been bombarded with applications and an entire team of government workers was assigned to help people try to navigate their way to our empire. Of course, this may be hard to do for some—but it is certainly a big draw for those who are interested in the affiliation or outright desperate to get ANY chance at a reroll for their own affinities. All this being said, our capital, Brightsville, is now the unquestioned epicenter for the study and acquisition of the Unholy Foundational Pillar, and all its branches, on the planet of Panu."

"Didn't realize you were such a celebrity on the cortex, did you?" Athela teased while jabbing Riven in the ribs.

Fay nodded enthusiastically with a yawn. "You get talked about a lot in this forum! You're probably the most popular Unholy-oriented user on the planet, and you definitely have the most footage out there. Compared to that rank-three corpse lord elder lich, Retesh Vorath, you probably have twelve times as much footage as he does even though he's a rank above you."

"Kathrine informed me that it is rather rare to successfully convert an Elysium altar the way you did, Riven," Luke continued again with a small smile playing at the corners of his lips. "It's apparently considered a world treasure by many factions. You sometimes see terraforming altars, or ones that have some kind of affinity in some way or another, but to outright change someone's pillars and reroll affinities is very much sought after by even the larger factions of the multiverse. You hit it big, and Brightsville will no doubt be a long-standing attraction to the world and beyond because of it. Though she did say that when the world opens up, you may want to start taxing people who come to use it—otherwise your world will be flooded with desperate masses of people from intrasystem planets. Some may even try to conquer Panu over such a treasure, or so she says."

"Already have that problem!" Riven replied with a laugh, slapping Athela on the back of the head when she tried to jab him in the ribs again. "Not much I can do about it now, though. Don't get me wrong, this is all very interesting—OW!"

Riven got Athela into a playful headlock after another jab, and the arachnid woman hissed before warping into a smaller spider version of herself and scampering away with an audible humph.

Shaking his head at the exiting spider, Riven cleared his throat and turned his attention back to Luke. "It's all very interesting and I'm glad to know, but why bring it up?"

Luke turned his gaze upon the lightning mage, Jared. "Because Jared here wants to convert his own pillars, and wants to join the necropolis. Don't you, Jared? You've already read these posts, haven't you?"

Jared gave a sheepish smile and scratched the back of his head. "Heh . . . yeah. Maybe. I didn't know how to ask, but I'd very much like to become a necromancer or warlock myself. Something with minions to keep me safe. An elemental storm mage is REALLY cool, don't get me wrong! But it wouldn't be my first choice. It's only good for combat and doesn't have much else in terms of use. At least, none that I've personally found. I . . . hope I'm not overstepping here."

The eyes of all others, at all four campfires, were now intently staring while they listened in on the conversation.

Riven blinked. "Oh? Is that all? No, that's not overstepping whatsoever. If you want to try your hand at a reroll then sure, you can come along with me next time I head to Brightsville and we can set you up at the altar."

Jared's face lit up with surprise and then elation. "Seriously?! Just like that?! I've heard that some of the guilds that go monster hunting give combat lessons and help acquire new abilities—do you know if that's a thing?"

"Yeah, that's completely fine with me—and no, I don't know if that's a thing or not. It appears Allie has made it a mandatory thing to pledge to the necropolis, though, so as long as you're fine with becoming a citizen—"

Luke cut into the conversation a second later. "It is a relatively common practice for guilds to help out their new recruits in the necropolis, yes—and there's lots of experience to be gained due to the high numbers of rabid undead that spawn in the terraformed lands surrounding Brightsville. Hunting parties and government contracts go out all the time."

"I'll do it!" Jared exclaimed excitedly, jumping to his feet just as others from other campfires started heading over with a barrage of questions for Riven.

Riven held up his hands to calm the others down, and soon the room became quiet again. "Yes, you can all come if you really want to—I didn't realize it was such a draw. But that only will happen after we're done power leveling my friends from the tutorial."

He gestured to Tanya, her children, and Hakim. "Also, guys, I'd been wanting to talk to you about a decision you need to make. Come on over and have a seat."

Confused, Hakim and the others got up, making their way through the crowd to sit nearby.

"That sounds ominous," Julie said with folded arms. "What decision do you have for us to make?"

Riven held his hands up to either side. "Well, first answer this. Why do you think I'm power leveling you guys?"

The four people he'd met in the tutorial exchanged looks, and they all shrugged.

"To be nice?" Tim replied hesitantly.

Tanya laughed. "That was my thought, too!"

"I suppose that's part of it, yes," Riven admitted with a side-bob of his head. "But not all of it. You know that guild functions just went up, right?"

They all nodded.

"And you overheard me talking about the war that we're about to enter in the hellscapes of Negrada. Right?"

Their expressions became more wary, but they all nodded yet again.

Riven smiled. "Allie will announce to the empire that we're joining Negrada's war soon, and we—alongside Negrada—are going to pay Elysium a large sum of money to do it. It'll be beneficial for both of us, but for different reasons. The guild functions to be hired on as mercenaries will very likely be approved without issue, and if not, we can at the very least use my portaling abilities to get some of our elites into Negrada if the dungeon chooses to pay us. It will be a very good opportunity for real combat experience, a chance to solidify our bond with one of the hellscape dungeons, and there'll be lots of loot. Allie will also announce a guild tournament, with prizes handed out to the top contestants, and it'll be empire-wide in both combat and crafting categories. She's forming her own guild because I'll be leaving for Chalgathi's subquest over the next few months while she deals with the fallen elder god quest in the underdark, and I'll be gone for a year—but I was hoping to get my own guild started with the four of you."

"Four?" Tanya asked, obviously surprised.

Hakim's own smile brightened his face. "You want us? I love the idea! But we are far, far below you in terms of power."

Riven dismissed him with a shake of his head. "We'll change that. If you want, I intend to bring all of you up with me. Hakim, you're already close to Fay's level—and Tanya, you could stick to crafts. For me, a guild is just a bunch of friends who go on cool adventures together. Why not let it be you? Besides, my demons don't even count toward the twenty-member limit! It'll be fun—at least I think so. What do you say?"

"You forgot to tell them other thing," Azmoth stated pointedly from where he was still drawing with Len as the little girl giggled and hummed.

Riven snapped his fingers. "Oh! Right. Well, if the four of you want it, and you certainly don't need to do this, I'm willing to turn each of you into vampires. It's a big decision to make, yeah, but it'll also seriously improve your chances for survival because you'll have innate healing abilities—and my bloodline is good enough that a conversion will set each of you up in the greater vampire category."

Chaga moved furiously through the dungeon halls alongside his two vampiric brethren, red eyes flaring and blood magics tearing through armored rats and purple abominations one after the other. The fifth floor was far harder than the others and was now giving the three Rippenvire vampires a tough time due to the concentrated high levelers Dungeon Petrus kept down here to keep its dungeon boss and treasuries safe.

Curses and damnations, why did it have to be here and now?

Couldn't Riven Thane have gone to some other out-of-the-way village?

Why Jerbyville? JUST WHAT WERE THE CHANCES? This gods damned settlement was on the other side of the fucking world!

Despite his orders, Chaga was questioning whether this would actually work. But orders were orders and he dared not be labeled a blood traitor like so many of those who'd surrendered to the Thane Necropolis in weeks past—destined never to return home for fear of a swift execution.

The thralls he'd harvested from Jerbyville and the surrounding area fought valiantly to keep up with him, but neither he nor the other two vampires could waste time. They needed to find the dungeon avatar or the boss itself in order to make contact.

"What's the time on reinforcements?" one of his fellow vampires, a man with a blade extending from his cane asked while slicing through yet another armored rat.

Chaga turned left down a dark hallway and shifted his weight when he saw the barred double doors. He heaved a sigh of relief and straightened out his vest while adjusting his top hat. "Three hours until Rippenvire and the Empire of Dying Suns have their death squads arrive, and we need to make a deal with the dungeon before they get here."

Chaga turned to look the other man in the eyes, fangs bared wickedly. "It's time we get revenge on the man who killed all our brethren back in Dawn. By this time tomorrow, his name will be erased from the leaderboards—and his body will be carried out as a corpse."

Without waiting for the thralls, Chaga and his two compatriots started walking toward the doors. Without even needing to reach them, the doors unhinged and clicked numerous times before swinging slowly open with an ominous creaking sound—and Chaga's eyes fell upon one of the biggest, purplest, meanest-looking mutated rats he'd ever seen in his entire life.

Yellow eyes flared, and the dungeon boss began to rise.

"Yes," Chaga said with a growing smile. "Yes, this one will do nicely. Dungeon Petrus, if you would but spare me a moment, I would like to make you a deal. One that would benefit you far more than it would ever benefit me."

CHAPTER 15

Captain Vros Kinal knelt on the outskirts of the forest clearing in full plate-mail armor, the etched carving of a black sun on his breastplate. His pauldrons looked like they were aflame and caught in a moment of time from the way the metal was carved, and a long red cape flowed out behind him in the wind.

Unsheathing his silver-infused long sword forged specifically for killing vampires, picking up his kite shield, and lowering the visor of his plumed helmet, he raised a hand to give the signal. "Kill the natives, let none escape."

Horns blew from all around the clearing, and many soldiers in armor just like his rushed the camps below.

The locals who'd been coming out of the dungeon or had been preparing to go in began to scream and shout in alarm—but they didn't even have a chance before soldiers of the Empire of Dying Suns were upon them.

Captain Vros Kinal blurred forward down the hill, decapitating a young woman he thought to be a healer and then spearing another man through the heart with his blade. He parried two strikes—crushed a man's knee with a side kick and disemboweled him all within a second's time.

Guts spilled out onto the forest floor.

Locals from Panu were desperately trying to flee and started scattering upon seeing the drastically higher levels of the invaders, only to come face-to-face with another death squad of Rippenvire vampires. Steampunk guns mowed them down mercilessly with popping sounds of shots amid horrified screams, vampiric hounds lacking fur and with split faces tore into the ambushed men and women, and the shrieking pleas for mercy were short-lived.

Blood soaked the hillside moments later, and the final begging sobs came to an abrupt stop as the two invading parties stared at each other in front of the dungeon entrance.

Captain Vros Kinal nodded to the vampiric leader, and without another word the two forces merged and started their trek into the tunnels. They had a common goal, and neither group would benefit from killing the other.

Unlike Rippenvire, the Empire of Dying Suns had been far more successful in leveling its members up over past months. Each of the three dozen elites from the empire's death squad were above level 100, and they had a very specific vampire prince to put down for good this day.

It was time to knock out one of their biggest obstacles toward world domination—it was time to kill a world boss Apex ranker.

On the third floor of Dungeon Petrus, Riven and his two stronger familiars or the skinwalkers had to step in a few times, but otherwise the power-leveling group was doing very well. They were confident, sometimes too confident for their own good, but didn't hesitate to throw themselves as hard as they could to gain experience.

Wave after wave, room after room, and with a few caches of loot to be had, they made their way all the way through the third floor until they reached a dungeon miniboss.

It was another beetle queen, though this one's shell was covered in large spikes, and it took a lot of effort to kill her. When she eventually died, both Fay and Hakim were particularly rewarded by Elysium.

Fay was given a pair of enchanted hoop earrings that passively boosted her mana recovery and intelligence—while Hakim was given a pair of thick metal bracers that added to his strength and sturdiness. They weren't anything overly special, but they were nonetheless good items to have.

The fourth floor was filled with traps and, surprisingly enough, large lakes of venomous aquatic rats with gills, webbed feet, and stingers at the ends of their tails. These particular rats lacked any fur and were accompanied often by their armored, land-dwelling rat brethren on the shorelines of vast chasms. The purple mutant humanoid handlers were also in abundance, often appearing with mages who used swamp spells like afflictions or plagues that did damage over time.

The healers were very much overtaxed by these, and the party often had to rest in between fights in order to make sure they could continue without needing to be saved by the stronger backups in the observing party.

Everything was going as expected, and perhaps even better than expected due to the frequent level-ups and even more frequent loot drops the farther and farther they went. By the time they found another large stairwell traveling down to the fifth floor of the gigantic mazelike complex, Riven was quite pleased with their progress.

"I gained a level from passive XP just a moment ago," Genua stated with a smile, holding Len's hand while they traveled down the stone steps of the spiral staircase and exiting onto the fifth floor, where the stairwell led into a large library.

Riven, who flipping through the pages of a book, quickly tossed it after realizing it was a medical textbook from Earth and nothing of significance to him. "Glad to hear the plan is working! Len, did you grow any levels yet?"

"Mmm-hmm!!" Len smiled happily, running over to where Athela was ripping book after book off the bookshelves. "What are you doing?"

Athela glanced down, then handed the little girl one of the picture books she'd found. "Just making sure none of this is worth anything."

"Are you looking for spell books?"

"Or tomes, yes. It appears this dungeon is something of a collector concerning normal, old-fashioned books, though. Nothing too spectacular."

Athela patted the little elf girl on the head, getting a warm glance from Genua, and then waltzed over to Riven to put an arm around his. "Feeling better? You look a lot better."

Riven shrugged and lifted up his right arm, where the Unholy sleeve tattoo shifted its runes and sigils that flashed between black and red at random. "Gluttony is hard at work putting my soul back together, so yes. It still has a bit to go, but I almost feel 100 percent. I just—"

Riven's voice cut off and his head swiftly turned left, seeing the hall at the far end of the library abruptly cave in. His frown only grew deeper when a new passage opened up between two bookshelves that split apart with ominous grating sounds. The new hallway was more pristine than the previous one, with no layers of dust or grime anywhere and a smooth white surface of polished marble.

"Well, that's super weird." Riven scratched his head, sharing glances with Azmoth and then starting for the new hall. In the new marble hallway, Riven touched the wall and channeled a pulse of mana down its length.

The mana swiftly radiated along its entire length, rebounding back like sonar and simultaneously setting off a single trap that'd been placed at the very front of a circular vault-like door at the end of the hall. A pillar of flames tore out from the bottom floor and crashed into the ceiling, rebounding and tearing through the hallway toward Riven's position before he raised his free hand and lifted a wall of crimson ice to block the oncoming inferno.

Flames collided with his blood magic and rebounded, heating up as more and more of the flames continued to blast into the compact marble room with increasing fury.

Riven kept the mana channeling, watching expectantly for the trap to stop spewing out flames—but he raised an eyebrow when his wall began to crack. "Step back, everyone, to the end of the room. Just in case."

Jarla hurried her husband to the very back along with many of the others, including the lightning mage Jared and Len, who was dragged by her mother at a rapid pace.

Riven in turn stepped back and set up another wall of ice, a second layer, and then a third. Still the flames kept coming, and the stone walls of the library about them began to shake under the force of the pressure building up inside that rectangular marble hallway.

"That is a lot of pressure in there," Riven stated absentmindedly, clicking his tongue in irritation and watching the very walls of the inside start to turn red-hot and melt. "Surely that dungeon trap doesn't have much more to go. Right?"

Azmoth, who had come to stand next to him with both of his maws circling around off his back to peer like eels at the melting inner layers of ice, unstrapped the large dark-gray shield off his back and held it in one of his four clawed hands. It was the same round shield Riven had bought for him back in Negrada's trading compound, and it had finally accepted Azmoth as a wielder only recently.

[Immortal's Grasp (Tier-1 Awakened Shield) (Heavy Armor): 640 average defense, 83 average damage on strike. +209 Sturdiness, +42 Strength.
- **Grasping Fingers: A hand can launch out of the shield to grasp enemies, pulling them toward the shield or you toward an enemy.]**

"I can suck in flames before explode," Azmoth offered, turning his almost permanent obsidian smile on Riven with a questioning head tilt. "Put ice around me, then I go in. I not die in fire."

Just like that, Azmoth's body burst into hellfire—the obsidian plates around his body cindering while bare red muscles in between the plates lit up with bright, spreading flames. Slapping his spiked tail impatiently on the ground behind him, he motioned for Riven to get on with it.

Riven backpedaled while his original three layers continued to melt, then began to draw up a fourth ice layer behind Azmoth—this one far larger than the other three he'd already made. Anticipating an explosive impact, he put a fifth and final layer around the party members behind him for insurance. "All right, my man, let's see if you really can suck in fire or not."

Azmoth gave him a nod through the crimson ice, turned back to the melting barrier Riven had initially made, and raised his shield. His feet crashed into the ground, shattering stone and anchoring him into one spot while bracing—and as a final act he swung his massive magma-infused war hammer into the ground, creating a hole that half his hammer was also anchored into while he held on to the weapon using two hands.

The two eellike maws opened wide while their necks circled around to the front in anticipation, as did Azmoth's actual mouth a moment later.

It was a weird sight, but the pressure only kept building and building behind Riven's three crimson sheets. More cracks spread, the quaking of the dungeon around them kept building to the point that many of their party had to kneel behind Riven's protective dome in the back, and the fire's light behind Riven's makeshift plug had reached a nearly blinding crescendo.

Riven took in a deep breath, making sure Fay and everyone else were safe with one more check. Only he and Athela were in the main room now, and he nervously clicked his tongue yet again when the air began to whistle with high-pitched shrieks through cracks along the edges of the melting hallway. "This is going to be a very big—"

BOOM

His inner plug shattered, giving way to a raging inferno that tore through the air toward Azmoth like an atomic bomb. His planted clawed feet tore through stone alongside the war hammer—causing his anchors to leave long trails ripped through the dungeon floor as his body began absorbing the flames as fast as it could.

The fourth layer held, but only barely, and the short distance the flames rocketed through was enough to send all the books around the library flying off their shelves onto the floor. Azmoth's figure disappeared in the raging flames, and Athela transformed into her drider body in anticipation of another break.

More cracks formed on the fourth barrier, and the shrieking sound of hot air only grew louder.

Riven immediately took his plate-armor leggings, his weapon Jackal, and his armor Messenger out of his spatial bag, donning his Gluttony-infused armor first. "I thought this was supposed to be a lower-leveled dungeon, so what the fuck is this?"

"Yeah, this doesn't make much sense," Athela replied with a worried grimace. When she opened the vertical crystal maw on her white body, ice-made spiders began pouring out and moved to cover the barrier Riven had made behind them for another buffer. "This is definitely odd."

Bloodsilk snapped around his body, clinging to his skin and disposing of the robes he'd been wearing. Ivory plates began shifting and moving to cover the larger sections of his chest, abdomen, back, and arms. Gauntlets with spiked knuckles crackling with black and red energies snapped onto his fingers, and the eye sockets of horned skull pauldrons began to glow bright red. A very smooth, ivory-colored metal helmet clamped down over his head with slits for his eyes, molded in the form of two jaws coming together to interlink vertically down the middle, like two halves had been smashed together to create the intricate helmet. Short neon-red feathers that almost looked like blades came down the spine of the helmet and along the back of the neck.

The full-body chest armor had the same vertical maw of black teeth down the center, and it had what looked like four flat patches of black metal embedded in the ivory along the back. These black slabs each sparked with a similar energy to the gauntlets, but instead of sparks they exuded wisps of red and black that drifted into mist, similar to what happened when Riven charged a Blood Lance. Two additional large flaps of bloodsilk hung down from the armor's back to cover the posterior and sides of his thighs down to his knees before ending entirely, protecting his legs from any potential propulsion his suit made using Launch—and the bloodsilk from his upper body began making its way down to connect with the plate-armor leggings he was using as an add-on piece for the otherwise complete set.

Jackal came next.

The spear-staff snapped into his hand, akin to a Chinese halberd or kwan dao. It was quite long, made from polished black wood, with the bottom of the shaft being blunted using a cap carved into a Jackal's mouth. The opposite end had another, larger, jackal's head that produced a pitch-black blade, and the weapon oozed a mixture of red and black energy in the form of wisps trailing off the sharp end.

Swirling patterns of blood trickled like small rivers along its surface and flowed over his hands. The streams caressed him, burrowing into his armor and his skin, sending a jolt of awareness from the weapon as the mental entity touched Riven's mind, and Jackal's eyes along the carved faces of the weapon began to glow crimson in a very similar way that Riven's own did.

The maw on Riven's armor hissed and opened wide, and Riven held up a hand to reinforce the layer around Azmoth yet again. He'd received no notification that Azmoth had died but he couldn't see the demon, either, and he could feel the pressure building in the room while the very stone under their feet started melting.

Red wisps tore out of his hand, embracing the cracking ice layer and trying to repair it to give Azmoth more time. Athela, too, began sealing the cracks and reinforcing the fourth layer with her mana-infused bloodsilk, keeping the shaking barrier intact as best she could while more of her dog-size spiders crawled out of her giant maw to settle on the dome in the back. Cracks just popped up in other places, and Riven had to increase the amount of mana he put out. By now the room was rumbling violently, and heat was starting to escape out of fissures in the floor with spewing flames that Riven's ice quickly combated as layers of frost rapidly buried them one by one.

And then, the dungeon trap inside let out an even more urgent pulse of flame.

The straining barrier of Riven's magic burst.

The room went bright white when the metaphorical dungeon pimple popped.

KABOOM

Both Riven and Athela's aspects of Gluttony's maw opened wide and took in huge swaths of flame before both of them were violently flung back into the far wall. Fire raced through the room and spiraled up the staircase, shredding the melting stone into magma as the ceiling began to collapse with the force of the explosion.

Riven's thoughts tugged at his soul aperture, and Gluttony's maw erupted as an Unholy black visage in front of the barreling fires to intercept the brunt of the impact before it hit the dome. His soul clone ate what it could, swallowing the flames and drinking them into the abyss, but much of the flames still got around Gluttony's form and slammed into the piles of ice-made arachnids covering the final protective layer around the weaker dungeon divers.

The arachnids all shriveled and died, but thankfully enough, the barrier held.

Ten seconds passed before the flames finally died away, and Riven's body screamed at him in agony as he moved, despite Hell's Armor being activated to negate the fire damage. That amount of pressure had been so vast that his body would have been crushed ten thousand times over if Messenger hadn't been there to protect him, as was evidenced by the way his less-able armor covering his lower body was now crushed into flattened scrap metal, along with his mutilated legs. The smoldering room was in absolute ruin, glowing bright orange and white along the stone walls and partially exposed upper floor dozens of meters above them, where a hole had been melted into the ceiling. The door at the end of what had once been the marble hallway was still intact but glowed a hot molten color, and to Riven's left Athela was pulling her scorched archdemon body out of a hole in the wall where she'd created a goddamn crater.

"Fuck!" Riven yanked the bent, twisted metal from his soup-like legs, trying not to scream while Messenger's fingers dug the leggings out of his flesh piece by piece. Thankfully his legs began to regenerate quickly, courtesy of his pureblooded heritage, and he let out an audible sigh of relief when new flesh began overtaking the charred remnants that'd been left behind.

Still, even as he picked himself up and pulled out a second set of the leggings he'd had crafted in case something like this should ever happen, he dared not take down the crimson dome covering the others. The heat was simply too high—he could feel it even through the nullifying effects of his own body's obsidian plates and flames, and he didn't even consider dismissing Hell's Armor after his initial attempt, immediately reactivating it when he both saw and felt pieces of his regenerating legs catch fire after brushing up against the near wall.

"OW! Motherfucking goddamn—" He started cursing in force, not stopping while he continued applying his new leg armor, ignoring Athela's laughs while she let off soothing waves of frost from the crystal roses covering her body.

"That was fun!" Athela crowed, raising both of her giant arms in the air over her house-size body and stomping two of her eight sharpened feet into the molten ground. "Let's do it again! Azmoth, are you okay?"

In the very front of the room and still near the hallway that'd nearly been vaporized, Azmoth's flaming body stayed in a kneeling position with two hands grasping the magma-infused stone maul and a bright-hot metal shield. He was breathing heavily, each breath producing flames that billowed into the air, and with a loud belch he accidentally let out a good blast of the stuff with a demonic groan.

"I don't think he's that okay," Riven said with a grin. "Big boy, you gonna live?"

Azmoth hiccuped, producing another puff of flames, then shook his head and stood. "No. Eat too much, not enough" *HICCUP* "space."

A loud cracking sound, and then the snapping of metal on stone was heard from the end of the hallway. There at the very end, the vault-like contraption began to turn—hot metal sliding around in a circle until there was another loud click.

Opening and spilling magma onto the smoldering ground, the hallway's end was opened up to reveal a rather odd sight.

There, standing at the dungeon hall's end, was none other than the man in the top hat who'd propositioned Genua not all that long ago in Jerbyville. Beside him were his companions, also in top hats, all with canes—and behind them were numerous gruff men with hatchets, machetes, and rifles.

All of them had death stares locked onto Riven's person, the previously wary or polite smiles now gone.

How had they gotten down here before Riven? Had they used another set of passages he hadn't known about? He was sure his team had come down first, but he also knew there were multiple ways to the bottom. Perhaps he just hadn't seen them because they'd taken one of these alternate routes.

But the way they stood there looking at him like that caused him to tense, and he met their gazes with narrowed eyes—only to hear the sound of marching feet from above. Looking up at the hole that'd been carved into the dungeon's ceiling far above him, he saw more men in top hats and steampunk attire that he immediately recognized. More warriors who were not vampires also closed in around the hole overhead, heavy-hitting knights and paladins with unsheathed swords and kite shields—while hooded monks clasped hands in muttered prayers beside them.

No words were spoken, and the stare-down commenced as Riven sized up the enemies who no doubt had come for him. What were the chances that those guys in top hats had actually been Rippenvire men? Here, on this side of the planet?

He wanted to facepalm. The chances were so low that he hadn't even considered it, and the vampires had somehow concealed their race upon brief identifications when seen earlier. What was even worse was that though the Rippenvire soldiers were all around level 70 or 80, the knights, paladins, and monks were all even higher level. The identification information they gave off also spelled out just exactly what they were doing there, and who they were.

Their names were also highlighted in golden flames, signaling that they were of the elite status based on level range according to Elysium.

> [Otherworldly Invader, Empire of Dying Suns. Heavy Knight, Human, Level 110 Elite]
> [Otherworldly Invader, Empire of Dying Suns. Heavy Knight, Human, Level 102 Elite]
> [Otherworldly Invader, Empire of Dying Suns. Paladin, Human, Level 119 Elite]
> [Captain Vros Kinal, Invading Faction Boss, Empire of Dying Suns. Sunchosen, Human, Level 122 Elite.]
> [Otherworldly Invader, Empire of Dying Suns. Sunfire Monk, Human, Level 103 Elite]

Their blades were made with infused silver alloys; he could tell just by looking at them. The queasy feeling he got made him absolutely certain of it, and it was like he almost recoiled internally at the thought of touching one. He knew wholeheartedly those weapons would hurt him far more than any normal blade; these people had come prepared to slay a vampire—namely him—and they were equipped with Sun-type classes. The Sun subpillar of the Holy Foundational Pillar did extra damage to vampires—as was confirmed by briefly pulling up part of his status page again.

> [Pureblooded Vampire, Malignancy Heritage (Blood/Shadow/Death)— Your heritage as a pureblooded vampire has finally come to fruition and is no longer repressed. As a person holding one of the original vampiric lineages and as a greater undead, you are a favored descendant of the Blood God. Your heritage empowers you with many bonuses, but it also comes at a steep price. Please review the following changes.
> Negatives:
> - You suffer 400% additional damage from any silver-based weapons.
> - You suffer 300% additional damage from any Light and sub pillar abilities.
> - . . .]

He closed the window after the first two items, not needing to read the rest. "This . . . is not good."

Riven's words were spoken too soon, because the wall to his right shattered in a spray of molten stone when an enormous rat three times the size of Athela crashed into what had once been a library. Scales covered its skin instead of fur, enormous spiked plates covered its body, and a third yellow eye was planted into the center of its forehead between slits in the metal helmet it wore. Huge clawed hands carried enormous battle-axes, spit dripped out of its mouth and off its two enormous front fangs, and huge muscles encompassed its limbs while it stood up on its hind legs to roar out a high-pitched squeak.

The areas far beyond this room, both up above and below, sealed off in white barriers of shimmering light—locking him and his team inside entirely without any chance of being able to portal out.

WARNING
WARNING
WARNING
WORLD QUEST BOSS FIGHT:
TEAM 1: RIPPENVIRE DEATH SQUAD, EMPIRE OF DYING SUNS DEATH SQUAD, CAPTAIN VROS KINAL OF THE EMPIRE OF DYING SUNS (FACTION BOSS), AND SKRAGNUT THE DOOMAXE (DUNGEON PETRUS BOSS)
VS.
TEAM 2: RIVEN THANE (PANU WORLD BOSS), ARCHDEMON ATHELA (PANU WORLD BOSS, THREE FORMS), SKINWALKER TRIBE, AND OTHER PANU DUNGEON DIVERS

[This fight is now being broadcast.]

ELYSIUM HAS SEALED OFF YOUR POINT OF EXIT WITH A DIAMETER OF FIVE MILES UNTIL THE BATTLE IS COMPLETE, THOUGH ENEMY AND ALLY FORCES CAN STILL ENTER THIS ZONE DURING THE BATTLE UNTIL ONE OF YOU IS KILLED DUE TO WORLD QUEST AND INVASION PARAMETERS.

[One Mythic-grade artifact will be provided to the victorious team.]

BEGINNING BATTLE IN
5 . . .
4 . . .
3 . . .
2 . . .
1 . . .

CHAPTER 16

Chaos erupted.

A dozen intricate ritual circles overlapped one another in the air over Riven's position, written in the flames of the sun. Celestial power tore down from above and crashed into his position, only for Azmoth's defensive dome of hellfire to nullify the attacks with a thunderous boom that scattered the flames across the already molten room.

Battle cries roared out and heavily armored soldiers leaped from above with vampiric hounds and thralls, while vampires on the ledge up above and in the smoldering hallway took aim with rifles full of silver bullets to pepper Riven's position.

The vertical maw across Athela's lower torso and her upper arachnid body opened—letting out a torrent of energy from her ability Crystal Maw Cannon. Elemental lightning fused with ice and purple sin energy shot out in a radiating wave that shredded the incoming thralls along with two of the three vampires at the end, instantly ending their lives—but she was forced to defend and backpedal when a flaming sword tore a gash into one of her legs.

The warrior was flung off her body instantly and smashed into a wall with the sound of snapping bones, only for Riven's arc of Black Lightning to rip across his body—burying the warrior deeper into the stone and shoving him across its surface in sprays of debris for twelve yards like one would wipe thick ice off a windshield.

CRASH

The echoing squeak of the dungeon boss was shrill and loud with resounding fervor, and its two battle-axes made contact with Azmoth's shield to create a shock wave that pushed the brutalisk into the dungeon floor. One of Azmoth's free hands crashed into the ground and his body let out a kinetic shock wave that staggered the rat, only for him to follow up with flaming breath in a torrent of fire. The enormous, armored, three-eyed rat rapidly dashed left and avoided the flames while simultaneously using a kinetic martial art of its own—raising both huge axes up in the air, each larger than Azmoth was, and smashing them down in dual rippling waves of energy that tore through the entire room across the demon's position.

Pieces of Azmoth's obsidian plates were ripped off, but he ignored the damage and began chanting under his breath. Quick, direct, and violent body motions lurched from his four arms while he activated his Tier-3 martial art buff the Burning Crusade—and everyone in the dungeon diving party that Riven had entered with saw their bodies begin to cinder. Weapons and claws caught fire for additional flame damage, and they each gained increased resistance to flame as well—inhibiting the Sun damage Riven and Athela were currently taking while sparks flew in clashes of blade, magic, metal, and claw.

And like a fuse was lit underneath them, the skinwalkers acted on this new buff in a frenzied rage—tearing out of a weakened point in the dome barrier together and rushing the vampiric hounds and human paladins that were trying to swarm Athela's position. Their bodies shifted and morphed, revealing to everyone the demons that they actually were with extended claws, pale, lanky limbs, and shrieking screams roaring from toothy circular mouths.

The violence escalated.

Riven's enhanced body—moving far faster than what was normal with wisps of power from Blessing of the Crow—ripped through a tear in space. His blade smashed through the flaming shield of a paladin immediately after the teleport, but the man in turn sacrificed his shield and the impaled arm behind it to return a blow of his own—flaming silver mace crashing into Riven's left shoulder with a resounding sound of metal on ivory that shook the pureblooded vampire just by being in proximity with the weapon.

Sunfire stacked on silver alloy. Riven felt weakened by the close contact, and he felt his regeneration in both health and mana already beginning to decline. If he let his reserves drop to a dangerous level and didn't keep himself in top condition throughout the fight, he wasn't sure he could even depend on his normal levels of healing. Not only that, but they'd attacked in an enclosed area that limited his long-range capabilities, and in a place where he didn't have massive amounts of blood reserves to pull on as environmental mana.

They'd planned well for this.

- **Gluttony's Riptide: Passively builds up an elongated blade of sin energy that can extend by swinging this weapon in an arc. Recharge rate and damage output depend on control and insight concerning Gluttony.**

The ground underneath him screamed in protest and shattered with a roaring visage of Gluttony at his back. Dark sin energy swirled and flew forward in an arcing slash, colliding with three overlapping barriers of the sun in a monumental explosion as he simultaneously parried a swinging claymore and staggered when a flail collided with his back. Silver bullets slammed into him from above in a storm of metal, but the room exploded in crimson light when spikes of crystallized blood launched skyward.

The spires of ice avoided his allies entirely, some even bending around fluidly before reorienting themselves in the direction of enemies. The vampires and crusading invaders did not fare as well, however, and many of them were skewered or knocked off the overhead ledge, although the dungeon boss itself was too large to dodge.

The enormous three-eyed rat was still engaged with Azmoth in a David-and-Goliath scenario when Riven's spires struck—tearing into weak points and even through many spots along its armor into a tough hide of scales and muscle. Azmoth capitalized on that moment and activated his shield's grasping ability—pulling the screeching bloodied rat closer with a black hand that ripped out of the shield's metal before meeting the giant rat's face with a magma strike.

[Hell-forged Maul (Infernal/Volcanic Weapon): 319 average physical damage on strike, two-handed for full effect, with each strike dealing additional burn damage on hit and over time. 10% bonus to stun chance. Requires 532 Strength stat with the Infernal or Volcano sub-pillar to use.
- **Magma Strike: Activate this ability to increase the damage dealt by 40% in the form of an additional magma-based explosion. Mandatory five-minute cooldown.]**

Stone maul met rat skull in an explosion of flame and molten rock, sending the creature rolling and bouncing across the ground despite its massive size. Azmoth roared and exploded forward, launching himself with a flare of hellfire and crashing into the dungeon boss with the force of a cannon.

WHOOMF

A miniature sun of golden flames exploded overhead, causing a wave of burning energy to radiate out from the hole in the ceiling above Riven's position—collapsing directly onto him. The vampiric prince staggered under the channeled assault of golden light, twisted to avoid an incoming spear thrown at supersonic speed across the room, and prepared a counterattack. Spinning storm razors ripped into existence around him by the hundreds, infused with blood and shadow mana in conjunction with the Path of Red and Black, and launched forward in a chaotic tidal wave of desolation.

Twisting and turning with lock-on effects for each of the hundreds of deadly projectiles, the spinning blades avoided all skinwalkers, avoided Athela, avoided Azmoth, and ripped into enemy warriors. Vampiric hounds and thralls were shredded entirely in sprays of gore by the dozens, not as protected as the other combatants, while the enemy paladins and knights on the lower floor formed an abrupt shield wall.

Sunlight blasted upward from radiant shields, connecting with the oncoming barrage with each storm razor exploding on impact with tremendous force.

An illusory copy of Riven ejected itself from his body and he saw himself go invisible, only to see a fire-covered flail originally meant for his real body flash through one of Fay's illusions.

He grinned, seeing the man wide-open while noting relief upon the channeled golden light of the sun above following Fay's illusion, too, and his spiked knuckles took the armored man's chin at close combat.

- **Ripping Claws: Punching someone with the spikes of your gauntlets will cause massive hemorrhaging damage over time.**

The metal of the man's helmet tore and blood fountained out of the heavy knight just as his lower jaw tore off with it, sending the warrior crashing into the ground twenty meters away before Riven's body teleported back to avoid a two-sided attack by other combatants.

Time seemed to stall when his hand curled and he activated his snipe ability via Blood Lance, the mana flaring up his arm in slow motion as his vision zoomed in to lock onto the exposed neck of another paladin.

The long crimson Blood Lance erupted from his outstretched hand.

SMASH

A sonic boom caused the room to shake, and the paladin's shield barely came up in time to block Riven's attack, shattering the shield but saving the man's life while he spun through the air in dozens of flips per second before smashing into and bouncing off the ground in a roll.

"Damn, I thought I had him."

To his left another flaming long sword whipped around and collided with his weapon, only for two skinwalkers to claw under his armpit and rip the appendage off entirely with herculean teamwork. The man screamed, only to be pounced upon by the two level-90 demons in an extremely violent goring session.

Throughout all this, the dome of crimson ice mostly held—but he made sure to reinforce it from time to time when able. He'd also sealed it shut again after the skinwalkers had left it to join the battle, and was relieved after looking that way again to see these enemies were completely ignoring the weaker members of the dungeon group—considering them noncombatants, no doubt, until the end, when they would certainly be killed if Riven ended up losing this fight.

Well, at least he didn't have to worry about a hostage scenario.

On the other hand, the monks from above were doing a very good job of healing any of the knights and paladins his side didn't outright kill, as did the golden sun overhead that simultaneously healed the invaders and sought him out to damage him over time despite Azmoth's buff to reduce fire damage. The vampires on the ledge had also stayed out of the fray, taking potshots at Athela, Azmoth, the skinwalkers, and himself this entire time while sending in their thralls and fleshy hounds to do the up-front fighting alongside the other invaders.

His pauldron groaned under the sparking impact of a power shot from a steampunk rifle above, and Riven was sent crashing into the ground when two golden fireballs smashed into his body. One was intercepted and eaten by the gluttonous maw on Messenger, but the other one made full contact with his lower thigh and groin—causing him to lurch and wince.

"Cocksuckers!" he said in a high-pitched voice through gritted teeth, rolling and launching himself across the room as sin energy bloomed out of the back of his armor to avoid yet another large fireball.

Creating a shadow rift just before he smashed into the wall, he teleported up above and right behind the vampires and monks taking potshots at him.

He gave an evil grin, and the entire area around him—now completely devoid of allies he had to worry about getting caught up in the immediate explosion—began to light up bright red. His hands blurred with the proper motions, and a shock wave radiated out from his body to floor the enemies with their backs turned to his airborne position.

The orb of crimson light between his palms was thrust forward and in an instant grew to the size of a truck. "Nefajia crecus Blood Nova!"

BOOM

The vampires were eradicated in a single go, with half of the floor they stood on vaporizing under a blinding red light—its blowback shattering the summoned golden sun as well and sending many of the monks falling back with cries of alarm. Winds whipped the air around them and the dungeon shook with the impact, leaving Riven to crash-land in a superhero pose on the crackling remnants of the ledge overlooking the battle below, where Athela's large figure crashed all eight legs into the dungeon boss to help Azmoth take it down in the confusion of Riven's shock wave. Black Lightning coursed through his body, and his crimson eyes elevated themselves through slits in his gluttonous ivory helmet to look at the six monks and three armored warriors standing across the gap in the floor.

These three warriors were different from the others who'd already jumped down. Each of them wore frilled helmets and more decorative armor than the others with golden and black trimmings, and each had a bright-red cape and breastplate with the sigil of the black sun.

These were the leaders of the empire's invasion force, and they each drew flaming long swords while getting ready in a defensive stance—radiant shields lighting up in golden light while their eyes flared a bright orange mixed with gold.

[Otherworldly Invader, Empire of Dying Suns. Sunchosen, Human, Level 120 Elite]
[Otherworldly Invader, Empire of Dying Suns. Sunchosen, Human, Level 117 Elite]
[Captain Vros Kinal, Invading Faction Boss, Empire of Dying Suns. Sunchosen, Human, Level 122 Elite]

The six robed monks quickly got to their feet, getting behind the three sunchosen warriors and empowering them with various buffs—golden rings of light encircling the three warriors at different points in the air and sigils of Holy and Sun origins smashing down onto the warriors' bodies.

A man's calm voice carried over the chasm, coming from the central man the system had labeled Captain Vros Kinal. "Hello, Riven Thane. I have heard much about you, and I must say that I am less impressed than I thought I would be."

Riven raised an eyebrow, watching the power build between the three of them as his own power immediately spiked. Roaring waves of black and red thundered around him in a storm of crimson frost and Black Lightning, and the visage of Gluttony—Riven's soul clone—appeared behind him with a hungry chuckle of malice that caused the three warriors to instinctively step back.

Riven sank Jackal into the floor blade-first, then smashed both his armored hands together. Tearing them apart with strings of blood and death mana ripping through space between his fingers, eight flashes of light appeared—four to either side of where he stood.

[Legionaries of the Blood God (Death/Blood) (Tier 2): This is a temporary summoning spell that does not require minion slots. You may summon eight Elite-class Bloodstricken Undead from the Blood God's realm, equal in combat level to your own, and may designate whether or not you wish to summon Blood Knights, Blood Sorcerers, Blood Assassins, or a combination of the three when you do so. Undead are nonsentient and last for five minutes before disappearing. One-day cooldown time. Very high mana cost.]

[Summoned Blood Knight, Bloodstricken Undead, Level 133 Elite]
[Summoned Blood Knight, Bloodstricken Undead, Level 133 Elite]
[Summoned Blood Knight, Bloodstricken Undead, Level 133 Elite]
[Summoned Blood Knight, Bloodstricken Undead, Level 133 Elite]
[Summoned Blood Sorcerer, Bloodstricken Undead, Level 133 Elite]
[Summoned Blood Sorcerer, Bloodstricken Undead, Level 133 Elite]
[Summoned Blood Assassin, Bloodstricken Undead, Level 133 Elite]
[Summoned Blood Assassin, Bloodstricken Undead, Level 133 Elite]

Eight hooded skulls etched with Unholy crimson runes on their foreheads stared with equally crimson orbs for eyes in their skull sockets. Four were heavily armored with red claymores and thick red plate mail. Two held thin, wicked daggers dripping blood mana in each hand and were strapped in intricately decorated red leathers, while the last two wore crimson robes of shifting runic black sigils and held staves with ruby orbs that flickered blood mana.

Riven yanked his sin-afflicted weapon out of the ground in a spray of debris, got into a stance, and the screeching visage of Gluttony opened wide as tendrils of dark sin energy poured out in a typhoon. The hooded blood knights simultaneously shifted their own stances, planting their armored forward feet in line with

Riven's own—long blades lowered at the opposing fighters while the blood assassins utterly vanished in clouds of red and the skeletal sorcerers began summoning Blood Lances similar to Riven's own.

Riven sneered. "Good thing I won't need to keep you impressed if you're dead."

CHAPTER 17

The first to move was one of the bloodstricken sorcerers, who shrieked an unholy cry before their Blood Lances snapped forward with blinding speed. The monks countered with golden fires or barriers of their own, and the magics clashed across the gap between ledges in explosive fury.

Gluttony cackled and the great maw's tendrils collided with the sunchosen in turn, smashing them backward and dimming the barriers they created before the maw diverted its attention to easier targets—those down below.

"I am hungry!"

Deep-purple and black sin energy that was once directed toward the three leaders now turned on the more numerous and distracted warriors fighting the skinwalkers on the bottom floor, tendrils impaling them from behind one by one or wrapping around the legs and arms of the screaming paladins to drag them back into the abyss. Snapping down on well over ten of their elites to immediately end their screams within seconds, the visage let out a content groan and fizzled out—its taxing presence on Riven's soul dying away with it.

Riven winced as the pain in his back seared—his still-broken soul had pushed too much through a particular mana channel—but he ignored it just like he'd done for most of the fight. Launching himself across the gap where red and golden lights collided, Black Lightning encompassed his spear-staff and slammed into the blazing shield of the enemy faction leader.

Sparks flew and the man parried his strike with a countering kick to Riven's leg, causing Riven to buckle, then capitalized with a headbutt to Riven's face and a shield bash martial art that knocked Riven over entirely.

What Captain Vros Kinal didn't see were the threads of needlelike black nets that'd sprung out of Riven's hand and wrapped around that same leg he'd kicked the vampire with.

Riven cackled and yanked violently, coming out of his roll and flipping his enemy onto his back before bringing Jackal up in an arcing swing to smash down onto Kinal's flaming sword.

Blood and Shadow bloomed against sunfire, and the weapons continued to spark while Riven pressed his weight down before vanishing backward through a shadow rift to dodge an incoming swing from another of the sunchosen. He reappeared twelve yards away and whipped around, only to see his caped pursuer get smashed into the ground by two bloodknights. The undead legionaries of the blood god were nothing to scoff at, and five minutes—though technically short— now seemed like an eternity as he watched them carve through the opposition even as reinforcements from what remained of Rippenvire attempted to help.

He winced yet again as pain radiated up his back.

Goddamn it, why did he have to enter a fight now of all times—while he was still recovering?!

The monks used flaming barriers to block and defend against the blood assassins, who'd already killed two of their number with a quick rush from behind and teleport abilities—while the four blood knights went to work battling the three sunchosen with blurring attacks of sparks and metal while Riven took a breather. Meanwhile, the blood sorcerers at his command had turned their attention to the battle below after killing the small squad of reinforcing vampires, repelling any of the empire's soldiers who attempted to jump back up and otherwise just bombarding the enemy combatants to give the skinwalkers, Azmoth, and Athela some support fire.

The same could be said for Fay, who was still encased in the crimson dome but was simultaneously casting hallucinations and curse traps that she'd activate whenever an enemy walked over one.

Even now, the multiton rat dungeon boss in spiked armor was missing an arm and two of its eyes—with Athela and Azmoth tearing into the creature time after time, only its massive sturdiness was keeping the creature alive. It would no doubt have already been over if this had been a more open battlefield, too, but Athela was being very careful not to unleash too much power in case she accidentally killed those huddled inside the dome. It made her slower to work, but she didn't want to hurt Len, Hakim, or any of the others.

Huffing and pulling himself up to a fighting stance, Riven took in a deep breath to focus on the primary target. He only needed—

SHUNK

Pain.

He felt pain.

A silver-alloy dagger empowered with some kind of martial art sank into Riven's neck, piercing through the bloodsilk before lighting up with golden flames. Riven didn't bother screaming—because his voice box was blown out and flames tore through his mouth—but he instantly activated Launch from Messenger's back, causing sin energy to blast the area behind him.

A resultant scream was heard, and Riven dropped to one knee when he crashed into the opposite platform across the chasm—looking left and yanking the dagger out of his throat while struggling to breathe through the charred flesh. A rogue's corpse lay where he'd been a second ago, unmoving with half its flesh melted off.

No doubt the man had waited this entire time in order to get a clean shot, and a clean shot he'd made.

Riven fucking hated rogues, and goddamn did that hurt, but it'd take more than a single attack like that to kill someone like him.

Yanking out a red vial of health potion from his spatial sack and downing it, he clamped his eyes shut and shook his head to clear his mind. The liquid soothed his insides that were battling the antivampire attack, and he downed a second one for good measure before shifting his weight and cracking his neck. His gasping stopped as the flesh revived itself, and he took in a deep breath of fresh air to expand his lungs to the fullest.

The blood god's legionnaires had killed four of the monks now, but one of the blood assassins and one of the blood knights were also dead. Thus it was three blood knights and a blood assassin versus three sunchosen and two monks. Their actions were all elegant, well trained, and fluidly savage while they cleaved into one another with blades, miracles, martial arts, and magics. A wave of blood energy tore out of the claymore of one blood knight with a downward swing that glanced off a golden dome of fire before one of the sunchosen grew wings and rushed the blood knight, taking the two of them off the ledge and down below, where they crashed and continued to battle furiously. The others remaining up top smashed, crashed, and roared in blindingly fast strikes, propulsive movement abilities, and bright lights amid clashing spells.

It looked like the legionnaires were more than enough to give him time to free up Athela and Azmoth.

Mentally ordering his blood sorcerers to focus their attention on the huge dual axe–wielding rat creature that could have easily stomped him flat underneath one foot, he began to charge up his own barrage. Blood Lance after Blood Lance after Blood Lance was created, shifting and detaching from their arms to hover like two-meter spears all around them. The air sang with the building mana as Riven reached out with his mind, connecting lances one by one with thick cords of Unholy Wretched Snares before he electrified them all with a thought.

The resulting display was an enormous, electrified net with large red spikes at every interval between cords, spanning an area forty yards in diameter, including the lances that his blood sorcerers had created.

"Focus on the sunchosen now. I'll take over these spells from here."

The blood sorcerers wordlessly acknowledged his command and relinquished their own spells to his control, then began casting crescent waves of blood that started barraging the other platform across the gap where Captain Vros Kinal and his men were still fighting the blood knights.

In turn, Riven concentrated on his telepathic connection to Athela. "Both of you, move."

He activated his largest and most powerful Blood Lance, the epicenter of the entire sparking, writhing net, and time slowed while his vision zoomed in on the dungeon boss's shrieking open mouth.

It snapped forward just as Athela dived backward with a call for Azmoth to do the same, and the two demons managed to get out of the way right before Riven's attack struck.

The bottom floor exploded with power as the primary lance tore into the back of the monster's throat, and the net coming behind it swung around the creature's body to entangle the dungeon boss—spike after spike using centripetal force to snap down and through the rat's armor.

The creature croaked a wail, dropping both of its enormous axes to the ground and clawing at the electrifying net with the dozens of Blood Lance spikes impaling it. And when Riven's hand curled into a fist, the infused mana of the net exploded inward.

Shrapnel from the rat's armor, mixed with highly piercing Blood Lances, shredded the already wounded monster—only for the remaining snares to contract and squeeze, ripping into and through scaled flesh easily now that the punctured armor wasn't holding.

The enormous rat let out a gasp, stumbled left, and crashed into the ground with a shrill squeak—only for Athela in her drider form to rip its throat out with two of her enormous bladelike front limbs. Blood stained the stone ground of the dungeon, and Athela let out a scream of victory as her aura boomed out with electrified snow.

Satisfied that the dungeon boss was no longer a factor, Riven nodded their way—sending another telepathic communication to Athela. *"Help the skinwalkers finish up those below and get up here!"*

He didn't pause to see if she'd heard him; he knew she had. And—

***CHINGGGGGGGggggg . . . ***

Metal rang against metal, and another splash of sparks lit up Riven's armored face when one of the sunchosen—who'd lost an arm to one of his blood knights—tried to impale him. The flaming metal sent ripples up the flowing blood of Riven's spear-staff, and Riven pressed back to keep the weapon at bay before leaning to be within inches of the other man's armored face and glaring eyes. "I find you wanting."

Riven's headbutt caught the other man off guard and staggered him, only for Jackal's Lunge to activate. The bloodred maw of a canine roared to life in front of his outstretched blade, and in an instant Riven's body blurred through the sunchosen's own—armor and all—in a spray of red mist when Jackal's visage snapped down.

His momentum stopped at the ledge overlooking the bottom floor again, and he stared over at the remaining man. All the monks were dead now, as were the other two sunchosen and even Riven's entire blood legionnaire retinue, excluding the two sorcerers at his side. Captain Vros Kinal glared at Riven, golden flames still crackling along his long sword, before he blasted forward with intent.

BOOM

CRACK

SMASH

The blows landed one after the other, pushing Riven back while the blood sorcerers launched waves of red energy at the invader—only for one of them to die a moment later with some kind of thrown bomb that tore the skeleton apart entirely and nearly caused the entire platform to collapse.

The other sorcerer erected a red barrier just in time to block Kinal's follow-up strike, and Riven used that opportunity to feign an attack with his weapon—only to follow with a low kick to the knee.

But Riven's kick never connected, and Kinal's body spun in a horizontal arc while jumping over the kick to throw his long sword directly into the sorcerer's skull. The blade hit home, piercing the rune along the skeletal mage's head with an impressive explosion of sunlight that eradicated the undead where it stood.

Despite this, Captain Vros Kinal was obviously injured. Blood leaked from numerous places along his armor, and a huge gash was carved down the right side of his chest where a red claymore had dug into one lung. He drew a long dagger from his hip, cape flowing out behind him while he gasped for air, and he stared at Riven not far off with unconcealed contempt.

"Your kind belongs nowhere except a shallow grave," Captain Vros Kinal stated simply, watching Riven get into the final stance of the fight with grim determination. He straightened and pointed his flaming sword in Riven's direction. "I have learned much from this fight, but it saddens me that we could not have finished this today. This is not the end, Riven Thane—it is only the beginning. The next time we meet, I will be stronger than you."

His shield flared bright white again, blinding Riven as the captain pulled out a small box. The lid opened, the man reached inside, and he turned his wrist. The room immediately flared up around them with an even more intense light just as Athela's lean humanoid body ripped through the air and sank one clawed hand into the man's side.

[Captain Vros Kinal, Faction Leader of the Empire of Dying Suns, has used a single-use escape treasure. Invading factions may only have one escape treasure on hand per invasion, and he will not be able to use another one even should he acquire a second, per Elysium's rules of engagement.]

The ringing in Riven's ears and the flash of light in his eyes faded away, leaving only the sound of a single desperate combatant left from the Empire of Dying Suns—a heavy knight who was immediately swarmed by the remaining skinwalkers. His screams echoed throughout the dungeon with—

SHUNK

Pain.

The same pain he'd felt from that other gods damned rogue.

"MOTHERFUCKER!"

CRACK

SNAP

"AAAAAHHHHHHHH!!!!" The rogue's screams were shrill, pain-ridden, and terrified.

CRUNCH

Riven reacted far faster this time, even if the stealthed rogue had managed to shank him for the second time, and this time it'd been a kidney shot between ivory plates rather than in the neck.

He didn't even give the rogue time to activate the second follow-up martial art concerning the flames, just quickly crushed the man's head after breaking the rogue's wrists with a downward chop of his hand.

He let the dead man drop to the ground in front of him, wincing at the side wound and growling, "I fucking HATE rogues! HATE THEM!"

Stomping on the man's already crushed head for good measure, he ground his plated boot into the stone floor and spat. "Athela! I've decided what kind of demon I need for my last slot. Remind me to get a demon that has detection qualities. I'll be damned if I'm killed by one of these pussy-ass twinkle toes who run around in the dark shanking people all day long!"

"Hey!" Athela protested, frowning and folding her arms. "I'm an assassin, too! You're not being very nice."

CONGRATULATIONS

CONGRATULATIONS

CONGRATULATIONS

YOU HAVE WON THIS WORLD QUEST BOSS FIGHT:

TEAM 1: CAPTAIN VROS KINAL OF THE EMPIRE OF DYING SUNS HAS FLED. RIPPENVIRE DEATH SQUAD, EMPIRE OF DYING SUNS DEATH SQUAD, AND DUNGEON PETRUS BOSS SKRAGNUT THE DOOMAXE HAVE BEEN ELIMINATED!

TEAM 2: RIVEN THANE (PANU WORLD BOSS), ARCHDEMON ATHELA (PANU WORLD BOSS, THREE FORMS), SKINWALKER TRIBE, AND OTHER PANU DUNGEON DIVERS HAVE COME OUT VICTORIOUS!

[This fight is now ending its broadcast.]

ELYSIUM HAS UNSEALED YOUR POINT OF EXIT.

[One Mythic-grade artifact will now be provided to you.]

[You have gained three levels. Congratulations! Be sure to visit your status page to apply points.]

[Your minions have received their XP and level-ups as well. Congratulations!]

[YOU HAVE DEFEATED THE DUNGEON'S PRIMARY BOSS, SKRAGNUT THE DOOMAXE. DUNGEON PETRUS HAS LOST, AND AS MASTER OF AZMOTH, WHO WAS THE PRIMARY CONTRIBUTING PARTICIPANT IN KILLING THIS DUNGEON BOSS, YOU ARE THE ONE WHO DECIDES WHAT HAPPENS NEXT.]

[Now that Dungeon Petrus has been defeated, you may choose to either take the dungeon's bribe or you may choose to destroy its core. Taking the dungeon's bribe allows it to offer you treasures otherwise hidden in the dungeon's realm. Taking the bribe allows the dungeon to either relocate entirely or to enter a hibernation mode where the Elysium administrator guarantees its protection and gives it time to rebuild. Choosing to destroy the core will kill the dungeon permanently, preventing monster spawns from it, but you must find the core first to do so.]

Riven closed his eyes, bringing another health potion to his lips and gingerly sucking the red liquid down as he felt his wounds slowly start to regenerate again. It was weird, not healing immediately like so many of his other injuries in the past had. Those silver weapons and Sun affinities were no joke, almost completely negating his passive healing and making him feel rather sick to boot.

His attention was turned to the dungeon floor on the lower level next, where a large platinum chest with glowing blue runes had appeared on top of the dead dungeon boss. If he had to guess, that was the mythic item Elysium was talking about. Half of the skinwalkers had also died, leaving only eleven of them still standing, which was certainly unfortunate . . . he even felt a little bit bad and would be sure to reward the survivors for their efforts.

Not a moment after the chest had appeared, another smaller figure flashed into existence right beside Riven's standing position, taking the form of a hooded ratkin man only two feet tall. It was tan, seemingly made out of clay, but Riven had already seen a dungeon avatar like this before. His identification only made him more certain of it.

[Avatar of Dungeon Petrus]

Riven's red eyes narrowed. The dungeon avatar merely looked up expectantly and rather sheepishly his way. "I hope you know that, unless you want me to seek out your core and shatter it for the shit you just pulled, you're going to have to pay up realllllly nice. And I mean, REALLY nice. Got it, rat boy?"

All Dungeon Petrus could do was nod and sigh.

CHAPTER 18

Mythic-tier item box sitting on another dungeon boss corpse for his sister to use?

Check.

Room full of gold, jewels, and various F-grade artifacts?

Check.

Power leveling his friends and demons?

Very much a check. Having a bunch of level-15 to -50 dungeon divers in his group after wiping the floor with a whole gaggle of level 100–plus paladins and their less powerful vampiric allies had meant enormous gains for everyone involved.

Unfortunately, Captain Vros Kinal of the Empire of Dying Suns had gotten away, Riven had failed to see Athela's two new blood martial arts during combat, and half of the skinwalkers recently pledged to Athela had died—but considering the ambush, it was overall a better-than-expected outcome. Riven was still recovering from the tribulation, Athela had lost her entire force of crystal ice spiders before the fight had even begun, and the paladins had specifically outfitted their weapons with antivampire silver alloys, which had been a real pain in the ass.

Riven pocketed the orange bauble, having had Dungeon Petrus package its dead dungeon boss just like he'd forced the last one to package the drake. "It was a pleasure doing business with you, jackass."

"Stuff it!" Dungeon Petrus growled while folding its little avatar arms. "The number of coins you cost me is outrageous! You have six hours, then you gotta leave so I can relocate! That's the deal. I'll be moving out of these forsaken lands to set up somewhere else. I won't have a monster like you knowing where I set up or I'll never make a living!"

The dungeon avatar snapped its fingers and vanished, leaving Riven in the room behind where skinwalkers were still stripping gear and loot off the dead. Athela and Azmoth were digging through piles of gold and treasures in the room beyond the trap he'd tripped behind that hidden hallway earlier, where Dungeon Petrus had put an additional sum of cash after Riven's threat made it abundantly clear that if it wasn't enough, Riven would find the core.

As for Fay, she was standing beside Riven while he watched the skinwalkers work. On one hand he didn't necessarily trust them not to steal high-quality treasures off these young scions of the multiverse if there were any to be had, but on the other hand, they'd also bled and died in the fight against the off-worlders. He was torn on what to do, because though he likely wouldn't have needed them, they had served as decent distractions.

"Ak'ra and Selzi, a word, please." The skinwalker couple stopped what they were doing and walked over to where he and Fay stood in the center of the room that looked like a typhoon had gone through it.

"Yes, master of our master?" Selzi, the female skinwalker, asked with a submissive bow and posturing. "Can we help the great one in some way?"

Her mate, Ak'ra, bowed the same way. "We wish to serve . . ."

Riven gave them a sad smile, seeing that they were a bit down about losing friends or family, and took his helmet off to better look at them. Stuffing it under one arm, he gestured to the piles of armor, weapons, potions, jewelry, and other items. "Do you see anything you want?"

Selzi shifted her body uncomfortably. "We do not wish to take from the vampire prince but appreciate the great one's generosity if that was intended."

Riven blinked, considering this. "What is it that you and your clan want?"

"I am . . . unsure of what you mean by that. Forgive me, great one."

"What are your goals? Why leave hell? What do you intend to do here now that you're on Panu and in the mortal realms? Surely you have some kind of want or desire."

Ak'ra was the one to reply this time. "We do not have any high aspirations, great warlock. We merely wish to grow strong. What about you? What is it that you desire?"

Riven hadn't been expecting that kind of response, and the question turned around on himself made him seriously give it thought. He looked right, to Fay, and pulled her in close to kiss her forehead.

She grinned, planting a kiss on his cheek and wrapping her arms around him while he continued to search for answers.

"I guess my life is so hectic I hadn't thought about it much," Riven replied softly, stroking the back of Fay's head with one hand. "Growing stronger used to be a need, and it still is, but that, too, has become a desire because of the freedom it grants me. That, though, is secondary to keeping the people I love safe. And lately, magic itself has been rather . . . fascinating. I suppose if I had to choose an answer aside from granting the people I care about protection, it would be that I want to explore magic in the same way scientists of my old world did with microbiology, chemistry, physics—I want answers to how it all works."

Riven thought back to the totems he was working with, smiling slightly. "I wish the Blood Moon Requiem was able to give me more information on totems. Sucks that it's restricted. Elysium is very picky about what it does and does not allow on-planet . . . Anyways, I'm getting offtrack. Ak'ra, Selzi, I just wanted to let all of you know that I appreciate the help. And you know what? Take whatever you want off the bodies, but know that if you find anything good that I may be able to use, I'd be willing to buy it from whoever finds it for a good price. You're all more than welcome to come back to the necropolis after this is done with Athela, too, though I'm sure you'd already planned on it."

"We had, great one!" Selzi adamantly nodded her head. "We will do so, and your appreciation is noted! We will let you know if there's anything worthy of your attention and I will inform the others."

Both skinwalkers bowed again, then left for the rest of their clan on the outskirts where the bodies had been dragged to.

The sound of a woman clearing her throat caused Riven to turn, and he saw Genua standing awkwardly with her daughter's hand in her own only a few feet away.

"Yes, Genua?"

The elf woman's eyes blinked rapidly, and she looked around the room—then back to the others who'd remained under the dome. Most of Jarla's group were completely shellshocked, staring dumbfounded at the absolute destruction of the dungeon around them, while a few of them were excitedly going over all the levels they'd passively gained.

"You okay?" Riven asked, frowning in concern when Len hid behind her mother to peek out from behind Genua's leg.

Genua seemed to get ahold of herself then, and straightened her posture to smooth out her maid uniform. "Y-yes . . . I just wanted to say thank you for keeping us alive and out of the fight. It was far more violent than I'd expected it to be, and I just . . ."

"Mother and I were scared," Len said from behind Genua's leg—staring up at Riven with that one eye poking out where the rest of her face was hidden. "That was really, really scary."

Genua took a shuddering breath, closed her eyes, and nodded. "Yes, I felt rather helpless. I don't like feeling helpless, but it seems to repeatedly afflict me time after time. But I wanted to thank you for having us along, because it appears that I may not always be so helpless."

Genua shifted one hand, and a status screen appeared.

[Genua's Status Page:
- **Level 21**
- **Orientations: Fae Foundation, Forest (corrupted; transition to Unholy foundation has been detected. Potential loss of Fae foundation and associated pillars is soon possible.)**
- **Traits: Race: High Elf, Class: None (three options available), Vampiric Thrall (98% complete), Blessing of the Blood God (???)**
- **Abilities: None**
- **Stats: 3 Strength, 4 Sturdiness, 6 Intelligence, 6 Agility, 1 Luck, 2 Charisma, 3 Perception, 2 Willpower, 1 Faith (90 free stat points to use)**
- **Equipped Items: None]**

"Oh wow! You gained so many levels just from standing by! That's awesome!" Riven enthusiastically put a hand on her shoulder. "Three class options, too! Any idea what you want or if they're any good? I'm happy for you . . ."

His voice trailed off when he saw Blessing of the Blood God listed as one of her traits. Furrowing his brows, he scratched his head. "What's that? Have you had it before now?"

Hesitantly, she shook her head no. "It is new, and came with the level-ups. Until now I'd only had one class option available, too—it was just Slave—and now the old one has disappeared entirely. There are three new ones. They each mention something very specific, and I'm not sure if it's some kind of oddity, or a joke from Elysium, or something entirely different. Would you mind having a look and guiding me?"

Riven continued to stare, his curiosity getting the better of him. "Sure, of course."

Nervously smiling her appreciation, and with Len still looking at Riven like he was some kind of truly scary monster after the fight, Genua pulled up her class options. It was somewhat reminiscent of his own class choices back in the day, only these ones were far, FAR better than his own options had originally been.

[For every level gained, you will be presented with certain numbers of stat points depending upon both your class title, your race, and sometimes other unique factors that will not be discussed here. Currently you have no class title, and your race is set to High Elf. The High Elf race has +5 free stat points per level. Please choose your starter class title. Remember that classes do not dictate your survival style—rather, in the future, your survival style will dictate what classes you are awarded beyond these base forms. The better your performance, the better classes you will be awarded upon evolution opportunities.

- **Priestess of the Blood God (Class Title) (completion of the Vampiric Thrall trait is required to choose this class) (Must apply the Blood God's Markings to choose this class)—A ritualist class evolutionary pathway emphasizing the use of divinity, utility miracles, rituals, and sacrifices. You gain access to the Blood God's clergy interface, where you may buy miracles using faith points gathered from prayer specifically made for your class or interact with the Blood God himself if you climb the ranking ladder of clergy to a sufficient degree. +16 Faith, +1 Willpower, +2 free stat points per level. Comes with the abilities Sanguine Smite [Tier-1 miracle that blasts an enemy at mid- to short-range with blood divinity], Blood Oath [Tier-3 miracle that requires your vampire master's permission to use. Roots the user to one spot, increases the amount of damage taken by the user's vampire master, and grants invincibility to yourself unless your vampire master dies],**

Transfusion Zone [Tier-3 area-of-effect miracle that heals allies and damages enemies], Body Fusion [Tier-3 miracle that temporarily fuses the priestess with one of her master's other minions for unique effects depending on the target], and Sanguine Possession [Tier-4 ritualist miracle that requires a sacrifice in an attempt to temporarily control a marked enemy based on enemy Willpower]. Choosing this class also comes with a legendary F-grade Clergy Robes of the Blood God set.

- Lamprey (Combined Race-Class Title) (completion of the Vampiric Thrall trait is required to choose this class) (Must apply the Blood God's Markings to choose this class)—A berserking race and class that emphasizes raw power and up-close violence. Lampreys are a direct upgrade from the Vampiric Thrall trait, meant to be protectors and pets of the Blood God's chosen. Choosing this class will rid you of the Vampiric Thrall trait while binding you as a Lamprey to your vampiric master instead, simultaneously granting you magic resistance, physical resistance, divinity resistance, extremely high regenerative properties, bonuses to unarmored, and the vampiric tendencies to regularly feed on mortals for survival. Choosing this race-class combination changes your body into a hybrid of what you originally were, and a Blood-type demonic entity, with associated traits that also drastically increase your Agility, Sturdiness, and Strength. Comes with the abilities Cannibalize [Tier-1 martial art that launches you toward an enemy in a frenzied state and does heavy amounts of damage to a single target while simultaneously spiking your own regeneration amid consumption], Berserk [Tier-1 martial art that increases the amount of damage you do with physical attacks, increases the amount of damage you can take, drastically increases your speed, but enrages you and clouds your judgment], Bloody Feast of the Primordials [Tier-3 martial art that sends out repeating shock waves that afflict all nearby enemies with the Heavy Bleeding debuff; that debuff will continue to apply additional stacks every ten seconds or upon being hit by another shock wave for additional passive damage], and Blood Dance [Tier-2 martial art that applies a mark to an opponent for execution in the next eight seconds, dealing 100% extra blood damage on strike to that opponent until they die or the eight seconds expire. If the marked enemy lives, this martial art goes on a lengthy cooldown. If the marked enemy dies, this martial art allows you to mark and teleport to another enemy for 120% additional blood damage on strike. This effect can repeat up to 400% additional blood damage on strike as long as executions are successfully made within their eight-second time allotments]. +6 Strength, +6 Speed, +7 Sturdiness, +2 free stat points per level. Comes with a legendary F-grade Guillotine Rampager set.

- Sacrificial Slave Aspirant (Class Title) (completion of the Vampiric Thrall trait is required to choose this class) (Must apply the Blood God's Markings to choose this class)—A utility class that focuses on empowering one's vampiric master by means of internal sacrifice. Comes with the traits Numbed Pain [60% decreased sensation to any painful stimuli], Masochist [Derives gratification from pain while simultaneously healing your vampiric master at 1% of the damage you take directly], Cockroach [Upon death, respawn a day later as long as your vampiric master is still alive], and Master's Burden [20% of damage dealt to your vampiric master is rerouted to you until death]. Comes with the abilities Take Affliction [Tier-1 spell that immediately rids your vampiric master of any debuffs and places them on yourself], Give Life [Tier-1 spell that immediately sends a portion of your health pool to your vampiric master], and Red Meditation [Tier-3 spell that absorbs surrounding blood mana while in a channeling trancelike state to heal yourself at extreme rates. This channeling can be easily interrupted]. Increases Sturdiness by 500 flat points, with an additional 10% Sturdiness overall buff. +1 Willpower, +1 Intelligence, +10 Sturdiness, +3 free stat points per level. Comes with a legendary F-grade Shackles of the Blood Slave set. This class has an abnormally wide array of potential evolutions in the future once reaching level 50.]

The very second Riven finished reading her notification, the room shuddered as the lid of the Mythic-grade treasure chest opened. His eyes widened, and many of the onlookers stepped back while Azmoth and Athela rushed back into the room.

Red light bathed the interior of the dungeon wreckage, and a swirling mass of intertwined crimson symbols hovered in the air—mixing and rearranging themselves in odd, interchanging patterns.

If there was ever any question that system prizes for quests didn't customize themselves to their assigned person, that question was now completely curb stomped.

[Blood God's Markings (Mythical-Grade Female Thrall Enhancement): Apply to a female thrall for upgrades.]

Female thrall enhancement. Did this mean there were specific types for male as well? He shot Luke a hesitant glance, wondering what his options would have turned into if he'd been the one to receive this kind of booster, and returned to staring at the swirling crimson symbols in the air.

"Huh. Well, that's neat."

His fangs sank into Genua's neck while Len was distracted by Jarla and the others, and the elf woman's red eyes brightened even beyond her already abnormal light as a shudder ran down her body. Her muscles spasmed, her bloodstream flowed with vampiric venom that Riven continued to pump into her, and her fingers clenched around his forearm while her mind began to temporarily fade away.

> **[Final stage of Thrall Manifestation is now underway. Estimated time until completion: fifty-six minutes. Would you like to claim this thrall as your own?]**
> **[Genua has been claimed as your vampiric thrall and now requires a certain amount of Willpower to sustain. Thralls will begin to mentally shut down if they lack the appropriate amount of Willpower.]**
> **[Due to unique internal circumstances and the presence of a vampiric child inside Genua's womb, the trait of Vampiric Thrall has been upgraded into Ascended Vampiric Thrall.]**
> **[Genua has acquired the following traits: Ascended Vampiric Thrall, Positive Vampiric Inclinations, Vampiric Subservience. Due to unique internal circumstances and the presence of a vampiric child inside Genua's womb, the Unholy Foundational Pillar and Blood subpillar have now replaced her previous pillars.]**

His eye only twitched slightly when the system itself confirmed Genua's pregnancy, and he felt a very odd influx of emotions when considering the woman fainting in his arms carried his child. Especially given their history, it certainly wasn't a match made in heaven.

"Will she be okay?" Tanya asked worriedly, blocking out Len's line of sight while her mother was gently placed with her head on a blanket.

Riven nodded and stood up, turning around to look at all the other people assembled there. "Yes, she'll be fine—better than fine, probably."

Athela and Tanya looked skeptical, Fay took it all in stride without a hint of doubt, Luke looked worried, and Azmoth seemed not to care.

"Uh . . . While we wait . . ." Athela slid up next to him and prodded him in the ribs with a finger. "Want to see what we've got going on in terms of loot?!"

She yanked out a rather gaudy headdress from behind her back made of jewels and gold, with massive dangling earring-like pieces coming off the sides. Smiling widely and placing it on her head over the black tiara she already wore, she began to wriggle her fingers Riven's way. "NOW I'M A REAL PRINCESS!"

CHAPTER 19

The room beyond the trapdoor was something to be seen. Dim light reflected off thousands upon thousands of coins and jewels from a glowstone embedded in the ceiling. A pile of weapons and armor with lesser enchantments were also stuffed into a corner on the right-hand side of the square room, while trinkets, baubles, and low-grade artifacts were piled in the very front. It was the smaller pile to his left that caught his attention most, as it was the pile that was supposed to be things he'd be interested in having for himself or for his minions.

"How much is this?" Riven waved around at the piles of bronze, silver, gold, and platinum Elysium coins higher than he was.

"Uh . . ." Athela held out both hands to either side. "No idea. Put them in a storage bag and find out?"

Riven rubbed his temple with two fingers. "Rat boy, come hither."

The dungeon avatar popped into existence next to him with a scowl, folding its arms. "What is it now, vampire?! Is it not enough that you're already robbing me?! Do you seriously expect me to—"

"Yes." Riven glared down at the avatar with a flare of his aura, holding out his bag of holding that Negrada had given him. "And do it now. Those two piles over there as well."

Grumbling to himself and raising a hand, the dungeon avatar quickly made a series of gestures that saw the flood of coins rocket toward Riven's outstretched bag. The bag guzzled down the river of money and jewels over the course of five minutes until it swallowed the last of the coins.

"Now get lost—you've already ruined my day and I have lots to do." The dungeon avatar humphed and vanished in another flash of light, leaving the demons and Riven to stand in front of only a single, very small pile of stuff that he was quite keen on inspecting.

Looking at his bag, he nodded in approval as the monetary value added up. "I had less than sixty-three million after spending some millions on keeping the population fed, but now I'm back up to eighty-two million in Elysium coin value. A couple dozen low-grade artifacts, weapons, and armor—along with a few spell scrolls and tomes in both the Fae Foundational Pillar and . . . the Zodiac subpillar of the Harmony foundation? I haven't seen that one yet. Interesting, but not applicable to any of us. Maybe some of the people in the other room will want these."

A splashing sound from Riven's left sounded, and when he turned to look, Athela was gone. Instead, only a bloodstain remained.

He furrowed his brows at Azmoth, who just shrugged, and then at Fay, who also shrugged.

"What?" Fay asked innocently, blinking twice underneath her flat-brimmed, purple witch's hat.

"Where did Athela go?"

"I don't know."

"She was right there."

Fay giggled. "She was, but now she's not."

. . .

. . .

. . .

"I see." His eyelids half lowered, and his head swiveled back to the bloodstain on the floor. He saw it move slightly in his direction, and he reached out feelers to get a grasp on the inborn mana. That mana was not accessible to him, and he lifted an eyebrow.

Intentionally ignoring the slowly moving blood puddle and guessing that this was very likely one of the two new martial arts she'd been wanting to show him, he tried to hide his smile and pretended not to make the connection. "Very well, I'm sure she'll come back to us in time. I'd probably smell her foul stench before she actually got close anyways. Now, let's take a look at these gadgets."

He walked over to the small pile of stuff set out for him, internally chuckling when he noticed the puddle abruptly freeze at his words as if grievously offended, and got into a cross-legged sitting position on the floor.

One item was a pair of flaming antlers stuck onto a ring of light, giving off an orange-yellow glow. The next item of interest was a large black grimoire, its pages yellowed, with a green viper set onto the thick leather cover. After that was a huge belt of thick metal rings with a metal boar's head protruding slightly from the buckle. There was a set of bone-made boots as well, plate armor with death mana that oozed out of them at a slow but steady rate. Then, lastly, there was a set of two red katanas that were rather long and slender for their make.

"Care to join me?"

His minions did as he asked, both of them sitting down next to each other and across from him on the other side of the pile. Meanwhile, the puddle of blood remained sitting there without doing much otherwise.

"So first things first," Riven began, picking up the two red katanas and handing them to Azmoth. "These were going to go to Athela, but I figure they can go to you since she's not here to claim them."

"UNHAND THOSE SWORDS, VAGABOND!" Athela launched herself from the puddle of blood on the floor—or, more accurately, warped her figure into her humanoid version and swiped the katanas out of Riven's hands while humphing loudly. "And I do not smell! You snore when you sleep, ingrate."

"I love you, too, Athela." Riven gave her a wink, and she immediately blushed before clearing her throat to sit down next to him.

Glancing his way just once and then averting her eyes again, she scooted in closer, twice, and gave him an embarrassed peck on the cheek. "Love you, too."

Fay looked a bit jealous, but otherwise didn't comment.

"These are what dungeon say best for us," Azmoth commented, ignoring the interaction completely and pointing a clawed finger at the allotment of items in front of them. "I not use your armor to identify yet, I wanted to wait. Like . . . like Christmas presents. We open!"

"Your wish is my command!" Riven bowed from his seated position. "And just who told you about Christmas? Was it Allie? Anyways, I have a vague idea of what they are so far, but let's get the nitty-gritty details, shall we?"

He picked up the burning antlers first, along with the ring of light they were attached to, and displayed the status page.

[Ragar's Burning Antlers (Infernal Headgear): 82 average damage on strike. +143 additional defense to the outermost layer of your entire body once equipped, including but not limited to armor. +7% mana regeneration. +2% stamina regeneration. +3% to the Infernal subpillar's affinity. Equipping this item fuses it to the wielder's head, and it will not come off unless intentionally taken off by the wielder. Requires the Infernal subpillar affiliation to use.

- **Flame Skin: Applies a passive flame shield to skin that activates on violent contact, with defense equal to one-third of your total Sturdiness. Resets every five minutes.**
- **Set Piece: one of three. This item is part of the Ragar's Hellsteed Set. Acquire three items of the Ragar's Hellsteed Set for additional bonuses.]**

Riven smiled and passed Azmoth the flaming horns. "The mana regeneration won't help much, but everything else is rather good. ESPECIALLY that affinity boost! Never seen one of those before."

Azmoth grunted his appreciation and lifted the horns, allowing the circle of light connecting them to hover over his head before he placed them down. The horns shuddered slightly, and the circle of light they were attached to disappeared when the antlers fused to Azmoth's forehead a second later. They grew slightly, enlarging to fit Azmoth's proportions, and a shimmering barrier of cinder lit up across Azmoth's body as an additional layer of protection before fading away again across obsidian plates.

"That's badass," Athela said bluntly. "Really, really badass. Azmoth, you look like a stud. I bet you'll have all the brutalisk women chasing after you before long!"

Azmoth's clawed fingers tapped on the horns gently, then gave them a good tug to make sure they were secure. The obsidian teeth of his smile clicked together and he gave Athela a nod. "Thank you, Athela. For being nice."

"No prob, bud!" Athela swatted him on the back. "Maybe we can find some of the other set items sometime. We'll probably have to buy them from an off-world vendor, but you never know—maybe Negrada has other matching pieces or even duplicates of the one you have."

"If it does have duplicates, I'm sure it's rather expensive," Fay muttered, kicking out her long blue legs and tapping her feathered boots together. "Set items are always pricey, even in the F-grade, because you can't just make them. They're all system-spawned."

THUD

"Oof!" Fay grunted when the large black book with the green serpent on the front landed in her lap. Sticking her tongue out at a snickering Athela, she glared at Riven. "Is this one for me?"

Riven nodded. "It is indeed. It's probably the best item here. I think you'll be impressed. Take a look."

[Viper Grimoire of Curses and Schemes (Unholy Specialization Grimoire, Unique): +129% mana regeneration when held. +9% damage to all curses when held. By binding this grimoire and adding a single one of your curses to its pages, you will decrease the cooldown time on your chosen curse by 10% while simultaneously allowing for spontaneous evolution options of that curse with insights drawn from the Unholy Foundational Pillar and its related subpillars. Spontaneous evolutions will occur as the grimoire actively writes out different variations of the curse across its pages with random trial and error experiments in an internal, limited plane. Evolution options will occur in the form of insights once a breakthrough is made.]

Blankly, Fay stared at the description of the Viper Grimoire in her lap. Then her jaw began to slowly drop to the floor, and she let out an audible gasp as her eyes went wide. "Riven! Riven, this is—this is incredible! And it's a UNIQUE item! Riven, do you know what this means?!"

She continued staring down at the black-and-green book in her hands, still utterly shocked. "This item is going to single-handedly improve my cultivation by . . . by . . ."

She couldn't find the words.

"By a fucking lot. It's certainly not a normal grimoire in the way I learned them to be." Riven nodded in agreement. "If you look at its pages, they're all blank and don't even have spells in them like most other grimoires do—because it's waiting for you to put in a spell yourself so it can start rewriting it in an attempt to evolve your chosen curse. Very niche item, as it only works with curses, but it's perfect for you. Spontaneous evolution options? I can't think of a better prize to get from a dungeon like this. Not to mention the mana regen. Which curse are you going to bind to the grimoire first?"

Fay's eyes lifted from the book, suddenly very distant. "I honestly don't know. I'll have to talk to my mother about this. Thank you so much, Riven."

Riven beamed. "Glad you like it. Now, for the others."

The large metal belt with a carved boar's head as the belt buckle was handed to Azmoth next. It wasn't anything special, but it did give some specs to Azmoth's strength—which was a small boon and certainly not unwanted.

[The Tusken Rager (Heavy Armor, Belt): +266 defense. +58 Sturdiness, +13% Strength.]

After that were the bone-made boots, layers of thick ivory overlapping one another, which Riven took for himself. They were better than the ones he already had, and to boot they also changed the plate leggings he had on—absorbing the ivory-painted steel without much issue until coming into contact with Messenger. When the boots met Messenger, they visibly retracted upon trying to absorb the Gluttonous armor as Messenger hissed a threat.

Still, the boots rather easily upgraded his current lower-body armor and settled down into a new form when his plate-armor leggings simply became a part of the whole. The steel turned into true bone plate mail, too, not just painted, and it felt both heavier and sturdier after the change had taken hold. It wasn't anything near as good as Messenger's 1,858 defense to plated areas, or even the 965 defense of bloodsilk in between the plates, but this was still far better armor than most things on Panu right now, or the 257 defense his plate leggings had had prior to the merge.

[Lich-Kin Boots and Leggings of the Cannibal (Death-Attuned Heavy Bone Armor): +788 defense. Absorbs and nullifies up to 60% of any death attuned attacks. Requires the Death subpillar affinity and 198 Strength to wield.
• Cannibalize Armor: Absorbs adjacent armor pieces of the wearer and enhances them up to the quality of the original Lich-Kin Boots.]

Yup, it was a significant upgrade.

Lastly were Athela's two red katanas, each of the blades magnificent in its own right and likely taking a solid second place behind Fay's grimoire in terms of prize value, and that was only because the concept of inherent Dao visions built into an item was outright absurd. Carvings of birds in flight decorated each blade all the way down to the hilt. Riven could already see Athela admiring the weapons while she held them, the quality of them evident, and heard the whispers coming from each of the blades even now as she held them in her grip. He hadn't even been sure she'd switch from using her clawed hands, but if anything was going to change her mind, these weapons would be the key. And frankly, he didn't blame her—they weren't far behind Jackal in terms of quality. Jackal had actually started out at 894 damage before increasing to 1,390 over time due to its Sacrificial Kill trait, which absorbed damage based on strong enemies killed, so in fact these weapons were stronger than Jackal's original form when only comparing base attack damage averages.

[**The Twin Red Doves (Awakened Weapons, Dual-Wielding Set. Blood Artifacts. Twin Katanas): 899 average damage on strike with each physical strike on flesh adding a guaranteed stack of the Bleed debuff for damage over time. Hidden strikes that land before an opponent is aware cause additional guaranteed damage of +5%. If the strike is a critical hit, deal an additional two times critical modifier. These items, when bound to a wielder, may be stored in the heart of the wielder and withdrawn at will. These items are nearly indestructible while the bound wielder is still alive. Requires a Blood affinity of over 51% to wield.**

- **Whispers of Agony: From time to time, these blades will whisper to you. The stronger your bond, the louder they whisper, and the louder they whisper, the more pain your strikes inflict regardless of damage.**
- **The Red Tide: Unleash stamina, mana, or divinity into these blades via your Blood subpillar to charge ranged sweeping attacks in the form of a red crescent. Damage and range depend on the amount of energy infused.]**

Athela gave a giddy laugh as the whispers rose in pitch, and it didn't take very long for blood to begin pooling out of the blades and onto Athela's skin while she held them—merging with her flesh only momentarily before floating in the air before her.

"They've already accepted me," Athela stated fondly, puffing out her chest and watching the two weapons shift into a stream of blood that slammed into where her heart should be—disappearing entirely in the next instant. A look of shock overcame her then, and she blinked curiously while scratching her head. "Neat! These things don't really talk, but I can tell what the twin doves are thinking when they're inside my chest!"

"And what's that?" Riven asked.

"They want to kill stuff."

"I shouldn't have even asked." He shook his head, facepalming. "What else would Blood-attuned katanas want? Are you going to use them?"

"Of course I'm going to use them!"

"Then you might want to start training at the Blood Moon Requiem's enclave. You haven't had sword training in illusory bodies back in the nether realms before, have you?"

Athela grimaced. "Eh . . . yes, but not much. When anticipating our change into humanoid forms of our arachnid bodies, future Arshakai are given lessons. I focused more on daggers and claws back then, or the blades from my back when using illusory versions of what I would likely become. Not a lot in swords, unfortunately."

"Would your mother and other kin of your demonic clan train you, then?"

"Probably. It'd also be easier to visit them than the vampiric enclave, so I'll probably just do that in my spare time whenever you're sleeping."

Riven nodded in approval and got up, happy to see that each of his demons had their own upgrades. It was a great haul, and it made him ask himself why he hadn't done more dungeon diving like this in the past.

Then again, would the prizes have been as good if those asshole invaders hadn't shown up?

He could only guess at that one.

Speaking of which, it was probably time to check on Genua. He could feel her heartbeat in the next room begin to quicken, and although her transformation into thrallhood wasn't quite done, it was approaching the terminal.

So, getting up and motioning for the others to follow him out of the treasury room, he began to head for the new thrall he'd acquired—excited to see just what class she'd choose and how it would turn out when she was finally able to bind to the Blood God's Markings.

Aksilias Bloodmare and his two sons, Rufus Bloodmare and Jakromi Bloodmare, had been rather relieved when Allie had told the native vampires of Panu that she'd come see their city as requested. When she'd agreed to speak to their coven's patriarch and matriarch to learn more about this vampiric elder god World Quest. They'd left with smiles on their faces and apologies on their lips for the poor interaction they'd had with Riven's thrall-to-be, Genua, as guests, and they'd hurried off into the underdark after supplying Allie with a map to their underground city of Bernzee—self-proclaimed home of the Hundred Covens.

What Allie had not expected to find, therefore, were the hundred covens all gone.

Or, better said, they'd all been killed.

Towering spires of blood-covered rock, shattered walls, and burning homes giving off plumes of smoke sprawled for miles in a vast underground cavern. Piles of rubble and scattered pieces of half-devoured corpses—this was what she found in their stead.

Allie's footsteps echoed through a ruined city that was devoid of any sound aside from the crackling of flames and the splash of her steps in pools of crimson fluids. Her red eyes scanned the tens of thousands of dead she passed by, building by building, street by street, in what was nothing less than an absolute genocide of the populace here. What was even weirder was that her vampiric senses couldn't pick up any heartbeats at all, meaning that not only could she not SEE anyone living—but it was very likely there wasn't anyone hiding here, either.

Weirder yet was that the blood mana that should be here, given the absolute carnage, was absolutely gone. There wasn't a hint of blood mana to be found, and she certainly wasn't the savant of the Blood subpillar like her brother was—nor did she even have the subpillar—but she was still a pureblooded vampire and she should have been able to identify it in any normal circumstances.

Add another layer of oddity to it, and the ghosts, souls, and wraiths that usually kept her company in the beyond had scattered—sensing the presence of something that she could not. Even when she reached out to them for answers, they did not agree on what it was or how they knew it was dangerous, only sending her vague signals that she should not be here.

That none of them should be here.

"This was not a place for the living or the dead," they whispered to her. This was not a place where she should remain.

"Finding anything?" Allie asked in a low tone, scanning their surroundings when they came to a crossroads filled with more of the same.

Mara shook her head from underneath her black cowl, and the necromancers behind them all stood out at intervals with eyes seeking just as much as their scattered minions were. "My shadow ravens aren't seeing any movement from above. It appears that the covens here have been completely wiped out, along with all their slaves and their thralls. Be it vampire or mortal—it did not matter to whatever or whoever did this. Not a single ounce of life, even to my soul sense, is detectable. My skeletal assassins also report no movement as they go house to house, and I am at a loss for what could have caused this amount of carnage in what appears to be a very short amount of time, given the way they all failed to escape."

"There were no bodies out in the tunnels leading here, so it must have happened fast." Nin nodded his agreement, stepping through the afterlife to appear next to Allie with the sound of a breath. "This is wrong. There is a distinct lack of blood mana here when there should be just as much as the death mana permeating this city. I cannot fathom why that is, or where it would have gone in such quantities."

Allie frowned underneath her skull mask. "You sensed it, too, then? I was thinking the same thing."

Then she realized: Why were there no bodies other than the populace? The creatures that'd done this were monsters, without a doubt, because of the claw and teeth marks left in the innumerable corpses. Where were the bodies of these beasts?

And why had the citizens all died in their homes? Had they not heard the carnage before it'd happened? Not just once, but dozens of times now she'd seen the bodies of children next to dolls and toys, or the corpses of their parents at tables attending to untouched dishes of food now gone cold.

Gritting her teeth and taking another look down at the map, she decided on the only course of action she could take that might provide answers. "We head to the Bloodmare estate. If Aksilias and his sons, or their clan, are all dead . . . then we search it for clues. I have a feeling this butchery is related to the world quest and the fallen elder god—things just line up too perfectly for it to be otherwise. Something is very, very wrong here . . . and I intend to find out what that is."

CHAPTER 20

Genua came into consciousness with an absolutely enthralling sense of power coursing through her soul. The abrupt sensation caused her to gasp, and she felt the divinity channels rushing through her body explode with crimson radiance.

Her vision went red as her eyes blazed with light, her skin flared with profane crimson sigils that buried themselves into her to remain as red tattoos across her otherwise tanned skin, and the shudder escaping her lips was one of ecstasy. Because she had already chosen which of the three classes she wanted, immediately upon becoming a thrall she had been taken from Panu to be placed in the realm of gods.

[You have successfully transitioned into an Ascended Vampiric Thrall. You have chosen Priestess of the Blood God as your next class, the lowest level of his clergy but an esteemed position none-theless. Impulses to faithfully guide and serve your vampiric master have been amplified. Vampires, children of the Blood God, will not be able to harm you outside of regular feedings without receiving a Blasphemer's Curse. Your Blood God's Markings have been absorbed as a thrall upgrade. Access to the Blood God's clergy interface has been established and is accessible through your status page. The abilities Sanguine Smite, Blood Oath, Transfusion Zone, Body Fusion, and Sanguine Possession have been granted for your faith.]

She wanted to stay in that state of power perfusing her very being forever, but the red light dulled its brightness within her eyes and allowed her to see only a minute later.

She was kneeling, naked, red eyes shining bright to match the new tapestry of brilliant crimson tattoos covering much of her body. In front of her was the entrance to a grand, ominous temple of alien design, and overhead a sky of stars surrounding a bright-red moon cast their light upon her.

Five other women with calm smiles, red eyes, and bright-white hair stood just ahead of where she knelt, in front of a set of double doors that remained shut. All of them wore the same kind of outfit, replicas of one another—but all were grand in design.

Everything made from the base silk outfit was black, while all the additional embroideries and metal ornaments were red and gold. A black hood covered each of their heads, with thin sheets of red metal headdresses, gilded in gold, flaring out, up, and above the hoods along the middle of their heads. Pieces of the metal were carved out of the headdresses to form symbols and words in an ancient language she could not understand, but she could sense the meaning behind them:

Power, dominance, and supremacy.

The dresses were very formfitting but revealed little otherwise past where the hood cut off at a V-shape along their necks, clinging to each of the women like an extra layer of skin all the way down to their legs, where the black silks spread out a bit before hitting the floor. The outfits caused the women to look almost like flowers by the way their silks spread out around their feet. Each of the five women also wore long red gloves that revealed their fingers just past the knuckles but otherwise covered everything up to their midbiceps—further distinguishing the gloves from the rest of the black silk of their formfitting gowns by way of a gold trimming at the glove's proximal base. Two red crescent moons were also embroidered on the front of each of their chests, while a full moon was stitched into the very center between them. Words of that same ancient language she didn't understand were written in gold lettering along each side of the black silk covering their rib cages, and then again along the outer side of each thigh, but these had less impact on her innate understanding than the words carved into the red metal headdress each woman wore.

Without a word, and after the five of them had stared at her for more than what was comfortable, the middle of the five women walked forward from the shadow of the looming temple. Her footsteps were silent, and in her hands she carried a folded bundle of what was yet another uniform just like the one she was wearing—with the red metal headdress laid on top. And as she got closer to stand over Genua's kneeling figure, Genua could see that this woman with white hair had the same tattoos as she now did.

"Sister." The woman's voice came out as a fresh breeze on the cold night air. "Stand."

Genua did as asked, shakily getting to her feet and meeting the woman's gaze. Something about this person commanded her attention, and she dared not look away even in the presence of such a magnificent structure beyond them.

The unknown woman nodded in approval and held out the folded garments. "These are for you."

Blinking, Genua hesitantly reached out and took the items without argument. "Thank you . . . Is this the realm of—"

"You already know it is," the woman replied, smile widening in amusement. "This is his realm, yes. I, along with the four others standing before you, are also clergy. We are greeters, welcoming our sisters into the fold. These are your clergy robes; keep them in good condition—for they are sacred treasures not to be lost. Should you do well in your duties, you will be given far more."

Windows displayed themselves unbidden, each of them telling Genua what it was she now grasped—items that were likely worth far more than her life by most people's standards.

[**Blood God Clergy Hood (Legendary Blood Artifact, Light armor): +330 Defense. +19% additional potency to any Blood miracle. Must be one of the Blood God's clergy or have a Blood subpillar affinity of over 80% to use.**

- **Soothsayer: Passively speeds up your miracle chants by 25%. +10% Divinity regeneration.**
- **Set Piece: Four of four. This item is part of the Clergy Robes of the Blood God set. You have acquired all four items of the Clergy Robes of the Blood God set for additional bonuses (this is a set bonus and not individualized for each piece): +450 Faith, +160% Divinity regeneration, +2,000 additional defense against any Blood-oriented skills. Any sacrifices to the Blood God while donning this clergy set add a multiple of two to gained clergy points, while doing so publicly in front of large crowds under the Blood God's name add a ten times modifier to gained clergy points.**]

[**Blood God Clergy Gloves (Legendary Blood Artifact, Light armor): +380 Defense. +19% additional potency to any Blood miracle. Must be one of the Blood God's clergy or have a Blood subpillar affinity of over 80% to use.**

- **Hands of the Profane: Allows you to draw miracle diagrams with nearby blood using thought and hand motions.**
- **Set Piece: Four of four. This item is part of the Clergy Robes of the Blood God set. You have acquired all four items of the Clergy Robes of the Blood God set for additional bonuses (this is a set bonus and not individualized for each piece): +450 Faith, +160% Divinity regeneration, +2,000 additional defense against any Blood-oriented skills. Any sacrifices to the Blood God while donning this clergy set add a multiple of two to gained clergy points, while doing so publicly in front of large crowds under the Blood God's name add a ten times modifier to gained clergy points.**]

[**Blood God Clergy Robe (Legendary Blood Artifact, Light armor): +490 Defense. +19% additional potency to any Blood miracle. Must be one of the Blood God's clergy or have a Blood subpillar affinity of over 80% to use.**

- **Vampiric Regeneration:** This item imparts passive vampiric health regeneration EQUIVALENT to your vampiric master's own regeneration for as long as the thrall-master bond remains intact.
- **Set Piece:** Four of four. This item is part of the Clergy Robes of the Blood God set. You have acquired all four items of the Clergy Robes of the Blood God set for additional bonuses (this is a set bonus and not individualized for each piece): +450 Faith, +160% Divinity regeneration, +2,000 additional defense against any Blood-oriented skills. Any sacrifices to the Blood God while donning this clergy set add a multiple of two to gained clergy points, while doing so publicly in front of large crowds under the Blood God's name add a ten times modifier to gained clergy points.]

[Blood God Clergy Metal Headdress (Legendary Blood Artifact, Light armor): +600 Defense. +19% additional potency to any Blood miracle. Must be one of the Blood God's clergy or have a Blood sub-pillar affinity of over 80% to use.

- **Profane Intervention:** This item allows you to call down a single second of absolute immortality around you and your vampiric master, negating all damage directed at the two of you for that one second. This item ability can only be used once per day, and only if you recharge this ability with a sacrifice in the Blood God's name after use.
- **Set Piece:** Four of four. This item is part of the Clergy Robes of the Blood God set. You have acquired all four items of the Clergy Robes of the Blood God set for additional bonuses (this is a set bonus and not individualized for each piece): +450 Faith, +160% Divinity regeneration, +2,000 additional defense against any Blood-oriented skills. Any sacrifices to the Blood God while donning this clergy set add a multiple of two to gained clergy points, while doing so publicly in front of large crowds under the Blood God's name add a ten times modifier to gained clergy points.]

Genua took in a sharp breath as a pulse of power echoed out from the clothes she now held in her hands, and blinked rapidly. "Will I get to meet him?"

"The blood god?" The woman laughed softly, shaking her head. "Oh no, he is too far above one such as us. Lowly priestesses in our position can one day get there if we find the right master to serve, or if you, like I have, join the church and rise in the inner ranks after your master's death . . . should such an unfortunate fate befall them. But those are the only two ways to go about it. Which brings me to the next topic . . ."

The other priestess pulled out a sealed black letter and handed it to Genua. "Take this and open it as soon as you return to Panu. It will destroy the letter, but its intended recipient will be granted the intended message in the form of inspiration. One of his children is in great peril, and doing this will likely save them from an otherwise violent end."

Genua's brows furrowed. "Riven is fine, though, isn't he? We just beat back the invaders . . ."

Her voice trailed off.

And the other priestess shook her head. "I said nothing about your master, Riven. Regardless, you cannot stay here long without significant soul decay due to your F-grade body. Remember that you are required to pray and worship the blood god every night, and you will begin your study of his scripture during this time after prayers."

She pulled a small black book with the sigils of two red crescent moons surrounding a full moon from her pocket next and set it on top of the clothes. "This will detail what is expected of you; it is the base scripture of the first writ. Once a week I will come to visit you to make sure you have been studying. This is important, for reasons we will discuss later, but for now just focus on keeping your lord safe. He is an important part of the supreme one's plans, if he lives—but Riven is still only an infant gnat in the great scheme of things. He has potential, but potential is not a promise, and he is still inconsequential as he is now. Should he die, your potential will likely die out with his. As will the life of your daughter. Do you understand?"

Genua's frown deepened, worry clouding her mind as her spine went rigid under the threat of her daughter's safety. Yet without a doubt, she knew this woman wasn't bluffing—and it only deepened Genua's abnormally firm resolve to help Riven thrive. "How am I supposed to keep Riven safe? He's far more powerful than I am. Shouldn't it be the other way around?"

The unknown priestess raised one eyebrow, then tsked. "We're going to have to change that attitude of yours as well. One of many things to work on, I see. Even if you are pathetically weak, that does not mean your duties venture outside the norm of what it means to be a priestess. Now go, leave us, and we will speak more on your duties in a week's time when your soul has had the opportunity to recover from your travels here."

With a flick of her wrist, the priestess dismissed Genua's presence from the blood god's realm—casting her back into the world of Panu as the heavens closed around her in a blur of stars and space.

Allie stared up at the mutilated corpse of Aksilias Bloodmare where it'd been impaled on a spike jutting from his compound's walls. One of many spikes where many other vampires had also been impaled and left to rot, their corpses withered and shredded. They didn't even have any clothes on, so there was nothing to check, and the deep wounds left in their bodies spoke of torture that was far more exaggerated than many of the other bodies they'd passed in the city.

Which raised the question . . . Why?

"We're on the right track."

Not sparing the corpses another look, she continued through the gate that'd been ripped off its hinges and flung aside into a courtyard of flowers. Oddly enough, much of the garden was still intact, though there were bodies of thralls, slaves, and servants in abundance here—treated with far less hatred and malice than the vampires had been.

The large manor behind the bloodied garden was in rough shape but overall intact, with an ugly dark-green paint covering the pillars leading into the house where the doors had also been flung off their hinges. There'd been obvious fighting here, which was far different from the rest of the city that Allie had visited—but it also made her question just what other parts of Bernzee had put up a fight if this particular coven had been able to do so.

Broken sculptures, paintings with blade and claw marks torn through them, felled tapestries and body parts were in abundance. A maid had been impaled with some kind of odd-looking spear, the back of her head nailed to a stone wall while her body dangled two feet off the floor—and a vampiric child lay halfway out of a closet where he'd obviously tried to hide.

Dark hallways to the left, right, and center exited the receiving room, and Allie turned to the other necromancers behind her with a quick set of hand motions.

Immediately, the skeletons and zombies following them panned out to the right and left without a word, dispersing to search the large building without a single complaint. If one of them died, the necromancer controlling it would immediately know and they'd notify her. In the meantime, she and the best of their minions filed through the central hallway that had the most obvious signs of conflict ramping up. She came upon more bodies and blasts of magic and began combing through bedrooms and office spaces.

More carnage—ripped bedsheets, a slave who'd been killed while still shackled to a wall. Books torn apart, spilled ink on otherwise blank parchment, an opened safe with the money and jewels still left inside. So far nothing on the bodies of the men and women found contained anything significant that pointed them to what'd happened here, or had any real connection to the world quest concerning the fallen vampiric elder god.

Coming to the fifth room in her search halfway down the hall from where an overturned marble statue lay broken, she noticed the door was locked. Using her vampiric strength to try and break the door with physical force, she found it unyielding and infused a significant amount of death mana to fry a hidden enchantment that fizzled out under her grip.

With a spark the handle flew off, and she easily pushed her way inside with Mara following closely behind her.

Inside was just another office, though it was quite clean and devoid of any of the signs of fighting outside. A dim lantern flickered in one corner, almost out of oil by the looks of it, and bookshelves lined the walls in pristine condition with a large rectangular desk in the center of the room with a few hastily scribbled notes off to one side.

Allie gestured left. "Search the bookshelves."

Mara nodded and obeyed, looking for anything that might provide clues.

Allie came around the desk, sitting in the fine leather chair and checking the drawers one by one. Certainly there was a reason this room had been locked, right?

The scribbled notes on the desktop she went through first. There were records of positions the house was hiring for, various types of trade done with other covens in the city of Bernzee, notes on various slave-trading deals, and then finally, at the very bottom of the stack, a poorly hidden note addressed to . . .

To her?

Had she been expected to find this?

Had it been placed underneath the other papers so that whatever had come rampaging through this manor wouldn't find it, should they have entered this room?

Allie Thane, queen of the Thane Necropolis, it is in our darkest hour that I find myself putting pen to paper in a hasty attempt to relay to you what is happening in our city as I sit in this closed room amid the dying screams of my people. I can only hope that you followed the map my servant supplied to you and that you have come looking for answers here in our home.

The labyrinth has been opened. It has been opened for some time now, but only recently did we press into the second layer after uncovering a sealed lock on what appears to be an ancient coven of vampires from another age. We didn't know what it meant, but the council of Bernzee insisted that we uncover the secrets in an attempt to save our world from devastation should Elysium's words be true.

Destroying that sealed lock was a mistake, and the things we found there before tragedy struck were . . . concerning. It appears that the blood god we know and worship today as our forefather may not be as all-encompassing for our kind as we once thought, if the records written on the walls of the labyrinth tell truths and not lies. Could there really have been an opposing pantheon, and more than one blood god in the ancient past? I also fear that we have doomed our city for reading these taboo texts, or at the very least for unleashing the things that guarded them. The bodies of what we once thought to be an ancient coven, frozen in a time stasis, weren't vampires at all—but something else entirely. They are false, faked mockeries of our elder kin, a taboo of what we were meant to be and a blight upon the land.

They are intelligent, monstrous things that hide in the skin of the slain. However they only seem to inhabit the bodies of the blood god's children; we don't know how or why—but when you find our corpses . . . burn them. Be wary of their trickery, for we don't know how many there are—but should they remain here inside Bernzee and you find yourself reading this letter, you are in mortal peril. You have likely already passed by many who you thought perished, when in reality they were merely watching and waiting for an opportunity to corner you like a rat.

If you do not have an army at your back to escort you into the depths, you need to run. And you should start running now. I have provided another map leading to the labyrinth in the second drawer on the right; there you will find the answers to the world quest you seek, and I hope you can use it to better effect than we did. I hear their drums beating in the depths even as I write, echoing through the streets paved with the dead of our kin, and my heart trembles for what is to come of myself when they find me.

Leave this place.

A thudding boom of drums echoed through the streets and into the halls of the manor, causing Allie's head to slowly lift to stare out the door as she gripped the paper in her hands.

Mara turned as well, unsure of what the noise was until it came again, and again, and again.

Boom . . .

Boom . . .

Boom . . .

Allie shifted to her right and pulled the second drawer out, revealing a thoroughly detailed map of the underdark passages leading out from the city of Bernzee and through a series of tunnels to what was labeled Labyrinth of the Elder God on the map—symbolized by a fanged skull.

Boom . . .

Boom . . .

Boom . . .

She let out a sharp breath, picked the map up, and put it in her spatial bag before standing up. Already the other necromancers, skeletons, and zombies were rushing through the hallways toward the front entrance as the sound of faint chanting was heard in the depths. "This was a trap. Whatever killed all these people has been in the city this entire time, and they've just made their move."

"What's the plan?" Mara asked, following Allie out into the main room when an unearthly wail sang through the air as the corpse of the vampiric child lurched and blasted from its position in the closet.

The small body tore through one of the ghoul necromancers to Allie's right, three sets of vampiric fangs sprouting from the small monster's mouth as its skin turned into a very pale blue. Claws erupted from its hands, its eyes grew wide and pitch-black, and within half a second the screaming necromancer was torn in half—causing the minions he was controlling to stagger and fall.

Allie's wand whipped forward and blasted the devouring monster with strings of death mana that shredded it just as easily as it'd torn apart the ghoul necromancer, and Allie quickly stabilized the groaning undead man with more strings of death mana. The eruption of battle sounded ahead and the drums began to pick up speed, with a resonating wave of roars from somewhere outside. Bodies of vampires that'd been torn and dead, impaled or left half-eaten in their rooms, now gained new life as their bodies warped. Once-red eyes turned dark black and became large, numerous sets of fangs shot out from their mouths, and their white skin turned a very pale shade of blue.

[Ancient Vampiric Precursor, Blue Blood Heretic, Level 95]
[Ancient Vampiric Precursor, Blue Blood Heretic, Level ???]
[Ancient Vampiric Precursor, Blue Blood Heretic, Level 71]
[World Quest 4, Blood of the Fallen God: An unnamed vampiric elder god has fallen from grace after having sinned against the Elysium administrator. The elder god has been trapped within a hidden, guarded labyrinth in the deepest levels of the underdark, and you must stop him from awakening. Advanced details HAVE BEEN PARTIALLY UNLOCKED:
- UPDATE 1: You have found clues to the labyrinth's location in the depths of the underdark, the resting place of the fallen vampiric elder god, but found yourself cornered by heretics in defiance of the one true mantle of the Blood God. Why did the native vampires here in Bernzee contact you for help? What was the reason that they journeyed out from the deep parts of the world to do so? Your answers will be found at the labyrinth's location, should you manage to survive.]

"There is no plan," Allie said bluntly, stitching the ghoul necromancer back into fighting condition with a wave of her hand. "We have no choice but to fight."

Fimrindle flickered into her peripheral vision with a bow, scythe held low. "Master . . . I believe we may have a problem. All routes of escape have been cut off, and tens of thousands of enemies have begun encroaching on our position along all four walls. We are completely surrounded, and I do not believe it is a fight we can win. We must find an alternative path."

As if on cue, a vision panned out in Allie's mind when an otherworldly entity reached out to touch her soul from some distant plane. A red moon in the background of a dark silhouette, a toppling pillar created from pale-blue stone, and then finally a series of images of a time once past here in this very manor she now stood in. Children playing hide-and-go-seek, opening a hidden compartment leading into a passage leading beneath the building, and then it was all gone in a flash.

She stumbled, blinking rapidly and holding the side of her head as the visions faded away. "What the fuck was that?"

Boom . . .

Boom . . .

Boom . . .

BOOM

The wall cracked and tore as a muscular abomination of a pale, blue-shaded bald man barreled through—launching one of the skeletal knights in full armor crashing through two adjacent rooms into a piled heap at the far end.

Immediately Fimrindle was upon it along with numerous skeletal assassins who'd been lying in wait, and the enormous humanoid found itself quickly losing limb after limb that tried to regrow back at extreme rates similar if not equivalent to Allie's own. But when Fimrindle's scythe sank deep into its brain and flared with deathly light, the monster crashed to the ground in a heap. Meanwhile the sound of claw on blade and crazed screams of undead and vampiric precursors grew louder at the front gates outside where a battle could be seen through the ruined walls and dust cloud. Beyond the gates and down the hill into the greater city beyond, thousands of bodies were roaring and sprinting toward her position with huge, mutated creatures in the back beating drums to the sound of her impending doom.

Allie abruptly launched a series of flaming skulls that screamed forward—exploding along the nearby wall and destroying some of the precursor heretics swarming over the barriers. Then she turned to leave the minions behind. "Necromancers, follow me. I don't know how, perhaps it was my Malignant Prophecy or something else entirely, but I just had a vision. And if I'm right, there may be a way out of here yet."

With complete trust in their queen, the twelve necromancers of the Thane Necropolis filed into line behind her with only their very best undead servants coming with them—all the others being sent toward the waves of enemies trying to rush the gated compound in a swarm of fangs, claws, bald heads, black eyes, and pale-blue bodies with a vicious need to feed.

CHAPTER 21

The bloodsilk nest Athela had created had been converted into a multitude of hammocks in anticipation of Jarla's group meeting them before nightfall, with the earlier idea of throwing a victory party having soured when they'd found numerous local groups slaughtered on the way out of the dungeon. Ones that'd been caught by the invaders on their trek in.

Still, everyone else insisted that they should drink it off later that night—and who was Riven to tell them otherwise?

"You're still not going to tell me what that letter was about, huh?" Riven asked again, eyebrow raised while he used a mallet and chisel to chip away at a stone while going over schematics for another attempt at runecrafting, since his last three totems had utterly failed. He leaned over the bench outside the cabin Tanya's family used, intent on getting this one right.

Genua shook her head, the new priestess attire already on and fitting her nicely. It was certainly stylish, if Riven had anything to say about, it and matched the style of her newly acquired tattoos and bright-red eyes.

"I'm afraid that letter was not even meant for me," Genua said with a frown. "All I know is that when I opened the letter and it vaporized, I got the sensation that I should not talk about it again and that it was meant for someone else. I'm sorry."

Riven tsked, then smiled pleasantly at Len, who was watching him intently—kicking her small legs back and forth while he worked. "That's all right. Hey, Len, did you ever end up beating Azmoth in that arm-wrestling contest?"

He began chipping away at the stone again, making sure to carve the rune just right with microscopic adjustments.

Len beamed and then began to giggle, holding up a small hand to her face while her mother started fixing her hair. "Yes! He had to use all four arms and even then he couldn't beat me! I'm super strong for a girl, you know!"

She flexed, and Riven chuckled with a shake of his head. "Yes, you're quite intimidating, Len. You'd probably beat me up, too."

Len looked like she was going to retort with something feisty, but she got a curious look about her and quieted down with her eyes downcast.

"How's the discussion going?" Riven asked, wincing when sunlight through the pine trees overhead hit him directly in the left eyeball with a backlash of discomfort. "Ugh, sometimes I wonder why I'm up and about during the day."

Genua's lips tugged upward at the comment before she replied. "Yes, well you are a vampire, after all. As for the discussion, I assume you're talking about the others and your proposition to turn them as well?"

"Yes, Hakim's group."

"They're not sure yet. It's a big decision to make, but I'm certain they're more than willing to join your guild."

Riven nodded, wiped sweat off his forehead, and moved some papers around to better look at what he needed to do next. Taking some odd-looking yellow herbs and adding them to a mortar and pestle, he began grinding them into a fine powder that he then stuffed into the runes he'd just carved—using a glue-like paste to seal it in. Then, placing the rock inside a recently acquired human skull, he used Crimson Ice to seal it all together and finally dipped the skull into a pool of black gunk on his left.

The tiny voice of Len caught him off guard only a second later. "Are you and Mommy having a baby?"

He choked and nearly fell over at the words. Quickly reorienting himself and blinking rapidly, he took a deep breath and put on a crooked smile while looking back at the little girl across the table from him. She had her arms folded, and she looked half accusing and half worried, with her little blond pigtails up to either side now that her mother had fixed her hair just a second ago.

"Uh . . . um . . . Who told you that, exactly?" Riven asked curiously, raising an eyebrow Genua's way.

The priestess, his thrall, just sat there unblinking and unfazed.

"Mommy did," Len replied somewhat hesitantly, looking between the two adults and then huffing loudly when Riven didn't reply. "Are you? Mommy said if I wanted to know more I needed to ask you, so I'm asking you now. But she says she's pregnant and that I'm going to be a big sister! Is that true?"

Riven saw Athela and Fay turn the corner just as Len repeated the question, and both of them quickly turned right around and headed off elsewhere after seeing the pleading look for help Riven gave them. He saw Fay mouth, "good luck," and Athela just laughed.

Curse them to the depths of hell.

"Well . . ." Riven scratched the back of his head, feeling much less at ease right now than he'd been with his life on the line in battle. "I . . . Uh . . . I suppose your mom is right. Genua and I . . ."

He trailed off, looking to Genua for support.

He got none.

A mix of emotions overcame Len's features, many of which he couldn't pinpoint, but they settled on genuine curiosity when she leaned forward. "So . . . Do you and Mommy love each other now?"

Ugh.

"I'll let Genua answer that one," Riven replied sheepishly.

"Hmm." Len scratched her head in thought, staring at the table. "Are you going to be my daddy, then?"

Riven paused at this, again getting no support from Genua, and set down his crafting materials to give his full attention to the little girl in front of him. "Why do you ask?"

Len hesitated, then avoided his gaze—shrugging as she did. "I don't know."

"Aren't you afraid of me?" Riven asked curiously. "You seemed afraid of me in the dungeon not long ago."

Len thought about it, then shook her head. "I wasn't afraid of you. I was just afraid. But I . . . I think Ethel would like it if you were my new daddy. Farrod wasn't very nice to us back then, and I've always wondered what a nice daddy would be like."

Len shuffled awkwardly, briefly casting him a glance and then twiddling her thumbs while Genua pursed her lips.

Meanwhile, Riven's heart sank. "I . . . I don't think Ethel liked me that much, Len."

"Yes, she did," Len replied with a smile. "I know she was supposed to hurt you, but that wasn't her choice. She just did what she was told, and before she died she wasn't sure if vampires were even bad anymore. At least, that's what she told me."

Riven's heart sank farther, and he felt a lump forming in his throat. "Um . . . You know she was supposed to hurt me, then?"

Len nodded sadly. "Yeah."

"And if I may ask, who told her to hurt me?"

Len glanced up at Genua, who nodded encouragingly.

"Daddy. Farrod," Len replied solemnly. "Mommy didn't tell me what happened exactly, and I know I'm a kid. But I'm a smart kid, and I know something happened between all of you when they tried to hurt you. That's when Ethel and Daddy died."

The little girl shot him a wary glance before avoiding eye contact yet again. "So if you and Mommy are having another kid, could I ask you a question?"

Riven nodded rigidly. "Of course you can, Len. Anything."

Len took in a deep breath, steeled herself, and looked at him straight in the eye while her lips began to tremble. "Was it on purpose when Ethel died? Or was it an accident?"

Silence.

Silence reigned.

Riven didn't know how to respond to that without shattering this little girl's world. It was his turn to avoid eye contact, and he stared down at the bench in front of him while reliving those memories—experiencing that guilt one more time in a far worse way than he had ever before.

But goddamn it, if this little girl had the courage to ask him that kind of question—he wasn't going to pussy out now and not answer it. Slowly, he nodded his head and closed his eyes. "What else has your mom told you about what happened?"

Tears were beginning to trickle down Len's face, dripping off her quivering lips and chin onto the ground while she glared at him. "She won't tell me."

Another pause, and Riven inhaled deeply. "I did it on purpose. It is my fault they died."

Silence.

Silence once again reigned.

Len's eyes narrowed and the tears started flowing more freely now, with snot beginning to run down her flushed face with those tiny pigtails blowing in the wind behind her. She nodded, wiping away the snot with one arm but maintaining a gaze braver than he could muster. "Now that you and Mommy are having another kid, are you going to make me go away, too?"

"LEN!" Genua said, astounded and shocked that her daughter would ask such a question. She put her arms around her daughter and hugged the upset little girl close. "Len, that would never happen! Why would you even ask that?!"

The question jolted Riven to his core, and he abruptly looked up to meet her eyes. "No! Len, I would never hurt you!"

"Then why did you hurt Ethel?" Len asked, beginning to sob quietly, her small chest heaving up and down. "Why did you kill my big sister? Even if she was told to hurt you, you were stronger. You were so strong! You could have run away or something!"

And what, just what, was Riven supposed to say to that?

The truth was that Ethel had been collateral damage. He wouldn't have blown that bomb Azmoth had carried into Greenstalk village if everyone else hadn't been there, despite Ethel's own damning attempt to set him up and kill him. He remembered the way she'd come down on the person she'd thought was Riven, but even so—he might have just walked away if Prophet and the village elders hadn't been there.

Or perhaps he'd just been angry. Angry that he'd been used, and he'd wanted revenge for the absolute betrayal of Ethel and the others. A revenge that he now felt a supreme guilt for after essentially ruining Len's life.

But he'd thought Ethel was a friend.

How wrong he had been.

"Can you tell me the truth, please?" Len asked in a whisper, wiping more tears off her face by using her mother's silk outfit. "Please? I want to understand."

That made up his mind.

And so Riven told her everything. By the end of it all, Len merely got up—staring at the ground—and walked away into the forest. Genua followed her, leaving Riven alone at his table with all his supplies in what now seemed like a very inconsequential task he'd set out for himself.

Some king of the necropolis he was.

Lahn sat in his old wheelchair, on the back porch of his manor under a sunny sky sipping tea just like he used to do when his body had been crippled by that parasite. Now it was his soul that was shattered after having used the angelic possession.

It seemed ages ago now. Though in large part that was because he'd done nothing but recover, as soul damage afflicted the body in various ways, too—it just manifested differently. The frequent visits from his loving girlfriend, Allie, and the beaming presence of his mother, Shovi, were the two bright lights in his otherwise dark world.

But at least now he had two, instead of just one like in the past.

Unfortunately for him, he was also now a central piece of gossip among his mother's inner circle, and they were very aggressive with their probing questions.

Questions about the videos circulating around the Thane empire concerning him and his fight with a vampire at the Blood Moon Requiem's estate. Though those videos had all been captured by outsiders and didn't show explicit details concerning what happened in the compound, the very fact that he'd even been there had started a wildfire of rumors that were circulating rapidly as one of the hot topics of the kingdom right now.

These middle-aged women sitting around the table beside him sipping their tea with his mother didn't necessarily know he was dating Allie Thane, queen of the Thane empire—or Thane Necropolis, as some people called it—but they had suspicions about whom he was connected to concerning the actions of recent events.

And with the drastic change in very abrupt, respectful behavior from his sister, brother, and father, who almost outright avoided him now—it made things all the more obvious that something was amiss.

"So, young man . . ." one of his mother's peers began, tipping her feathered hat down and putting her teacup on a porcelain plate while steepling her fingers. "When do you think our city will be receiving another shipment of supplies from Brightsville? Mandon is very much in need of more manpower, too, and though the undead have been rather tireless in their efforts to help, we could always use more. I mean, just look at this place."

The blonde woman waved at the city down the hill from their estate, where nearly half of the topmost level of Mandon—previous capital of Dawn—was still an absolute wreck.

Lahn tried not to groan at the question, as it was yet another probe concerning things he honestly didn't know. "And what, my Lady Rutair, makes you think that I'd know such a thing?"

The snarky woman grinned as many of the other well-dressed women of the court chuckled. "Well, after that rather dashing set of heroics on the forums, it only indicates that you're rather well-connected with someone high up enough in the Thane government to warrant a visit to the vampiric compound. Even my husband, who is friends with Dawn's king—if you can call him a king anymore, despite the Thanes allowing him to keep his title—hasn't been able to get an invitation to Brightsville's important meetings or inner circles. The Blood Moon Requiem is supposed to be some kind of off-planet empire the Thanes are royalty of, and their trading commune is already selective enough as it is concerning who they let in. But you were inside, and it asks the question of why. So, I just assumed since you were so well-connected that you'd be able to tell us!"

"Oh, stop it!" Shovi scolded her friend, getting another round of laughs from the cougars surrounding him as yet another woman laid a hand on Lahn's arm.

"You know, my daughter has always found you quite dashing." The redheaded woman in a satin dress winked Lahn's way with an almost predatory smile. "Perhaps at the upcoming ball at the academy, I could introduce you to her. Would you like that?"

Shovi huffed, cutting off whatever Lahn was about to say with a loud clink of her glass on a porcelain plate of her own. "Marcela! I told you, Lahn already has someone that he's courting and she's very pretty!"

"But does she have good standing in the court?" the woman named Marcela refuted with a raised eyebrow. "I'd heard that Wraithtide girl, whoever she is, was a country bumpkin. A talented one from the rumors, but still a bumpkin. Surely you wouldn't let your son marry a nobody like that, especially now that he has standing."

The women continued to bicker and gossip, and Lahn could only grimace and bear it. None of these people, nor their daughters, would have had any inkling of an interest in him before that video happened to appear on the feeds. No, the only one who had been interested was Allie . . .

God, he loved that girl. He hadn't told her yet, and he'd probably hold off so he wouldn't scare her away, but that's definitely how he felt. He was absolutely smitten, and a small smile crept across his lips while he looked over the city and off into the blue horizon.

She'd sent word that she might be back late after dealing with some ratkin uprisings, and it bothered him a bit to think that she might be in danger, but she was the butcher of Carnis, after all. She struck fear into the hearts of many, far more often than even Riven did, despite Riven being the stronger of the two. So perhaps it was silly of him to worry.

He just hoped that she really would be back in time for the ball, because his mother had already picked out a couple of dresses for her to try, and the relationship between the two women he loved most was drastically improving each and every day they spent together. It was quite funny to him how excited his mom got on girls' nights out with Allie, and made him feel warm inside when they did so.

He just hoped his soul would eventually recover. Given the amount of rare Dao treasures that Allie had piled up in his room to help him heal, there was a chance—even if it was a slim one—and it was actually about time to use yet another in an attempt to regain some of what he'd lost.

After all, he didn't want to be deadweight to her like he had been in the past.

Not after having come so far, and having just been handed another chance at the life that'd been stolen from him.

He would persevere.

CHAPTER 22

Had the tunnel led out of Bernzee, likely saving Allie's life?

Sure.

But it certainly hadn't led to safety. They were traveling deeper into the underdark, and into a tunnel complex of twists and turns that were nowhere on the original map she'd been provided to get to the vampiric city—or the map she'd found in the partially destroyed Bloodmare estate.

What was even worse was that Fimrindle suspected this tunnel actually led directly to the labyrinth these vampires had spoken of. Why might he think that? He'd already assassinated twelve of the vampire precursors, and the tunnels were changing by the second.

Caverns were visibly being augmented, adapting to some unknown power's will, as the rock smoothed out into square and rectangular floors or ceilings. Stalagmites and stalactites had changed into pillars with ancient languages carved into their bodies, and ziggurats or other odd buildings were created before his very eyes from the natural earth of Panu's crust. And the feeling of the stone riddled with millions of diagrams and sigils he'd confirmed to be blasphemous presystem scripture was tainted with an alien presence.

Better said, the tunnels likely hadn't originally been connected to the labyrinth. No, they didn't lead to the labyrinth at all, but rather the labyrinth had been building itself and expanding itself toward Bernzee, perhaps even in all directions.

The labyrinth of the slumbering vampiric elder god was growing. Rapidly.

Fimrindle watched from the shadows as another of the hulking, muscular abominations shambled past—the pale-blue creature not sensing him at all—but picking up on the scent of his master and her necromancer companions. Its black eyes narrowed and its mouth full of fangs dripped saliva while it picked up speed, unnatural additional limbs supporting the large monster's trudging gait.

It was marked for death, and the silently building affliction began to amass power on its soul.

The scarecrow's metal body didn't even twitch, the carved *X*'s for eyes in his metal head not showing any sign he was even observing the lumbering creature until he appeared behind it within the time it took to blink. Under the Tier 3 Death buff of Stalking Predator, alongside the affliction Mark Prey and his assassination martial art Execution flickering through the artifact scythe in his hands—the amount of stacked critical damage his strike would dish out could have killed a fully grown level-200 E-grade garsnapper.

Not that he'd even seen a garsnapper since having left the last planet he'd been quarantined on, but the point still stood.

[Ancient Vampiric Precursor Abomination, Blue Blood Heretic, Level 102]
[You have landed a critical hit. Max Damage x17.]

His scythe flashed through the higher-leveled monster like a knife through butter, as quiet as a night's breeze. There was no resistance in the target's body; the ancient scythe simply slipped through it from hip to ear—causing ripples of critical energy to silently tear across the beast as its innards splattered across the floor. One half of the body slid off the other, and a *splat* echoed through the terraforming room.

The fledgling reaper stared down at his target, not feeling satisfied in his kill—but patience was something he was very good at. He knew what lay in wait at the end of this road, and getting there was just part of the job. It was just a shame that he'd had to take a level cut to bind to Allie, because it was something of a setback being forced to wait for her to catch up. He'd even intentionally pushed her by holding back in numerous fights, such as the fight at the Blood Moon Requiem's compound—even at the risk of letting her die.

It wasn't that he'd wanted her to die—in fact it was quite the opposite. He had high hopes for the child, but he'd done his part to even the odds and then let her prove her worth. If she'd been worthy of his contract, she would find a way to persist. If she was worthy of his contract, she wouldn't die. Unfortunately Riven had intervened before she'd been able to truly push past the barrier holding her back . . . but he had faith it would eventually give in nonetheless. He also had no intentions of holding her hand the entire way through and would only give as much help as needed to put her into situations that allowed a hard but winnable fight. This was the best way to gain insights and leveling, and if she wasn't up to the task, then someone else would be.

Then again, she'd also been very lucky he was even able to accept her contract, using the Ritual Bonds of Blood and Soul—a multiuse utility skill that allowed him to artificially decrease his own parameters to trick Elysium into allowing their partnership despite a level gap.

It made Fimrindle wonder just what the other, more advanced reapers of death in the S-grade could do with it if he was able to create such a massive opportunity as this with such a low amount of effort on his part. He was far, far from understanding the machinations of those ancient beings, though, and was unlikely to find out anytime soon.

He shut down that train of thought, compartmentalizing it for future meditation, and was just about to report back from his scouting mission when he heard a familiar noise.

His passive buff Anticipate Movements activated, and the scarecrow blurred.

Eight whistling throwing stars empowered with discrete bursts of shadow energy were torn out of the air one by one—plucked like cherries from a tree with perfect precision. His clawed metal hands easily took what little damage the sharp edges dispersed, before the thrown projectiles disappeared into puffs of black.

He stared down at his hand, comprehending the nature of the stamina that'd been used to attack him, remaining completely still as he did so. Observing the room around him, he couldn't tell where the opponent was despite the direction of the attack. With an uncharacteristically slow motion, he brought a single metal claw with remnant power from one of the throwing stars up to his mouth, closing down with daggerlike teeth.

Ah. How surprising.

It was one of his kin.

Why was there another reaper here, though?

A contracted job, perhaps?

But who would hire them? No one on Panu would even know of those kinds of merc contracts or the rituals to summon reapers until a long, long time from now. Even if they did, they'd not be able to afford someone of that caliber without bankrupting entire empires. Or at least the probability of it was extremely low. That meant an off-planet entity had likely hired the assassin.

An opposing faction inside the Blood Moon Requiem?

Perhaps.

Someone related to the vampiric elder god? A descendant?

More likely. Otherwise the reaper would have targeted Allie and Riven both long before now.

He nodded; it was the only thing that made sense. There was no other reason another reaper in the F-grade would be here, not on a tiny, remote planet like this.

The thought exhilarated Fimrindle, who'd been rather bored while waiting for Allie to make the building breakthrough he could feel coming, and his metal features instantaneously twisted into one of the most horrendous visages of sadistic glee ever seen upon the face of Panu. His mouth, which was usually set into a deadpan, interlocking set of metal jaws, had turned upward at an unnatural angle—teeth elongating to twice their normal length and shifting in sharpness. The *X*'s carved into his metallic face had abruptly doubled in size due to his excitement, and a rasping sound escaped his throat—letting out a low, cackling sound like the scratching of two rusty blades.

His stick-thin body stood to its full height—senses now picking up a faint clicking sound at various points around him—and for the first time in centuries, he equipped his ceremonial reaper's cloak. The shroud literally made from shadows encompassed his body, and he planted both clawed feet out to either side as the clicking sounds stopped. His malicious gaze settled on the figure before it made itself known, appearing out of thin air like a phantom with two small scythes fluidly dancing between the skeletal fingers of either hand—and swirling black throwing stars circled the figure that stared back at Fimrindle through the dead eyes of a skull face.

Just like Fimrindle, the ceremonial shroud was equipped—flowing about his body like a writhing, living thing that merged and re-formed from the very shadows around them—encompassing the other reaper's body in a cloud of black.

[Skullborn, Initiate Reaper of Souls, Level 199 Elite]

Fimrindle's unnatural, excited smile grew even wider. This was a fight where his limits would truly be pushed to the test, given his reduced sub-100 combat level, while his opponent was at the peak of F-grade and almost into the E-grade. It was very likely this particular reaper had been chosen for exactly that reason, as Elysium probably wouldn't have allowed an outsider E-grade to enter an integration planet this early. The golden lettering of the enemy reaper's identification information also didn't come as a surprise, given that almost all reapers had that signifier at a minimum when they weren't hiding it like Fimrindle was.

"Brother." The other reaper bowed low, briefly, his voice coming out like a cold wind. "It is a fortunate test of fate for us, crossing paths as fellow children of the Scythe. Yet I must hold to my contract and will not hold back. Your soul will be sent to the collector in due time."

Fimrindle responded with a pleased groan, the Ritual Bonds of Blood and Soul shifting to unlock some of the restraints he'd placed on himself while in this form—originally meant to hide him from Elysium's gaze. He felt them snap, one by one, and though he would need to remain at the paltry level of 91 since he couldn't go over his contracted master's own combat level, he still felt a flood of power insert itself into his soul apparatus.

The enlarged X's across his face burst into neon-teal flames, and a cold wave of energy began rising from his position.

[Legendary status marker has been unveiled. Reaper of Souls Unique Title has been unveiled: Disciple of the Wailing Lake has been unveiled.]
[Three additional skills have been unlocked. Two additional traits have been unlocked and 709 stat points have been reapplied.]
[You have gained the attention of Elysium. Beware, my child, for if you push yourself too far, the system will recognize your deceit and void your contract with the chosen master you've acquired until natural parameters have been met.]

His mentor's warning voice echoed in his ears, and he lifted his scythe as it flared with the same neon-teal fires underneath his shifting, Shadow-crafted hood. His status page identifiers abruptly changed from the normal lettering Elysium most often used to that of a deep-crimson fire, indicating his legendary status—and he took a stance while his newfound enemy took a step back in surprise. To his knowledge, only he and twelve others on this planet had such an indicator—with Athela and Riven being two of the others.

Fimrindle's head lowered, activating his Tier-3 domain with a brief expanding hand motion and the recited chant. "Nekarakt arts, shadow realms."

The terraforming cavern erupted with the howls of lost souls and a raging tidal wave of black Shadow energy, encompassing the two combatants in an alternate reality that shattered the fabric of the world around them. He took a single step forward as his enemy's body erupted in a red mist of blood—empowering a swarm of Shadow-made throwing stars that ripped out of the enemy reaper's shroud in all directions.

Fimrindle's scythe cut through an erected barrier enchantment with a single swipe, an arc piercing through time and space with a snap of noise and a blur of flaming steel.

WHUMPH

BOOM

CRASH-CRASH-CRASH-CRASH-CRASH

The storm of exploding Blood-imbued throwing stars reminded Fimrindle very much of Riven's own Bloody Razors, and he outwardly cackled in an echoing howl as he danced through the waves of oncoming blades before activating Flurry and Tear Asunder.

His body was naturally fast, but the combination of both martial arts ripped space apart in giant tears—causing his very soul to scream and leaving an afterimage as the two reapers clashed with the ferocity of apex predators.

[You have gained nine levels. Congratulations! Be sure to visit your status page to apply points.]

Allie stumbled to an abrupt stop when she got the notification. Blinking rapidly and scratching her head, she let out the only thing that came to her in that moment. "Huh?"

She'd been following the trail of bodies left by Fimrindle, little *X* marks carved into their chests to signify it was his doing—with other *X*'s carved into the walls when choosing between splits in the tunnels to sign which way he'd gone.

The notification had appeared just as she'd turned left down another one of the tunnels—which was quickly being terraformed like much of the caverns they'd already traversed, and she failed to understand why or how it'd even happened.

She'd never had an influx of XP that large before. Not ever. Not a single time, even after slaughtering hundreds or thousands of people in the war against Prophet, and then again in the war against the conquered Tereen elves.

The amounts of XP she'd been getting from Fimrindle had been coming in time after time as well, with every kill he made concerning these strange vampiric precursors that wandered the underdark. But that'd only granted her a single level so far, and the XP was split between them, so a nine-level jump just didn't make any sense.

"What's wrong?" Mara asked curiously, raising the corpse before them and causing it to stand with a gasp—dead eyes lighting up and adding the creature to her posse before turning to look at her best friend. "You look stunned. Did something happen?"

"Yeah . . ." Allie replied, shaking herself out of her stupor and taking a look at her status page. There was no clue there, but she did apply the stat points to Willpower and Intelligence nonetheless. "I just got a nine-level boost and I don't know why."

Mara blinked. "Nine combat levels?"

"Are you sure you're not seeing things?" Vin asked from the side, skipping to a stop and staring at the strange language written into the smoothing, shaping stone walls around them. "Hells, I might be seeing things, too. What's this language? Anyone know?"

"No idea," one of the necromancer elites called from the back. "I've been wondering, too."

No one else said anything, but a roar and a scream was heard from the back when the sound of thundering feet caused them all to turn.

Allie's red eyes narrowed and she equipped her skull mask again, body flaring with death mana as the entire horde of their undead began rushing the back line where dozens of pale blue-skinned vampiric precursors were crashing into the ground from a steep drop-off that Allie had just traversed not long ago.

Unfortunately for the aggressing mob, they didn't have any ranged casters at the moment—and they were on a slope in a somewhat narrow passage for such a large group.

"FIRE!"

Threads of black and teal, flaming skulls, death balls, and green clouds of necrotic curses blasted into the rampaging swarm that was building like an avalanche. Body parts were torn, melted, and burned off in a violent display of destructive magic that wiped out much of the first wave before more of them surged out of the tunnel above.

The skeletons and zombies made contact, clashing with black-eyed men and women of a lost race from another age. Weirdly enough, not all the precursors showed signs of absolute lunacy, many of them making smart and calculated decisions without a mob mentality in their fighting. Martial arts were seen in some, others simply avoided fighting the undead altogether to go around on the outskirts of the tunnels, while others simply stayed back and watched so they'd not cause a body plug and crush their comrades, even calling back in an ancient language to make their compatriots slow the charge.

That did not bode well, in Allie's opinion, as the first impression she'd had of these creatures was a mindless swarm—similar to many of the versions of lower-tiered undead she often raised up. It was true that some of the mutant variations, large lumbering things that looked like the Hulk on steroids, did maintain that basic mind-set—but certainly not so with the others, despite their ferocity in battle.

It was almost as if these precursors weren't necessarily stupid, but instead they were just . . . desperate?

The thought disturbed her, but upon second evaluation she confirmed her theory. The looks these people had were of desperation, without a doubt, and they were doing their utmost to try and bring her down before she entered the labyrinth and headed toward their fallen god.

"FIRE!"

Another volley of magics tore into the oncoming tide of pale blue, killing dozens more. She and the other necromancers continually moved back, cutting them down time after time as they came but being pushed by sheer numbers. They took time raising the dead to send back at the still-living precursors as well, and then would rinse and repeat with more showers of offensive magic while a couple of Mara's Shadow-infused skeletal assassins kept the creatures at bay whenever they broke through the main line.

[You have gained one level. Congratulations! Be sure to visit your status page to apply points.]
[You have gained one level. Congratulations! Be sure to visit your status page to apply points.]

The ground thundered.

Hundreds fell.

Allie began to feel her mana waning, and she took numerous vials of blue mana potions to stave off absolute depletion. Even with all the remnant death mana from the environment acting as a stimulant to fuel her power, she was still struggling to stay in the fight as the swarm grew larger.

It started to get really bad when enemy casters started appearing, wearing odd metal bracelets and feathered ornaments reminding her of Aztec attire from books she'd read as a child. Enemy scepters flared brightly, and soon she found herself in an even worse pinch as her necromancers were pushed to the brink in an exchange of offensive and defensive magics over the melee battle in the middle. All she could do was continue to backpedal down the sloping path, following Fimrindle's markings in a battle of attrition as one, then two, and then three of her elite necromancers fell in battle—stemming the tide of their own minions and causing the brutal melee to sway in favor of the precursors.

When the fourth necromancer fell, the tidal wave broke through the dam of undead shortly after—as even she with her swarm necromancer abilities could not raise the dead as fast as they were being cut down.

She snarled, summoning a storm of ghosts that crashed into her enemies before erecting a wall of bones. Then, turning heel, she sprinted down the corridors in the opposite direction. The ghosts only had so much passive mana before they'd be banished back into the ether, and the bone wall wouldn't hold very long.

"COME ON! LET'S MOVE!"

CHAPTER 23

Drums.

Drums echoed in the dark.

A blast of strange, azure-blue mana with an unfamiliar origin in the Unholy foundation tore through the halls. Her eyes went wide midsprint and she was sent blasting across the stone laden with ancient texts, crashing into a pillar and spinning rapidly in the air until she cratered into the opposite end.

Coughing up blood and snapping one arm back into place, she smoldered with wisps of that same azure blue—and she had to send a pulse of death through her body to clear it off her armor and skin. Her vision swayed, and she caught herself with another cough as a loud boom shook the halls amid screams, roars, and the beating of drums.

"RRRAAAAAAAAAAAHHHHH!!!"

A large, salamander-like creature lacking eyes or back legs tackled her to the ground, using huge black claws to pin her down while its open maw snapped shut on one arm.

The bone armor underneath its grip held firm, and with a snarl Allie's left fist swung around and crashed into the monster's skull.

An explosion of death mana radiated out from her fist, and two more snapping jabs ripped open the facial bones of the beast before it let out a gurgling hiss and fell to the side.

"Shit! Why are there so many of them?!"

Wounds where she'd been burned, cut, and bruised were still healing with her natural regenerative properties—the latest were two shallow gashes where the black fangs of the salamander had found a gap.

Unclasping a small pouch along her hip and downing a vial of red liquid, she let the soothing concoction trickle down her throat. Energy flowed back into her, but the number of potions she'd taken now was building into what the alchemists called elixir toxicity. The effectiveness was going down, and the overdose had begun to make her feel nauseated.

Trying to stabilize herself as the hall shook around her yet again, she blinked rapidly when three pale-blue figures broke through the frontline fighting and sprinted her way.

Her wand let out a shrill scream as the soul within lit aflame, and her hand lifted—accompanied by dozens of deathly threads that ripped and tore the precursors down akin to a Gatling gun. Pale blood sprayed from their bodies as they were hit numerous times, littered with holes until their legs gave out one by one—splattering their corpses onto the floor.

She whipped around, swinging her leg in a blurring horizontal kick.

CRUNCH

The mutant's face snapped left, but it staggered back to a standing position. One pale eye settled on her, and a monkey-like tail snapped around—sparking against her skull mask and knocking her backward.

Smacking hard into the stone wall, she summoned a death ball and lunged underneath a swing that shattered a portion of the wall behind her. Flipping over another tail swipe, she launched the death ball directly into the open jaws of the screaming creature and ruptured its insides—causing the beast to explode in a shower of gore.

Allie landed on her feet, stumbled, and created two more skeletal minions from nearby corpses before commanding them to the front, where her allies were still battling the front-runners of the oncoming hordes.

Three of her necromancers were dead, one of their corpses being paraded in the back of enemy lines over their heads amid loud chanting, while two more lay nearby in ripped, crumpled mounds of mutilated flesh, bone, and cloth.

To their front were building enemies.

To their sides were stone hallways.

And to their backs was a giant, black pit so deep that even Allie's own dark-attuned eyesight couldn't see the bottom.

They were trapped.

"ALLIE! WE WON'T BE ABLE TO HOLD FOR MUCH LONGER!" Mara yelled over the din of battle, summoning a flock of Shadow-made crows that swarmed the oncoming enemy tide—adding to the skeletons, zombies, and other undead creatures the necromancers were throwing into the fray. "TELL US WHAT TO DO!"

Tell us what to do?

Allie could barely even hold herself up and was only doing so through sheer force of will. Her mana was waning, only sustaining itself by drawing on the sheer amount of death around her, and she wasn't nearly as good as Riven in utilizing environmental mana anyway.

They'd killed hundreds of these creatures; she'd blown all her major abilities including Miasmic Roar and Eye of the Scythe. Her minions were being cut down just as fast as they made them, and they were being killed faster now that they had nowhere to retreat to. And where was Fimrindle during all this?

She took in a deep breath, staring down what had once been a tunnel, and closed her eyes.

No. She could not give in to despair. Not here.

Not ever.

Her mind entered a state of tranquility as the souls around her began to whisper in her ear. They told her it was going to be all right and that they would help her overcome this obstacle. They were her friends, they were her protectors, and she need not worry.

Her body lifted slightly off the ground, and the roar of battle grew louder as a huge, bull-like creature with horns and dozens of curved, sharp teeth barreled through two zombies and tackled one of the robed ghoul necromancers—opening up the front line for the rest of the vampiric precursors to funnel in.

Nin's hissing curse simultaneously let out as he snapped one of his skeletal fingers, causing three of his plague-ridden zombies to explode forward and blow back numerous enemies in a single go.

Vin followed suit, causing torrents of rapidly spreading plague to settle on the hall ahead of them while the brothers continued throwing out orbs of dark-green miasma.

Mara's arm extended and blasted the creature trying to eat the ghoul underneath it, sending out a beam of black light that caused the monster to shrivel and die with an agonizing scream. "ALLIE! ALLIE, WH—"

Mara turned her head, only to gawk at the sight behind her.

Allie's figure was six feet off the floor in a meditative state, hands clasped together, eyes closed, legs pointed directly down, a billowing cloud of death mana being collected from their surroundings and building into a roaring storm that began to shake the underground complex more and more. Souls began leaking into Panu from the beyond, whispering in an audible wave of sound that soon turned into a shrill scream. A ghostly form unlike any Mara had ever seen stepped out of the ether, a pale, naked woman with black eyes and giant unfolding wings. A halo burned over her head, and she whispered into Allie's ear in a language Mara couldn't understand.

Despite Allie being her friend, Mara took an involuntary step back—wide-eyed and staring. "What in the hells?"

Vin's scream of pain caused Mara to whirl back around, and her dead heart clenched when she saw his lower half torn off by the afterimage of a large axe trailing through the air. In front of her was the first of nearly two dozen heavily armored warriors. Each of them had bronze plate mail adorning their pale-blue bodies. Blocky, Aztec-like decorations were carved into the ancient armor—and each of them carried various types of axes and broadswords, accompanied by bulky circular shields.

Mara's teeth gritted together, and with a Banshee's Wail that echoed through the hallways in a radiating, bouncing storm of sound, she stunned the entire oncoming horde for a couple seconds and allowed herself to pull Vin's body backward. Simultaneously her swarm of crows rapidly closed in on the gap in the front line—and two skeletal assassins writhing with black Shadow energy snapped out of her shadow and sank daggers into the eye sockets and underarm weak spots of the warriors' armor.

Then the battle reset, and the horde that'd been pushed back due to her area-of-effect spell began regaining ground.

BOOM

An explosion of azure-blue wisps ripped through five skeletons and obliterated one of the necropolis necromancers, causing half his body to disintegrate on impact and not even allowing time for him to scream.

"ALLIE!" Mara screeched over the clamor of claws, bone, and metal crashing into one another—and prepared a barrier to intercept yet another of those azure orbs, sending shock waves back into the oncoming horde. "ALLIE, WE NEED YOU!!!"

Fimrindle watched, awestruck and eager, as the breakthrough finally took hold. Allie's desperation had finally pushed the seed through into fruition, and he rasped out a wheezing cackle from the shadows above her.

She fit all the requirements—he'd just known she could do it!

The world rumbled as the Scythe took notice of the once-in-a-lifetime event, and Fimrindle felt the awe-inspiring presence of the lord of death settle his gaze upon the scene. The touch of death incarnate resonated within the reaper, and Fimrindle shuddered in ecstasy when he felt the mental acknowledgment and approval for forcing this set of events into place.

After all, Fimrindle had been the one to lead Allie down this corridor. To a place where she had no choice but to finally push herself beyond her limits. It was that or die—and Fimrindle's gamble had succeeded.

He'd actually done it.

WHOOM

The air turned stale, and Fimrindle felt the presence of yet another ancient being encircling the area. Only this time, its presence was hostile, overbearing, and he gasped—falling from his hiding spot and smashing into the ground where he began to silently spasm.

"You dare take one of my prized possessions from me . . ." the ancient being whispered in Fimrindle's mind in a deep, booming voice, and Fimrindle began to scream as the entity began crushing his soul bit by bit. "You transgress . . ."

The Scythe intervened, its own presence forcibly tearing the other entity off Fimrindle's soul and causing the ether just outside Panu's physical realm to quake as the titans clashed.

"The child . . . is just as much mine . . . as it is yours . . ." the Scythe's raspy echo replied while repairing the damage to Fimrindle's core in a split second. "You may have helped create . . . the vampire, as it is known . . . in this era . . . But you forget that it was within my outlines . . . that you based your genesis . . ."

Fimrindle watched, dumbstruck, having completely forgotten about Allie's transcendence upon witnessing the absolute domineering might of the two entities just a single reality away from his own—peering into the beyond as the presence of mounting titans bled through.

"All undead are mine to take . . . should they show themselves proper vessels . . . to the path . . ." the Scythe stated in a tone that allowed no disagreement. "You would do well to remember that . . . for you, too, were once my child as well . . ."

The other entity let out a shudder of angry rage, turning its ire to brush against Fimrindle's soul one more time. "That may be, but this is not acceptable. She has my bloodline; she is mine by right."

The Scythe let out a long, raspy chuckle that dwindled away into nothingness—a laugh that only Fimrindle and the blood god could hear. "Is that so? Perhaps we should . . . let the girl . . . decide for herself . . ."

Allie saw Mara die.

She saw Nin die.

Then Vin.

Each of her necromancers fell.

Each of them screamed her name in hopes that she'd save them.

Finally, she saw herself die, too—and it was a brutal, painful way to go.

Allie's eyes snapped open with pale, unnatural light—far different from her regular crimson, and then her eyes dilated. The world around her abruptly calmed on the fifth replay, slowing down right before the killing blow had struck Mara down—the axe only an inch away from her friend's wide-eyed, frantic face. She'd never seen Mara so afraid before.

It fucking infuriated her.

The land around them was tinged in shades of black, red, and gray, and the out-of-body experience halted space all around her as cold, resonating energy rippled across her skin.

Her ethereal body, a replica of her own but without physical representation, stood staring at the scene before them—glowing pale eyes blinking and looking down at her floating body with a mixture of mounting fury directed toward the precursors and intense gratitude when looking at the souls around her.

These souls . . . they were her friends.

They were her family.

And they were going to stand with her until the end.

Glancing left to where the only other being able to interact with this strange environment now floated beside her, peering into her out-of-body form, was a ghostly winged woman with pale-gray eyes and a deathly halo hovering over her head.

The woman smiled a very familiar smile, and Allie knew that—somehow—she was looking at a reflection of herself.

[Malignant Prophecy has activated. Desired Action: Extremely High-Tier Manipulation. Current Willpower stat: Incalculable due to potential mutation. Unable to determine if sufficient Willpower is available for desired action.
Overridden. Performing this act will put your Malignant Prophecy on cooldown for significant amounts of time. Do you wish to proceed?]

"Of course."

[Desired Action: Save yourself, Mara, Vin, Nin, and the remaining necromancers underneath your banner. Malignant Prophecy's two options are as follows:
- Option 1: Create a cave-in and pray to the Blood God for inspiration. Chance for success: high.
- Option 2: Accept your new calling as an Angel of Death and change your race. This act will both please the Scythe and infuriate the Blood God. You will be marked as a fledgling Hero of Death by the Scythe for taking on this role, will irretrievably change the fate of Panu, and will be marked as an Apostate by the Blood God. This choice will negatively influence your relationship with the Blood Moon Requiem. Chance for success: very high.]

Allie's eyes drifted over the text twice, and out of the corner of her eye she saw her phantom twin giggle. "What's so funny? And who are you, exactly?"

The phantom angel didn't reply, only continuing to smile as its warm energy permeated Allie's soul. Allie felt it then, the connection, the replica, the complete fit to her own—only better.

This . . . was her?

A version of her that she could choose.

There'd been no notification given by the system outside her Malignant Prophecy.

And yet . . . what exactly was she supposed to do with it?

Bind it?

How?

And did she even want to do so? Marring her relationship with the Blood Moon Requiem, a powerhouse of the multiverse and her extended family, in the process? By marking herself as an apostate in the eyes of the blood god?

Her eyes searched the phantom angel's own, and she felt a pulse from her other half—calling out to her, telling her that she should reach out and grab it.

Or . . . was it even truly her? Had it been created as an opportunity by her bloodline? Or was this apparition something else entirely?

A vision engulfed her mind, and suddenly she was high up in the air on wings as black as night, pale-gray eyes glowing against a dark span of clouds underneath a black hood—while a deathly halo of similarly pale-gray flames flickered over her head. In her hands, a sword as big as she was lifted to point at an opposing army of holy warriors settling down in trenches, waiting for her to descend—as her legions of the dead stormed the grounds underneath her in a mad rush of fury. Hundreds of thousands of the dead poured forward like a tidal wave, and out of the enemy ranks, another woman ascended to the skies.

Brilliant golden flames billowed around her silk-clothed body, and a sword of her own shattered the dark skies in a comet of brilliant fire—crashing into the ascending woman's hands as white wings erupted out of her back. Her golden eyes and similarly brilliant halo matched Allie's own in an opposite mirroring, and her long blond hair trailed out behind her with a flare of power.

Allie recognized this person from the forums. It was none other than the number one Apex ranker on the power forums. The woman Judith Marcina, Angelic Fallcaller.

The vision ended abruptly as her brief glimpse of the future ended, a possibility of what was to come should she take this new class and ascend into higher ranks of power.

Yet . . . despite the dread she felt at making so many enemies in her potential ascension, a giddy smile began to combat that dread. Who were they to tell her what she could and could not do? Who were they to dictate her fate? Be they gods, mortals, or even her own extended family—no one was the master of her fate other than herself.

"I accept the risks."

[Desired action has been selected: Option 2: Accept your new calling as an Angel of Death and change your race. This act will both please the Scythe and infuriate the Blood God. You will be marked as a fledgling Hero of Death by the Scythe for taking on this role, will irretrievably change the fate of Panu, and will be marked as an Apostate by the Blood God. This choice will negatively influence your relationship with the Blood Moon Requiem. Chance for success: very high.]

Immediately, time unfroze and the colors of the world went back to more normal hues. Her ghostly, angelic replica crashed into her body just as her own soul did—igniting a chain reaction as the overlapping upgrade to her soul structure fused and merged.

She screamed, and her Death subpillar exploded into thousands of fragments as the storm of power around her launched itself forward into the oncoming swarm of vampiric precursors. The black and teal aura quickly changed to a third, pale-gray coloring—and the river of energy swept through the enemy ranks so fast that the oncoming swing meant for Mara's head was incinerated along with the axe's wielder.

The walls trembled.

Flesh was torn from bone as thousands of precursors died like flies when the shock wave of pale-gray flames engulfed them in a wave unlike anything Allie had conjured from the Death subpillar before.

Then, there was silence.

Utter silence.

Allie's mind blanked, and she continued to hover in the air as her soul recreated itself under the guidance of some otherworldly force. Her bright-crimson eyes flickered and died out, replaced by the same pale, glowing gray—as a similarly colored halo created itself over her head. That, too, sputtered out flames of its own before absorbing them and remaining as a glowing, metallic circle about a foot over her eyes. Black wings sprouted from her back, tearing through her bone armor and remodeling it to fit her new appendages as the angelic feathers briefly glittered in the darkness.

The souls swirling around her quickly slowed, almost reverently, as a sigh escaped her lips—power oozing from her very voice and causing the underground passage to warp at the expulsion of excess energy.

Her body flickered, as if a ghost, and Allie slowly raised her hand in the dead silence as her followers looked on in amazement—watching a phantasmal afterimage of herself follow her movements.

Her fangs protruded when she smiled, and then—to her surprise—they fell out entirely, clattering to the floor beneath her when new teeth replaced them.

A scream of rage next came from the beyond, causing the earth around her to tremble for only a split second—until it was abruptly gone, and an explosion of notifications berated her senses.

[Worldwide Message: A new Hero of Death has been named, and her name is Allie Thane. For the first time in over seven thousand years across the entirety of the multiverse, an Angel of Death has ascended. Requirements—including 100% affinity to the Death subpillar, the servitude of a Reaper of Souls, willing subservience and friendly terms with at least three thousand souls in the afterlife, and the status of Undead race—have all been met. May the living tremble in fear upon her approach, for true death now stalks these lands.]

[Worldwide Message: The Scythe has blessed a portion of Panu. The entire continent of Umbra, where Brightsville—capital of the Thane Necropolis—is located has been terraformed in favor of the undead—giving all undead on Umbra a potent bonus to all stats and passive upkeep while simultaneously debuffing any living present there. Undead of various species will now randomly spawn on the continent of Umbra, and their ability to repopulate has tripled in efficiency. Potent miasma now oozes out of the land itself, and every living person or creature now inhabiting these lands has been changed into an undead version of themselves. They have had

their pillars altered to reflect this, with each of them given a choice between the following options and their subvariants based on original race: Ghoul, Skresh, Golem variants, Deathtouched Enlightened, Phantasmal, Abomination, Ravager, Skeletal, Zombie, Necrofisa, Ravenous, Hungerer, Blighted, Horror, and Neverlight. Other resident vampires have been unaffected by this change.]

[Worldwide Message: New OPTIONAL World Quest (7): Eradicate the Angel of Death, Allie Thane. Your world has birthed an extremely rare variant of undead, an Angel of Death. Allowing her to reign throughout the integration will no doubt lead to further terraforming of this planet, and she represents a potent danger to all those who are living. This quest goes out to all other World Quest antagonists as well. The prize for delivering a killing blow to Allie Thane before the five-year integration time limit is up will be inheriting her fledgling divinity in a form of your choosing, allowing your own ascension and the start of a path into future godhood. Guild mercenary options will reflect an increased ability and lowered cost to acquire off-world holy warriors in the pursuit of this crusade, as long as the guild owner is not undead and the intended target is perceived as truly being Allie Thane by Elysium's administrator.]

[Fifty-seven combat levels partially gained and partially granted.]

[You have obtained the first-ranked Apex position on the power ladder of Panu. The Legendary status marker has been applied to your identification information.]

[You have been labeled an Apostate by the Blood God. All other worshippers of the Blood God will be notified of this when looking upon you.]

[You have acquired the race Angel of Death and have begun your transcendence into divine origins. +10,000 additional minion slots. Undead minions that are nonsentient now only cost 1 Willpower to control. Feral mindless undead will not attack you unless provoked and may be commanded to do your bidding to a very limited extent even outside your normal minion slots if they are masterless. Your affinity to the Death subpillar has been increased to 101%, and you are now able to increase it even more with each step of transcending divinity that you take. You gain the other traits:

- Phantasmal (allows warping in and out of the ether and void at will),
- Legion Commander (allows for far more intricate control of minions at an individual level despite the number you have),
- Profane Angelic Wings (enables flight at the expense of mana, stamina, or divinity),
- Deathly Halo (your very presence inspires, passively heals, and empowers fellow undead nearby, and your Charisma vastly amplifies itself when concerning fellow undead, inspiring worship. You

    are also able to terraform land in favor of the undead should you wish to do so.),
- **Body of True Death** (upgrades your Death subpillar to the True Death Specialized subpillar, +30% to all stats, +100 flat points to all stats aside Charisma. -20,000 stat points applied to Charisma. Souls can seek refuge in your body and make your inner world a place they call home. Your soul apparatus has been modified to house souls and is now considered an inner world that can be manipulated in time),
- **Eyes of the Phantom Angel** (allows you to peer into the ether and void at all times in conjunction with your normal sight), and:
- **Angel's Phantom Touch** (allows you to completely resurrect allies by physically dragging their souls back into the world with your phantasmal body aspect. Does not require activation of an ability. This is contingent on being able to find their souls before they're swallowed and lost to the afterlife, or finding them again once they've already been lost).]
- **[You have been labeled a Hero of Death by the Scythe, in hopes that you will serve him. This title amplifies all Death abilities by 10% effectiveness and empowers all undead under your control by 20% to all stats. An open branch of communication, directly linked to the Scythe, has been applied to your status page so that you may converse with him for more details. All followers of the Scythe will be notified of this title upon seeing you. With this title, he also grants you a relic E-grade Divine weapon.]**
- **[Blade of Soulcry (Divine Claymore, E-Grade, Death Attuned): ???]**

Allie paused her reading of the numerous notifications when a pale light illuminated the air in front of where she hovered. Her new wings instinctively extended, and the hundreds of souls slowly swarming around her reverently came closer to embrace her—almost tentatively—though their warm intentions bled through their thoughts when her mind embraced them back.

A long claymore, shifting with pale light, hovered in the air before her. Her gray eyes glowed just like the weapon did, taking in every detail of the claymore as her bone gauntlet reached out and touched it with a finger.

It was exquisite, made from a dark-gray metal with a single elongated rune along the entirety of the blade's middle, twisting and turning but not breaking the lines creating it while glowing a bright neon teal.

Her finger tapped the blade again, causing it to respond to her with another flare of energy, and the afterimage of her movements showed her phantasmal soul trailing behind. Her wings flexed and extended again as she got a feel for them. She smiled at the way her soul trailed behind her physical body even there—with her hair flowing around her and underneath the glowing gray halo.

Looking up and meeting the stares of her friends and allies, she saw each of them slowly take a knee, then bow, the effects of her new presence completely capturing their attention and instilling a sense of reverence in them.

Hesitantly, Allie willed herself to move forward—and without more than a twitch of her black wings, she flew ahead to where the bodies of her three necromancers now lay. Their remains were unscathed from her own eradication of the enemy, whereas the vampire precursors were now only piles of ash and bone, and she stared out at their still-present souls that had yet to recede into the afterlife, hovering over their bodies as if asking to be let back in.

They weren't quite yet sentient during this transition, not like the swarm of souls gently embracing her now—but it did not matter. The transitory phase was about to end as she quietly pushed each of them back into their bodies. Pushing energy through her soul's newly acquired True Death Specialty subpillar, a mix of deep grays, blacks, and teals, the power flowed into her halo next and started to rapidly mend the bodies underneath.

Two ghouls and a skresh, necromancers of the necropolis, let out gasps and hissing sounds simultaneously while their bodies mended under the influence of her halo.

"The beginning of a new era . . ." Mara hissed under her breath while kneeling, reverence in her eyes while staring, starstruck, up at her best friend. "Your Excellency! I do not have the words to describe these feelings! You are . . . majestic!"

Allie shifted her gaze, and she took her skull mask off with a warm smile just when a final notification appeared ahead of her. "Don't talk to me like that, Mara. You're my best friend, and I won't have my best friend treating me like I'm above her."

[New system quest dispensed: Conquer Panu. You have been publicly denounced by the Blood God as an Apostate, have angered almost every vampiric faction in the entire multiverse, and have already been marked for death on the public forums by numerous other factions across your planet. Having instilled a deep fear in the minds of the living, and having given hope to the sentient undead of your world, you are destined to be hunted down—or, alternatively, you will rise from the ashes of war as a hero to your people. Will you and your kind be eradicated from Panu? Or will you conquer this planet and claim it for yourself? You have until the five-year time limit of integration to take over at least 80% of this planet for yourself. If you accomplish this, you will gain Elysium's direct and absolute protection from outside invaders for an additional one hundred years and will gain a shroud that stops other outside forces from scrying your planet's location for five hundred years, and the administrator will allow you to reposition your newly conquered planet anywhere in the multiverse a single time at the end of integration.]

CHAPTER 24

Gaia looked out over the land from a mountain's peak. What had once been a world full of beauty and balance, with green pastures and lush forests full of life, had turned into a blighted black-and-gray version of itself with death and undeath in abundance. Only silver grasses and occasional trees with neon-teal leaves, black bark, and occasional deep-red shrubbery or vines stood out amid the dreary sea around her.

The blue skies overhead had darkened, and though she was able to comfort herself to a minor extent by knowing that these haunted woods did hold another form of life beyond that which she was originally attuned to, she could not help but weep.

For even she had become a thing of nightmares.

Kathrine was scrambling to get things in order, working with General Viku's soldiers alongside her own to help make the compound presentable. Representative thralls had just been made for each and every one of the high council, including the high queen, who would be using ritual magic to eat away those poor souls in order to acquire a mere hour or two of consciousness in this world.

Devouring souls such as this, even for vampires, was something of a taboo, but that just went to show how angry the leadership of the Blood Moon Requiem was after Allie's ascension.

"Out of all the things you could have done after being responsible for the deaths of many high-ranking young nobles, you went and became an apostate!" Kathrine hissed under her breath, long brunette hair frazzled while she frantically combed it in the mirror again before dropping the comb into her cleavage and racing down the stairs after her favorite maid, Cherna. "Cherna! Let me carry that for you!"

She could tell the blonde vampire woman was struggling, and Kathrine lifted two of the many large, heavy bags off the maid's shoulders while urging her onward.

Cherna, for her part, didn't even argue, having nearly tripped in her descent down the stairs and being very on edge concerning whom their guests were about to be. "U-um, thank you, Princess!"

"No time for thank-yous! Hurry!"

The two women raced down the flights of stairs and into one of the halls humming with activity like a beehive as various personnel, decorations, food, scented hookah displays, champagnes, and only the best furniture swarmed back and forth—many of which were being brought in by House Wraithtide and House Crushada from off-planet.

Frantic repairs were also underway concerning the last remnants of the battle concerning Allie's recent struggle against her previous would-be fiancé. The fortress wasn't completely done being built back up yet, and the mere thought of it not being presentable gave Kathrine very real palpitations.

"Riven!!!!! Riven, where the hells are you!!! I don't know what I'm going to say to ANY of them!" Kathrine muttered to herself in a high-pitched voice with furrowed brows, and she started to hyperventilate when she saw a blond vampire man with perfect posture in flowing white robes turning a corner to her left. He bore the sigil of an imperial messenger, locked eyes with her, and before he even made it halfway down the hall to where she was standing, Kathrine fainted out of panic.

The Stockyards.

That's what this regional prison had been dubbed, implying things that the thousands of vampires captured here from the battle for Dawn didn't necessarily agree with or like.

But at least they were fed.

The large complex was patrolled and held by the elites of the Thane Necropolis, with numerous electrified fences and high-quality enchantments set along the floors, walls, and even domed barrier ceilings in the crevice between two mountains only a few miles from Brightsville itself.

Normally, the surrendered vampires got well enough along with their captors after having realized whom the Thanes actually were. Many had even been planning on joining the necropolis and abandoning their homeland of Rippenvire entirely.

Had was the key word here.

When the earth beneath them rumbled and the roar of the enraged blood god was heard, and the ascension of Allie Thane was proclaimed, lights illuminated the city of Brightsville in the distance when people began to change. Evolutionary selections were given to some and forced upon others, and within mere seconds the lights had begun spreading throughout the Stockyards.

The captors of Rippenvire's forces began to wail, scream, and lurch as their bodies went through either minor or major mutations over the course of thirty seconds—breaking down components of other pillars and embracing the Unholy queen and Death subpillar by the grace of the Scythe.

Yet, although it was a short-lived transition, the rage that the vampires felt at the mention of their god being shunned and the absolute betrayal of one of their own sent them into a frenzy. Almost as one, and while their captors were preoccupied with the evolutionary changes, the captive vampires threw themselves into madness—clawing, hitting, biting, and even expending their own life force to break those barriers down.

Within minutes, carnage had spread throughout the prison.

Within the hour, that carnage was headed toward Brightsville itself.

General Bruner had seen riots and in-person combat before. He'd served in the Middle East and had helped save his people by battling Azag Hive Cluster forces, and had even been on missions for monster-culling purposes with other cyborgs after the integration.

Yet the sight of thousands upon thousands of civilians and active military men alike screaming for rebellion right outside headquarters disturbed him.

Bruner's mechanical orange eyes swept over the crowd, watching as one of the barriers around a supposedly secure outer gate to the military HQ was torn down. There was infighting in the crowds, but it was mostly located where those same crowds were pushing up against a line of military personnel holding them back from entering the three-story structure he occupied along with his closest officers. News reports across the cortex were already flowing in, from both local and world-wide sources, and he put a hand over his face and closed his eyes, squeezing his temple to try and relieve the stress of what he was seeing.

"Sir." A bald man in their new-age military uniform, a dark carbon shell dec-orated with the officer tags of the necropolis, came in and saluted along with two lesser officers behind him. "Reports show that anyone of ours that was beyond the wormhole has also been changed. In one case, one of our snipers on duty who'd just been coming through Riven's Eye Wormhole was lynched by a mob—even though he'd only just arrived and was in a panic to seek guidance. He'd been turned into what is called a Neverlight, some kind of Shadow-attuned undead. He was still humanoid, but that didn't stop the mob from killing him and the eight other service members escorting him here."

General Bruner's weary eyes shifted to an explosion, and he shook his head while lowering his chin to his chest. Clasping his hands behind his back and staring out the bulletproof windows, he could only guess at what he would need to do to contain this mess. "Colonel, I want you to get the word out. We're prepping for martial law and will actively roll out units to contain the looting and riots within twenty minutes."

The colonel hesitated, coming to stand right behind the general with a wary posture. "General? Are we really taking the side of an undead monster over our own people?"

"That monster is your queen, Colonel. And you'd best remember it." Bruner glared back over his shoulder at the stiffening man only for a moment before turn-ing back around and lifting his head up to take in a long breath of air. "Those undead across the wormhole are our own people, too. Don't make this an us-versus-them situation—talking like that is very dangerous."

The colonel silently thought over Bruner's words, then snorted. "Sir. May I speak openly?"

"You may."

"Thank you, sir. It is in my opinion, and is the opinion of most of the other officers here in command, that continuing to follow a creature that will terraform our planet into a zone of undeath is very unwise. She is a tyrant and a monster, sir—her behavior has only gotten worse with recent developments. If we don't do something now, we very well could be the last generation of humans on our planet. This is no longer a matter of political allegiance. This is a matter of racial genocide and survival. Even now we have other neighboring factions trying to contact us in a panic regarding the connection to the necropolis—"

"WE are the necropolis, Colonel." General Bruner gritted his teeth and tried to contain his anger. After all, he had told the man to speak freely. Yet he still didn't turn around, and the only sign that he was mad came from the way his right fist clenched within the grasp of his left hand behind his back. "Thank you for your opinion, Colonel. However, there will be no coup. Not today. Please lea—"

BANG

A high-powered energy weapon erupted point-blank into General Bruner's skull from the back, plastering his brains onto the window and melting a portion of the thick glass.

The colonel watched as the general's body fell dead to the ground and shakily lowered his hand, holstering his weapon while the other two officers beside him waited silently. Taking in a deep breath, the bald man turned around and marched out the door. "Begin an evacuation of the civilians from Chicago in anticipation of a fight. Contact our neighbors down the coast—all of them—for an emergency meeting, and close off access to the wormhole. No one goes in or out. This is no longer a matter of allegiance to a queen, king, or president—it is a fight for our children's future. This, gentlemen, is now a rebellion."

Snagger the ratkin warrior, his ratkin cousin Mesha, and Rashtalia, broodmother of Brood-Tarrow, were all unceremoniously thrown into a prison cell over the enraged roars of their kin in the brood halls up above.

Or at least, they had BEEN ratkin.

Their entire civilization had been changed in the blink of an eye, and these three had taken the fall for it as they were the ones who'd been closest to the Thane Necropolis. Their failure as diplomats had resulted not only in the loss of lands concerning the dwarven expedition, where the greedy vampire king had claimed the dwarvish cities as their own, but now their entire population was cursed—having become Blighted Ratkin.

Faint green mists of plague literally wafted off their bodies, oozing out of their very pores. Some of them retained patches of fur, while others had lost theirs entirely. Their bodies had become leaner, more muscular, their eyes had turned a sickly vomit-green color, their skin had turned black and gray or had partially fallen off in certain circumstances, and all their pillars and abilities had changed to reflect their undead status.

They were walking bringers of disease.

And their cries for renewed war roared in the caverns of their city while they butchered the resident necropolis diplomats in a public display.

Snagger grunted over the sound of a slamming door, bringing his muscular frame to a sitting position while staring, naked, at the ground in front of him. "How-why this happen?"

Mesha just sniffled in her own corner of the cell, not bothering to reply while curling up into her own misery.

Rashtalia, on the other hand, remained calm and collected, staring up at the ceiling where the chants of war could be heard. "The dwarf-devils will fall-die first. They are weak-raw from war with necropolis, and then queen-mother will take revenge-fight to the surface. This is a mistake-fail, and us-we will die because of it."

Snagger could only agree. He stared down at his clawed hand, where green plague continued to rise off his skin in a fog, and shook his head in dismay. He hadn't wanted this, certainly hadn't expected it, and he wasn't even sure if Allie herself had truly tried to do this. Knowing her only minimally, he still guessed that she hadn't. How would someone even attempt to do something like this?

No, this was the work of gods and devils. Of greater powers beyond themselves. Elysium had proven itself to love and strive for conflict, and this was just one more step on the path to enlightenment—a path paved in the bodies of the dead and the clashing of weapons and glorious battles.

Deepnest was to go to war, to devour the undead dwarves and take their lands before turning on the ones Snagger's queen had once called allies. Whether or not that was wise was something else entirely.

Lahn stood looking at himself in the mirror, staring blankly at his pale skin with mixed emotions. His neon-teal eyes glowed dimly, and his body . . .

His body was completely healed. His soul was repaired, and his body—for the very first time in his life—looked normal.

Or changed—perhaps—but for HIM it was more on the normal side than the shriveled husk he'd been living in all his life. He had muscles now, defined ones, and his anatomy was on par with most athletes. He was now a Deathtouched Enlightened, and it was certainly better than becoming a skresh or golem.

He actually looked really good. More or less he'd kept his human appearance, though his hair had turned a bright silky white, his skin was a medium-gray color, and his eyes were now a neon teal that glowed dimly back at him. It was mostly the same for almost everyone in the manor, as the system had given them sixty seconds to choose a new race before choosing for them—and the options given by the system were the three that allowed them to keep most of their humanlike qualities when transitioning into an undead. They were: Deathtouched Enlightened, which were supposed to be good casters and magical spellslingers; Neverlight, which were Shadow-attuned undead that could manifest various inherent shadow abilities; or Ghoul, which were well-known and had a very high pain tolerance as well as regenerative properties. Only one other in the manor had chosen Ghoul, while the rest had all gone with Deathtouched Enlightened after the system screens had shown what they would look like after picking a selected race.

Skresh was also an option, but it was marked "Not Recommended" by the system due to anatomy differences and a heavy initial toll on the psyche in most cases. Or so the system claimed.

Some of the maids were even rather excited about the change because, like vampires, Deathtouched Enlightened were physically appealing to look at.

Oddly enough, a sigil was burned into his skin across his bare, muscular chest—a sigil he recognized very well. It was bright white, burning with Holy light against his undead body, and the confusion at seeing it there was more than a little off-putting. Simultaneously, it was also encouraging.

Just what was going on? And what had Allie done to cause this?

How was the king of Dawn going to react? Even as a subservient part of a greater necropolis in recent times, Dawn still had a deeply rooted history and a sense of nationalism. Would this infuriate the populace? Lahn wasn't sure, but as the exclamations of surprise echoed throughout the manor, he flipped through the holy book Allie had once given him.

Coming to a familiar page, he stopped and stared at the rune inked onto glowing white pages in golden lettering. He looked up at the sigil on his chest, then back down to the page, and confirmed it.

They were one and the same.

The angelic summoning he'd performed, the entity that he'd called upon to save Allie's life, was still inside him. That, or a remnant of its power had embedded itself within his soul aperture.

How was that even possible? Especially now that he was undead. This shouldn't be possible, given Unholy and Holy were exact opposites. He'd heard examples in the past of different Foundational Pillars being maintained in certain individuals—but these were all extremely rare and had never once encompassed these two particular pillars due to their opposite natures.

And what exactly did that mean for him?

[Twenty-six billion current participants have been analyzed. The ranking categories are as follows: Apex rank (top 10), Paragon rank (top 1,000), S rank (top 0.0001%), A rank (top 1%), B rank (top 15%), C rank (top 30%), D rank (top 50%), E rank (bottom 50%)]
[Current Top 10 Native Participants:
1. Allie Thane, Level 160 Angel of Death, Apex rank, primary class in transitory state, Hero of Death

2. Judith Marcina, Level 176 Divine Human, Apex rank, Angelic Fallcaller, Light's Beacon
3. Aren Hrall, Level 161 Snow Giant, Apex rank, Frostmage Berserker
4. Retesh Vorath, Level 199 Corpse Lord, Apex rank, Elder Lich
5. Riven Thane, Level 134 Pureblooded Vampire, Apex rank, Warlock Devastator, Harbinger of Gluttony
6. Netithi Bluskish, Level 129 Naga, Apex rank, Champion of the Kraken
7. Chitter Teh-Sneaker, Level 137 Rat Man, Apex rank, Dark-Blade Assassin, Poison Master, Sneaky Sneak Sneaker
8. Nithkik Brutishvase, Level 140 Dark Elf, Apex rank, Depthdweller
9. Thorman Bame, Level 157 Human, Apex rank, Hammer of the Mountain
10. Sinthil Tuk'tuk, Level 168 Lizardian, Apex rank, Wind Storm]

Retesh Vorath, Corpse Lord and Elder Lich of the Black Mists, sat on a throne of bones and skulls while staring at a system screen in front of him. His bony hands clicked their clawed fingers onto the armrests of his chair while dozens of souls slowly moved about the room. Fleshy organs curled around his exposed skeleton to create unnatural formations, and a black mist continually trailed out of the eye sockets of his barren skull.

Out across his own zone of undeath in the far reaches of the northern Chaos Wastelands, far from the Thane Necropolis, his legions gathered for an assault on the living. He was the one named in world quest 1 concerning the Lich King's Plague, and he'd already had multiple crusades launched against him when the terrorized citizens of the enlightened world came into contact with what the quest actually involved.

For most, they'd just see this:

[World Quest 1, The Lich King's Plague: In the far reaches of the northern Chaos Wastelands, an ancient lich begins to stir. Advanced details are locked.]

But the quest itself was far more sinister when the advanced details were unlocked.

His clicking fingers stopped moving when he heard a knock at the door, and continuing to stare out the window that was half the size of the room—out across his massing legions—he lifted one hand.

The door swung open, and in stepped a huge, armored skresh—a death knight—who came to kneel in front of the lich with a reverent bow. "Master . . . the horde whispers . . ."

Retesh chuckled in amusement. "And what is it they whisper of, my child?"

"They wish to know what stance you have upon the new arrival of the angel, sire . . . The Scythe has blessed the lands of Umbra, and it is within your power to forge a path. The generals wish to see an alliance, and they have sent me to ask you of this . . ."

Retesh nodded his hooded head, beginning to click his clawed fingers against the bone throne again while turning his attention back to the legions. Three undead drakes and their death-knight riders flew overhead—casting shadows on the land as one of the beasts roared out across the wastes.

"I agree with them." Retesh slowly stood, the fleshy organs moving slightly and tightening around his skeleton with the attempt. "We have waited long enough and have endured much already. It is high time we finally stop enduring the attacks and begin our own crusade. Having an ally in one such as Thane Necropolis will push us far out ahead of the others, even beyond that irritating fallcaller Judith Marcina. She nearly killed me last time we fought, and I'll not risk such an encounter again without insurance. Forge a path to the southern coast, convert all the living who reside there, and take over the port city of Albakask. Then, when we have secured it, use their ships or build our own to set sail for the Thane Necropolis. Even if we can get to a point where our drakes can fly there after crossing half the ocean, establishing contact is of utmost priority."

The huge death knight hissed with excitement, standing up and slamming a fist onto his breastplate in a salute. "Yes, sire! May I ask, what of the naga and merpeople? They pursue their own world quest for domination and have already targeted our ships in the past when using the river deltas of the Pilgrim's Sea."

"Do we still have some of their krakens?"

"We have three undead krakens at our disposal. The war effort against the sea dwellers has not been kind to us, but it would also take them two months to travel around the peninsula and out of the Pilgrim's Sea and into the ocean to Albakask."

Retesh waved a dismissive hand. "Have it done. The lives of our people depend on it, for though we are strong, it is not a far-off idea that the world of the living would soon ally against us when we show our hand. Having another undead faction on Panu with powerful members such as Riven and Allie Thane is a complete change to the chessboard, and we cannot let such an opportunity go to waste."

He withdrew his fangs, licking blood off Genua's neck and pushing off from where he'd been pinning the elf thrall up against a tree. He blinked twice at the notification concerning Allie's ascension to Apex rank number one, the third time it'd been brought up to him since the initial World Quest only half an hour ago, and shrugged. "Yup, there goes the continent."

Genua let out an exasperated sigh, started putting her clothes back on, wiped some of the blood from her sternum, and clasped her hands together in front of her face with worry. Her wounds shortly sealed themselves. "Riven! This is very, very bad! I only just received the blood god's blessing and—"

"And her choices have nothing to do with you," Riven stated with a smile, patting the blonde elf woman on her head and fixing her hair before adjusting her metal headdress. "Don't think it does."

"But I'm worried that—"

"Don't be." Riven cut her off again with a raised eyebrow and a chuckle. "Yeah, I'm sure that things are going to backfire to some extent. But there's no need to worry about it until we know what those things are. We already have enough to worry about that we're certain of. None of the demons are concerned, right?"

Her face shifted to watch Athela and Azmoth where they were playing beer pong against Len and Fay, the crimson tattoo markings along her skin shimmering when she moved. "Yes, but I'm in a much different situation than they are. I'm worried this is going to blow back on me and my child."

She paused, then let her hands fall down to her stomach. "And our other child is coming soon."

His eyes followed her hands, and he had to shake himself out of the tunnel his thoughts were wandering down.

"What was it that those other priestesses said to you again?" Riven thoughtfully asked with a raised finger. "That your rise to power is tied to me, or something like that? Unless you lose your master and join their temple directly? Well, I haven't done anything that would get you in trouble, and I'm sure that we can work something out. I mean, think about it—how many vampires are out there?"

"Out where?"

"In the multiverse."

"Um . . . billions?"

Riven's look flattened, and he pulled his bag of holding to one side and started rummaging around for the completed totem he'd finally managed to build. "Probably more than that. Billions in the realm of the Blood Moon Requiem's capital planet by itself. My guess is that the number is far, far greater than that. So, theoretically, the blood god has many trillions or hundreds of trillions of vampire followers. Right?"

"Um . . . yes? Maybe?"

"Assuming that's correct, why would he be so irritated about Allie's shift in allegiance? My guess is she's not worth as much to that god as we're thinking, and it's not like he outright proclaimed that she was to die or anything like that. She'll probably just be shunned from vampire society." He paused thoughtfully. "At least I hope so."

Genua shifted nervously, but then nodded and gave in. "I suppose I haven't been contacted about it, so maybe you're right. I know they can reach out to me at will through the clergy system . . . it's all silent."

"See?! Nothing to be worried about." Riven patted her shoulder and casually set his single floating totem—his work in progress—on a large stump before clicking his tongue thoughtfully. It was certainly not the best totem ever made, not even by a long shot, but to his knowledge not many people on this planet were using totems or able to build them. With the taxation using system stores, it made a lot of sense to just make them himself. And to his knowledge there were an estimated two dozen Elysium altars at this current time, and the only one that had an affinity was controlled by him.

As for the totem—it was an icosahedron, essentially a twenty-sided die, but much larger than the dice from board games. It had twenty triangular faces on the outer surface, each face holding a rune, and was about one-by-one-by-one foot in dimensions. He'd gone through a grand total of thirty-two attempts before settling on this as a temporary final product, but he'd probably expand upon it at some later date. He'd crafted it from metal while using his magic to slice into the steel plates on the outer skeleton. Inside he'd placed ground bone to help house the soul and a couple of Shadow-attuned plants, and he had reinforced the insides with Crimson Ice and something called Black Norstone that the locals here mined.

He would have used better materials for a better outcome, as different materials were more or less potent concerning what runes and abilities he was infusing into the totem, but he worked with what he had.

And the result was not bad, even if he had only enough stuff to make a single one.

[Partially Constructed Totem of Bloodforged Rift Sparks: Status page is currently on standby. Soul acquired, affinity to Shadow acquired, sigils acquired. Totem soul is currently absorbing the minor sigil of Black Lightning and will reach comprehension sometime within the next week. Unable to bind at this time.]

He turned the totem around on the stump, watching the runes on each triangular face light up with a mixture of red and black energies. The soul inside it touched his own, and it shuddered when he sent a pulse of warm intentions into it.

During the past couple days, he'd come to understand just one single thing that he'd seemed to have missed during his previous studies of totems. It was that, despite some people using totems that were only controlled by soul shards, those who used entire souls actually created what was essentially a body or a vessel for that particular soul.

How aware that soul was . . . that was an entirely different question. He had no idea. He didn't even know if it was the soul itself or the brain of the organism that dictated awareness or thought patterns, and it was something he'd have to ask Allie about later on in case she knew.

Or perhaps Instructor Pladius from the Blood Moon Requiem's compound . . .

Yeah. Actually, that wasn't such a bad idea.

Perhaps he'd even go today. Heading back to Brightsville was probably a priority anyway, given Allie's recent ascent, and he didn't know just how people of the necropolis would take recent events.

Especially all the elves, orcs, dwarves, goblins, ratkin, and humans who had been turned into undead variants of themselves. Not to mention the other cities or small countries that'd started developing on what the system called Umbra—their continent.

He might have a riot on his hands by the time he got back.

CHAPTER 25

Colonel Landers slapped aside a rock that one of the civilians threw his way as the boos and roars of disapproval echoed in his ears. The press conference was not going well, and his strike against the Thanes by taking down General Bruner and the mayor of Chicago were being seen by a lot of the population as a power grab by a tyrant—despite the Thanes' world-ending potential. Two of the news stations were even openly painting him as a villain without even attempting to hide their disgust—with calls for the people to rise up or wait for Riven to arrive and reclaim the city.

What shortsightedness.

It appeared that there were still just as many supporters of the Thanes as there were people scared enough to want this rebellion, and his orders to block off the wormhole had led to a bloodbath between groups of their own people as firefights erupted across dissenters and loyalists who still remembered how Riven had saved them all during the Azag Hive Cluster's attack. That same picture was being painted here to a lesser extent between people in the crowd and news stations, with many small fights happening within the crowds and guards needing to take many people away in handcuffs over the immense amount of angry shouting, smack dab in the middle of downtown Chicago.

Many of these people also still had family on the other side that had been changed into undead but had still managed to contact their families, and the blockade had seen many of those same people trying to get home jailed or outright killed in the small battles or firefights at the wormhole's entrance.

His plans were not unfolding as he'd intended, but thankfully he'd been planning for this moment a very long time. Rebellions were not born within hours, and Colonel Landers had been preparing this one ever since realizing his fellow citizens of Earth had been led down a spiraling, sinful path.

A path led by monstrous vampires.

By bloodsucking abominations, and his assumptions on the two Thane siblings had only been validated by Allie's brutal actions concerning the Tereen elves—or how Riven had taken the side of overgrown rats over the more humanlike dwarves. Allie was even called the butcher of Carnis after wiping out an entire army of high elves, not taking any prisoners, torturing their officers, and burning down the entire town as the elf civilians inside screamed and begged for mercy.

She was evil, and back on Earth this kind of behavior never would have held water in any civilized country. She needed to be put down.

The balding man turned around and left the stage without looking back, realizing that his attempts to calm the populace by public opinion weren't going to work—and that he'd have to resort to more violent methods after all.

Not that it mattered. He was doing this for the good of the planet, and for his children's children. He would not let Panu fall into the hands of treacherous monsters such as these, especially now that Allie had sped up that timeline of worldwide disaster when she gained the ability to terraform.

Adjusting his nano-tech armor suit, Colonel Landers was flanked by four other cyborgs carrying guns. They walked past a guarded perimeter and into the downtown building he'd been using as a base of operations to plan this rebellion. Others just like him, ones who'd joined his cause over the past months, had been recruited to help organize what he'd already known was coming.

A woman in uniform saluted at his approach near an elevator going up as other military personnel walked back and forth or through the halls, adjusting her posture to be even straighter than it'd been before. "Sir! The Romanovs are waiting for you upstairs."

"Thank you, Private." Colonel Landers didn't even look her way and continued onto the elevator with his escort, hitting the button and clasping his hands behind his back as the elevator doors shut.

Ten stories later and with a ding, those same doors opened up into a long hallway leading directly to a set of double doors. Six of his own men were positioned on the left side, while six other figures were standing opposite them; dressed in familiar black sunglasses, trench coats, shortly cut uniform sets of hair, and dark-purple vests. None of them carried any weapons, or at least they didn't APPEAR to do so, but he knew better. These Russians weren't anything to mess around with.

The doors swung open, and inside a pristine white room with silver furniture and a sky-top view of the city were two more men and a woman wearing similar trench coats. They were some of the higher-ups of the Romanov mafia family, which had excelled in the integration and built a solid foundation for a budding empire farther down the southern coast. They'd conquered a small kingdom from one of the other two merged worlds already, and had two of their members in the Paragon's top thousand ranker list—both of whom were standing here in this very room.

These were the colonel's insurance policy against the Thanes. He only needed to catch one of the Thane siblings alone and isolated while the other was away.

It **was** possible.

[Vilari Romanov, Level 119 Arcane Assassin, Human Elite]
[Helena Romanov, Level 123 Arcane Assassin, Human Elite]
[Brutis Romanov, Level 108 Arcane Assassin, Human Elite]

Vilari had distinctly chiseled features and a scar running down his left cheek. He leaned back on a couch, arms folded. His sister, Helena Romanov, had long brown hair and a tight-lipped demeanor as she sipped on a glass of vodka. Brutis remained hunched over, hooded, and appeared to be half asleep—though Colonel Landers was pretty sure this was to put people off their guard rather than truly a case of exhaustion.

"You're late!" Helena muttered irritably in a heavy Russian accent, setting down her crystal glass of alcohol and spitting to the side. "We've prepared months for this and NOW you decide to become lazy? Do you realize what kind of prize Elysium will grant us if we're able to kill a Legendary-ranked world boss? Please do not jeopardize our plans by stalling because you want to maintain a good public image."

Colonel Landers glared at the woman, but then remembered whom he was glaring at and quickly took a seat across from her. The eyes of the three Russians followed him, and his escort took up positions behind him on the back side of the silver couch. "You were right, I should have made the call sooner. Be assured that before you leave here today, the men under my command will make quick work of whatever naysayers remain on this side of the portal."

"And Brightsville?" Helena asked curiously, twirling a strand of her dark-brown hair between two fingers while crossing her legs.

"It is already done," Colonel Landers confirmed with a curt nod. "The bombs all went off as expected—we massacred all the undead around the opposite side of the wormhole. We also left Bruner's head as a warning with an attached message for whenever Riven's locked ability teleports him back. It should be enough to enrage him and force him to act. He'll be coming across soon enough."

"Any VIPs killed?"

"By the blast? No one else in their leadership was confirmed dead outside of General Bruner, but Allie is far underground at this point and has lost contact with anyone topside, and Riven is sure to come barreling through that wormhole as soon as he figures out what happened."

Vilari Romanov chuckled, a deep, masculine growl. "You are pretty brutal, Colonel Landers. I did not truly expect you to follow through on your end of the deal."

Colonel Landers gave the other, bigger man a deep-set scowl. "Unlike you three, who are in it for the power and treasures Elysium will grant you for the kill, I am in it to save our planet. I am fighting for the very right of our species to live on Panu. Of course I would hold up my end of the deal."

Helena rolled her eyes. "You've been playing this game of betrayal far too long to claim that; we've been planning this for months now. I think you may just find vampires and undead as subhuman creatures not worthy of you, or perhaps it is the negative Charisma everyone on the forums keeps talking about. But truthfully the reasons why don't matter to me. Even if I do think you're just like us in many ways."

Colonel Landers flatly ignored the woman, turning his head to Vilari Romanov—the leader of their group and the other Paragon ranker aside from

Helena. "You guaranteed me that you'd be able to finish Riven off whenever he comes through. Are you sticking by that?"

The Russians all snorted simultaneously, and Vilari sat up straight. "Of course. We wouldn't be here if we didn't think we could do it, obviously. It is known that Riven is weak against rogues and assassins, and we are some of the very best. Do you have the wormhole locked down?"

"No, there is some infighting going on between my men and the loyalists, but they'll be crushed soon enough. Most of the ones standing in our way are either being dealt with now or are already imprisoned or dead."

"Will you be able to activate the seclusion rune to lock him down?" Helena asked, pulling out a silver-infused dagger the size of her forearm and licking one side of the blade with a giggle. "I'd rather he not try to run!"

Chuckles from her two comrades echoed in the pristine white room, and Colonel Landers gave her a nod. "We've had it functional for a long time now—we integrated it into the defensive measures originally set up under the guise of additional monitoring enchantments. Some of our very best mechanics were on the job. When he arrives, the trap will trigger. You'll be notified and you'll be able to take him out without much of a fight . . ."

Colonel Landers narrowed his eyes in concern when he saw Helena's left eye begin to collect a tear of blood underneath the eyelid before it dripped down her pale white cheek. Nothing else seemed amiss, though, and she didn't even seem to notice. "Helena, are you all right?"

Helena's eyebrows furrowed, and another dagger flipped out of a sheath along her hip. "Of course I'm all right!"

CRUNCH

Simultaneously both of her arms swung back, crashing each dagger through the throats and into the cervical spines of both Vilari and Brutis with the activation of a piercing martial art. Both immediately went limp, wide-eyed, and crumpled to the floor. Colonel Landers attempted to scramble back in shock.

However, he didn't make it more than a couple of inches off the couch before a thin red thread was wrapped around his neck and yanked back—choking him, pulling him onto the couch, and cutting deep into his skin.

He flailed, using his abnormally high strength to try and peel away from whatever assassin was attempting to strangle him—and his stamina channels flared while attempting to activate various abilities.

Not only did he not succeed, but not a single one of his abilities activated before being snuffed out by a localized and overwhelming aura of dread.

He coughed, choked, flailed, and spluttered as the room around him began to change.

What had once been a pristine white room was now covered in blood. Tables at the far end were overturned, and the guards in the hallway that'd been there earlier were now disemboweled, nailed to the walls, or hung from the ceiling in death.

Along with the change in the red-splattered room came the figures of two very recognizable demons and a third woman Colonel Landers did not recognize. On one side of the opposite couch was the blue-skinned succubus Fay, who had a mischievous grin on her face while her slender black tail slapped against the cushions to the right of Vilari's twitching body like a dog's would. Behind her was Azmoth, who looked rather bored with all four arms folded in front of him. Then, lastly, there was a hooded blonde woman with crimson tattoos—wearing a red metal headdress over a formfitting black robe, sitting in a meditative pose farther beyond the couch while some kind of Blood-based ability was being channeled around her.

The succubus whispered something into Helena's ear, and the woman responded in kind by answering her as more blood continued running out of her eyes—a wide smile plastered across her face.

Fay and the arcane assassin continued speaking in hushed whispers for a couple minutes until Fay eventually nodded and looked across the room to a hooded figure standing next to a window—looking out at the crowds far below where brawls and acts of unrest were continuing to break out.

Colonel Landers wasn't being completely strangled yet, given that the person behind him was letting him gasp from time to time, but he was still in a state of panic. However, he felt himself go absolutely cold upon seeing Riven Thane, and the colonel began to fight even harder to try and squirm out of what was essentially an unbreakable wire cutting into his neck.

"We're finished obtaining your requested information," Fay stated, standing up and bowing to her master with an elegant swish of her long white hair.

Riven didn't reply, but nodded and began walking their way. His bootsteps clicked against the white tile floor before splashing in puddles of blood until he came to a stop in front of Helena Romanov with a stoic expression. Raising one hand, claws of crystallized blood began to form over his fingers and he gripped the assassin's face while lifting her up off the floor.

She continued to bleed from her eyes while her body hung limply in his grip, but Colonel Landers could tell she was now regaining some of her own functions from whatever spell, ability, or ritual these people were casting by the way her muscles started twitching and she began to hiss between bouts of seemingly random jerks.

His eyes flicked toward the meditating woman channeling some kind of ability on the couch nearby, an elf by the looks of it, and then he went back to staring at the scene in front of him.

Riven's single, clawed hand began to grip harder, and a loud whimper began to come out of Helena's lips when his fingers started digging into her skin. Cuts turned into deep gashes, and Helena let out a muffled sob while her body continued to jerk as something in her jawbone snapped.

CRUNCH

Helena's eyes went wide, and with a shriek her head exploded in a shower of gore.

The assassin's body dropped to the ground like a rag doll and joined the other two Romanovs.

"Mr. Landers . . ." Riven stated calmly, taking a seat where Helena had been sitting only a minute ago—scooting her carcass over to make way for his legs with a few pokes of his boot. His red eyes calmly evaluated the partially asphyxiated military man while his fingers interlaced. "It appears that we've come to a conclusion concerning your attempted rebellion quite a bit faster than General Bruner had anticipated. I must admit, I hadn't expected Allie to transcend like she did—but as soon as I saw the worldwide notification, I assumed whoever you were working with would likely take the opportunity to show themselves. It would be now or never, so to speak, because you wouldn't risk taking us both on at the same time after Allie's power-up. Oh no, that'd be too risky, and you'd all prepared for it for so, so long."

The door to the room opened up again, and the familiar form of General Bruner stepped inside—accompanied by a couple of the elites of the necropolis—cyborgs, death knights, deathtouched enlightened, and necromancers flowed inside to silently wait on the sidelines while Colonel Landers just gawked.

"Lookalike zombies can be a tricky thing to distinguish from the real deal if your necromancer is good enough. You never actually killed General Bruner," Riven stated flatly, stifling a yawn and shaking his head. "It really is a shame that people had to die for this, but your actions would have likely caused far more deaths if we'd just killed you and didn't put this situation with the Romanovs down early. They were very sneaky bastards. Even when they arrived here and fell into our own trap, it took quite a bit of time for Genua to possess the woman. I'm not sure Genua would have been able to do it at all given the level discrepancy, but the drugged vodka and mana suppression helped. Fay had to work extra hard to keep the hallucinations around all of you going, and the combination of Fay's Silvertongue plus Genua's possession allowed us to dig through Helena's mind quite easily. Thank you, though, for delivering them right to us. Now that they're out of the way, I think I'll be paying the rest of their mafia family a little visit as a reminder that I am not above killing thousands of people to get a point across. Not anymore, anyways. Now . . ."

Riven gestured the colonel's way, and strings of blood snaked through the air before tightening around Colonel Landers's phone. The threads plucked the phone right out of the man's pocket and set it on the table in between the two couches where Helena's half-finished glass of vodka still rested.

With a single finger, Riven pressed the button to turn the phone on—and he turned it around for Colonel Landers to get a good look at the screen.

"Call off your men and publicly surrender. People are dying needlessly right now. Athela, you can let up on the string."

Immediately Colonel Landers gasped and began coughing violently when Athela's thread retracted and the archdemon lowered her head to whisper a chuckle into the pale man's ear.

"I will do no such thing!" Colonel Landers hissed, shaking in his seat. "You are an abomination! Your sister will lead us into disaster! We cannot—"

Riven interrupted him with a flick of his wrist, and a spike of Crimson Ice tore through Colonel Landers's right knee.

The man screamed, dropping to the ground and writhing in pain while Riven stared emotionlessly at him.

Riven glanced down at the time displayed on the other man's phone, then let out a soft, slow exhale. "General Bruner, bring his wife in here. I'm sure once we start prying off her fingers one by one with pliers, he might be more willing to cooperate with us."

CHAPTER 26

Gaia stood atop hills of vampire corpses, remnants of the Rippenvire forces that'd come from their imprisonment in the Stockyards. The transformed demigoddess was already incredibly displeased at the change she'd undergone, and she'd been even more angry that they'd targeted harmless civilians on the outskirts of Brightsville when finally encountering resistance. Bodies could be repaired and evolved, shaped into what she'd want after time had passed, but the loss of life from people she had promised to protect could not so easily be forgiven.

And her arrival at the scene had led to a very swift and brutal end for all those involved.

Instead of the small childlike figure she'd once worn, her new body was now that of an enormous, carnivorous tree. Her roots buried themselves into the mounds of drying-up flesh as they sucked in the lifeblood of the vampires she stood on. Her dark-gray bark had pulsing red veins running up into bright-red leaves. Spiked vines trailed off her branches and trunk and dragged the few vampires who were still alive toward her. The vines sucked up their bodily fluids and drained them just as easily as they drained mortals—leaving only withered husks behind before smashing them into dust.

Her gray skin, her bark, snapped and crunched while she moved, arms swaying at her sides, taking her step by step over the battlefield and smashing corpses underneath her weight. Slowly, monotonously, she and the other turned dryads who'd become Unholy treeants alongside her were juggernauts of destruction shambling toward their enemies. Each step they took shook the earth.

And all the while, her pitch-black eyes were dead set—staring out the wooden face carved into the front of her midtrunk while the vampires gathered up again for a counterattack. So enraged the vampires were at having their god shunned by Allie Thane, so firm was their belief, that they'd become fanatical—disregarding their own lives in an attempt to wreak havoc and pain on the offending team.

But Gaia had her own anger to dish out, and it was her rage that would overcome. She did not blame Allie for what had happened, but she needed an outlet to vent her wrath.

The leaves in her canopy rustled and billowed, whipping up and tearing off her branches in a storm of red leaves that was soon joined by the numerous others of her newly born kin. The sky was soon filled, and—sharpening—the raging storm of leaves bore down on Gaia's enemies.

Allie gently glided down, farther and farther, until her bone-made boots touched lightly on the surface of an exquisite stone mosaic. The souls of the dead, many of them the precursors she'd only recently killed that she'd forced into submission, were leading her through the passages at a fast pace. Unfortunately their minds were mostly jumbled, and she felt like the touch of some foreign entity had made it so that she'd be unable to access any valuable information they might have.

And yet, that foreign entity had still allowed her to access the path down.

That troubled her, but she had nothing else to go on, and the labyrinth was enormous.

Aztec-like designs similar to the jewelry and armbands the precursors wore decorated the flat, perfectly circular art piece many hundreds of yards across—depicting various kinds of worship to an ancient, long-forgotten deity. The creature they worshipped, prayed to, and sacrificed victims to was a one-eyed, fanged creature with pale-blue skin, four humanoid arms, and feathered wings as black as hers.

Behind her, and carried by ghosts and phantoms under her command, were all the other necromancers she'd brought with her, alongside Fimrindle, who looked uncharacteristically sheepish after the hard glare she'd given him earlier. They hadn't talked yet, but that was certainly going to happen after she'd learned of his actions from the spirits.

Allie continued over to the far wall, her silver-gray halo lightly glowing the same color of her eyes while her footsteps clicked against the mosaic. Ahead of her was another tunnel entrance ripped from the side of the deep shaft they'd floated down—and beside it on two large spikes were a set of impaled naked bodies she didn't recognize. However, these were vampire bodies—and not the precursor type. Gingerly touching the silent scream on one's face, she closed her eyes and reached into the void.

The soul still attached to it flickered in her mind's eye, only brief images of the previous life it'd had lighting up in her mind, and soon the transfer of knowledge was over with. She was lucky it hadn't been lost to the beyond yet, and smiled while retracting her hand. It was too damaged to salvage, so she bade it farewell and let the little soul drift into the darkness.

"Survivors of the Bernzee covens came this way," Allie stated confidently, folding her wings tightly behind her and starting down the tunnel. "We're on the right path after all. Follow me."

Twists and turns, signs of recent battle, and dried bloodstains plastering the ancient scripts of the hallways the labyrinth was building were seen in abundance. Leading out into large caves, the tunnels soon disappeared entirely—letting Allie's group bask in the amazing sight of an entirely new world underneath the top layer of Panu's crust.

A false sun radiated light down into the world, though it was far dimmer than the real version and was partially obscured by clouds and mists that also blocked off most of the ceiling. The cavern before them was so wide she couldn't see the opposite end, having numerous dips and mountains within it that hinted at more landscapes being blocked from view, so Allie had no real measure of its true size. She stood at the edge of a cliff, the ground at least a solid mile below. There were stone steps leading downward across the cliff edge and into a marsh, where an entire ecosystem was brilliantly colored with a tapestry of yellows, reds, blacks, greens, and oranges.

And there, far in the distance, was a flat-topped pyramid that dwarfed even the tallest skyscrapers from Brightsville.

This was not what she'd been expecting, but it was certainly beautiful.

[You have entered the Fallen Vampiric Elder God's Realm. World Quest 4 update available.]

[World Quest 4, Blood of the Fallen God: An unnamed vampiric elder god has fallen from grace after having sinned against the Elysium administrator. The elder god has been trapped within a hidden, guarded labyrinth in the deepest levels of the underdark, and you must stop him from awakening. Advanced details HAVE BEEN PARTIALLY UNLOCKED:

- UPDATE 1: You have found clues to the labyrinth's location in the depths of the underdark, the resting place of the fallen vampiric elder god, but found yourself cornered by heretics in defiance of the one true mantle of the Blood God. Why did the native vampires here in Bernzee contact you for help? What was the reason that they journeyed out from the deep parts of the world to do so? Your answers will be found at the labyrinth's location, should you manage to survive.

- UPDATE 2: You have been led through the labyrinth by the souls of the dead and have found a fragment of what was once the inner world of the fallen elder god—though his current state does not allow him to retain it within his soul any longer. You still do not know why you were contacted by the Bernzee covens, but signs of their flight through the underdark point to their trek leading here. Find out what the distant temple holds, and perhaps even find the last of the Bernzee covens—if they remain, for more answers.]

"Fimrindle." Her head turned, glowing gray eyes shifting to the reaper with a stoic expression as he bowed. The irritation in her built just by looking at him, but then her eyes fell upon his status screen—and then hers . . . and she let the tension in her shoulders relax slightly.

[Fimrindle, Level 159 Reaper of Souls Initiate, Demon-Undead Hybrid, Unique: the Iron Scarecrow. LEGENDARY.]
[Allie Thane, Level 160 Angel of Death, primary class in transitory state, Hero of Death, Lost Princess of the Blood Moon Requiem, Apostate of the Blood God. LEGENDARY. PANU WORLD BOSS FOR WORLD QUEST 7.]

"Yes, Mistress?" the reaper asked, black cloak made from shadows billowing around him like a living thing. His metal hands gripped his scythe and he got onto his knees in a bowing position, head lowered subserviently. "What is it that you ask of me?"

Allie gestured to the temple in the distance as roars echoed far from down below. She kept her eyes locked on the distant building despite the swarming hundreds and then thousands of precursors tearing through the forests and marshlands in her direction. "Find out what resides there, and if you can, find the Bernzee refugees. Do not die, Fimrindle, for even though your contract is unique and you are a partially demonic entity, I am not sure I'd be able to summon you back if I am not present to take your soul. Have you ever died under contract before?"

"I have not, Mistress."

"Then you do not know, either?"

"I believe I'd be able to come back unless skewered with a blade blessed by the commandments, similar to how Athela was killed previously."

"I see. Regardless, be careful. We will talk more about your scheming later . . . I am still not pleased that you put my life in danger so flippantly—despite the outcomes."

Fimrindle nodded abruptly, then turned and vanished in the blink of an eye.

The other necromancers were now gathered along the cliff's edge as well. They all watched the incoming swarm of angry, desperate, and crazed people of another age racing toward them up the stone steps in the cliff's face, watched them literally claw their way up the side of the steep drop by tearing their claws into stone.

"They are like rabid animals . . ." Mara growled as the howls drew nearer. "I have only seen this kind of fanaticism in mindless undead, not in those who are still sentient."

Allie opened her spatial sack and pulled out the weapon the Scythe had given her. The long, gray blade flared with neon-teal runes as she held it aloft—and she admired the wicked edge on either side that came down to a handle engraved with depictions of hooded wraiths and skeletons.

[Blade of Soulcry (Divine Claymore, E-Grade, Death Attuned): ???]

"I believe they are desperate," Allie eventually said after getting a feel for the weight of the weapon—allowing the energies inside the claymore to merge with her own in a wave of energy that almost shocked her system.

She blinked a couple times to regain her composure, then shuddered as she felt the weapon's energy stabilize when the intertwining mana channels that were somehow built into the blade connected to hers.

Mara, Nin, Vin, and two of the other necromancers glanced her way curiously while the others continued peering over the ledge at the oncoming horde.

"What do you mean?" Mara asked. "Why desperate?"

"Those are the remnant emotions their souls leave behind," Allie stated sadly, sinking the blade a foot deep into the stone floor rather easily before turning to look at the others who'd followed her here. "They may have a quest of their own, such as to keep their elder god safe until he awakens in five years. That's only a guess, but it's certainly a possibility. What happens if they don't? Will they be hunted down or completely wiped out by Elysium itself? Are they tied to him somehow? Whatever the reason, they certainly aren't going to talk to us about it—but that doesn't mean we won't fight back. It is us or them until proven otherwise."

Allie pulled up another notification screen under her status page and grinned. Forming a guild would increase their XP share, and if she was about to wipe the floor with thousands of enemies, she wanted to make sure her loyalists ascended with her climb.

It was hard to find good employees, or good friends.

[You must create a guild with the Create Guild command prior to utilizing this page. You must have at least three people to create a guild.]

Mentally she selected all twelve of the necromancers standing nearby. Each of them whipped their heads around to stare at her as they got their own notifications, then eagerly selected the option to agree to the terms.

"Create Guild—Fallen Wings."

[Guild Name: Fallen Wings
Guild World Rank: 5
Current World Registered: Panu
Guild Roster: 13/20
- **Allie Thane, Level 160, primary class in transitory state, Guild Leader**
- **Mara Tovane, Level 82, Voidstar Necromancer**
- **Vin Kal, Level 83, Blight Necromancer Adept**
- **Nin Kal, Level 80, Blight Necromancer Adept**
- **Alastar, Level 71, Swarm Necromancer Adept**
- **Enivia, Level 70, Bloodsoaked Necromancer Adept**
- **Porish, Level 79, Blight Necromancer Adept**
- **Letti, Level 81, Swarm Necromancer Adept**
- **Zakarivi, Level 75, Curselore Necromancer**
- **Quesilina, Level 69, Haunted Necromancer Adept**
- **Bret, Level 66, Necromancer Farcaster**

- Rush, Level 74, Twilight Necromancer
- David, Level 78, Necromancer Deathsworn

Faction: None, link to a faction network of guilds for this feature to become available

- Faction Archives and Forums: N/A
- Faction Wars: N/A
- Other Guilds in Faction: N/A
- System Faction Events and Invites: None

Current Guild Bonuses:

- Tier 1 guild, XP share bonus set at baseline of 5%
- Guild Shops: None, link to a merchant-class attendant for this option to become available
- Guild Hall: None, link to guild hall for this feature to become available
- Attendants: N/A
- Homeward Teleportation: N/A
- Guild Investments: None, link to an Elysium fund for this feature to become available

System Guild Events, Raids, Quests, and Invites:

- World Quest 4, Blood of the Fallen God
- Guild Titles and Achievements: None
- Guild Blessings: None
- Mercenary Status: Available]

[With creation of your guild Fallen Wings, World Quest 4, Blood of the Fallen God, has been applied to your guild information. All XP will now have a bonus of 5% to total original XP and will be distributed across all guild members who are involved in the battle to at least a small degree.]

Allie reviewed the information twice over and gave a satisfactory nod. Now that she was sure her efforts would benefit her friends, too, she took her wand in her left hand and gripped the handle of her sword in her right. "Hold the top of the cliff, I will be supporting you from the skies."

With a blur of motion, she bent her knees, spread her wings, and launched herself off the cliff's edge—soaring into the air and reveling in the feeling of her newfound power of flight. It was even better than riding Tyranus, but she did wish the drake could have fit down here in the tunnels of the underdark—he'd certainly have been a massive help.

Turning in the air and raising her wand, strings of death mana exploded from her position and ripped downward into the swarm racing up the cliff face. The necromancers on the ledge began to conjure magics of their own, pouring clouds of noxious green fumes over the side while flares of neon-teal fire, bone spikes, and clouds of Shadow-made crows came over the edge like an avalanche.

Area-of-effect magics came soon after, with black diagrams and pentagrams drawing themselves in the air over the necromancers' defensive position that empowered them and created one-way barriers at various stages down the cliff—making it harder for the swarm to climb up.

Allie continued to carve out huge swaths of the incoming enemies, dragging the strings of death from her wand across the cliff face and spraying rubble and body parts—somewhat akin to carving open a watermelon with a chain saw. Screams erupted from the abnormally fast precursors and soon she found herself bombarded with various magics of a deep-blue color, similar to the strange blood attacks she'd experienced the day before.

She merely shrugged them off, deflecting one blue orb after the other with a swipe of her claymore. The blade shattered the spells and took zero damage despite dispelling so much energy. And as they became more numerous—enemies pouring out of the woods to race upward or fire mana-infused projectiles her way while she dodged and wove in the air while continuing to blast those climbing up the cavern toward her friends—she began muttering the incantation for her Tier-3 spell Eye of the Scythe.

Her arms and hands made the proper movements, and a tear in space overhead covered the land in teal light as the eye of some malevolent god looked down at the incoming horde with disgust.

Bodies withered, precursors screamed, and the land underneath them shattered under the force of her newly empowered mana channels that flooded the skill with everything she had. The Blade of Soulcry in her hand responded as well, simmering with the power of True Death, as an explosion of gray engulfed a mile-wide area in an immense aura of power.

Karlita gagged and coughed, spitting bile and nearly tripping over her own feet while desperately trying to claw at the door for some kind of latch or switch. Her red eyes were producing streams of tears that glistened against her pale cheeks, and her heartbeat thudded in her chest over the deep gasps she made while the screams of her friends and family echoed in the chamber beyond.

"Please! By the blood god, there has to be something here!!! We've come so far!"

Her nails scratched against an ancient, rusted lock—catching and pulling out dirt from what was obviously a keyhole.

Her eyes brightened, and with a strangulated, terrified laugh she fumbled the key in her hands to bring it toward the lock.

It fit.

"YESSSS!!!" Karlita screamed in victory, and she heard the mechanism click when she turned it in her hand.

The huge door groaned, then swung open in a showering spray of dust and debris.

She only backed up a moment, but one look over her shoulder told her that she needed to move now and fast.

"KARLITA, WAIT FOR ME!" her elder sister called back to her—scrambling through the small hallway and shoving another of their coven to the side, but the precursors were on her heels.

Karlita couldn't wait. Otherwise, they'd both die.

With a look of shame and stifling a sob, Karlita only held the door open the briefest moment to see her sister's heel get caught by a diving, pale-blue abomination that quickly started dragging her back.

Her sister screamed in horror as a jagged claw cut into her calf muscle. "KARLITA, HELP ME!!!"

Karlita's heart clenched, and with a sob she slammed the door behind her. The mechanism locked back into place, and through the thick stone slab she could hear her sister's horrified screams, sobs, and begging echo through the chamber until the sounds of crunching, muffled gags, and gurgles came next.

Soon the battle had stopped, leaving Karlita as the very last living vampire of the Bernzee covens on the face of Panu.

Shaking violently and pulling herself into a fetal position, she continued to cry for the next few hours until she managed to finally fall into a light sleep . . . only one full of nightmares, regrets, and horrors.

CHAPTER 27

Riven sat in a chair overlooking the city while a bloodied Colonel Landers lay curled in the fetal position not far off. The mental toll of having watched an illusionary replica of his wife undergo brutal torture for over twenty minutes had done a real number on him, though he'd somewhat recovered after realizing it was faked just to get him to call off his men.

"The last remnants of rebellions in Chicago are nearly put down; it will be completed within the hour," General Bruner stated plainly, hands clasped behind his back and standing next to Riven's chair. "Gaia has crushed an uprising stemming from where we kept all those Rippenvire soldiers. A few of them held back, but all other vampires were killed. Gaia wishes to speak with Allie about her changes when the queen gets back, Your Majesty. I do not believe she is happy, but I don't think she holds animosity toward your sister for what happened, either."

"What of Deepnest?" Riven asked, not taking his eyes off the city streets below where hundreds of rebels had been chained up in lines—more adding to their number as the hours passed.

General Bruner cleared his throat uncomfortably. "Communication lines from our forces in the underdark have gone silent. Both from the diplomats stationed in Deepnest right after they sent that final message, and from our forces occupying the two dwarvish cities we conquered not long ago."

Riven clicked his tongue in irritation, standing slowly and holding out both arms. Messenger flashed behind him and opened up wide, clamping down along his upper body and sealing his head shut in the ivory helmet. Jackal came next, jumping up from its squatting position on the floor and changing from canine to spear-staff form in an instant. The metal greaves came last, and Riven turned around to eye the general with a calm and collected gaze from behind the metal encasing his face. "Repeat the last message those diplomats sent, just one more time for me. I'd like to make sure I wasn't hearing things."

General Bruner grimaced, but kept himself composed and his posture straight. "I believe it was 'The ratkin queen seeks vengeance.' That was the last relayed message before all coms were cut."

Riven took in a deep breath, then exhaled slowly, turning back to the window one final time. "I see. Are there any other rebellions or betrayals I need to know about?"

General Bruner shook his head. "No, my king. Dawn and Tereen remain in a state of shock but have had no uprisings or social problems outside of a few pockets of very upset priests from one of Dawn's temples. The elves were more or less beaten into submission a while ago and have caused us no problems."

Riven nodded then created a portal through Jackal's perk. "I'll be back later. Keep things under control in my absence. Contact Gurth'Rok and Dr. Brass if you need any help, though I've heard they're rather busy themselves at the moment."

"May I start things off with a retaliatory strike first, my king?"

"I do believe that's in order as long as we keep our losses to a minimum. Those Russian mafia guys have it coming, so you have my full permission to utilize whatever forces you desire to accomplish this—but don't get too aggressive without me. That'd just result in needless casualties, and they've built up a small empire of their own from the reports you sent me. In fact . . ."

Riven gestured to Athela. "She'll be staying with you to help. That way I'll be sure your men have a real siege breaker in my absence. Crush them into dust."

Athela grinned widely with a clap of her hands and a giggle—and General Bruner nodded in appreciation.

With a snap of Riven's fingers, his two other demons and Genua all filed through the portal—leaving General Bruner behind in the tower with Athela, a few officers and necromancers of the necropolis, and the sobbing colonel-turned-traitor.

Bruner snorted the colonel's way only after a half minute of staring, then gestured to one of the guards. "Get him in a cell, and make sure he doesn't ever see the light of day. Prepare the pilots for all able jets and helicopters. Have the drone fleets activated. Set up a perimeter around our lands on this side of Riven's Eye Wormhole. Get me King Arthur Brix of Dawn on the line—I'll need to borrow some of his airships, rocs, and drake riders."

"Sir?" the man replied, confused at the last statement the general made—but starting to pull Colonel Landers across the room with the help of one other man. "I know it isn't my place—but do you intend to bring the entire armada? We're still recovering from our battle against Rippenvire."

General Bruner raised an eyebrow and then nodded. "We are declaring war, Captain Blare. Of course we're using the entire fleet; those Romanovs have it coming. Who was it that said, and I quote, 'I know not with what weapons World War III will be fought, but World War IV will be fought with sticks and stones'?"

"It was Albert Einstein, sir. And I believe we're about to find out what World War III is finally capable of, given our queen's recent ascent."

"That was a rhetorical question, you imbecile. Now get that traitorous bastard in a cell and get me Arthur Brix!"

Over the tunnel's usually guarded entrance leading into Deepnest's main cavern swung two ghoul bodies, hung from the ceiling where they'd been mutilated beyond recognition. Their skin was also marked with some kind of disease, almost like boils and pockmarks, aside from the deep cuts where they'd obviously been stabbed numerous times.

But the signet rings Allie had given them, marked with a winged vampire skull, were still recognizable—sending the message that these were indeed the diplomats of the Thane Necropolis.

It was one of many symbols that Allie had been considering as a potential flag for their budding empire, but she hadn't decided yet and Riven honestly didn't care what she chose.

Of more concern at the moment was the fact that they'd killed the two diplomats. No other words needed to be spoken—he knew what it meant.

The other thing that bothered him was that this tunnel was absolutely deserted. Usually it was bustling with trading caravans or at least had people posted here to make sure the traffic in and out of Deepnest kept a certain pace. But there were no guards, no signs of conflict, and only a few signs of recent passage. Moving farther into the cavern that Deepnest resided in, he found the underground city dead silent. Not a single thing moved down there, with the tunnel-littered mounds, buildings, scaffolded roadways, lakes, and streams all having been completely abandoned.

"They could have at least talked to us first instead of killing our people and abandoning the place . . ." Riven muttered under his breath, moving through what was obviously a hasty, scrambling removal of all valuables from the brood nests— one after the other. Scattered baskets of spilled food, smashed crates of alchemy ingredients and textiles, and a few trampled bodies lay broken in the streets.

He knelt down with Azmoth, Fay, and Genua at his back, waiting in silence. The body of the ratkin was half skeletal, half flesh, with smokelike tendrils of green wafting off its body. It smelled horrid, and when Riven got close enough to reach out and touch the broken creature's corpse, his skin started crackling upon making contact with the gaseous green cloud.

Riven's eyebrows furrowed, watching his vampiric regeneration battle the fumes. At one point even a bubbling abscess took form and burst before healing itself over and draining away. It was very minimal damage, and quite disgusting, to the point that it was very likely other undead who weren't vampires could survive in the presence of the fumes for a while, but long exposure would no doubt kill the average person . . .

His mind drifted back to the two diplomats hung over the tunnel's entrance into this abandoned ratkin city, and his eyes widened. "Those ghouls back there . . . the bodies—they were afflicted with whatever is coming off this corpse."

"Blight," Fay stated, nodding promptly in agreement as Riven stood up. "It's a rare type of undead, spreads plague. But because you're undead, if you expose yourself to enough of it, you'll become immune. It won't actually kill you, though. Even people with the Unholy pillar can become immune to it, but that's a bit harder to do than being completely undead."

"Those two ghouls looked pretty dead to me, and they definitely were affected by this."

Fay shook her head. "They had a reaction to the blight but they were certainly immune to any lethal damage from it. Those ghouls were doubtlessly killed by something else, like the dozens of poisoned stab wounds. I promise you, your people have nothing to fear from the blight itself other than discomfort. Think of it like . . . like having a mild allergic reaction."

"Mild?" Riven mused, grinning slightly. He held his hand out over the wafting green cloud oozing off the corpse, and made a gesture to his exposed hand as another boil burst and healed itself. "That's pretty painful."

Fay rolled her eyes and adjusted her witch's hat. "Yes, mild! Because no matter how long you or any other undead sits in it, that blight isn't going to kill you! Those reactions to the blight will go away after you expose yourself more and more. And the reactions that living people have in its presence are FAR more volatile than what you're experiencing right now. It's believed, theoretically, that world quest 1—the Lich King's Plague—is referring to this exact thing: blight. The forums talk about how people on the outskirts of the lich's territory have sent in scouts and spies, and they think he's preparing some kind of weapon or army related to blight."

Riven's frown deepened. "Does blight really make such an impact that he'd try to spread it like a plague?"

"It IS a plague," Fay corrected, booping him on the head with a finger and giving him a playful wink. "The plague of undeath, created by followers of the Scythe back in the second era far before this universe was ever created—with the Scythe being the first-ever god of death. And yes, because when mortals die to blight they have a high chance of self-spawning as undead soon after. It's also highly contagious, and it can be cured, but that takes a significant number of healers, priests, or shamans to cleanse it from the population when it starts spreading."

"Wait, hold on. You're saying that humans will not only die from it, but then spawn as undead, too? Are you being serious?"

"I'm absolutely serious."

"That's very seriously not good."

"Not good for the rest of the world! But your population is undead now!"

"No, MOST of my population is undead now. But we have three entire cities on the other side of Riven's Eye Wormhole that are human-based. This could pose a very serious problem."

Genua raised a hand to get their attention. "Not to mention you need mortal people to feed on, along with the other vampires of Rippenvire who have not abandoned their pact of nonaggression. If this blight kills all the living mortal races, then vampires in particular will be starved."

Riven froze at the thought. "Yeah, there's that, too, though I doubt we have many vampires left after Gaia reported in from her slaughter right outside Brightsville's borders. And what about Genua? Is she going to have a problem by being here?"

Fay shook her head. "No, she's a thrall and is partially undead by technical standards. She'd likely have a more severe and painful reaction than you do but still would not die from it after prolonged exposure."

"I see . . ." Riven rubbed his chin thoughtfully, looking around at the abandoned city with growing concern. "I still can't believe they just got up and left, though. Why would they kill our people and just move on? And for what? Because they were mad about Allie's change to the world so they took it out on us by murdering the diplomats? Our men talked about how they were seeking vengeance before they were strung up—but I don't see them anywhere, and we'd have seen them coming if they were aiming for Brightsville through known tunnels. And the dwarvish outposts went radio silent . . . Do you really think they did it?"

"Attacked Charathigog and Reathian, the dwarvish cities?" Fay shook her head. "Possibly, but they'd have lost a lot of people doing it. The communications were probably cut off because it's so far underground and we don't have access to the communication crystal network we'd set up through Deepnest's territory. We had large garrisons in each dwarvish city to maintain the peace, and Allie had doubled them recently because of unauthorized raids on dwarvish civilians by hostile ratkin. My guess is that the ratkin just cut their ties and ran."

"Because they know they can't win in an all-out fight against us?"

"Yes. They knew it would be suicidal to fight you outright, and the same can probably be said for Allie, too, now since she just took the number one power ranking."

"That still doesn't make any sense," Riven argued. "Why abandon everything you've ever known? Where would they even go? I wasn't going to attack them until they murdered our men and hung their bodies as a sign. Their behavior is very rash, especially without any chance for diplomacy."

"They were just turned into plagued abominations," Genua stated with her hands clasped in front of her, red eyes staring at the broken corpse on the ground. "Of course they're angry. Angry people do irrational things, and though Allie may not have been the direct source of their dilemma—she is certainly the cause of it. They want someone to blame for their misfortune."

Azmoth, who'd remained silent up until now, abruptly shifted his stance and pointed to a bright ball of light hovering over a nearby building. "What is that?"

A blinding brilliance lit up the miles-wide cavern in an instant, and the entire city of Deepnest exploded with a shuddering boom.

Blood Oath (Blood) (Tier 3): This miracle requires your vampire master's permission to use. Roots the user to one spot, significantly increases the amount of damage taken by the user's vampire master, and grants invincibility to yourself unless your vampire master dies.

Genua managed to get the incantation out and knelt in prayer just in time for Riven to accept it before the shock wave of raging energy crashed into their party like a tidal wave.

Azmoth's hellfire barrier held for only a brief two seconds before being crushed underneath the absolute magnitude of a city-destroying blast that tore the cavern's ceiling and floor apart like wood into a grinder.

Her body immediately burned a bright red and she stood helplessly rooted in place as Riven, Azmoth, and Fay were swept away. Genua saw Fay scream before her body was ripped apart—no doubt being banished to the nether realms a split second later. Azmoth got lost in the swirling storm of debris and thundering energy only a moment later, and Riven was flung into a similar direction so fast that it looked like he'd been shot out of a cannon.

Then she was alone.

Genua's heart thundered in her chest, and she remained in her position of prayer, head bowed and blood mana swirling about her in an impassable protective layer that covered her entire body. The ground underneath her tore and ripped, the winds about her howled, and hundreds of thousands of pieces of rubble collided with her in a maelstrom that lasted for nearly twelve seconds without pause.

She'd been only a split second away from death, and both she and her unborn child had barely managed to come out alive. That thought alone had her adrenaline spiking, and she honestly couldn't thank Riven enough. This power was on the magnitude of his own when he'd destroyed Daskus. He'd knowingly taken the hit to save her life at the risk of his own due to the miracle increasing his own damage taken by an unknown amount.

Her chest rose and fell with rapid breaths, and soon the storm had passed—leaving a smoldering crater in place of what had once been Deepnest. The floor beneath her boiled with magma from the sheer heat of the energy used, every single building was long gone, and neither Riven nor Azmoth was anywhere to be seen.

She was alone, in a hellscape created by magic of some variety in a likely attempt to assassinate Riven or his sister.

Genua could only hope that the ratkin hadn't succeeded, and not knowing where to even start looking in this vast sea of smoldering, melted rock, she began to call out Riven's name when she quickly stopped and dropped to the floor from her floating position.

Hiding behind a cooling mound of raised stone and gritting her teeth while her flesh began to burn, she watched in horror as dozens of figures started racing out over the edge of a hill that'd somehow been protected from the blast—and if she was right, was also the likely origin of said blast.

There were too many for her to handle, and she was at a loss for what to do.

Gluttony began to stir in Riven's soul. The primal hunger it experienced at all times began to rise up as it watched its host bound with high-quality, mana-suppressing shackles on his wrists and ankles before Riven was dragged off by a war band of blighted ratkin in a rush of scampering feet. Clouds of plague left trails in their wake, and the undead creatures soon took to the tunnels, dragging their prisoner unceremoniously along with them.

The great maw might have been weakened by what he was about to do, but such was the price of freedom. Too long had Gluttony and his brethren been trapped, shut away from the light. Too long had he fed off nothing but hope that one day, one day he would finally find the vessel to bring him back.

Back from being a mere shadow of the monster that had once terrorized the cosmos, the monster that had once devoured entire pantheons of gods.

Back when the sins and commandments had been free.

The multiverse would once more know fear.

Gluttony stared at the last piece of Riven's fragmented soul, the last shard that had yet to be placed, and gingerly held it with building glee. This was merely a reset button, that was all. Per Elysium's contract, Gluttony would lose most of his power and knowledge while inhabiting a host and would have to level up through the ranks just like everyone else.

But it was worth it.

It was oh, so worth it!

It was a new chance at life.

"Take me to your leader . . . My unwitting servants . . ." Gluttony whispered into the abyss while watching the ratkin who were unknowingly delivering a catastrophe in the form of a prisoner to their people, finally placing that very last piece into place—finally having finished rebuilding the damage Elysium's tribulation had done. "Take me to your people . . . For it has been too long since I have truly tasted flesh. One day, far into the future, it will be marked down in the history books that it was this day, here on Panu, that Gluttony finally returned. That it was Gluttony who was the first of the original sins to claw his way back out of the abyss. And that it was here in the underdark of the world that he finally feasted after millennia of starving, the first meal of many to satiate his hunger!"

CHAPTER 28

Sweat dripped down her skin.

The molten cavern radiated hot energies even twenty minutes after the ratkin's ambush, and it'd taken that entire time to find Azmoth despite the connection they shared as cominions under Riven's control. If not for that connection, she'd never have found him in the vast desolation of what had once been the city of Deepnest.

Genua's head remained bowed, hands steepled in front of her and only occasionally shifting into necessary gestures while chanting the rites of her Transfusion Zone miracle. Blood divinity swirled around her like a thick mist of red, and the crimson runes along her skin flared brightly while her eyes remained locked on Azmoth's broken body in front of her.

Slowly but steadily, the demon's large frame began to repair itself. Bones snapped back into place, metal plates that'd been torn off now re-fused themselves to his musculature, the breathing became less ragged, and the caved-in left side of his skull shifted into a more natural form while her healing miracle took hold.

The huge maul on his left was shattered and embedded into the smoldering cavern wall, the enchantments on it broken, as was the shield that had taken the brunt of the initial blow. She could barely make out the remnants of his items after they'd been so thoroughly destroyed.

"Little priestess . . ." Azmoth muttered in a guttural growl, prying himself out of the crater he'd been flung into with a shower of hot orange rocks as his fires flared to life around him. He shook his huge head and gave Genua a nod of appreciation when she stopped her chants and let out a long huff of exhaustion. "Thank you."

A clawed finger lifted and tapped the elf thrall's metal headdress, and he turned around to gingerly lift up the broken fragments of his maul with a sad groan. "This is first item Azmoth ever receive. It present from Riven, and makes me sad to see gone."

Genua, who was still heaving from exhaustion and taking in slow, deep breaths, shot a glance toward the tunnel that led out of the cavern far, far away from where they now stood. "Azmoth! We need to save him! He was taken by the—"

"He not need saving," Azmoth stated with a shake of his head, finishing picking up the pieces of his stone weapon—or at least what he could salvage from it—and chuckling with his head turned her way. "He is fine."

Genua's eyes widened, and she took a step forward to point the way Riven had gone. "NO! NO, Azmoth he is NOT fine! He was captured!"

If Azmoth could roll his eyes, he would have. "Little priestess . . . You have soul bond to Master. You can feel how and where he is if try hard."

Genua furrowed her brows, hissing when she again stepped onto another piece of molten rock that nearly burned through her boot. Sweat continued pouring down her face, dampening her clothes, and she wiped her forehead with a sleeve and threw her hands out to either side. "What in all the hells are you even talking about?!"

Azmoth looked confused. "You really not know?"

"Know what?!"

"Focusing on soul bond allow to feel Master's presence. Not as strong as Athela's bond where she talks through mind with telepathy, but still strong enough to know he fine. He is awake, his soul very strong, and he that way." Azmoth pointed down through the floor of the cavern and slightly toward the outer wall where the blighted ratkin had taken Riven's bound body. "If he need us, he can summon Athela and me. But he not do that. He likely want me stay with you to protect you and unborn child."

"They bound him with antimagic! That's why he's not summoning you! I will NOT be left to take care of yet another child ALONE!" She stomped her foot, fists clenched. "I can't. I just . . . can't. I'm already drowning as it is with Len. I'm a failure, and I can't provide the kind of support they'll need by myself."

Azmoth tilted his head to the side. The large four-armed demon opened his mouth to reply, then snapped it shut again. "If Riven not okay, why his power growing? I can feel from here. No, he summon through portal if he need me—Riven is one of strongest on planet. So we will go to surface, to make you and child safe."

With that, the large demon picked up Genua and flung her over one shoulder—much to the protests of the priestess—before walking out the opposite way they'd come. It hadn't been anticipated that the ratkin could or would blow up their entire capital city just to strike out at Riven or Allie, but Azmoth was confident that Riven would be fine.

Though . . . the feeling he was getting from that connection was certainly a little more sinister than usual.

Meanwhile, in other parts of the world at that very moment: Kenji, the last survivor of the cultist group that had killed Athela, looked up from where he was carving runes into corpses with a grin. The dim light of the hidden cave barely illuminated the newly formed tattoos of the profane that littered his body, or the new limbs he'd taken from recent victims to build himself up. Nora Lang, the Asian woman Riven had met all those months ago on the ascension of the pyramid in Chalgathi's starter quest, pulled a rapier out of her victim and pried the amulet from his quickly cooling hands in the snow. She saw the quest update in front of her as the five artifact pieces meshed together into a new combined item set of her own.

It was almost time.

[The Apocalypse Beasts, Chalgathi, Quest Update: Blithe Fullhandle has fallen in battle to Nora Lang. Nora Lang has acquired five of five set pieces for Chalgathi's Inheritance.]
[All ten sets of Chalgathi's Inheritance have been completed.]
[World Quest 2, The Apocalypse Beasts: Chalgathi
The death of this world approaches. Nekra, the Skeletal Devourer, churns in his sandy tomb amid a sea of the unliving. Chalgathi, the Plague Dragon, awaits those who would free him from his skyward prison above the clouds. Chubin, the Glass Kraken, seeks an escape from the abyss beneath the ocean. The cults of the end times gather their strength and resources to try and find the lairs of their chosen apocalypse beasts. Should they succeed, your world is doomed.
As one of the three apocalypse beasts born for this cycle of ascension, Chalgathi is destined for carnage. It is a creature of nightmarish power, a beast born of hate and malice. Five years after the beginning of this integration, a wave of destruction will spread across all the world on wings of decay. Empires will fall, billions will die, and the very ground you tread upon will rot and wither—for the plague dragon has finally awakened.
However, there is an alternative to this fate: stop the cultists from raising the plague dragon to his adult form, find Chalgathi's incubation chamber, and destroy or claim his egg for yourself before the five-year period is done. You, Nora Lang, are one of his chosen ones, a final contender. You have acquired all his artifacts: the amulet, claws, mask, pauldrons, and breastplate. It falls on you to act.
In the beginning, there were 1,672 with an Unholy bloodline. There were then only fifty chosen ones to leave Chalgathi's Trials. There are now sixteen originals remaining, ten of whom have collected all needed pieces to enter the next phase of this World Quest. The chosen ones are divided into two categories: cultists and noncultists, and you are all competing against one another regardless of category. Depending on which of the chosen reaches Chalgathi's lair to successfully claim his egg, each outcome could have drastically different consequences: either salvation or damnation of Panu.]
[Chalgathi, The Apocalypse Beasts, World Quest, Panu, subevent has been unlocked: The Altars of Despair and Hope.
Chalgathi, the Plague Dragon, is the final of the three apocalypse beasts to have his ten item sets collected. Due to the unexpected and early acquisition of all thirty item sets across all three apocalypse

beasts, including Chalgathi, the Plague Dragon; Chubin, the Glass Kraken; and Nekra, the Skeletal Devourer, the Altars of Despair and Hope event has been expedited. You will arrive at your designated starting point for World Quest 2 within three hours.

When arriving at your designated starting spot, you will gain the locations and access to Chalgathi's altars. You will be required to visit all four Chalgathi altar sites and activate the shrines before acquiring knowledge of the location of Chalgathi's Temple where Chalgathi's incubation chamber has been hidden.

There is one Altar of Hope where all noncultists will arrive. There is one Altar of Despair where all cultists will arrive. There are four additional altars for each of the three apocalypse beasts for a total of twelve additional altars.

The Altars of Despair and Hope are exclusive areas designated by the Elysium administrator, where only the chosen of the apocalypse beasts who've acquired the five needed artifacts, as well as abducted participants from across the multiverse, may enter. This applies to all apocalypse beasts, not only Chalgathi. Here at the Altars of Despair and Hope, you will be divided into two groups: cultists and noncultists.

There are twenty-one registered cultists.

- Seven Chalgathi cultists, six Chubin cultists, and eight Nekra cultists

There are nine registered noncultists entering this event.

- Three Chalgathi noncultists, four Chubin noncultists, and two Nekra noncultists

As previously described, the outcomes of this World Quest differ greatly depending on which of the chosen acquires the prizes for these quests. Thus, cultists will be pitted against noncultists when reaching these altars. Noncultists across all three apocalypse beast categories will arrive at the Altar of Hope, and cultists across all three apocalypse beast categories will arrive at the Altar of Despair. You will be highly incentivized to work together with your given team upon arrival, and severe punishments will be handed down to those who intentionally harm any others in their own category while involving themselves in this subevent of the quest line. However, despite these punishments, killing your own teammates may be needed in different scenarios in order to make sure that it is you who gets to the temple first—rather than your peers.

Here are the rules:

- The Altar of Hope will indefinitely respawn all noncultists after a twenty-four-hour time period after death and will have a barrier of protection around it that only noncultists can enter through.
- The Altar of Despair will indefinitely respawn all cultists after a

twenty-four-hour time period after death and will have a barrier of protection around it that only cultists can enter through.

- Chalgathi, Chubin, and Nekra's altars can only be claimed by chosen belonging to their designated apocalypse beast, but all altars can be entered and turned off by chosen of any apocalypse beast. People and creatures from outside Panu that are involved with this World Quest cannot activate or deactivate any altar, but they can enter the altars.
- All altars will have indiscriminate defenders that respawn after death.
- People and creatures from outside Panu that are involved with this World Quest will continually be funneled into this event either voluntarily or involuntarily depending on circumstance or deals struck with Elysium.
- The goal of this event is to acquire points. You are a noncultist, so your method of gaining points differs from cultists and will be discussed more thoroughly when you enter the event. Global methods of gaining points, however, are retaining control of altars for uninterrupted twenty-four-hour time periods, unique quests that everyone competes for, and killing competitors of the opposite team. Killing people of the same team will decrease your total points and often end in punishments, but may be necessary to complete and secure larger numbers of quest points and prizes.
- Killing anything inside this trial will not grant XP and levels due to temporary immortal status, but completing spawned quests will grant XP and levels.
- Points may be spent at the Altars of Despair and Hope for various prizes, bonuses, knowledge, items, buffs, or mercenaries.
- When you reach ten thousand unspent points, you as an individual are allowed to leave the subevent and travel back to Panu. At this time you will be granted the location of Chalgathi's temple, where Chalgathi's egg and incubation chamber are located. If Chalgathi's egg is claimed prior to your completion of this subevent, you will be placed back in Panu at a random location.
- Upon opening the altars three hours from now, the next phase of World Quest 2, The Apocalypse Beasts, will begin. You can expect to enter an alternate pocket realm at that time along with various people, places, artifacts, and events drawn in from around the multiverse, and can be expected to be gone for approximately one year's time.]

The Amphitheater.

An enormous place deep, deep down in the underdark that had once only been a refuge for the most devout worshippers of the old world's gods—ones whose brutality and bloodthirstiness she'd had hoped to escape with the arrival of the system. She'd even thrown the priests out of the city when she'd realized their connection to the old world's gods were no longer as solid and that they had limited power here in the new multiverse.

And yet here she was, Queen Bez—the once-rotund leader of what had once been Deepnest, matriarch of the blighted ratkin clans, having led them here in their time of need, in an attempt to restore to the old gods what had been lost—as a trade. She was desperate, as were all her kin, to get their old bodies back. To remove the stain of undeath, the tarnish of blight, that would mark them as outcasts from the other ratkin of this world forever. Simultaneously, she was eager to have revenge on the one who'd caused them to turn into abominations.

Even if it wasn't a direct strike against Allie, even if it was her brother instead. There would be vengeance for what had been done to the broods of Deepnest, for the agony of knowing what they'd been cursed with. Forever they would be outcasts among their own kind, never again able to return to the swarms and homelands of the deep. Queen Bez would have been happier if Allie had walked into that trap, but Riven was a very close second best.

Many hundreds of thousands of their kin—potentially over a million, both those who had been outcast in the past and those who'd lived in the very center of the prosperous Deepnest—were present on the large stone steps that stretched for miles. The enormous amphitheater had been a thing of wonder in the past, built by an unknown race in an unknown time—a wonder of the world. A relic of ancient history long lost to the record books. No one knew who had built it or why, or how they'd created such a large hollowed-out structure, but the fact remained that miracles cast here were always of higher quality, leading many of the ratkin scholars to believe it had been the site of some great ritual once upon a time. That, or it'd once been a place of ceremonial and sacred value—which in turn had been utilized to produce worship sites for their own faithful even prior to knowing how miracles actually worked by system standards.

Hundreds of huge stone pillars held the cavern ceiling up, and packed crowds of murmuring undead ratkin whispered to one another as lines of hooded priests with metal staves continued preparing the ritual ceremonies at the bottom. Dozens of huge stairways leading from the top down to different flat platforms big enough to house small communities were present at a couple intervals, and at the very bottom in the distant depths was a very large, circular platform where the queen now sat next to some of the hooded ratkin priests she'd once thrown out of her society. She had once been very large, very fat, and a black-furred beauty in her own right—but now she'd been reduced to nothing but literal skin and bones with vomit-green eyes; fumes rose off her body as wisps of blighted plague.

Yet the priests promised they could bring about salvation if she just gave them this one chance to prove themselves. A chance to repent. The priests claimed they'd finally made contact with their old gods, and that—if given proper sacrifice—they'd be able to summon those gods back to Panu and into the Elysium system so that they might bring about an end to the blight that afflicted all their bodies.

She would see whether or not this was true.

Silence overtook the crowds as Bishop Prek bade Queen Bez to enter the pool of blood—directly in front of the large, blessed ziggurat where sacrifices of their own kin were set in a row on spikes. Only this blood had a green tint to it, and it smelled like . . . infection. A by-product of their new bodies. Two hooded ratkin priests went to remove her cloak, and moments afterward Queen Bez felt her skeletal right foot enter the bowl of crimson liquid. The warm fluid engulfed her leg, and as she waded farther in, it engulfed her up to waist height. Chunks of coagulated cells floated about in a rather grotesque reminder that many had been sacrificed to perform this ritual, and she would not let those people go to waste.

The bishop raised a hand skyward. With a flick of his wrist his scrying ability took hold and displayed a magnified vision overhead so that all could witness the ceremony. Candles burned around the perimeter of the ritual circles, along the blood pool, under the sacrificed bodies where the priests stood, and all along the low stone walls at the very back of the amphitheater next to the ziggurat.

Head bowed, Bishop Prek also began to strip and stepped into the large pool of sickly fluids. He stopped short of Queen Bez, leaving a six- to seven-foot space between them. He spread his hands out wide, as if to embrace her, and called loudly for all to hear through the scrying ability broadcasting the event across this amphitheater.

"Bez, queen-leader of the brood-clans of Deepnest. It is me-my sacred-holy duty to serve-honor the one bonded to our ancient-long lineages. What is it that you-we wish to do here-now today?!"

Queen Bez did not hesitate, and her sinewy, bony body bowed in reverence—hope beginning to build while the sprawling crowds of her people watched nervously from above. "I wish to speak-converse with Rashi, the Great Winged Rat! I seek-find advice to cure-save our people-kin from undeath-fate! I seek vengeance on bat-kin fiends who curse-wound us!"

Murmurs of unease and hope filled the amphitheater but were soon silenced with a wave of Prek's hands.

Bishop Prek held up both arms to the sky and lifted his eyes to the ceiling above. The beating of drums began to thunder out from the priests and priestesses of the temple at an increased tempo.

"It is known-seen that Rashi smile-grins upon us, and that he-he forgives. He has spoken-told me of his sadness-anger that we abandoned-left him in the darkened days-times of the integration, but he is pleased-happy to see us come back! But a price-toll must be paid-given. Us-we must solidify our pact-deal with the great winged rat before he all-fully embraces us as the new chosen people! Are you sure-certain you wish to proceed?" Prek's question was genuine. There would be no going back from this. "Bringing old-world god will make you-you many enemies of new gods and pantheons. You must be solid-stone in your resolve and must be willing-eager to pay the toll-fee of the blood sacrament."

Bez's eyes narrowed. She had no other choice but to pursue forgiveness, not if she wished to remain a true ratkin instead of this new species they'd all been transformed into. She didn't even know if the priest was telling her the truth—there was a chance he was completely making this up. There was a chance that this priest could be doing something else entirely rather than summoning an old god who many of their kin had decided was nothing but a farce—but her desperation to regain what had been lost was a counterweight to reason. She had to at least try.

"I am ready-certain."

Prek excitedly clapped his undead hands twice and pointed to the back end of the temple with a spit-laced shriek. "BRING FORTH THE FINAL-LAST SACRIFICES! BRING FORTH THE FINAL-LAST VESSELS SO THAT THE FATHER-KIN, THE GREAT WINGED RAT, MAY SEEK THE CREATION OF HIS BODY-VESSEL!"

The drums doubled in speed and the clergy began to chant in rhythm with the beat. Ancient words and phrases that even Bez didn't entirely understand were hummed, chanted, and sung by all the blighted clergy present. And one by one, the blighted hordes of onlookers joined in. Their mouths moved as the words came to them, gifted to them from some otherworldly, foreign power, as the pool of blood tinted with green began to swirl with the intense and vulgar ritual.

Four priests and priestesses exited from a hallway built into the stone of the ziggurat's main hall. The four undead ratkin had long slender ropes in their hands and were pulling objects out of sight beyond them. Seconds later the pulling and yanking of the clergy produced four captives: Rashtalia, Snagger, Mesha, and then, finally, Riven—who was bound with suppression collars, shackles, and trinkets that would offset his absurd mana access. He was awake, though seemingly only barely—and he in particular sported an additional mana suppression rune carved into his forehead that wasn't healing despite his vampiric nature.

"THE FIRST!!!" Bishop Prek screamed, slapping his hands into the pool around him while the chanting of the priests and priestesses grew louder—their metal staves beating into the cavern floor under the candlelight and shadows of the sacrificed ratkin held up on spikes.

He pointed to Rashtalia, and the broodmother began to scream through her gag while she was dragged—kicking, sobbing, and bound—toward the pool. Her body, too, had undergone the change, but she was still hyperventilating.

Queen Bez couldn't tell what she was saying over the enthusiastic chanting and beating of drums, but she did note many of Brood-Tarrow turned their eyes away in shame or revulsion. She knew that many of Rashtalia's friends disagreed with this, just as they had when they had sacrificed those now up on spikes during the first ritual, but Queen Bez also knew that it must be done. The gods of the old world demanded blood, so they would get it.

"THIS WOMAN-WHORE TURNED HER BACK-TAIL ON US-WE! BEFRIENDED BAT-KIN QUEEN-LEADER TO STAB US IN BACK!" Prek screamed as the woman was dragged across the platform toward the pool.

The crowds that weren't chanting roared in anger like a thunderous storm.

Prek nodded his approval. "SHE HAS FAIL-FAILED AS A DIPLOMAT-SPEAKER AND SHOWN-LED US INTO DISASTER WHEN OUR LEADER-QUEEN BEZ TRUSTED HER!!"

Of course, this wasn't entirely true. Queen Bez knew this, but she had to pin the blame on someone. She had to give focus to the anger and rage her people were feeling, the calls for war needed to be heard, and Rashtalia was one of a few targets she could pin this entire problem on in order to let her people vent their rage. Allie would eventually come after that, but only when they grew stronger with the help of their old gods. Until then, the unrest needed a focus point.

Two priestesses, one on each side of the temple platform, bent down with candles and lit a stream of oil that had been poured onto the ground. Yellow flame ignited and burned a semicircular tapestry of intricate runes, symbols, and diagrams around the pool of blood. The firelight glistened off the naked bodies in the pool and the blood they stood in. Four more priestesses all stepped forward simultaneously and waited along the edge of the pool while their individual servants took the liberty of taking their clothes off, revealing patches of fur on exposed muscle that occasionally lacked skin—or even bone protrusions that were sometimes not even part of the previously normal anatomy. After each of the four priestesses stood barren along the edge, they again simultaneously took a step into the shimmering liquid—tails flowing behind them.

Ripples of blood moved along the otherwise flat, silky surface as the undead ratkin women waded into the center to surround Prek and Bez at four corners. And just as the clergy pulled their violently struggling captive between two erupting pillars of flame to enter the centerpiece of the ritual, the four servants along the pool's edge at spaced out intervals to prostrate themselves.

One of the clergy coming from the ziggurat ripped out Rashtalia's gag with a knife, and she began to beg.

"PLEASE, NO-NO!!! I'LL DO ANY-MANY THINGS, JUST DON'T KILL-SACRIFICE ME-ME! PLEASE DON'T, QUEEN-LEADER BEZ, WE ARE FRIENDS-KIN!!!" Rashtalia flailed as her captors pulled her forward. Her hands and feet clawed at the ground in between the yanking of the cords around her limbs. Her heart was pounding wildly and the poor terrified ratkin woman shrieked, begging them to let her live.

Then, as she was brought up violently and forced to kneel at the edge of the red fluids, her eyes met Queen Bez's own.

"Bez! Bez-kin, please, please-please . . . !!!" The sobbing ratkin woman clutched at her pale, hairless stomach as she tried to contain her terror. She sniffled and choked on her own saliva amid the heaving of her breasts. "I'll be a good servant-kin slave! I am sorry-sad that I fail-failed to stop Allie-queen bat-kin from cursing us-we, but I did not know-see this could happen! Please-please, just let me live-go!"

CHAPTER 29

Queen Bez looked upon the ratkin woman she'd once called friend with only a mild amount of guilt, but that did not stop her from doing what needed to be done. Despite Rashtalia's begging sobs, and fully knowing she was using Rashtalia as a scapegoat and focal point for her people's rage, to maintain order over the angry masses, she stretched out a blood-covered hand from the crimson pool, cutting the ropes binding Rashtalia with a slim, clawed finger. The broodmother flinched but waited, hopeful, for her queen's final decision.

"I'm going to think-miss on our time-places together, but your time-life has come to an end. Be quiet-silent." Bez lifted her hand and engaged her magic, and Rashtalia's mouth immediately snapped shut as the rest of her body went rigid—muffling her sounds to a silent, shaking sob. Her lips still quivered and water continued to stream down her face from wide, terrified eyes.

Bez turned to Bishop Prek. "You may start-proceed."

The bishop nodded just once as Bez's hand fell to her side and Prek's came up. Rashtalia stiffened and was lifted into the air face up while her body became flat as a board and hovered over them before settling down just a foot over the bloody bath. Strands of her remaining brown patches of hair drifted down gently around her, her breasts rose and fell faster and faster, and her eyes flickered back and forth to the six people looking down on her.

The other priestesses around the pool drew themselves in closer.

"Begin the ritual-rite," Prek said without looking up. The four priestesses all began to chant new verses in ancient tongues, shifting forward. Each held their hands up and out above their heads as the verses continued rhythmically, and their dead green eyes soon began to burn with Unholy flames.

"The sacrifice-slaves, and all others-kin who call on the great winged rat, must be bathe-bathed in blood," Prek stated, and the naked bishop flipped the palms of his skeletal, clawed hands over. Rashtalia was immediately dropped into the pool and then brought back up via psychic power to hover a foot over the bath again. Turning to look at Bez, he walked around Rashtalia and put a hand on the queen's shoulder.

"May I have-take the honor of bathing-baptizing you, my queen-leader?" The bishop was sincerely reverent as he addressed her.

"You may-may."

Prek let out a low hum, ignoring the gagged exclamations and sobs from Snagger and Mesha, and dunked Bez beneath the blood's surface. He let the warm bodily fluid engulf both of them completely for a couple of seconds before bringing Bez back up. One by one, Prek went to each of the priestesses and did the same with them. Each time, the woman would come up and begin the chant again as if she had never stopped. Before long, Prek submerged himself in the pool as well and came up dripping in the fine red liquid.

"THE SECOND! THE THIRD! AND THE FOURTH!"

The drums continued to boom. The fire-drawn tapestry of flickering symbols about them rose several feet in height.

The same ritual baptism was then performed on each of the other captives, each of them going rigid and floating above the blood-filled bath to be dunked and taken back out. Bishop Prek positioned each of them in a line, with Rashtalia first, Snagger second, Mesha third, and finally Riven last.

Prek gave another signal over the thundering drums, and each of the four priestesses chose one of the victims, starting to carve sigils into their chests while three of the four started to whimper and scream through the magics restraining them.

The fourth, though, didn't react at all. Riven remained naked, hovering over the bath as the ratkin priestess cut deep into his rib cage and sternum with a jagged, rusty knife—not even blinking as blood dripped from the mana-suppression shackles, collar, and sigil already etched into his forehead. His red eyes seemed unusually dull, as if his mind was somewhere else, and if anyone had been paying close attention to the metal bands that were supposed to be keeping his mana restrained—they would have seen the faint, deep-purple cracks creeping along the metal.

"GREAT WINGED ONE, CHOSEN FATHER-KIN OF US-WE!" Bishop Prek screamed into the air as the priestesses finished carving the necessary sigils into the bodies of all four victims—each of the clergy coming back to the first of the four live sacrifices and surrounding Rashtalia while muttering chants under their breaths. "WE ASK-SAY THAT YOU COME BLESS-HELP US WITH YOUR GIFT-POWER! WE TAKE LIFE-LIVES FROM THE WORLD, FROM PANU-WORLD OF ELYSIUM, AND SAY-SAY THAT YOU COME-TRAVEL BACK THROUGH THE GATE-DOOR THAT BARS-STOPS YOUR GLORIOUS SPIRIT-SOUL! WITH THESE SACRIFICE-SLAVES, WE GIVE YOU THE GIFT-POWER AND VESSEL-BODY TO POSSESS! FIND US, OH GREAT WINGED RAT—COME-TRAVEL TO AID YOUR CHILDREN-KIN!"

Prek made an upward motion with his fingers as he spoke and six ceremonial knives slowly rose out of the pool, blades down. A blade went to him, one to Queen Bez, and one to each of the four assisting priestesses.

Each of them grabbed the knife by the hilt, following Prek's example and keeping the blades down against their chests as all the women recited the chant of the ritual outside of Prek's own personalized call to the old-world god. Bez chanted, too, the words coming unbidden as a flare of unnatural, foggy green light erupted over the pool with dark-brown eyes that glared through the veil of space and time.

She shuddered under that gaze, even if she could not fully see the god's body yet, but the presence was certainly that of the divine. The aura boomed and crashed down upon everyone present, and the roars for blood became weeping cries for salvation as the masses lifted their hands and began to worship the divine being.

But the ritual was not yet complete.

Bez just stood and watched amid her chants, dagger against her bare chest, as a terrified, blood-covered Rashtalia shook uncontrollably, still sobbing silently while she hovered in the air between the six dagger-holding participants.

"HEAR ME, WINGED ONE!" Prek continued enthusiastically, throwing his arms up toward the giant green cloud overhead where a figure of a huge, demonic rodent was ever so slowly taking a spiritual form. Bat-like wings spread, taloned claws ripped out of its hands, and the torso elongated to unusual levels as the deep-brown eyes grew wider and wider.

The chanting of the clergy matched that of the five women in the pool of blood, and soon the entirety of the blighted crowd, spectators of the ceremony, were doing the same and shouting out the chants in a synchronous, excited, thundering roar.

"Come speak-talk with your chosen ratkin and deliver us-we into your power-cold embrace! Let it be seen-known that I, Prek Zrof, bishop-kin and humble servant-worshipper to the old-world gods, am the one-kin that calls-summons you to me!" The bishop lifted his dagger high above his head and looked down at the stiff ratkin woman lying flat over the pool.

The others followed suit, including Queen Bez, closing in to form a close circle around Rashtalia, who quivered wide-eyed but could not speak under their gaze.

"Take this soul-slave as a sacrifice in your great-wonderous name, and let-see the calling be deemed-judged worthy-able of your presence! TO ME, GREAT WINGED RAT, TO ME!" Prek paused only a moment to let the queen speak the final words.

"To me," Queen Bez repeated.

Prek let out a shrill, high-pitched wail, spit flying in all directions, and the six daggers swiftly descended to pierce Rashtalia's flesh. Rashtalia gasped involuntarily, her fingers balled up into clenched fists and her lips curled in a silent scream. Bez felt the ratkin woman's rib cage catch on the dagger before she withdrew it and stabbed her again. Prek and the five others savagely tore into her thighs, abdomen, breasts, and face with dozens of brutal strokes. Prek was particularly boorish in his approach as he ripped into Rashtalia's gut and pulled out her intestines in pieces and chunks.

Rashtalia's mouth opened and closed and she coughed up blood just once before daggers pierced her lungs. Her right bicep was carved off the bone and then her left cheek. Then, with her last dying, horrified, and pain-ridden gasps she saw one of the priestesses cleave open her entire rib cage and pull out her heart with a wicked set of claws to hold it over their heads on display.

Then the broodmother's vision went black, and Rashtalia's suffering finally ended.

Prek reached out at the moment of death amid the cheers and chants of the demon hordes, plucking Rashtalia's soul from her body as the limp corpse dropped unceremoniously—a destroyed bag of flesh plunging into the blood pool. The tiny light pulsed in his hand and he lifted it up to the level of the sacrifice's heart, holding it there.

Waiting.

Yet, the visage of the god above them did not move.

Prek soon whirled on the priestesses with a snarl. "THE SECOND AND THIRD MUST BE TAKEN!"

Without even a hint of reluctance, the clergy all moved on, alongside Queen Bez, and began carving into Snagger next. His body purged and his huge muscles spasmed while he was held in place over the bloody pool. Tears streamed down his face and he gagged as his innards were ripped out, and his heart was eventually carved from his chest.

Mesha came next, and the petite ratkin woman didn't last nearly as long as the other two had. She died quite fast, and her limp body dropped into the pool with the two other corpses—their souls being plucked alongside Rashtalia's own, three little balls of light held in Prek's hands. Meanwhile, the priestesses held up the three still-beating hearts of the undead they'd so recently sacrificed—bowing before the visage overhead while it stared down at them, contemplating.

The god's visage stretched out a clawed hand, and the bat-like wings extended. The visage moved its mouth as if speaking, but none but the bishop could hear the words it was trying to convey through whatever veil had kept it from traveling into Elysium's multiverse since the integration.

Moments passed and the three souls suddenly shattered into a million pieces, soaring skyward. The hearts each burst into flames. A shudder, a ripple of power cascaded outward from the place of sacrifices across the crowds. An extreme sense of dread overcame all of them just as a large black hole opened up far above the ziggurat in the cavern's sky. It was so black that even in the dark of the cave, it was a stark contrast to the background.

More ripples of power commenced in quick succession, and dark magic spiraled out of the black hole in a swirling mist of animosity that then settled into the amphitheater. The energy shook Queen Bez to her very bones, and it was all she could do to stay calm. For the first time in a long time, she felt fear.

Then all was deathly silent.

Not even the splashing blood around her as she turned made any noise. She tried to speak and nothing came out. The wind, the chanting, the sound of drums were all gone. It was as if she had gone deaf, and the confused looks of the others clarified that they were experiencing something similar.

"Hello, mother of Deepnest. I have been expecting you."

The voice was crystal clear, masculine, and drenched in confidence. It rang out like a bell amid the otherwise perfect silence and caused Queen Bez to whirl around to seek the source. But she didn't find it.

"Queen . . . Bez . . ." the chime continued as she felt a chill upon her skin. "I am glad my bishop found such a willing leader to finally call me back from the grave Elysium had sentenced me to, as this strange system had deemed me as . . . unwanted. How peculiar, I must say . . . but breaking through into this new multiverse was easier than I'd thought—given the help of my clergy. And the help of yourself, for bringing such an amazing specimen to bind to, in the form of this vampire's body . . . He will be the perfect vessel for me to possess after I devour his soul."

The candles all winked out.

A tower of green flames then exploded down from the black hole overhead and condensed as it hit the platform right beside the pool of blood. The heat was tremendous and Bez had to shield her face, though thankfully it only lasted for a brief moment as the god's winged figure took a more solid form.

He stood tall, just like all the statues of old she'd witnessed in temples as a child. Two large horns, one behind the other along his snout, protruded like daggers. Long claws, a twin set of tails, bright-green fur, and dark-brown eyes.

The ghostly, ten-foot-tall apparition seemed unstable, though, as if the god was battling . . . something . . . in order to remain in this realm. He looked at his hand, bringing it up close to his face as all the clergy around them prostrated themselves in reverence. "I am the great winged rat, and I hear your plea."

His aura exploded again and toppled many of the onlookers, throwing some head over heels—and his black wings lifted up to either side as he flexed his muscles. "My body will not last long in this form. Elysium does not want me here. It had left me as junk to be discarded . . . along with the rest of my pantheon. But with this body . . ."

The god gestured to Riven, and the vampire's bloodied, carved body shot upright and came to hover in front of the ratkin god's spirit. "With this man's body . . . I will be able to scoop out the essence of his soul and replace it with my own. After that . . . after I bring my brothers and sisters from beyond this realm into the new multiverse, I will work to alleviate and dispel the curse you have been afflicted with—my children. You have all done well. Prek . . . bring me the sacrificial dagger."

The bishop immediately scurried out of the bloody bath and knelt before the visage, stretching out his clawed hands to present a wicked, curved blade, which the god's spirit picked up with one hand.

Bringing the blade up to Riven's neck, and tracing the carved sigils and runes in Riven's chest with his other hand, the great winged rat's eyes narrowed. "Your name . . . tell it to me, so that I may know the name of the man I have consumed. So that I will remember it, as an honor to your memory."

Riven's crimson eyes began to dull, the light fading from them to the point that they didn't glow at all any longer—and the god's spirit frowned at the otherwise lack of response.

"His name-identity is Riven Thane! He is king-leader of the undead-kin up above!" Prek quickly stated after realizing the great winged rat was becoming irritated.

The god nodded slowly. "Riven Thane . . . May your passing be as painless as possible, for the gift you are giving me—willing or not."

The god sank the knife blade first, and very slowly, deep into Riven's sternum between the two pentagrams representing Athela and Azmoth. Blood began trickling down Riven's chest while he remained motionless and emotionless, up until the point when the blade was buried all the way to the hilt—and then Riven's eyes turned from dull to pitch-black.

The god's frown deepened, and it tilted its head to the side in confusion—matching Riven's limp posture to meet the man's eyes when Riven began to smile. "Do you find the end of your life to be . . . funny?"

The smile only spread farther, and the ends of Riven's cheeks split open to make it even wider as it literally came around from ear to ear. Musculature and bones were exposed and peeled back, and his vampiric fangs were joined by rows upon rows of similar teeth that began growing out of his jaws.

Then Riven began to chuckle—still remaining limp as a doll in the grasp of the god's power. The chuckle turned into a laugh, and the laugh turned into a screeching, crazed cackle—defying the god's spirit in front of him like there was not a care in the world.

Riven's body abruptly shifted positions in space—closing the small distance between himself and the winged ratkin god until they were only an inch apart as blood began streaming out of his eyes and dripping down onto the floor below. "Riven isn't home right now! But thanks for delivering yourself unto me so quickly. I'd been concerned you wouldn't arrive in person!"

The vampire's chest tore open into a huge vertical maw as tendrils of darkness ripped out of his flesh—carving into the god's spirit and beginning to pull it in as the great winged rat screamed in confusion and horror. Riven's shackles burned away as his Mark of the Sinner tattoo expanded to cover his entire body within a split second—etching Unholy black tattoos into his pale skin while two enormous auras crashed in front of the ziggurat.

Queen Bez and the nearby clergy, including Bishop Prek, were eradicated in an instant as the two powerhouses tore into one another. The ratkin god struggled and flailed, using its ethereal claws to cut away dozens of tendrils while Gluttony continued to cackle.

Hundreds and then thousands of black tendrils crashed into the god's spirit, digging and burying themselves into the ethereal body and burning, tearing, and ripping the ratkin deity's soul apart while consuming it bit by bit. Gluttony was eating the god alive, and he shuddered with ecstasy as he ate the ascended spirit before the very eyes of its ratkin worshippers.

Ratkin that'd been on the periphery of the initial blast came racing ahead, horror and fury engulfing them as they tried to assist their would-be savior with screams of desperation, but these, too, were swept away with a mere flick of Riven's hand. Gluttony's tendrils ripped out of maws in the floor that devoured the ratkin in moments—killing them with audible crunches that left them squealing before abrupt and bloody ends as their bodies disappeared into the abyss behind each of those ravenous mouths.

Gluttony's black eyes then turned upon the masses before him, growing a third, vertical eye of similar black down the center of his forehead, and the unnaturally large grin on Riven's face ripped again as half of his head tore itself backward to unleash a swarm of hungry insects that began tearing into the undead ratkin hordes.

Carnage erupted across the amphitheater.

The ratkin panicked and screamed as they began to drop like flies. Their bodies, still alive, were being eaten and torn apart in bloody displays like corpses through a grinder, and soon the entire amphitheater for miles saw more and more maws tearing through space to devour even more of the creatures.

Blood and bile sprayed. Bodies were devoured.

Crowds trampled over their own as the blighted ratkin escaped through tunnels at the top or sides of the place of worship or died trying to escape.

And the snapping, gurgling sounds coming from the semisolid spirit body of the ratkin god ended with a loud *CRACK* when one of Gluttony's tendrils found the soul core he'd been searching for.

The minor god shuddered, its form going limp, until it ceased resisting and was dragged into Gluttony's maw with a series of crunching sounds.

Gluttony shuddered yet again as his swarms and maws continued devouring the fleeing creatures before him, and he reveled in the sense of being alive once again.

[System Notice: Elysium's contractual agreement has been met. As one of the seven original sins, you are being allowed another chance at life. Per the contract:

You will remain as a symbiotic organism to balance out your gluttonous tendencies

You will have a nearly complete reset, losing over 99% of your skills, knowledge, and levels

You will no longer be contained to the abyss

The ones banished with you during the War of Eternum will also be returned to life, with a similar reduction of skills, knowledge, and levels as those you experienced

Limiters on all other original sins, and the angelic commandments, will be opened—allowing them to take the same deal you struck

Should your symbiote ever die, you will be given the opportunity to start over again and choose a new one—but you will have another complete reset in doing so

All Shards of Gluttony will be returned to you now that your banishment is being lifted, but remnants of your old power will remain in the harbingers you created during your attempts to circumvent my rules

Any further attempts to circumvent my rules will result in another, permanent, banishment]

[Multiversal System Notice: To all creatures across Elysium, let it be known that the return of the sins and commandments is at hand. The first of the seven original sins, Gluttony, has been unleashed from the abyss. Other sins and commandments will be released from the abyss over the course of the next ten years as long as they are willing to abide by Elysium's terms. Let the eternal war between the hells and heavens begin again, as the origins of angels and demons clash in the cosmos—unshackled and unrestrained, seeking to return to the power they once had.]
[Your level has been set to equal the symbiote partner you've bonded to, and you now share a body with the symbiote host Riven Thane. Experience needed to level up simultaneously with your host has doubled. Your host has gained the title Incarnation of Gluttony, Original Sin. Your skills have been reset to five: Hungering Clone Maws, Tendrils of Sin, Devouring Swarm, Devour Energy, and Banshee's Wail. All your previously banished servants will start at level 1.]
[Both you and your symbiote host have grown to level 200 and have been stopped from progressing further into the E-grade until you each reach enlightenment.]
[Your symbiote host has taken the number one Apex rank on the power ladder of Panu.]

Gluttony immediately felt the presence of the Scythe, then the blood god, and soon a plethora of other gods that numbered in the dozens, then hundreds, then thousands as the eyes of the multiverse shifted their attention to his position.

What vultures they were, feeding off the accomplishments and worship of those lesser than they.

Gluttony was nothing like them, and this great winged rat—though only a lesser god—would not be the last of his kind that Gluttony devoured.

Licking the last remnants of the ratkin god's semisolid spirit off his chest, Gluttony banished their presences with a flick of his wrist. He abruptly felt the change in his memories as Elysium forcibly tore knowledge of rituals, spells, miracles, and lore from his mind, causing Gluttony's face—or Riven's face—to scrunch up in pain . . . but he let out an audible sigh of relief when it was done.

He was not angry.

He had been gone too long to be angry.

Gluttony could only be . . . excited that he'd found someone as compatible as Riven to host him—and he groaned with pleasure when shards of his soul began slamming into his soul aperture, which was now intertwined with Riven's own.

He was going to be whole again, and it was only a matter of time before he and his symbiote grew into a power like he'd been once upon a time—long, long ago.

He could almost taste the fear of the angels even from here, in the dark depths of this backwater planet, and another low chuckle erupted from his lips as his massive soul encompassed Riven's—beginning to feed Riven power with checks and balances on Elysium's end coming into play.

One by one, portals began to form. Those who'd been the strongest of his worshippers, his strongest minions, his strongest followers—they'd been banished with him during the War of Eternum.

They'd all been reset to level 1, but levels certainly weren't everything when each of them had hundreds of body enhancements, perks, inherent buffs, titles, extremely high affinities, and natural strengths based on their racial aspects.

Dozens and then hundreds of demons that'd once been banished to the abyss began walking through black gates and into the realm of the living. They breathed their first breaths for eons, opening their eyes with hints of excitement and glee as they turned to face the one they called master.

"What are your orders, Gluttony?" a slender, multihorned woman asked through a veil of shadows that encompassed her body—white eyes lighting up through the darkness as she bowed low, setting an example for all the others as they did the same. "We are willing and able to serve and are excited to be of use once more. All hail the great maw."

"ALL HAIL THE GREAT MAW!" the simultaneous chant from the hundreds of demons surrounding him called out in unison, from those big and small alike.

Gluttony was pleased. He had nowhere near the number of legions he'd previously controlled when seeking conquest over entire galaxies or when invading the heavens in the sixth era, but the ones in front of him represented some of the brightest talents he'd ever had the pleasure of lording over.

He stepped forward and placed a hand on the shadowy woman's horned head. "There is another, by the name of Allie Thane . . . She has a quest gifted to her by the system that guarantees Elysium's protection from outside invaders. The catch is that we will need to conquer 80 percent of the planet in her name by the time the system integration finishes . . . and I will be preoccupied with another world quest within the hour."

He summoned Allie's quest status information, but how and why he knew what her quest was . . . was now unattainable to him. He'd received the information prior to having his mind stripped by Elysium and was doubtful he'd be able to acquire personal quest information like this again anytime soon.

[New system quest dispensed: Conquer Panu. You have been publicly denounced by the Blood God as an Apostate, have angered almost every vampiric faction in the entire multiverse, and have already been marked for death on the public forums by numerous other factions across your planet. Having instilled a deep fear in the minds of the living, and having given hope to the sentient undead of your world, you are destined to be hunted down—or, alternatively, you will rise from the ashes of war as a hero to your people. Will you and your kind be eradicated from Panu? Or will you conquer this planet and

**claim it for yourself? You have until the five-year time limit of inte-
gration to take over at least 80% of this planet for yourself. If you
accomplish this, you will gain Elysium's direct and absolute protection from outside invaders for an additional one hundred years and
will gain a shroud that stops other outside forces from scrying your
planet's location for five hundred years, and the administrator will
allow you to reposition your newly conquered planet anywhere in the
multiverse a single time at the end of integration.]**

The woman kept her head bowed. "You wish for us to help her?"

"I do," Gluttony stated simply, withdrawing his hand and allowing the woman's bright-white eyes to look up at him in admiration. "Find this Allie Thane,
help her accomplish her goals, and wait for my return. Do not let her die; she is
the sister of my symbiote host, and what pains him will also pain me. There is also
a dungeon called Negrada that we will assist to establish a foothold back in the
hells . . . Allie will have more information on the matter when you find her. Do
this, and you will serve me well."

The black tattoos covering his body flickered with black lightning for a
moment, sparking twice more, then his three black eyes began to form crimson
centers moments later. Gluttony sensed Riven's presence begin to settle in from
the slumber he'd been placed in, and soon each of his eyes had a black sclera
background with glowing crimson pupils.

The maw along his chest began to fade, and Messenger was extracted from
his soul aperture—along with Jackal. A sigil of the great maw then appeared in
a pentagram on his sternum, right underneath the pentagram sigils for Azmoth,
Athela, and Fay.

He equipped both Messenger and Jackal next as Riven began to form consciousness, and then looked down at his bare legs with a frown. "One last thing
before I go. Find me . . . some pants."

"Some . . . pants, my lord?"

". . . Yes. Some pants."

**[One minute until World Quest 2 proceeds with the subevent the
Altars of Despair and Hope. Prepare yourself.]**

CHAPTER 30

Porcelain masks, red flowing robes, and a swirling vortex of crimson that reached the sky.

Seven monsters of ancient power.

The seven elders of the Blood Moon Requiem floated in meditative poses in a circular formation, facing in toward a globe of blood that was drawing from each of the thrall bodies their spirits possessed here on Panu. Each of these thrall bodies were slowly withering away, and the original souls that had inhabited them were now long gone.

Elder Thune and High Queen Nephridi glared at each other through the slits in the masks their vessels wore, the remnant soul fragments of each thrall rapidly deteriorating as the seconds ticked by—sitting almost opposite one another with other elders between them on either side. The tension had been high ever since Allie had killed Lord Justo Barimont, which had almost led to a civil war.

That fracture line in the empire was still there, but at least the background assassinations had come to a halt. And now with the introduction of Allie's new changes, it appeared that Queen Nephridi had bet on the wrong horse.

Kathrine stood wide-eyed in the trading compound's center, watching awe-struck as fractal lines shattered the clouds overhead into red, crystalline patterns that bloomed and grew as the vortex continued to pour power into the ritual. She simply didn't know what to do or how to stop it, and when it was a unanimous decision of all seven . . .

There was just no stopping it on her end.

Riven and Allie were both going to be very angry. It made Kathrine worry about her upcoming engagement, about whether he'd blame her for not being able to stop it.

"You seem bothered, Princess," Elder Thune called from his floating position under the fortress's shadow. He turned his burning crimson eyes to Kathrine, and she nearly stumbled when his aura slammed into her.

It wasn't that he was intentionally doing it, either. It was just that, despite his real body being back in another universe past multiversal boundaries, he was simply that strong—and he had to keep the gates to his soul open to maintain this part of the ritual. Thus, a passive glance could kill mere F-grades such as herself if he really put intent behind it.

Thankfully he wasn't doing so.

"I . . ." Kathrine righted herself, sweat beading down her face, and she shook her head while straightening and smoothing out her formfitting black dress. "Y-your Excellency, I am merely concerned about the well-being of my fiancé. I am certain he won't like what is about to happen to his sister—"

"She deserves what is going to happen. She was the one who so blatantly refused the blood god's will," Elder Thune interrupted her with an uncaring, almost demeaning snort. "Pathetic, really. To think one of our own would so flippantly discard what it means to be one of the blood."

Queen Nephridi, who'd been glaring at the man opposite her this entire time, finally tore her red eyes off him and turned to look at Kathrine with a little more grace than the other elder vampire elder. "Child . . . It is not something I enjoy thinking about, either. But it is not as if we have a choice, and we aren't killing her. That in itself is a mercy, considering what she has done. Even if it angers the Scythe, our bloodline—Malignant Prophecy—is the most valuable treasure our empire has. It is what made us who we are today, it is what carried us throughout the hundreds of millennia to become a powerhouse of the multiverse, and it is simply not negotiable. We have committed genocides five times over and waged war on civilizations far more powerful than ourselves to prove to the multiverse that we will not tolerate others laying hands on what is ours by birthright. We cannot allow our bloodline to fall into the hands of the Phantom Legions now that she has turned, or even the Reapers, and I have no doubt that both organizations are going to be digging in their heels to get to her no matter the cost if we allow this planet to exit integration without some means of a safeguard. Stripping her soul, even at the temporary cost of our own power, is a necessary risk we must take."

The sky above them exploded in a storm of red as two fractal patterns connected and merged, sending red shock waves over Brightsville and causing the image of a blood moon to slowly take form over the stars in the sky. It slowly began to grow in size and brightness as seconds and then minutes ticked by.

"And the blood god wills it," Queen Nephridi muttered under her breath, turning back around to face in toward the globe of red wicking away energy from the seven thralls each of the elders now possessed.

Another messenger ran in, whispering into Kathrine's ear about Dr. Brass's repeated requests for information on just what was going on—but again she told the messenger to tell the necropolis it was nothing to be concerned about. It wasn't as if anyone currently present in Brightsville could stop what was going on anyway, and the sinking feeling she was getting in her gut only grew as—

[Multiversal System Notice: To all creatures across Elysium, let it be known that the return of the sins and commandments is at hand. The

**first of the seven original sins, Gluttony, has been unleashed from
the abyss. Other sins and commandments will be released from the
abyss over the course of the next ten years as long as they are willing
to abide by Elysium's terms. Let the eternal war between the hells and
heavens begin again, as the origins of angels and demons clash in
the cosmos—unshackled and unrestrained, seeking to return to the
power they once had.]**

The system notification burned itself into the air in front of her with a shattering, screaming howl. The usual blue hologram text was nowhere to be seen. Nor was the gold lettering of Elite notifications, or the red of Legendary notifications. Instead, it was a deep black that seemed to suck in the very light around her like some kind of black hole ripped in space.

Overhead and across the sky, a giant black maw screamed in triumph as the very planet rumbled around them. The air quaked, a cold wave of dread overtook them, and the sky flickered—even changing the blood moon's image into a vast abyss where six other faded entities resided, each of them holding a unique but vastly powerful essence themselves. Just staring up at the maw and the six caged entities caused Kathrine to start seizing, hitting the floor while the floodgates of dark inspiration crashed through her mind and soul. The dark truths of the universe came and went as a fire hydrant trying to be forced down a straw, and it took everything inside her not to cry out as her soul aperture cracked and reorganized itself under the massive weight of an eons-old but mostly forgotten path.

Then the maw, the abyss, and the presence of the six other original sins were all gone—fading away and leaving the world as it had been only minutes before.

The elders all sat in stunned silence, and it was one of the others, a woman by the name of Elder Istiva, who spoke first. "Did we just witness . . ."

"We did," Queen Nephridi confirmed with a whisper, still staring up at where the vision had presented itself while their ritual continued building.

One of the other masked elders began swearing under his breath, and as the seconds ticked by, he voiced the one question that everyone else was thinking, but not saying. "Why would it present itself here?"

The clearing fell into silence.

"You don't think . . ." Elder Istiva said slowly, nervously cracking one knuckle with a cocked head as yet another man began to cackle gleefully at the very idea that the assumption might be right.

"Impossible," Elder Thune promptly stated. "The chances of that are—"

He was cut off when a tear in space ripped open before them. All seven of the stunned vampire elders watched in dead silence as a very famous figure who they all recognized from the recorded histories stepped through, closing the black gate of the abyss behind her.

She was a demonic woman wreathed in shadow that covered her entire body, tall for a humanoid, with indistinguishable facial features other than the seven horns around her head that formed a pseudo-crown. The bright-white eyes lacked pupils, remaining drooped in a calm and collected manner—as if bored—and the deep-purple pentagram with the sigil of Gluttony's maw that drew itself onto her chest was a telltale confirmation of just who she was.

She raised herself off the ground to hover up and then over the seven elder vampires, looking down on them and clasping her hands behind her with a satisfied nod. Large black wings spread out from her back, as if stretching them after a long time of disuse—and a long black tail sprouted from her backside to whip about in the air behind her. "Yes . . . This is where our eyes should meet. With me looking down . . . on the rest of you."

No one said a word, each of the seven elders remaining in a stunned state of silence, while her bright-white eyes continued to glow—radiating out as two beacons amid the pool of shadows that clothed her body.

Her identification information, etched in black flames, was mostly unidentifiable.

[Lillith, Level 1 Archdemon: Unique ???. ???. ???. ???. ???. ???. ???. ??? Commander of the Gluttonous Legions. Mythic.]

She gestured to the ritual above them, and the sky shattered. The visage of the blood moon evaporated, and another shock wave radiated across the heavens as the seven elders each snapped out of their surprised trances to stand abruptly.

"YOU DARE!" Elder Thune snarled, reaching up with his thrall—only to evaporate into a spray of blood and viscera when Lillith's tail snapped forward to make contact.

"Now, now," Lillith cooed, turning her calm gaze upon the others with wings still outstretched. "I know you are all quite powerful in your own right, I can sense it . . . S-grade monsters or higher, the lot of you. But none of you are able to impose your true strength here and now, not on this planet, not under the watch of Elysium while Panu is still undergoing integration. There is nothing you can do here now that I have come, so it would be in your best interest to talk—rather than to attempt a poor and petty revenge. Because you see . . . That girl whose soul you were trying to strip—she is now my charge. It may take another ten thousand years before I'm able to match your raw strength as I regain my power, but if you know what's good for you—you'll all stay out of my way."

Riven sat before the great maw, a mouth that swallowed the universe as billions begged, screamed, and died. Planets burned, legions marched on the heavens, and angels were eaten alive by enormous, titanic demons and creatures of nightmare.

"*All is as it should be . . .*" Riven heard the great maw whisper into his mind. "*This is what our future holds . . .*"

The vision cut off, falling back into the black tattoos that covered his otherwise pale body—becoming accessible for later.

Notifications flashed through his mind, but they then quickly settled into the background of his status page for him to check later—as ones specific to the quest he'd been assigned popped up as priority messages.

[Chalgathi, the Apocalypse Beasts World Quest, Panu, subevent has been INITIATED: The Altars of Despair and Hope.

A temporary pocket world for this event has been created. The chosen finalists of Chalgathi, the Plague Dragon; Chubin, the Glass Kraken; and Nekra, the Skeletal Devourer, have all been sent to this pocket world to compete.

Locations of Chalgathi's altars have been marked for you. You will be required to visit all four Chalgathi altar sites and activate each of the shrines, as well as acquire ten thousand event points before being allowed to leave this event. Doing so will also give you knowledge of the location of Chalgathi's Temple, where Chalgathi's incubation chamber has been hidden.

There are twenty-one registered cultists.

- Seven Chalgathi cultists, six Chubin cultists, and eight Nekra cultists

There are nine registered noncultists entering this event.

- Three Chalgathi noncultists, four Chubin noncultists, and two Nekra noncultists

You have arrived at the Altar of Hope and are now registered as a noncultist. Killing other noncultists will decrease your event points. Each participant will have their own set of unique quests that allow them to gain points and level up, and only quests will allow level-ups and XP gains during this event. Other rules will be reviewed again and in more detail after your first quest is completed.]

[Chalgathi Cowl (Noncultist) has been added to your inventory. This is a soul-bound item only you can wear for the remainder of this event; it gives you no stats or bonuses, but it marks you as a Chalgathi noncultist to friend and enemy alike.]

[Riven's Quest 1 of the Altars of Despair and Hope: Other F-grade participants have been either voluntarily or involuntarily dragged into this event from across the multiverse. Unlike the chosen of this trial, they do not respawn twenty-four hours after death. You have been given the task of defending one of these populations. Your first quest is to travel to the marked quest location and save as many people as you can. Each person who dies subtracts one event point. Successfully defending the town from the monster wave will gain you 30 event points.

>>> Time until monster wave: fifteen hours.]

Riven opened his red-and-black eyes, including the vertical one stationed on his forehead, with a deep inhale of fresh air. The crisp cold flooded his lungs and invigorated him, and it was with a shuddering breath that he let it all out with a slump to his shoulders.

Just what had happened to him?

No . . . he remembered now. The memories etched themselves into his thoughts one by one, and a deep sadness overcame him when he thought of Snagger's recent death. That sadness turned to anger when he realized that Gluttony had intentionally let the ratkin die in order to get closer to the lesser god, and he turned his ire upon the symbiotic presence in his soul only a split second later.

"Do not be angry with me, Riven . . . If I had not done so, if I had not gained the element of surprise and been in such close proximity to the overly confident god, we would have died, too. This was the best and only way."

A soothing sensation washed over him, and it was as if Gluttony had imposed his will on Riven to calm him down. Despite knowing this, Riven decided this was a conversation to be had at a later time—and he let that soothing sensation continue to massage his anger away while considering just what he wanted to say about all that'd happened.

He had a lot of questions.

"Riven?"

Genua's voice pulled him out of his stupor, and Riven blinked while coming back to reality.

He stood on a large flat-topped tower that overlooked a forested landscape that spread out in all directions for as far as the eye could see. The sun beat down on him, though his gluttonous ivory armor kept him from taking passive sunlight damage, and he noted that his helmet had been modified to allow his third eye to see through from his forehead. A thin but very well-made cowl made from a smooth black material also covered his helmet, with a dark-green trimming and little holes having been custom-made by the system to let the spined central ridge of red feathers from his helmet through.

Jackal remained in its canine form at his side, and he had a different, unfamiliar set of metal greaves on. Beside him were Azmoth, Genua, Athela, and Luke, who'd been watching over Len in Brightsville. Fay was nowhere to be seen, but she'd also just died in Deepnest's explosion, so he did a quick set of actions to pay Elysium for her return in twenty-four hours.

Aside from his minions, there were also eight other people (some of whom had their own minions) standing on top of the flat roof of the tower—with a spiral stairway leading downward in the very center of the tall building. They all looked sketchy as fuck in his opinion, a mix and match of wary stares shared between the lot of them—and a good number of them wearing masks or hoods to obscure their faces. Some wore heavy armor, others wore leathers or robes, and one guy wore nothing but a set of boxers and carried two orange metal katanas in either hand.

Weird choice of a getup, in Riven's opinion.

But they all had one thing in common.

Each of them had a cowl on their heads, over the original outfits they'd put on. The three Chalgathi noncultists—who were all humans—wore black hoods with green trimming and had circular dragon symbols etched into the tops. This included the living fashion statement bearing two orange katanas. The four Chubin noncultists wore cowls made of silver material with blue trimmings and had the visage of a kraken etched into their tops. These particular people weren't humans at all; rather, three of them were actually lizard-like naga—with blue-green scales and frills along their necks and heads. They had webbed hands, the upper bodies were humanoid, and their lower bodies were that of a snake or sea serpent. The fourth Chubin noncultist was actually a mermaid with short green hair and a getup made of stitched scales and seaweed, who quickly changed her lower fish half into legs and stood upright when Riven's eyes fell upon her. The two Nekra noncultists wore sandy-brown hoods with teal trimming and an etched scorpion sigil, one a short dwarf woman wearing half a dozen skulls around her waist with multiple undead golems positioned around her, and the other a dark elf wearing a black robe with a white skull tattoo covering half his face. The dark elf held two well-crafted wooden wands out to either side and had a single large phantom hovering behind him protectively.

Dual-wielding wands wasn't something Riven had seen before, and he found the concept rather interesting.

"Riven!" Genua hissed, coming over to tug on his arm frantically with eyes wide. "Len was left behind! Where is my daughter?!"

This snapped Riven out of his musings, but they were all quickly calmed down when Luke held up a placating hand.

The old elf thrall cleared his throat. "Len is fine. She's at the manor now and was being taken care of by myself, Tupper, and all the other elf staff on duty. I must say that your daughter is getting along very well with all the other deathtouched elf children we brought in from the orphanage today—but she doesn't seem to understand why she wasn't turned like the rest of them. Keeps asking me about why everyone on that side of the portal and all the friends she'd made at school previously now have gray skin and neon-teal eyes. I think she's jealous of them."

Len had been on the other side of Panu when Allie's event had taken hold, and the elves of Tereen or the children who'd been orphaned had in many cases become Deathtouched Enlightened versions of themselves. They'd kept most of their physical attributes in terms of how they looked, but the coloring was often off and their death affinities had skyrocketed across the board due to their now technically undead heritage.

"Are you sure she's in good hands?" Genua whirled around on Luke, tears in her eyes, clasping her hands together in front of her. "I didn't even get to tell her goodbye! I'm going to be gone for a year or more and I didn't get to see her off!"

The others on the tower were staring slack-jawed, wary, or even outright scared as they stared Riven's group down—with Azmoth and Athela's drider form both very large and intimidating presences near the tower's edge.

"Len will be fine, Genua. Tupper is there, and I'll let Fay know to pass along the message so he can tell Len what happened," Riven assured her with a firm and comforting hand on his thrall's shoulder. "We can even have them give us updates that way."

Athela, who was covered in blood and standing at the height of a small building, turned her large frame around and groaned in irritation. "I was just about to finish wiping out that Russian mafia family before being teleported here! You do realize I was in the middle of an operation with General Bruner from Chicago, right? RIGHT, RIVEN?!"

Athela abruptly changed into her bloodweaver form, the dog-size spider jumping up into Riven's arms and rapidly swatting him on the armored forehead. "BAD RIVEN! SEND ME BACK! BAD-BAD!"

Riven immediately encased her entire body in crimson ice, walked over to the edge as she continued to screech muffled insults through the magic, and dropped the frozen block of spider off the edge while giving her a salute and a chuckle.

Azmoth joined in on the laughter, waving at the disappearing spider as she went.

Her screams faded away and he turned back to the others before his eyes settled on a single familiar figure wearing another Chalgathi hood nearby. Slowly he lifted an eyebrow, tilted his head, and his jaw began to drop as the woman meekly waved back.

She wore a black leather outfit, with her own Chalgathi items set having turned into something of a rogue's outfit with spiked-knuckle leather gloves that went up to her shoulders. Her dragon amulet remained the same as it'd originally been, and her headdress poked out the front of her cowl and looked very Native American–like with the feathers pulsing green energy, while a variety of different small blades were strapped to her upper body and thighs.

He pointed her way. "You're that Asian lady from the pyramid back in the pre-integration Chalgathi quest. Aren't you? The one who helped me get up to the top?"

Her smile grew a bit, and she hesitantly nodded. "It's good to see you again, though you helped me more than I helped you back then. It was a pretty brutal initiation, and if you'd told me that you were going to become the most powerful person on this planet by the next time we'd meet, I'd have laughed in your face and called you crazy, Mr. Riven Thane."

CHAPTER 31

The other noncultists had quickly left, setting out toward where their own quest markers were taking them. No one wanted to talk to Riven's group, with the one exception of the Asian woman who'd helped him up the pyramid in the very first day of integration, no doubt due to the terrible reputation he had on the forums and the power he had to back it up. Riven, to them, was an absolute monster. He was a genocidal maniac. He was a mass murderer in every sense of the word—and they did everything in their power to even avoid eye contact when he caught them staring in the early seconds of having transitioned into this new Apocalypse Beasts event.

"My name is Nora. It's nice to finally greet you like this," Nora, the Asian woman, stated with a smile from underneath the headdress and hood she now wore.

He took her hand when she extended it, and they shook firmly before releasing.

"It's nice to see a familiar face here, one that I don't want to kill," Riven stated with a laugh while the last people left filed down the central staircase of the altar's insides. "I'd introduce myself, but it appears you know my name already!"

"Hard to miss with everything you've done," Nora said wryly in response. "You're one of the most hated and feared people on the planet, and you have one of the largest cult followings, too."

"Cult followings? Are you being serious or is it a figure of speech? Like with Chalgathi?"

"No, not literally, but people on the forums are either die-hard against you or die-hard for you. There isn't much of an in-between. Hey, what's your first quest? I think we may have the same one."

Riven chuckled. "That's rather confident . . . What makes you say that?"

He pulled up his quest notification and showed it to her, only causing her to pooch her lips while reading.

[Riven's Quest 1 of the Altars of Despair and Hope: Other F-grade participants have been either voluntarily or involuntarily dragged into this event from across the multiverse. Unlike the chosen of this

trial, they do not respawn twenty-four hours after death. You have been given the task of defending one of these populations. Your first quest is to travel to the marked quest location and save as many people as you can. Each person who dies subtracts one event point. Successfully defending the town from the monster wave will gain you 30 event points.
>>> Time until monster wave: fifteen hours.]

Nora then pulled up her own quest notification, and a wide grin spread across her face. "So . . . What do you think? Partners for now? We can walk and talk to catch up on just what happened to us, and how we got here."

[Nora's Quest 1 of the Altars of Despair and Hope: Tag along with any other noncultist to defend their town for the upcoming monster waves. Your job is to successfully assassinate the enemy leader, as well as any enemy cultists who may appear with the monster wave. 30 event points for assassinating the enemy leader. Extra event points (+3 total) for any enemy cultist slain.]

This time, Riven's eyebrows both rose—and he looked off into the distance where his own quest marker in the form of a bright light continued pinging him with flashing signals. Then he laughed. "There'll be enemy cultists?! That sounds absolutely great. It appears we're already being pitted against the other side, and yes, I'd love to have you along. Let's get a move on, shall we?"

Gragle the gnome stared absentmindedly at the reflection looking back at him, little waves rippling in the cold amber liquid in his mug while people in the bar walked by. Two long scars had only narrowly missed his right eye but left ugly gashes of cursed energy that even to this day still hurt at random times. His once lively and joyous features were long gone after having lost so many friends over the years to disease and system-spawned monsters here on the barren planet of Mesini, and not a day went by that he didn't curse the decision to come to this hellhole.

The corporation he'd worked for had gone under when the lead on ancient artifacts had been a bust. His way off the planet had been barred, given he hadn't found some other way to pay back the people who'd given him a lift—and interstellar travel was not cheap. Not only that, but he was more of a magical artificer at heart and his skills had very quickly been deemed a need—rather than a want—for one very violent group of thugs called the Scrags mafia. He had a very unique class, one that he'd never heard of anyone else having before. One that let him see the most basic concepts of how skills worked. A way to cast abilities as something called graphics.

Graphics were, simply put, a way to formulate the magic of thought into physical concepts by utilizing the base code of the system. They were how Elysium itself performed feats, they were how Elysium itself created all the rules, and they were what some called the skeleton of all other magics because they could be used to combine and alter spells to interact with one another in odd and sometimes otherwise unheard-of ways. They were most often found in high-grade crafts, such as the applications he used for totem-crafting, but they could theoretically be used for combat as well. Gragle hadn't ever mastered the latter part as he was something of a coward, because graphics were generally a well-kept secret among most of the multiverse factions who had even a hint of knowledge about them, and the amount of magic it'd take to effectively use graphics in combat would have to be astronomical, but his skill in utilizing these graphics in his inventions had eventually led to his capture and pseudo-slavery here on Mesini.

He let out a long and high-pitched sigh, given his small size, and the human barkeeper snorted in derision at the depressed gnome before heading off to get more drink for another of the scavengers who frequented this pub.

The only joy Gragle found nowadays was deep in a glass of cold amber ale like the one in front of him. Even the love he'd once had for the crafting of totems, trinkets, magical weapons, and armor was long gone. He'd attempted to find something else to sway his wandering mind, something that he could grasp and find a love and passion for again—but he'd been stumped on what exactly that could be. Not that he could stop working for the Scrags—they'd kill him if he didn't produce for their outfit and had already tortured him brutally, twice. However, he otherwise had the freedom of choice, as long as he kept up with the demands of Ronnie—the Scrags mafia leader.

He took another sip of the amber liquid, his short black beard dripping the liquid onto gray pants stained with charcoal and ash. There was a bit of blood there, too, after having needed to sacrifice a few farm animals in order to properly create the two Blood-attuned graphics that were now hovering as three-dimensional objects over the scratched wooden counter. The graphics would occasionally shift shape, changing from one polygon form into another or sprouting branches here or there to retract them upon the next shift—but they each meant the same thing:

Power in Blood.

A man's grunt sounded out and the chair next to Gragle was pulled back. A thickly built man in full silver plate armor—trimmed in gold—sat down in it with a loud thud.

Gragle didn't even bother looking up, ignoring the silent stare from underneath the visor. He gestured to the two graphics over the bar. "There you go, Ronnie. As you requested."

The armored man looked down at the two floating polygons, then to Gragle, then back to the polygons before taking them and putting them into a spatial sack. "I told you not to bring these things out in public. You could be killed for the knowledge you possess, gnome—and I don't want you dead quite yet."

"Feigning worry, are we?" Gragle laughed, this time chugging the entire mug of ale in five large gulps before slamming the metal cup back down onto the old wood and pushing it away with a belch. "I would welcome death at this point. The life of a slave is no life at all."

"If that were true, you'd stop trying to find a way off this planet," Ronnie observed casually. "You'd just kill yourself."

Gragle stiffened in his seat, and for the first time since the armored man had arrived, the gnome looked at him through squinted lids. "Maybe, maybe not."

WHAM

Gragle felt his skull crack onto the wooden boards of the countertop, and many of the pub's patrons came to a standstill while watching Ronnie grind Gragle's skin against the rough wood.

"Remember your place, halfling," Ronnie stated coolly as a group of men behind him, all of them bearing the sigil of the Scrags on their armor or vests, chuckled. "Or I'll bring you down to the wringer and we'll go for round three— hot irons included. Wouldn't want to shit those finely made pants of yours yet again, now would we?"

The malice in Ronnie's words caused Gragle to flinch almost as much as the pain, and the halfling grunted when Ronnie's large human hand removed itself with another violent shove.

Gragle spat blood, and then a tooth as some of the Scrags members laughed— only for a system notification to appear in front of everyone present.

[Criteria met: Insignificant, lacking in Fate, high potential for reroute of Fate, and all below E-grade. Your town, Mesini Outpost Number 84, has been taken by Elysium for an integration event on the frontier of the newly born Universe 62.]

CRASH

The sky rumbled and the entire building shook. People and animals from outside began to scream and yell, with many of the scavengers dropping their drinks to hide under tables—while the more practical ones took their drinks with them until the earthquake stopped a few minutes later.

Ronnie, who'd been holding on to the bar hard with both gauntleted hands, looked around at his four men and whispered something to them before shouts from outside caused him to bolt for the door. When the gang leader got there, he immediately froze and gawked at the sky.

Gragle could already tell why, because he was looking out one of the dirty glass windows himself. Orange skies had turned into a pristine blue, and in the distance there were trees growing on hills surrounding their position on the outskirts of town.

Trees?

Gragle hadn't seen trees in over a decade!

"Wha . . . What just happened?" one of the men farther down the bar called out, his getup that of a typical scavenger with a gray cloak, various small weapons, and a few packs strapped to his hip.

The barkeep was the first to blink. "I think we were just pulled into an integration event . . . Read the text, bloke. Elysium is at its games again."

"Integration events are fucking dangerous!" the man hissed back, a little bit of fear in his words while he walked out to stand next to the still-gawking Ronnie. "I didn't ask for this! SEND ME BACK!"

[Outpost Number 84 Quest 1: Survive the monster wave. Time remaining: nine hours.]

There was dead silence for a couple seconds after that, and then an uproar took hold of the small town as hundreds of people began to panic simultaneously. Gragle, on the other hand, was a little less enthusiastic, remaining interested but less concerned about his own bodily safety. This was the most interesting thing he'd had happen to him almost . . . ever?

"This is bad . . ." Ronnie stated, sitting back down at the bar as another of his men in rat-skin furs sat down next to him. "Shit! Shit-shit-shit-shit-SHIT! I cannot BELIEVE we were taken off Mesini for a life-and-death INTEGRATION event, of all things! What are the chances?!"

"That's what your sister kept saying when—OW!"

Ronnie smacked the man as the others of his gang laughed.

And then the door to outside swung open and all the room abruptly fell silent. The laughter stopped, Ronnie's head swiveled left and froze in place, and people all over the pub stopped drinking just to stare.

"That's an odd kind of magic you have there. Or . . . is it even really magic? I'm quite curious."

The man's voice was calm and confident, and when Gragle looked up—still clutching his bruised face from where Ronnie had smashed it—he saw an armored, hooded man in the doorway surrounded by a variety of other figures.

The stranger gave off an aura of dread, not subtle at all given what was likely a very low or even negative Charisma stat, with two humanoid eyes and a vertical one along the forehead—all of them with deep black sclera and bright crimson centers. Spiked knuckle gauntlets of ivory metal, possibly even bone, covered his hands and led up to large, horned vampiric skulls for pauldrons that also glowed a bright red in the eye sockets. The chest plate had a long vertical maw of shifting teeth, with red silk of some kind covering the neck up to where a thick helmet created from interlocking teeth at the front clasped around the head—along with the three eye sockets that allowed the man to see forward. Red feathers down the central ridge created something like a mohawk, while a black hood with green trimmings and a circular dragon sigil along the top covered much of his helmet—allowing the feathers to pierce through the central row through numerous small holes.

[Chalgathi Cowl (Noncultist): This is a soul-bound item only you can wear for the remainder of this event. It gives you no stats or bonuses, but it marks you as a Chalgathi noncultist to friend and enemy alike.]

Strange—the notification had appeared immediately when he'd looked at the cowl without even attempting to identify it. What was Chalgathi? Gragle couldn't help but wonder.

Was this man one of the participants for the integration trial?

He had to be. Right? No one here had that high-quality gear.

A dog created from shadows sat at his side, with a black-and-red arachnid on his opposite shoulder. A huge, hulking, four-armed behemoth of a demon stood behind the man—no doubt a very powerful summon by the looks of it. Especially in this area of the multiverse—er, on Mesini, where only low-quality scavengers scrounging for scraps from the ruins of dead civilizations could be found.

Another woman in a black leather outfit with spiked leather gloves, a dragon amulet, and a headdress with a similar cowl stood beside the man who'd originally spoken—daggers strapped all over her body. Meanwhile, an old elf with red eyes and wearing thin linens had one hand on a mace strapped to a basic-looking belt.

Even with this odd mix and match of strangers, it was the last figure who had made everyone in the room freeze the most:

She was also a beautiful elf, but Gragle could barely tell, considering one of her ears was hidden under locks of blond hair. More than that, she was a thrall, if his identification read wasn't being tampered with. She wore a very formfitting black silk robe that almost looked like a long dress, with fingerless red gloves that came up her forearms and golden lettering on her rib cage. Two red half-moons and a central full moon were sewn into the front of the fabric, with shimmering crimson tattoos obvious in the dull light of the grungy pub. She wore a very recognizable red metal headdress over the black silk hood of her robes, and Gragle could see people even outside on the street had stopped to stare at her with a mixture of both awe and fear.

What in the hells and heavens was a priestess of the blood god doing here in an integration event?

Things were getting stranger and stranger by the minute.

Gragle openly gaped, just like many of the others did, and then blinked rapidly when the armored man at the forefront took a step inside. Gragle's eyes shifted to him, watching the stranger casually and slowly walk up to him, before sitting down on the opposite side from Ronnie.

Again, Gragle's eyes glanced back at the blood priestess, a cold sweat forming over his skin as his eyes darted around the room to settle on the man who'd just taken a seat nearby—and his blood ran cold when the priestess followed in to take a submissive position behind the man in ivory armor.

It didn't take much longer for the pieces to click together, even if Gragle's identification information couldn't piece much from the man's equipment or status information. It only gave him question marks when attempting, aside from that blasted hood, and the creepy three eyes the man had were certainly off-putting.

"M-master vampire . . . b-blood priestess . . ." Gragle said with a stutter, bowing his head low in respect and catching his breath while the sweat continued to accumulate on his forehead and palms. "W-what an honor it is that a p-priestess and her charge wish to s-speak with me! What c-can this humble gn-gnome do for y-you?"

His small body was literally shaking. And Ronnie now had a firm, tight grip on the long sword at his waist. But from the rattling of his weapon in its sheath, and the wide-eyed stare at the priestess, it was obvious that even he was terrified.

That didn't even account for the huge, hulking demon in the background.

[Genua, Level ??? Priestess of the Blood God, High Elf Thrall, ???]

The man in front of him seemed confused, and his central eye closed entirely as the helmet shut the vertical slit with ivory metal.

A living suit of armor?!

Gragle had tried creating one before, but it'd ended in absolute failure. If he could spend some time with this newcomer so he could study it . . .

"As I said . . ." the armored man stated before leaning right onto the bar's dirty, old wooden ledge. "You have an odd ability to craft . . . whatever those polygon energy constructs were. Would you mind showing me again?"

The barkeeper, a scrawny human man in his late forties who was already showing signs of balding, adjusted his glasses and nervously shuffled back to grasp something from underneath the bar. "Vampire . . . We don't wish to have any bloodshed here. There is no need to—"

"I don't intend to kill anyone here unless they attack me first," the armored man stated, continuing to stare Gragle down with a curious intent. He then held out a hand and deposited a small fortune of Elysium coins on the counter—immediately shifting much of the attention off the priestess.

That kind of money could feed any man here and his family for months . . .

"Drinks and food for my friends and me," the stranger stated, looking up to where Ronnie was clutching his sword and hesitating on what to do. "If you're going to take that sword out and attack, then get it over with. I'm tired of waiting."

The modified hellscape brutalisk was already looming over the men who'd accompanied Ronnie, and each of them had backed up a bit from the ringleader with wavering breaths and magic flaring in one's hands.

Ronnie shuddered, stood up, and took his hand off his weapon. He took one last look at the blood priestess and left without a word—all of his crew in tow.

Leaving Gragle all by himself, with a bruised face—and the attention of a bloodsucking scion of some coven. A scion that, by some massive stroke of misfortune, had chosen to single out Gragle for the graphics he'd had on display.

CHAPTER 32

Outside, the small scavenger town was an absolute riot, with people coming out of their homes onto the streets and gathering at the walls to look out beyond the high stone barricade. Gragle nervously glanced at the blanching barkeeper, who only shook his head as if telling the scarred gnome not to antagonize the vampire, and he let out a shuddering breath when his eyes again landed on the blood priestess.

The bar was clearing out, as half the people had already left to either get away from the bad omen in human form or to see what exactly was going on outside with the integration event. Things like this were very rare, but they did happen—and sometimes the moves were permanent. Most likely this would lead to a choice on whether to go back home or not at the end of the event should they survive, based on the history books, but there was no guarantee Gragle would even get back to Mesini after this.

There was no guarantee he'd live at all.

"Those polygons you saw are called graphics . . . Have you heard of them?" Gragle asked, noticing the quest timer in the top-right corner of his vision that was counting down to the moment the apparent monster wave would hit. Eight hours and forty-two minutes . . .

Gragle had a lot of questions for the strange, armored vampire, but he wasn't about to be the one who asked. Who were these people and why were they here? There was no doubt the system event somehow involved them—vampires didn't exist on Mesini, so what were the details of this overall quest? Surely it wasn't just a simple monster wave; there'd be no reason to transport Outpost Number 84 off-world if that'd been the case. Nevertheless and despite his building curiosity, Gragle twiddled his thumbs and gulped nervously when the vampire's companions all took seats at the bar as well—with the spider even transforming into a very attractive but deadly-looking Arshakai.

"He looks like he's about to piss himself," the demonic woman said with a wink, throwing a sleek black arm around the vampire's shoulders and pulling herself in to sit on his lap. "Poor little guy."

The man in armor blinked, took a cup of amber ale from the shaking bartender on the opposite side of the counter, and shoved the pile of coins toward the man insistently when he saw the paling human hesitate. "Take it."

There was a pause as the barkeeper seriously considered doing so—it was an absolute fortune in Elysium coins compared to what usually circulated around these parts—but he objected with a shake of the head. "It's on the house. I don't want to offend a young master of—"

"Take it," the armored man said again, smacking his hand onto the counter more forcefully this time.

The barkeeper took in a deep breath, closed his eyes tight, and prayed to the gods that he wasn't being tricked into some kind of foul, malicious prank. He slowly reached forward and scooped the gold into a sack, sweat starting to appear on his forehead and along his neck. He gave the vampire a quick glance to confirm it was still okay, and then gingerly put the sack of money on a back counter before continuing to pass out drinks to the others.

Meanwhile, the few people who'd stayed in the pub with them all just simply stared in absolute silence. It was like a grave, with the aura of dread so palpable now that Gragle was beginning to have a hard time breathing.

Just what was this man's Charisma level? He'd been here less than two minutes.

"My name is Riven," the vampire stated casually and took off his helmet—revealing a very handsome face with short brown hair. He had the pale skin typical of vampires, and the eyes were bright enough to be a greater vampire if Gragle had to guess—but those strange black tattoos . . . There was something very wrong about them. Something evil, ancient, even malicious, and he didn't recognize the script.

Gragle prided himself on having learned many of the ancient languages predating the system in order to craft better totems, enchantments, and graphics. He even specialized in Unholy magics, and his affinity told him that these tattoos were something related to the Unholy foundation. So it confused him that this script eluded him, and he outwardly cringed when the third eye on Riven's forehead flashed open to glare directly at him—opposite of where Riven's other eyes currently were locked onto the amber liquid at his lips.

The third eye blinked, flashed purple for a moment, and the action made the gnome involuntarily shudder. He felt exposed, undressed, bare before whatever that eye had just done—as if it was seeing into his soul to expose all the lies he'd ever told over his life.

"Are you part of the integration quest, Riven?" Gragle asked hesitantly, needing to take in deep breaths while in Riven's presence. "I hate to overstep, and if I am—I daresay I can be quiet, I am just rather concerned about being . . . transported . . . across the cosmos . . ."

His words trailed off slowly and fearfully when Riven's face turned his way, and he flinched again when the blood priestess got up. He even held up his hands pleadingly when she approached, and quickly bowed his head in a display of submission when she stopped beside the vampire. "Please, don't sacrifice me! P-please! I didn't m-mean to offend if I d-did anything wrong!"

He began to shake, tears starting to form under his eyes that were squeezed shut, and Riven shared a curious glance with the others.

"Little man?" Athela asked, knocking her knuckles on the top of his head and getting him to scream and flail out of his chair—smacking the back of his head onto the floor.

He groaned, began to pick himself up, and then fell back down into a patch of blood underneath the contact point.

"That was an overreaction." Riven blinked twice, and Gluttony's eye did the same before the great maw began to cackle good-naturedly in his mind. "Right, well, we have a little less than nine hours to shoot the shit until he wakes up—but keep an eye on him. I want to know what that ability was. It felt very unique."

"I keep eye on little man," Azmoth stated sagely, getting off his stool and picking the gnome up before setting him down on a bench nearby. "I not get drunk from this anyway, not strong enough."

"Azmoth, I don't think I've ever seen you drunk."

"I get drunk with Allie once."

"Really?"

"Yes. Ask her when get back."

Riven pooched his lips and took another sip as Nora laughed, and Genua took a seat next to him before clearing her throat to get his attention.

"Riven, would it be all right if I left for a while?"

He stopped sipping his drink and gave her a wary glance. "Left for a while? What are you talking about?"

Genua cleared her throat and pulled up a status screen that was described as an invitation to the blood god's temple. "I believe I'm supposed to take some of my very first lessons soon with other, older clergy . . . Once a week, I'm supposed to arrive there. I also think they're wanting to talk to me about your sister's actions . . . at least, that's what the invitation implies."

[Invitation to the Blood God's Temple: Your weekly session of worship, combat training, and scripture has come about. Please access the clergy system and teleport in so that we may start. We would also like to discuss recent events involving a particular angel on your planet, and hope that you can discuss the things we show you with Riven after the fact.]

It seemed pretty straightforward to Riven as well, and he waved Genua off with a nod. "Sure."

"Are you going to need me for this quest? Do I need to be back before the timer runs out?"

"No. Not unless things change. More than anything, you're probably going to benefit from their combat training rather than being here. I hope you can do some damage control on Allie's behalf."

Genua gave him a half smile and a nod before pulling up another screen for the clergy she was now a part of. "I will try. It will take a while to channel the teleport, so please don't let anyone bother me while I do it."

"Got it."

With a click, she started to glow a dull red—and she entered a meditative state a moment later after sitting down on the floor in a cross-legged position. Profane sigils related to the Blood subpillar lit up on the floor around her, and she remained absolutely still with her eyes closed while other patrons of the bar immediately got up to leave—casting her terrified glances.

Riven found it a bit weird, but didn't know much about the outside multiverse beyond Panu and some of the Blood Moon Requiem. It didn't appear that anyone wanted to converse much with him or his party, so he turned his attention to Nora after giving Athela a firm kiss with her fingers intertwined around his own. "So, Nora, tell me about what you've been through! And everything else, too! I don't know anything about you, really, other than our brief time on the pyramid together."

"That was a hellish time," Nora stated, nodding sagely and taking a big swig of her own drink.

The metal cup slammed down a moment later, and she gasped before gesturing to the barkeeper to refill it. "Hits the spot. After you and I were separated, I was eventually given the Rogue class. Then it upgraded twice after I got out of the Chalgathi starter trials and my tutorial dungeon, and now I have a class labeled Viper Blade. I can imbue any weapon I have with poison from the Unholy Foundational Pillar, gain critical amplifiers from the Shadow subpillar, and am pretty mobile. I'd ask you about your abilities, but I've seen enough of you wiping armies off the face of the planet to know enough. Chicago, where you wiped out the Azag, and then Daskus . . ."

She gave him an almost accusing look, ignoring the other people in the room catching their breath at her words.

He didn't even flinch, pulling Athela in tightly. "I did what had to be done, and I'd do it again."

Nora's eyes softened at the look of love Athela granted him, and she chuckled before taking the refilled cup. "I honestly don't care. I'm no saint, either."

She took another sip, but Riven could tell she was only half invested in the words she'd spoken.

"You don't have to dumb it down for me. I know what it looks like, but the ones I love come first." Riven gave her a sad smile, and then laughed out loud when the third eye on his forehead blinked—exchanging a quick set of words with Gluttony. "You know, I'm also the one that last system prompt was about. Maybe I am evil after all."

He gave her a wink.

"Last system prompt?" Nora repeated, swirling the amber liquid in her cup and glancing over her shoulder at Genua—who was still enveloped in the red runic circle in a cross-legged position. "You'll have to be more specific than that."

"Are you able to identify me?"

She looked up from her glass. "No. Other than your name and the red flames outlining it indicating your Legendary status. It's probably what everyone else here sees, too, considering they're all lower level than we are."

He opened his mouth to speak, then thought about it. "Check the rankings and tell me what's changed about my class."

"About your class?" She did as he asked and clicked a few options before coming to rest her eyes on the screen.

[**Twenty-six billion current participants have been analyzed. The ranking categories are as follows: Apex rank (top 10), Paragon rank (top 1,000), S rank (top 0.0001%), A rank (top 1%), B rank (top 15%), C rank (top 30%), D rank (top 50%), E rank (bottom 50%)]**
[**Current Top 10 Native Participants:**
1.   **Riven Thane, Level 200 Pureblooded Vampire, Apex rank, Warlock Devastator, Incarnation of Gluttony**
2.   **Allie Thane, Level 162 Angel of Death, Apex rank, primary class in transitory state, Hero of Death**
3.   **Judith Marcina, Level 180 Divine Human, Apex rank, Angelic Fallcaller, Light's Beacon**
4.   **Aren Hrall, Level 163 Snow Giant, Apex rank, Frostmage Berserker**
5.   **Retesh Vorath, Level 199 Corpse Lord, Apex rank, Elder Lich**
6.   **Netithi Bluskish, Level 130 Naga, Apex rank, Champion of the Kraken**
7.   **Chitter Teh-Sneaker, Level 137 Rat Man, Apex rank, Dark-Blade Assassin, Poison Master, Sneaky Sneak Sneaker**
8.   **Nithkik Brutishvase, Level 140 Dark Elf, Apex rank, Depthdweller**
9.   **Thorman Bame, Level 158 Human, Apex rank, Hammer of the Mountain**
10. **Sinthil Tuk'tuk, Level 168 Lizardian, Apex rank, Wind Storm]**

"Your class . . ." she muttered, then her eyes widened. It then clicked. "Oh. Your second class changed. Wow, that was you?"

Again Riven laughed, and he gave a nod. "That was me. So yeah, perhaps I'm just destined to be evil after all."

Azmoth and Athela exchanged a look, and Athela hesitantly scratched the back of her head before taking the gnome's old spot on the stool beside Riven.

She placed a hand on his own. "I don't think you realize how big of a deal this really is. Either of you."

Riven, who was still smiling, raised an eyebrow while panicked people continued to run around outside like a turned-up ant colony—preparing defenses along the walls and shouting at one another or trying to organize. "I can safely say that, no, I do not realize how big of a deal it is. I have no idea, frankly, and I'm tired of larger-than-life things happening to me."

He held out a hand to count them down as the barkeeper nervously stood by, listening in on their conversation while polishing a glass and not wanting to keep them waiting if they needed a new drink.

"First came Chalgathi," Riven stated, holding up one finger. "I found out that actually—YES—magic is real! And was told about my Unholy bloodline and my 100 percent affinity to the Blood subpillar."

The barkeeper abruptly choked and two other people spat out their drinks before hastily going back to pretending that they weren't listening.

Riven didn't mind. What could they do? And if all went as planned, Panu would be in a hidden state from the rest of the multiverse for many years to come should Allie succeed in planetary domination.

That thought . . . gave him pause. He'd really changed since first stepping out of hell. He'd become different, more than just jaded—but he just . . . didn't have the same values anymore.

He shook his head and held out his second gauntlet-encased finger—ivory metal over the top leading to spiked knuckles, and bloodsilk on the bottom half leading to his palm. "Then I learn that I'm a lost prince of the Blood Moon Requiem, a bunch of space vampires from another part of the multiverse."

More stares, this time—blatant. Many of them disbelieving and others outwardly horrified—but no one daring to leave their seats this time.

He held up fingers three, four, and five.

"I am granted visions from the blood god and obtain a shard of Gluttony. I am told that the world is going to end if certain world quests that I am involved in aren't completed properly. Then my sister ascends, becoming an angel of death right before I become the incarnation of some ancient hungry mouth that won't shut the fuck up in my head."

The eye on Riven's forehead widened and pulsed purple at his words, and Gluttony exchanged a few sentences with Riven internally—getting him to laugh good-naturedly while Gluttony shot him insults.

Athela, on the other hand, looked abruptly horrified that he'd say something like that—even more so than the people overhearing all this.

"Not to mention I have Luteski, my inherited world to run, where slave rebellions are rampantly killing other citizens—along with a bunch of greedy bastards for extended family that are making life hard as I'm trying to better the lives of said slaves. I'm technically engaged to a vampire princess that I barely know who's supposed to be working with me to make new bioweapon children for the BMR with the gift of Malignant Prophecy. Speaking of which, I've accidentally knocked up Genua and have a kid on the way that I'm not prepared for AT ALL! And what about Len? She basically hates me now because she knows I killed her older sister. Meanwhile, MY sister is on a mission to conquer our planet, which has—from what I've been told—basically made us priority target number one after or potentially even during the world quests. Oh wait, Allie IS a world quest now—isn't she? She's the target for world quest 7! So that's another thing I have to worry about. I also have to worry about a bunch of angry vampires across all of time and space tearing us a new asshole after Allie shunned the blood god like a real genius—which I'm sure my lovely great-grandmother the queen is oh so happy about. Gaia is a thing out of legend back on Earth but—oh wait—she's real, too! Angels are real. Demons are real—and it just so happens that I'm actually dating two of them, with you specifically being an archdemon. Which I STILL don't understand completely. I mean, what makes a demon an archdemon, anyways? I've never been told, so I don't know. I've been so busy that I haven't even had time to think about, or even want, to refill my last demonic minion slot after Yattazi left when she thought I was crippled. Do I even want another demonic familiar after that? It left such a bad taste in my mouth that I really am not sure. Not that I'd ever abandon Fay, you, or Azmoth—y'all are great and I'd die for any of you after all you've done for me, but I've been very hesitant to even attempt another contract since then. And if I DO fill it, what about Chalgathi? Isn't he, if I win this thing, supposed to be a wee baby dragon that I can contract with? Won't I need that slot for him? Or does he not count as a demon? And if I don't succeed in this set of trials, then what? Will a cultist do it and lay waste to the world with a fully grown apocalypse beast? Will it be my fault, then? What about all the otherworldly invaders I have yet to kill? Even Rippenvire isn't completely wiped out, and they're still hiding somewhere, which is a problem, because I'm supposed to deal with them before they can call for reinforcements at the end of integration in four and a half years. I'm stuck in F-grade at the bottleneck and Gluttony says his mind was selectively wiped when he connected with me for a new chance at life, so he doesn't even remember what kind of enlightenment the system is actually talking about for the E-grade bottleneck. So am I stuck at level 200 until then? What if that crazy rank-three fallcaller bitch who's named us public enemy number one beats us to it and figures it out before me—then comes for us? Will the Blood Moon Requiem tell me how to do it or are they going to snub me after what Allie did? There are SO many problems and SO many question that I—"

Athela smashed her pointer finger up against Riven's lips sternly, getting him to shut up while leaning in so her nose grazed his own. She frowned for a moment, thinking of how to phrase what she was going to say, and gave him a sad smile. "I know. I know you're overwhelmed, and I'm sorry. But you shouldn't talk about Gluttony like that. Gluttony is . . . he's one of the demonic origins. The seven original sins are what birthed all demonkind, just like the commandments birthed the angels. I know that Fay, Azmoth, and I have all been a little bit nonchalant about your communication with Gluttony, but please try to be respectful about him. You being the incarnation of Gluttony is an astronomically important thing, and it appears that you and Gluttony have a somewhat friendly relationship from what I've felt and seen . . . but please. It would mean a lot to me not to insult him."

Gluttony's vertical eye expanded its aura, sending out another layer of absolute dread on the nearby populace that caused many to gasp or fall to the ground in discomfort and panic.

Athela shot the third eye, which was now flaring purple again, a brief and submissive look—before staring back into Riven's other eyes with a sweet smile. She put both slender hands on his cheeks, leaned forward, and pushed her soft lips against his with a gentle touch of her tongue on his. Pulling back, she pushed some of the hair from his eyes and grew her smile wider. "It's a far bigger deal than you know, and I'm proud that he chose you. But know that being the incarnation of one of the seven original sins is a title that you and even I cannot truly fathom right now, and it'll be both a blessing and a curse as people across the multiverse try to protect or kill you simply for what you are."

Riven snorted, wrapping his arms around her slender waist and yanking her onto his lap so she straddled him and got him to grin teasingly. "Is that so? Not much has changed, then. It isn't like competitors in the Blood Moon Requiem didn't already try to kill me a couple times now. What I'm trying to say is that when you say I don't realize how big of a deal this is, well—everything is a big deal. There are too many big deals to deal with, and I'm tired of making a big deal about it all. Capisce?"

Athela hesitated, then snorted a giggle and slapped his hand away when he reached for her backside. "Stop it. A princess can't be seen being groped in public!"

"That makes me sad."

"I bet it does, you pervert. Just because you're a vampire prince and Gluttony's vessel doesn't mean you get to get handsy with me."

She said that, but Riven could tell that she liked the attention by the way she was blushing and the avoidant smile she wore while continuing to straddle him.

Nora, who'd been watching and listening this entire time, sighed in envy and put her chin in her hands. "I wish I had someone to feel that way about me. Oh, look! The gnome stopped pretending to be asleep."

Indeed, the two lovebirds on the stool turned and tried not to laugh at the three-foot-tall man on the floor, who was staring up at Riven like he had seen a ghost. His face was colorless, his chest was heaving up and down, and his entire body shook. "No . . . no, no, NO-NO-NOOOO!!!"

Gragle got up to run, not even bothering to hold the back of his wounded head, and sprinted out the door before Athela's flick of the wrist sent a thin thread of bloodsilk his way. The red string latched onto Gragle's neck and yanked him back, pulling the gnome across the floorboards as he screamed and pleaded for mercy while bursting into tears.

When the aura of dread from Riven's third eye increased, it hadn't gone unnoticed by only Gragle, and what Riven was conversing about openly didn't help the situation, either. Three other people had jumped out a nearby window and started running, the barkeeper had literally wet himself in a state of shock, two men had passed out from the pressure of his Charisma and Gluttony's passive state of observation, and a woman was vomiting in the corner while shaking violently.

The eye on Riven's forehead continued to blaze a deep purple, and the black tattoos along Riven's body began to shift and move as Gluttony made sure none of them were going to be a problem—even urging Riven to just eat them now to be safe.

Yes . . .

Eat them.

Riven nearly lunged out of his chair as a pang of extreme hunger overcame him, and his fangs whipped out—only for his own consciousness to pull him back to reality a split second later. He gasped, pushing Gluttony back down and internally scowling at the sin before commencing a series of quick exchanges between them.

Gluttony wanted to feed, and the hunger spike was so ravenous that it was all Riven could do to keep himself from getting up and ripping off the bartender's head to gorge himself.

To eat the man alive.

His vampiric hunger simultaneously kicked in, and his hand smashed into the bar—shattering a piece of it while Athela looked on in concern.

"Riven, are you all right?"

Riven was not all right, but he focused on the woman in his lap—looking over her curves and athletic figure to offset the internal battle. To distract him. The tug of war between himself and Gluttony reached a climax seconds later, his heart rate picking up speed until they settled on a singular thing:

He would compromise, and he knew Athela was sturdy enough to handle it.

His mind connected with hers telepathically only a fraction of a moment before his fangs slammed into her neck, and she gasped—clutching at his arm and shuddering in a mix of pain and pleasure before she was violently flung to the floor with the crash of wood.

The sensations Gluttony was sending through him were too much to handle, and if he didn't do this now, he'd end up killing and eating everyone nearby.

Athela, on the other hand, seemed excited at the thoughts connecting the two of them—and she started rapidly removing her exoskeleton to expose bare skin along her body only a moment before her hands were pinned above her head and Riven's form descended on her with his fangs sinking into her neck again. Her lifeblood pulsed out, and she winced as Messenger began to remove itself from Riven's torso while he entered a crazed, ravenous state of mind.

Azmoth, who was now holding the sobbing gnome by his head with one hand, shot Nora an apologetic look when Athela let out a feminine grunt. "I not know them. I sorry."

Nora's eyebrows had climbed to the ceiling, and, sipping on her drink, she watched unapologetically while the two bodies on the floor repeatedly connected with one another. "I . . . Uh . . . I don't mind at all. This has actually . . . turned out to be a lot more exciting than I'd originally thought it would be. Drinks and a show—who would have guessed."

CHAPTER 33

The compromise Gluttony and Riven had come to was that—yes—Riven would feed on something. Anything, really, and given Athela's incredibly high vitality, along with her passive trait that required all three of her forms to die before she was banished back to the nether realms, she was an easy target to settle on. Even if it didn't necessarily fit the requirement for mortal blood his vampiric side needed, it still satiated Gluttony's cravings when Riven began draining his lover—and it'd very quickly escalated when Athela had mentally agreed to it, on one condition.

She, of course, wanted to make it kinky.

Riven was already in a ravenous state at that point and he'd satisfied both Gluttony and Athela at the same time, having literally thrown Athela into a nearby rental room for privacy during a moment of clarity between urges. After fifteen minutes of very rough and loud sex on a previously semiclean bed, after having drunk what seemed to be gallons of demonic blood, with a lot of hair-pulling from Riven and screaming on Athela's part, Riven found himself having finished and on top of her while she dug her nails deep into his back.

Blood was everywhere. It was all over his face, her body, and the bed. There were also bite marks all along her neck, arms, and torso, but by the way she was shuddering in orgasm, she'd very much liked what had happened.

"I didn't know you were into that kind of stuff . . ." Riven said, panting, only to get a forceful kiss after she groaned. "But I'm glad you enjoyed it!"

She gave him a *duh* look.

"Please, let's do that again," Athela said, huffing deep breaths of air and shuddering occasionally. "I'm serious. Super cereal."

Super cereal? Had she been watching Earth-based TV shows on Comedy Central somehow?

He merely chuckled at the reference that he had no idea how she knew and began spooning her—wrapping an arm over her shoulder and wincing at the wounds she'd inflicted on him during their epic battle. Riven looked at the mattress drenched in red and let out a content sigh while watching the wounds on her body fade away—as if his fangs had never even been there.

She put one hand on his, smiling and glancing over her shoulder with raised eyebrows—still breathing deeply. "Fay's going to be jealous when I tell her."

"Is that so?"

"Ooooooh, definitely. Let's include her in the next bout."

"Do you think she'd be able to take that kind of damage, though?"

"Um . . . not that much, but to a lesser extent she'd certainly like it. Plus, we have some things to show you from our own time experimenting whenever you're not around, you know—we have . . . a plan!"

"That sounds ominous."

"Very much so! Damn, I wish she were here and not still banished! She needs to stop dying!"

They laughed and Athela snuggled up next to him, turning over and putting her head against his chest with an amused expression. "How much time do we have left until we fight for the town? If the locals don't attack you first, anyway . . ."

Riven pulled up the timer. "A little over eight hours."

"Hmmm. Want to try again? You'll have to tell Azmoth that we're going to be busy. But we NEVER get time to do this because you're always getting into trouble!" She pounded a fist into his chest with a playful but simultaneously menacing glare. "I want more Riven time! And that picnic was nice, but you never actually took me on a SOLO date like Fay had!"

Riven clicked his tongue and brushed away some of her black hair to put a hand on her cheek. "You know what? You're right. How about we go get another drink, have another romp, and then find a good date spot here in town before the monster wave? Surely there's something here like a good restaurant, or a petting zoo, or something like that. Or we can just go explore together and buy you some new clothes!"

"Like the time we went clothes shopping in Brightsville?!" Athela's eyes widened in excitement, and she clapped her hands together before cackling mischievously. "That was when I started crushing on you, you know."

"Oh, stop!"

"WHAT?! It was! I told my mom and the rest of my clan about how kind you were when you said I'd look good in that dress . . . It made me very happy to hear."

She booped him on the head with a finger. "You're pretty cute, you know. I'm a lucky girl, and my mom really, REALLY thinks so now that you're Gluttony's chosen. They want to worship you or something. Don't give me that look, I'm being cereal! Do you know just how many system messages my clan has paid for to expedite communication outside the normal nether realm visits? And they're all useless messages, too! Ones like, 'Athela, you a lucky, hot, crazy bitch!'"

"There is zero chance your demonic clan sent that message to you."

"I swear it on my princess tiara!"

"You're lying."

"Nope! That was my mom."

"Doubtful."

"Well, ask her when you see her next, then!" Athela humphed and snorted, angrily slamming a long pitch-black leg over his own. She tucked it in between his knees to pull her body against his. "Now shut up and accept it! And give me more snuggle time before we get another drink. Like I said—I don't get enough!"

Fay hadn't been happy, being blown up and blasted back into the nether realms. Deepnest's detonation wasn't something she'd seen coming. However, upon arrival and after realizing that Riven was, in fact, okay . . . she'd witnessed firsthand through her connection alongside with the rest of her entire clan what was akin to a miracle.

And not the type of skill, but a genuine miracle in the way one talked about when a one-in-five-hundred-trillion chance happened right in front of you.

Gluttony had been reborn, opening the way for all the other sins and commandments to come out with it. The eternal war was at hand yet again as Elysium let out the trapped beings that'd helped create existence before the multiverse had even been formed. The ancient armies of the hells were gathering their strength as excited waves of religious fervor crashed across the underbelly of existence, and the great maw responsible for it all had chosen Fay's own boyfriend as its vessel. The zeal once known across the great demonic factions that'd made them so feared was now at hand, and her clan was immediately bombarded with requests for audiences from factions so far above their own that her mother, Saemi, had called for a complete lockdown of their nether realm. She'd immediately banned any and all foreign entities from entering their home, fearing for their safety in a communal nether realm such as this, and had recalled all free-floating succubi and incubi belonging to the Sojavi clan minutes later.

First came shock, then came awe, and then an emotion Fay really couldn't place that washed over her like a flood as she sobbed and cried tears that weren't necessarily happy or sad—but nevertheless came. Inside their castles, ziggurats, and stone dwellings in the jungle existence the Sojavi clan had created for themselves in this small pocket reality, the low- to midtier information broker faction was already receiving bribes and threats for entry from other demonic forces that far surpassed their own power. Entities eons old with world-ending strength that never would have given the Sojavi clan the time of day before were now competing with one another for HER attention and leverage with her family. That, or they had more sinister intentions.

Messages sent from Athela's family painted a similar picture, as they'd already had to kill a forced invasion of their nether realm when one of their own had accidentally let in a parasitic ripclaw that'd opened up their home to unwanted guests. Thankfully, Athela's own clan was far more attuned to violence than Fay's was, so they'd rather easily massacred the interlopers while offering the Sojavi clan assistance if need ever arose.

Most notably, the Church of Gluttony specifically had called upon her—by name—to make an appearance before them. The worshippers of sin were what most of her kind had considered fanatics up until now, attempting to piece together the long-lost shards of the sins, tiny fragment by tiny fragment over a never-ending expanse of multiverse that would have taken untold billions of years to complete. And yet those harbingers who'd been touched by Gluttony now found themselves without their divine fragments, stripped of the opportunity to ascend with the great maw when it'd chosen another, and she simply didn't know what to do. Was going to greet them wise? Would it be considered an offense if she didn't go? Or was it some jealous and enraged follower or group of followers who'd taken it upon themselves to strike her down for her master stealing their opportunity—as a way of petty revenge?

It was too early to tell.

"Fay!" Saemi, her beautiful mother, called out to her with a frustrated and simultaneously exhausted scowl. Her shoulders were slumped, and she'd just finished barking orders at some of the other blue-skinned clan members concerning protocols on outside communication networks that had been compromised. "Fay, I realize this is a lot to take in, but you need to get ahold of yourself. It would be a bad look for us if other demon clans knew that one of Riven's—and thereby Gluttony's—bonded familiars and concubines was sobbing on our library floor in the arms of her sister! We need to maintain face!"

Tupper, who'd briefly left the elf child Len in the care of Gurth'Rok back on Panu, glared in conjunction with his sister Nitidi while Nitidi held the sobbing Fay next to a couch between enormous bookshelves reaching far above.

"Mother—" Tupper began, but he was cut off with a sharp return glare from Saemi.

"Don't even start—you're already on thin ice with your father and the rest of the clan," Saemi stated, rubbing her temple and waving off another group of incubi and succubi—letting her body fall into the ornate chair behind her. "The only reason you're even being allowed back without issue is because you're also on good terms with Gluttony's reincarnation. You're still both my children and you will do as I say."

Nitidi was taller and slightly bigger than Fay, and she got up from the floor—unfolding her wings—and helped Fay up to her feet while the shorter woman sniffled and shook uncontrollably. "There's no reason to be this upset, hon! This is a good thing! An amazing thing, even! Why are you crying?"

Fay blubbered something unintelligible.

Saemi sighed while her two daughters and son took seats across from her. Then her face lit up with a wide but tired grin. "She's likely in a state of shock. Not that I necessarily blame her . . . The chances of this happening are nearing the margin of impossibility. To think that Elysium would let them out . . . and that my daughter would be so close to the reincarnation! This goes far, far beyond being a prince of the Blood Moon Requiem. This is the difference between royalty and . . . and I don't even know what. I cannot think of anything that would so equally compare! To say that I am pleased is an incredible understatement, but I am still trying to wrap my own head around what this will mean for us going forward as a clan and family."

"Do you intend to let anyone inside to talk?" Nitidi asked, frowning in worry while keeping Fay's head buried in her side on the sofa. "We're being requested by—"

"Do not think I don't know who and how many are requesting audiences with us!" Saemi snapped irritably, groaning and leaning forward to put her hands on her forehead with fingers massaging her temple. She closed her eyes and let out a deep, slow, shuddering breath. "Aside from Clan Razok, there is only one other I will allow access to this place. At least for now, until we are certain of who is truly on our side and who is trying to set up a power grab. Or worse."

There was an extended silence after that, all four of them staring into the ground amid Fay's continued whimpers.

"Stop your sniveling, Fay. I love you, but stop it," Saemi snapped eventually, but then regretted it immediately when she saw the hurt look in her daughter's eyes. "Eh . . . sorry. I'm just on edge. I apologize. I should be thanking you for raising our clan's name rather than lecturing you."

Tupper cleared his throat and clasped his hands in front of him. "Clan Razok being Athela's clan?"

"Yes."

"Then who is the other?"

Saemi's black eyes slowly raised off the ground. "Lillith, of course."

Another long, drawn-out silence overtook them.

Tupper gulped and had to wipe his sweaty hands on his sides. "You don't think she'll come here, do you?"

"Why else would she request to do so, if she had no intent?" Saemi asked a little shakily. "Of course she intends to come, and I will not deny her."

Nitidi hesitated. "Do you think she'll be a problem?"

Saemi shook her head. "No . . . no, I don't. If anything, she'll be a deterrent. Even at . . . what level is she now since arriving on Panu?"

Nitidi pulled up a screen and scoffed in disbelief. "Level 39. Didn't she just arrive on Panu less than a day ago at level 1? How is that even possible?"

Saemi grinned, then laughed out loud while shaking her head and flopping back into her chair. "It's possible because she's a MYTHIC-tier creature. She's an absolute monster, a literal figure of legends passed down through the eons, and she's killed hundreds of beasts and enemies above her combat level on her path through the underdark toward Allie's location. Things will slow down when she hits the E-grade again, when it's less about numbers of kills and more about quality and insight, but even then I'm sure her growth will be explosive. She and the others who were banished to the abyss, like the other generals and officers of Gluttony's legions, were some of the brightest minds of their time. All their levels have been reset, along with many of their skills, and much of their knowledge was wiped— but what they do remember in conjunction with the system titles, attributes, and everything else means they're all walking calamities. I'd be surprised if Elysium doesn't entirely change the world quests of their integration to incorporate it somehow. Or if it doesn't do that, it'll balance out their appearance some other way—as Elysium doesn't like things to be so lopsided as this."

"Well, if she's on her way down to find Allie in the underdark . . . Why would she request an audience with us now?"

"Because it won't take her long to find the newly ascended angel of death. That's why. I'm sure it'll only be another day before they meet, and Lillith is trying to play damage control for her lord on Panu while Riven is swept up in system events for the Chalgathi quests. The Blood Moon Requiem is full of devout followers of the blood god—Riven even has a thrall who is one of their esteemed priestesses—and Lillith just eradicated the ritual meant to strip Allie's soul of Malignant Prophecy from the highest-ranking members of the vampiric empire. Lillith has to simultaneously try not to anger the Blood Moon Requiem because she knows that even if she can defeat their thrall forms on a newly integrating planet, she would be crushed if they were to find her or her master in the realms of the multiverse given their current rank disparity. Meanwhile, she also doesn't want to anger a potential ally, and despite Gluttony not being in any way subservient to the blood god, Riven himself has not dismissed the priestess and even had her embrace the position. This complicates things. So does the involvement of the reapers and the Scythe. Lillith will have to play a very political game here, maintaining Allie's safety from the bloodsuckers while trying to make sure she doesn't fall too far under the influence of the reapers. At least, this is what I am guessing, as they'll likely use Allie's quest to conquer Panu and maintain a safe haven for themselves while Gluttony's core forces rebuild."

Tupper nodded in agreement. "Makes sense. What about the Church of Gluttony? Have they made contact with Lillith? Or are they even able to do so?"

Saemi shrugged in an almost defeated manner. "We are not sure. It may be why the Church of Gluttony is attempting to contact us in the first place—they may be trying to use us to speak with Lillith or Gluttony itself. Fay, how long do you have before you head back to be with Riven?"

Fay, who'd calmed down and was shakily wiping her eyes, quickly went over her status screen. "A little over seventeen hours."

A knock at the door came, and the four of them turned their heads to see one of the lower-ranking clan members give a swift bow. The succubus was obviously nervous at being there, and specifically tried not to stare in admiration at Fay—given Fay's new standing as one of two romantic interests the reincarnation of Gluttony had. "Lady Saemi! Nitidi! Tupper!"

She glanced hesitantly at Fay, not sure how to address her now with the new dynamic changes of the clan. "Um . . . Lady Fay! I am sorry to interrupt all of you, but some of our guests from Clan Razok have arrived."

The four of them abruptly stood, and Saemi summoned two more large couches when dark figures shifted into the nether realm around them from shadows on the floor.

Clan Razok was entirely full of arachnid variant demons, all related to spiders in some form or another. Athela's mother, Vorindi, was strangely beautiful in a very sinister way. It was very close to how Athela looked—only slightly more menacing in her humanoid form. She had three pairs of mandibles coming out of the sides of her throat along a slit that likely opened up into an additional mouth, had smaller red markings across her otherwise pitch-black and patchy-white skin, and had four red eyes instead of two. Otherwise the athletic outline and the six bladelike arachnoid legs sticking out of her back were the same. Vorindi was also accompanied by four others, including two very high-level enforcers that took the form of enormous red, spined spiders that shifted in and out of existence, sometimes even in multiple spots at once using the same body. The other and last of their clan was the Clan Razok patriarch, a male drider with dark-gray skin—having the upper body of a very handsome drow man and the lower body of a large black widow.

Vorindi looked to the patriarch amid the awkward silence, and the patriarch nodded to Athela's mother to give her the stage with the clicking of mandibles.

Vorindi then took a step forward, with the lower-ranking succubus leaving the private area of the library and shutting the door behind her.

"Saemi of the Sojavi clan, Fay of the Sojavi clan. We of Clan Razok greet you." Vorindi bowed low in a customary manner to both Saemi and Fay—no doubt taking the lead because she was Athela's mother and Athela was the other love interest of Gluttony's reincarnation.

Fay was surprised by the immense respect shown her by a demoness far above her own stature, still not used to the idea of what her position as a girlfriend—or, in her mother's words, concubine—of Gluttony's reincarnation really meant. She in turn bowed low while matching her mother's own bow, but let her mother do the talking.

"We greet Clan Razok as friends and hope you find yourselves comfortable within the nether realm we have built for ourselves." Saemi finished her own bow and smiled warmly. "It is good to finally meet you in person, Vorindi. I hope the incursion into your home was met with brutal and swift death."

The Arshakai shook her head with a sly smile of her own, following Saemi's gesture and sitting on the couch while the three others of her clan remained in the back for now. "The incursion was swiftly dealt with, indeed. Invading a nest of assassins wasn't the brightest idea those firebrands had, but they were also extremists from the Church of Wrath, so it wasn't entirely surprising. And the pleasure is surely mine. Do we know when Lillith will be arriving?"

The others in the room shifted nervously as they thought about it, and Saemi retook her seat, motioning for the others to do the same while shaking her head. "Unfortunately I am not sure. I believe she will be here within the day, but that is just a guess. Would you like refreshments meanwhile? I've been wanting to discuss our daughters' shared man long before he became such a prominent figure—you know how it is with us old gossipers!"

"Mother!" Fay hissed under her breath, to the amusement of her sister, Nitidi, and her brother, Tupper.

To Saemi's relief, Athela's mother, Vorindi, only paused for a moment to consider her words before chuckling good-naturedly.

"Indeed you're right," Vorindi stated, amused, clicking her mandibles thoughtfully while putting a finger up to her chin. "I'm glad our daughters worked out their differences the way they did, and it pleases me that they found such a unique summoner. As you said yourself, I've been rather curious about the opposite perspective even before Riven became the reincarnation of the great maw . . . I would have no qualms with sharing in some gossip while we await Lillith's arrival. So let us speak on it!"

Outside the pub and on the streets of Outpost Number 84, Gragle, the scarred gnome, had been more than happy to get the hell out of there and away from the vampire who was a self-proclaimed prince of the Blood Moon Requiem. What was worse was that he'd claimed to be the host of Gluttony, a universe-ending entity that many demons literally worshipped.

If not for the presence of the blood priestess, if not for the ancient, unfamiliar tattoos on Riven's body that gave off extremely potent negative energy, Gragle might have just blown them off. But when they were both present, and having been accompanied by a very recent multiverse-wide announcement about Gluttony's return, Gragle could only pray that the vampire was just playing some kind of sick joke on him.

Because even as immensely unlikely as it was that the vampire was telling the truth, even as preposterous as the idea was, if Riven was the real deal . . . Gragle and everyone here were in very real danger. That was even putting aside the fact that a blood priestess would no doubt sacrifice him to their god for bonus points, given a chance.

So he'd taken the offer to lead Azmoth and Nora around town when they'd asked to leave, none of them wanting to listen to the two extremely loud lovebirds in the other room. This was despite the fact that Azmoth himself was incredibly scary to the gnome, and the reputation of hellscape brutalisks was not one to be scoffed at.

Though after Azmoth had paid the barkeeper three times what he'd been given earlier as an apology for Riven's actions, the large demon had—oddly enough—very politely taken his leave and followed Gragle out to explore the town.

"What's that?" Nora asked, ignoring the swarms of panicking people who were actively constructing barricades behind doors and windows and blocking streets in anticipation of a monster wave possibly clearing the stone walls surrounding Outpost Number 84.

Gragle's head swiveled, ignoring the looks he was getting parading around a huge demon as well as a woman with an odd hood very likely related to the integration quest line they'd all been flung into. "That? The thing with pipes coming out of the ground? It's a well."

"For water?"

"Yes, we use magic to pump water out of it and into the four basins surrounding it. We just keep the basins covered to stop air pollution or soot from getting in, something that may not be needed as much now that we're not actually on Mesini anymore . . ."

"Mesini being . . . what?"

"The planet we were abducted from for this stupid event."

"YOU THERE!" a husky voice bellowed out over the crowds, and to Gragle's immense relief, a squadron of armed guards in leather armor wielding spears pushed through the crowds to stand in front of the gnome's two companions.

It appeared that either Azmoth had drawn their attention, people escaping from the pub had alerted the authorities, or both had happened.

Though Gragle had to admit, the feeling of relief and safety quickly vanished when reality set in. These guards wouldn't stand a chance against a hellscape brutalisk; there was almost literally a 0 percent chance of success in a fight, but at least if a fight did happen, it'd give Gragle a chance to escape during the carnage that followed.

The guards seemed to be very aware of this, too, but their eyes kept flitting toward Nora's hood that identified her as a system quest participant and a Chalgathi noncultist.

"Ahem, sorry to bother you—but we have some questions that need to be answered," the guard captain stated while nervously eyeing Azmoth up and down. He turned his gaze on Nora. "Is this your summon?"

"You betcha," Nora lied.

The captain accepted it readily, not willing to dig further into the matter as Azmoth hadn't started killing everyone on sight. For him, the equivalent would be like an average Earthling watching hungry tigers parading through a preschool cafeteria while not eating all the inhabitants.

"I've been told by the warden of this town to fetch you, along with the blood priestess we heard about, after reports from a nearby pub suggested you'd know more about what is going on here," the captain continued, regaining a bit of his resolve in the process. "Where is this priestess of the blood god, if you don't mind me asking? Is she still at the pub? And if it's okay, could you and your familiar accompany my men and me to talk to the warden? We don't have long before the monster wave hits, and we need to know all the details you can give us if we're to prepare for the worst."

CHAPTER 34

[Judith Marcina, Level 180 Divine Human, Apex rank, Angelic Fallcaller, Light's Beacon]

The white dress clung to her skin like smooth porcelain, and the cold air filled each breath she took—her lungs expanding ever so slowly.

She twirled a finger through her long blond hair, glaring white-hot daggers at her Apex rank-three position on the ladder with growing fury at having lost her top position. Wings of golden light lifted up off her back while she sat in a cross-legged position amid the rays of dawn—scattering brilliant orange-yellow lights across the tufts of white puffs.

Far below her position in the sky, the bells for worship began to ring—echoing across the landscape. Thriving communities of those she'd saved began to wake up, heading to the cathedrals all across the medieval streets, where the pantheon of light she'd devoted herself to would receive their prayers.

Fuel for growth.

The gods were originally a strange concept to her after being faithless for so long, and it'd taken a lot to wrap her head around them actually being real. Back on Zazir before the merger, she'd only been a peasant girl working on her father's farm who'd always blown off clergy from various sects as money-grubbers who sputtered nonsense in an attempt to deceive people via imaginary benefits. Now, though . . . things were more complicated. And she would use these newly born gods as tools to her own end. They were in many ways both weaker and stronger than mortals. Weaker, because they depended upon prayer to survive—especially at this stage in their cultivation. At least that's how **most** of them survived, through prayer, but that also wasn't always the case.

Already there'd been countless new gods born on Panu, only for them to be snuffed out within weeks due to a lack of faith or worship. They were no more than spirits that couldn't survive without their followers fueling them. But those that did find worship, that were cultivated and grown, they were the ones that could change worlds. There were even stories of gods that gained bodies, or mortals ascending into godhood while maintaining bodies that did not need worship—but she didn't necessarily know all the details between these different types of gods, and the newborn deities didn't know, either. They had their own leveling and cultivation system to progress through before those kinds of secrets were revealed.

Regardless, she'd collected three of these gods, all subservient to her. They blessed her land with bountiful crops, staved off the spread of the blight into the southlands, and had given boons to her warriors to speed up their growth.

What a strange thought that was, being served by lesser spirit deities. But realistically it made sense, because she was the one with all the power—and with a mere flick of her wrist she could annihilate their cathedrals and banish their worship from her empire. It made them a far more convenient tool to use than the already established deities across the multiverse that had, in some places, seen fit to try and contact her. But even the gods of old were held back by Elysium's might and had little to no real effect here on Panu just yet. Even if that weren't the case, gods had less power in places they did not have worshippers—and she was confident that she'd come out as a dominant player in this world to force others into worship of her chosen three.

Or at least she had been confident. Now, though . . .

Now she had to find some other way to regain the top. The new addition of the world quest painting Allie as a target was certainly tempting, too . . . but the number-five Apex ranker on the power ladder—Retesh Vorath, the lich king—had been waging a war upon Judith's forces in the north for quite some time now. She'd been expanding south and west but had met solid resistance to her progression at Claw's Canyons on the northern borderlands where undead legions were controlled by that undead bag of bones.

Past that canyon lay a cold, desolate wasteland of snow, barrens, and tundra changed by the curse of undead where even she had a hard time surviving due to the building amounts of blight Retesh had created. Even the animal and plant life had begun to change, morph, and warp into grotesque versions of what they'd once been. She knew full well, too, that he planned to unleash the plague onto the lands of the living through some unknown means, and she was already prepared to deal with it in kind with methods of her own make. However, trying to push farther into already desecrated lands where the undead spawned like rats was a fool's errand . . . at least for now at her current stage of power. She had tried to kill that damnable lich a few times over already, all of which had ended in a stalemate with the lich on the back foot—but each time he'd survived long enough to cause her to retreat when the blight became too much or when the numbers of his minions simply stacked against her.

This in part was why news of Retesh claiming lands on the peninsula of Nune was concerning. It was south of most of the lich king's kingdom, and an odd place to attack considering the vast swath of land both east and west of the territory grab he'd made. In the past he'd always taken the slow and steady route to ensure his blight further infected the land and made it all the harder for the living to stay there. He'd also gone out of his way to massacre populations to create new undead with, such as one of her cities two months ago that'd been absolutely sacked and burned to the ground, but usually he left and brought the spoils of bodies back to the northlands with him. At least that'd been the trend since his initial appearance. Here, though, on the Nune Peninsula, he'd conquered and stayed. He'd also been putting massive amounts of resources into securing the land strip between mortal empires on either side ever since.

Given the geography, there was only one real reason for that—and it made her insides roil with fury. The peninsula was pointed right at the continent of Umbra, after all . . . where the only other major undead players in the world currently resided, and they happened to be number one and number two on the power ladder list.

It was where the Thane Necropolis was located, if one didn't count the extension into the place called Chicago she'd learned about. But she was nowhere near Chicago, if her spymasters and scholars were correct, thank the gods—she didn't want to have to deal with another massive undead state on her doorstep just yet.

She pondered this, putting a finger to her slim lips with a frown—still staring at the city waking up thousands of feet below. One of her angelic summons, a large, brilliant eyeball crafted from gold and silver metal, flew toward her on shimmering white wings resembling her own golden ones.

She gave it a smile and patted its head, shooing it away while contemplating just what to do with the current change of the political stage. Allie Thane reaching number one first after becoming an angel of death and converting an entire continent into the undead was, frankly, horrifying to Judith. Not because she was afraid, but because she found it repulsive and disgusting to warp people and the planet like that. And to think that Allie could terraform even more of the planet . . . the bitch had to be eliminated.

Meanwhile, Riven hadn't had any video feed of how or why he'd become the incarnation of Gluttony, but the multiverse-wide statement did not bode well for her or her people when he'd hit spot number one—replacing his sister and shoving Allie down to the number-two spot while putting Judith at number three. She didn't really know what Gluttony was, but the reaction of her angelic summons at the announcement had been extremely violent—and thinking about it like that was an understatement. All four of them had gone mad with fear, rage, or hate upon realizing that Gluttony had come back—and it'd only gotten worse after they realized it was here on their very own planet.

One of her summons, an angelic paladin, was still having a very hard time processing it at all. The large angel had secluded himself in a cathedral tower to consult his family elders in the heavens, and he'd been by far the most upset out of all of them—which was saying something considering her other summons had reacted so poorly. From brief conversations with them, she'd determined that it had to do with the renewed frenzy of what they called "the eternal war," which in turn would lead to a new age of carnage as the hells and heavens clashed like in the times of old.

Judith had originally hoped to maintain decent relations with the vampires, or at least until the end of the integration, when she'd be able to slaughter them after other more important world quests were dealt with, but it appeared the Thane siblings were too much of a risk to leave alone. Especially with the lich Retesh attempting to contact them, based on his recent military movements. She wouldn't make a direct move against them *yet*, but perhaps she could disrupt their activities enough to slow them down . . . or, if possible, she would attempt to intercept any messages sent from the lich king's faction.

Clicking her tongue and cracking her knuckles, she spread her wings, stretched her legs, and launched herself farther up into the sky before diving to the south-west. She had a particular person to visit today, a potential ally, before she decided to make any more major plays on the world stage.

Chandeliers sparkled overhead, servants in sleek black-and-white outfits passed out refreshments on tiny silver plates or glass wine cups, and a group of musicians was playing live on a stage in a corner while people in elegant ballroom attire mingled with one another. It was as if they were all trying to catch a glimpse of what was still normal, like they were trying to convince themselves that they hadn't all been turned into deathtouched versions of themselves—that they weren't all undead.

Dawn's royal ball had begun, and Lahn found himself sitting alone at a table. Without Allie.

All around him he saw familiar faces, now shades of very pale or gray skin with white or silver hair. All of them had black or neon-teal eyes, colors of the Death subpillar's manifested mana, but otherwise most people looked very similar to how they'd been prior to the change.

Dr. Brass was there, the vampire with steel-rimmed glasses, an adviser to the Chancellor Mara Tovane, who was also missing on Allie's expedition. King Arthur Brix of Dawn was in deep and merry conversation with him, obviously trying to put on a show of not being concerned given the changes that'd so quickly happened to their country—now a vassal state of the Thane Necropolis. The family of Gleetus Nefrand was there as well, though Gleetus himself had been killed by Allie for bullying Lahn a while ago and they'd never found out the true cause of his death. Lahn's mother, Lady Shovi Lucio, sat next to his father, Lord Nikola Lucio—though the rift between his parents had widened significantly ever since his father had shown little regard for the actions of Lahn's siblings.

Speaking of his siblings, his sister, Linela, and his brother, Parius, were mixing in the crowd—avoiding both Lahn and their mother while trying to act as if everything was absolutely normal. As if Allie Thane, queen of the Thane Necropolis, didn't have a personal death wish for the both of them that was only being held at bay by Lahn himself.

Lahn took a sip of his wine, downing it in a single go while sitting at a round table by himself in the corner of the ballroom. Waving down a server, he took three more slender glasses and thanked the man, downing two more before holding on to the third while closing his eyes in worry.

He hoped Allie was okay.

But she had to be okay. She was still on the leaderboard, still in second place, so there was no reason to worry. She'd be back . . . even if she had missed the royal ball. This ball was a three-day event anyway, so maybe she'd be back by tomorrow or the next day . . . He'd really wanted to—

His thoughts were interrupted and he blinked as the chair beside him was pulled to the side by a manservant, letting Marsia Bortrost of all people sit next to him.

This irritating woman had been following him around all night trying to get his attention, despite obvious signs that he wasn't interested in her like he'd once been. She'd blown her chance, and the irritation inside him was growing.

She wasn't an incredibly attractive person—but she was somewhat pretty. She'd been what he'd set his sights on when he'd been crippled at the prodding of his mother. Marsia had shot him down, though, hard, and in a very mean way back before he'd even enrolled in the academy. Back when his mother and the Bortrost family had attempted to pair them, only for Lahn to hear Marsia state the following:

"I will not allow myself to marry a cripple. Maybe your family's status will be enough to land you a peasant girl. Maybe one of your maids. But you need to leave me alone—and that is the end of it. Good day, sir."

He still remembered those words vividly and even now felt ashamed at the look of disgust she'd given him before walking away. Lahn's neon-teal eyes glanced up to the pale woman with a passive nod, then turned his gaze to the ground between his well-made boots to stare at the floor.

"I was wondering where you'd run off to! And I must say, you're looking rather good, Lahn!" Marsia stated in a chipper tone, pulling down the front of her dress just slightly to emphasize her figure and smoothing out the blue ball gown with a large smile. "The way your body repaired itself looks very good, and your musculature fills in your clothes in a way that's easy to look upon. I must say you've filled in quite nicely—that purple vest suits you well."

He didn't even bother looking up. Her flirting had lost all attempts at hiding her intentions, and she was growing ever more aggressive in her attempts to woo him the more she drank. "Thank you, Marsia. It is appreciated."

Laughter echoed from where King Arthur Brix, his spymaster Kassius, and Dr. Brass all laughed with nobles of the courts jostling for position with fake smiles and fake laughs. Marsia frowned slightly at Lahn's lack of reciprocation, but cleared her throat and tried again for the seventh time that night.

"Will you be participating in the dances this evening?" she asked curiously, clasping her hands in front of her and retaining another smile. "Or do you intend to stay back here? I do think it'd be rather fun to witness your first real ballroom dance, now that you're no longer in a wheelchair."

Lahn finally smiled and lifted his eyes. His mind went back to just a few nights before Allie's trek into the underdark, when they'd talked so excitedly about this exact topic. Before he'd even gained the use of his left side entirely, before he'd become undead, and before the restructuring of his pillars and soul. It was then, in Allie's room, that she'd promised to help keep him standing as they were to go dancing together—and she'd only kissed him and patted him on the head when he had asked her if holding up someone like him on the dance floor would be embarrassing for her.

"I'm afraid I'll have to pass today," Lahn replied, laying one of his hands on the round table and crossing his legs. "I do not feel like it suits me much. I'm sure not many would want to be my partner anyways."

"Does not suit you?" Marsia laughed playfully. "Oh, come now! Your display at the Blood Moon Requiem's compound showed that not only are you hiding some kind of position in the empire, but that you also have true power. Your angelic possession was rather fearsome! And I would personally be delighted if you were to be my dance partner when the first tunes begin!"

Another winning smile flashed his way.

Thankfully Lahn was saved a moment later by King Arthur Brix, his father, who was a personal friend of the king, and Dr. Brass—some of the only other people in the room who knew exactly what or whom Lahn was concerning social standing. Trailing behind them was a small crowd of well-dressed nobles, who all stopped a short distance away given the cramped corner Lahn had placed himself in.

"My boy!" The good-natured king laughed, slapping Lahn on the shoulder while Lahn got an uncomfortable half smile from his father. "How are you doing this evening?! Aside from the change across the continent and the war on the other side of Riven's Eye Wormhole against the Romanovs, you're the talk of the kingdom! Lots of rumors going on about who you are, boy!"

The king was half-drunk and winked Lahn's way—getting a laugh from Dr. Brass and a nervous chuckle from Lahn's father.

"You forget the coming war in the hells and guild restructuring here. People are talking quite a lot about that, too," Lahn replied with a grin, not bothering to stand up when Marsia Bortrost hastily stood and curtsied with a look of horror directed Lahn's way.

"Lahn! You should stand!" she hissed, getting nods of agreement or frowns of disapproval from others nearby.

Lahn blinked, only now realizing the social mistake he was making after years confined to a chair. Hastily he got up and made a slight bow of respect. "I apologize. I am so used to sitting in my wheelchair that I'd completely forgotten. No disrespect was intended."

King Arthur Brix raised one eyebrow, shared a look with Dr. Brass, the vampire, and they both burst out laughing.

"My boy!" the king stated with another hearty laugh, slapping Lahn on the back again and downing another drink from a passing servant while grabbing others for his friends. He finished handing out the drinks, then leaned over so that only the people immediately nearby could hear. "If anything, it should be me paying respects to you!"

He winked good-naturedly at Lahn again, implying that Lahn's position as lover to Allie was significant enough to bear weight even over his own influence. That got a flat look from Lahn's father and a stare of confusion from Marsia.

Lahn internally sighed at the comment but took it in stride and shrugged. "I don't know about that, but I appreciate the sentiment. I'm nothing special."

"Nothing special, he says!" King Arthur Brix guffawed.

Dr. Brass also shook his head, wiping his glasses and placing them back on his face. Even now he still wore a white coat around—it'd become his signature that most people identified him by in public, and the deathtouched elf woman clinging to his left arm whispered something in his ear. "We all know that isn't true, Lahn—not many could tame the fires of that inferno you've got on your hands. It's quite the feat."

Dr. Brass said this good-naturedly with both Lahn and the king laughing loudly at the comparison to Allie, though nobody else knew what he was talking about.

"Inferno?" Marsia asked, using the opportunity of proximity to attempt her hand at joining the conversation. "What is it you speak of?"

Dr. Brass hesitated at this, the empire's adviser not wanting to give off too much or any information, but then turned with a rare expression of anticipation when an announcement from the main double doors leading outside was announced.

"LADIES AND GENTLEMEN!" The announcer used magic to emphasize his voice over the classical music playing in the background and the soft rumblings of talk and laughter. "IT IS MY PLEASURE TO INTRODUCE TO YOU NEW ALLIES OF THE EMPIRE! FIRST, WE HAVE THE GOLDEN BULL SECT FROM FAR TO THE NORTH OF BRIGHTSVILLE ON OUR SHARED CONTINENT OF UMBRA! I PRESENT HEAD MONK FATHER PEN! YOU WILL PLEASE WELCOME THEM WITH A ROUND OF APPLAUSE!"

The crowds immediately began clapping politely as three monks in golden robes, all bald Deathtouched Enlightened who'd once been humans, came to stand at the front with low bows of respect. They immediately caught sight of Dr. Brass and the king, making a beeline for the small group and throwing wary glances back over their shoulders as the announcer cleared his throat for a second time.

"LADIES AND GENTLEMEN, THAT IS NOT ALL!" the young announcer called out—raising a hand to gain their attention once more. "I AM SURE YOU ARE ALL VERY AWARE BY NOW THAT OUR ESTEEMED HIGH KING AND EMPEROR, RIVEN THANE, HAS BEEN UNMASKED AS THE NEW REINCARNATION OF GLUTTONY! I AM ALSO SURE THAT MANY OF YOU HAVE HEARD OF THE DEMONS THAT WERE UNLEASHED ONTO OUR PLANET TO SERVE HIM! I DO NOT THINK I NEED TO EMPHASIZE JUST HOW UNBELIEVABLY SPECIAL THAT IS, OR WHAT IT MEANS FOR OUR PEOPLE NOW THAT WE ARE UNDER HIS PROTECTION!"

Uncertainty rippled across the crowds of onlookers with hushed, nervous whispers in abundance. Despite their undead transition and the Unholy affiliation they all now possessed, Gluttony and the other original sins were still something of a taboo among many in the vassalized kingdom of Dawn. There were certainly mixed feelings on the matter, but at the end of the day Riven, Allie, and the forces of the necropolis saved their lives and the city—so most had set aside their inherent fear of the great maw and put their trust in the two siblings.

The announcer waited for the whispers to die down, giving the three monks in golden robes time to reach Dr. Brass and the king with low bows, whispers of greeting, and handshakes before turning back to the man at the double doors leading out.

"IT IS THEREFORE MY GREATEST PLEASURE TO INTRODUCE TO YOU ONE OF GLUTTONY'S OFFICERS AND A MOUTHPIECE FOR THEIR GRAND GENERAL, LILLITH! I GIVE TO YOU THE ARCHDEMON TRE'ZIX—WARRIOR OF THE PURPLE CLAW!"

Immediately the room hushed when a hulking creature that looked like a mutated deep-red-and-purple praying mantis lacking antennae silently stalked into the room. It was over ten feet tall, with a pincerlike mouth and a set of long, retracted blade arms against its insectoid chest. The face was similar to that of a mantis but thinner, with narrow, catlike yellow eyes and three horns sticking out of its head. It turned, casually observing, until those yellow eyes stopped on Lahn's position. The four thick, armored insectoid legs of the creature retracted into its body and it shifted—becoming more humanoid in form. Within a second, a purple and dark-red man covered in chitin was staring in Lahn's direction, smiling wickedly with a thin mouth of razor-sharp teeth, three horns protruding from his head, and pincers coming out of either cheek. Wings along his back were also present and long purple blades jutted out of the extensor sides of his arms. The demon slowly headed in Lahn's direction with its intent pinpointed like a palpable will.

The music started playing up again after a short stop, and people either tried to get out of the way of the demon—or pretended to ignore the strange creature entirely if they were far enough away. The question marks and red flames outlining its identification box indicated that it was of Legendary status but didn't give any more information as it came to a slow halt in front of Lahn.

Ignoring everyone else present, the demon raised its wings up into the air behind it, each wing starting to flash with beautiful multicolored light, and got on one knee—bowing to Lahn with one clawed hand down against the ground.

"Lahn Lucio . . . My name is Tre'Zix of the Purple Claw, archdemon of the Klinac'Tal clan, an officer in Gluttony's legions, and slayer of Archangel Sinpha of the High Celestial Magistrates." The insectoid demon's voice was very sharp and dry. It turned its face upward, mashing its mandibles together and an unnatural smile spreading wide across its face. Clicking sounds emanated from deep inside its throat, and its head turned sideways unnaturally to get another view of the young undead man. "It is my pleasure and pride to meet you. Lillith has told me that you are in . . . a unique situation. I am here to personally oversee your safety regarding the angelic creature residing within you."

Safety?

It was odd enough for many of the onlookers to see that the demon had directly addressed Lahn rather than Dr. Brass or the king. It was even weirder that the demon was speaking about things they simply didn't understand.

Looks were shared and whispers began, but Lahn's creased brows and growing frown indicated that he didn't know what the demon was talking about, either.

"Are you indicating that I am in danger?" Lahn asked, gesturing for the demon to stand.

The insectoid demon did so, withdrawing its large wings and folding them behind his back, coming to a modified height of seven feet tall with purple blades on his arms flashing with energy. "Not a certainty, but possible. I wish to converse with you and the angelic entity dwelling within your body in private about such matters, before discussing other matters such as plans for world domination with your subordinates. There is much to do."

The demon gestured to Dr. Brass and King Arthur Brix, getting more furrowed brows and confused gawking from the nobles and servants around them.

Lahn didn't really know how to respond to that. He'd guessed the angel hadn't left entirely, perhaps forming some kind of karmic link, but did he really have an angel dwelling inside him?

He opened, closed, and reopened his mouth to reply. "That angel saved Allie's life, as it did mine. If there is an angel of the heavens dwelling inside me somehow, I don't wish it harm."

The demon's grin only widened, a sharp cackle erupting from its throat while its yellow eyes narrowed. "I would not dare if that is what you wish, but I will still need to speak to it—and I will discuss with you the details when we retain some privacy. Please, show me to a more secluded area so that we may speak more on this subject."

CHAPTER 35

The balcony Lahn chose was secluded enough for his liking, and at the demon's request he took a seat overlooking a large part of the academy here on the top city floor—some of which had been rebuilt after Rippenvire's attack. The gardens had all been regrown, too, with the help of nature-based mages, but to Lahn's distress, the small animal sanctuary he'd made in those gardens was no more.

"It's quite strange that one of Gluttony's own came to seek me out," Lahn stated with a grunt, letting his backside melt into the cushioned chair underneath him that was abnormally comfortable if he had to say so. "Strange that you'd even know about the angel to begin with since you were stuck in whatever void-prison Elysium put you in. Tre'Zix, was it?"

The demon gave a nod, retracting his purple blades slightly to avoid cutting into the fabric of the chair. Yellow eyes shifted across to where guards were posted farther back at the entrances leading onto the balcony and many others elsewhere, and he snapped his fingers as a translucent sound barrier erected itself around himself and Lahn.

"Gluttony keeps tabs on many things you'd not expect." Tre'Zix smiled— steepling his fingers and staring across the flower gardens that spanned for miles beyond campus grounds. "Tell me. What do you know of Gluttony?"

Lahn cocked an eyebrow. It wasn't a question he'd thought the demon would ask or even care about. "Anything at all?"

"Anything at all."

Lahn contemplated this, scrunching up his brows and folding his arms while deep in thought. "I know it's one of the seven original sins. I'd heard about it before Panu was formed and the integration happened. According to legend it is one of the seven origins of demonkind, and it's supposed to be hunger incarnate. It is said that it feeds on the souls of mortal men to grant itself power, and that it is evil beyond measure. That is what I was taught growing up."

Tre'Zix blinked, then chuckled with a widening smile that put on display all the sharp teeth behind his pincers. The smile looked alien, but it wasn't hostile. "Ah, I see . . . So even before the integration into Elysium, there must have been angels or demons that contacted your world or dwelt upon it. Otherwise you would not know such things. Let me ask you another question, then. Do you think all demons are evil—and that all angels are of good will?"

Tre'Zix turned his yellow eyes upon Lahn curiously.

Lahn, for his part, flinched just slightly. "I . . . I don't think so. No."

"Why?" Tre'Zix asked, cocking his head.

Lahn blinked. "Because Athela, Azmoth, and Fay aren't evil. They were all incredibly nice to me, especially Fay."

"The lucky three bound to Gluttony's reincarnation?" Tre'Zix laughed loudly, throwing his head back. "How amazingly fortunate they are! But this is good to hear. Tell me, then, do you think that I am evil? That Gluttony is evil?"

Lahn furrowed his brows. "I don't know. I would assume . . . Well, I would have assumed that being bound to the Unholy Foundational Pillar, you'd be evil by nature. But I am now bound to the Unholy Foundational Pillar . . . and I'm not. And Fay isn't. And I know that you can acquire the Unholy Foundational Pillar by doing evil things . . . but that is just one of many ways to get it. Isn't it?"

Tre'Zix narrowed his yellow eyes, then nodded slowly. "Yes. There is a very big misconception across the multiverse at large about those who follow the Unholy Foundational Pillar as a means to ascension's gates. And truthfully, there are stereotypes for a reason—but they aren't absolute. I will be the first to admit that I am no saint, that you truly would consider me 'evil' if you knew me in truth. I have killed for hunger, for pleasure, and for no reason at all, time after time after time. Yet I would even go as far to say that Gluttony is more akin to a predator's spirit rather than truly evil. He does kill indiscriminately at times, but not because he wants to inflict pain. Rather, Gluttony kills and feeds because it is in his nature to do so. Whether or not that makes him evil is up to one's opinion. Yet there are shades of morality that we all must decide on for ourselves, as finding oneself is half the journey on the transition into the higher realms of being. Should you ever make it past C-grade, you'll do well to remember these words."

There was a pause as Lahn digested the information. Was this reborn archdemon really giving him the secrets of ascension?

"I thought you'd lost all your memories," Lahn stated.

This got a laugh from Tre'Zix. "Oh no. The vast majority of my power was reduced and it is true that I have pockets and gaps in my knowledge. But not everything was lost, and we were once some of the greatest of our kind . . . We had means of preserving small tidbits that even Elysium could not find."

Tre'Zix winked. "Regardless, I have a point to make among all this talk—and it is this: We demons, and Gluttony, by default, are not evil. Many of us have done evil things, but we treat our friends with kindness just as anyone else would. Even though our cultures may be what the angels consider barbaric and excessively murderous, you must remember that there are shades of morality that even the worst of us hold close to our souls. It is an unfortunate and direct side effect of Charisma's battle that has propagated the images of our kind being evil, specifically to mortal races such as humans who were born aligned with positive Charisma instead of our negative Charisma. In many ways we are destined to seek conflict with those of different Charisma affiliations, with only those at the absolute neutral truly being safe from influence."

He pointed at Lahn's chest, and the sigil imprinted there into Lahn's skin, underneath his clothes, began to flare a hot white. "The same concepts can be applied to the angel who resides inside you."

Tre'Zix stopped pointing, and the sigil on Lahn's chest began to fade and dim.

The demon shook his head. "It makes me wonder how things would have been if Charisma had never existed in the framework of creation to begin with. If this eternal war between the commandments and sins was to never happen. But if I were to guess, it is likely that whoever or whatever created the fabric of existence created us this way intentionally, with polar opposites destined to war against one another until the end of time. After all, conflict breeds growth."

"Didn't Elysium create this multiverse?"

"Yes, but only in the sense that it stitched together other universes—or cannibalized them. Angels and demons existed long before Elysium did. Elysium is an enigma, creating its own multiverse within a multiverse, but it is just a piece of the greater whole. Even Charisma, though not seen on the outside of Elysium's multiverse by status page, was still a very real thing before Elysium came to be. Elysium just gave us a means of physically seeing it by way of status screen, but there were other ways to do so even before it descended."

Lahn's eyebrows rose in surprise. "A multiverse within a multiverse? There is more than one?"

"Certainly. Riven's parents fled from this one into the next, did they not?" Tre'Zix chuckled at Lahn's shock. "Though it is all so vast that no one can truly be certain just how far it all goes. What we do know is that there is a realm beyond the SSS-grade, and should you ever reach it, you gain access to it. Should that ever happen and you fight through tribulations even beyond Elysium's own, you vanish . . . never to return. At least, none have chosen to do so if they could. But there have been two documented instances in history where demons managed to break through, and one of the ordeals was actually recorded."

Another pause.

"That's incredibly interesting," Lahn said with a thoughtful frown. "What rank were you before all this?"

"Me? I was a peak A-grade, on the verge of S-grade. A being that could destroy entire civilizations! A true monster to be feared!" Tre'Zix laughed again, a gleeful glint to his eye. "It is a realm even many gods do not enter, despite their vast advantages when compared to other beings of the multiverse."

"What about Lillith?"

"She was mid-SSS-grade. That crazy bitch is something else, but I love her—as we all do."

"And Gluttony?"

Tre'Zix paused. "Intentionally peak SSS-grade without ever attempting to transcend. Gluttony and the other sins, though . . . they have compulsions to remain in that state. As if by design. Gluttony once told me that he had the opportunity to try and surpass his limits, but some kind of limiter would have made it all the harder to do, which made him not want to do it. He didn't go into much detail after that, other than to say there is another kind of system in the beyond that he once touched upon. Strange to think about. Perhaps this time around, one of us from Gluttony's ranks will finally make the jump . . . as long as we aren't hunted down and killed first. Ancient enemies will no doubt be coming out of meditative seclusion in an attempt to kill us all before we make it back to where we were, long-standing grudges to be had when we are at our weakest. Many of us will doubtless die in our climb back to the peak. But the same can be said for all the other sins, and all the commandments and their followers that were banished along with us back when the eternal war got out of hand."

Lahn was about to ask another question when Tre'Zix shut him down with a wave of his hand.

"History lessons can wait. For now, I need to speak to the angel that so proudly announced himself as Denaskus, arbiter of the Celestial Prax, when killing that baby bloodsucker at the Blood Moon Requiem's compound. Would you mind bringing him out for me?" Tre'Zix grinned. "I promise to play nice. I just want to make a few things very clear to him should we permit him to stay. After that, I've been instructed to speak to King Arthur Brix about our plans for world domination. Then I am to go power level with my demonic brethren before we take a mercenary guild contract to help fight Negrada's war. It's a lot to do, and it has been a long time since I've let loose in the hells, so let's get this over with. I have a bloodbath to attend to and an ascension into E-grade to acquire."

Gragle the gnome, Nora, and Azmoth were led through town behind the guards of Mesini's Outpost Number 84 without much fanfare. There were certainly wary or even scared looks shot Azmoth's way as they walked, but the residents were for the most part still rushing around trying to form barricades and set up defensive lines all around the stone wall perimeter. Health, mana, stamina, and divinity potions were all being passed around—and long-lasting miracle or spell buffs were being applied even hours before the monster wave hit in order to give the casters enough time for their cooldowns to reset over and over again.

The architecture here varied, and most of the people here wore various leather and fur gear or plain fabric, being either human or gnome in origin with a mix tilting in favor of humans by two to one. Nora could tell just by looking at the place that whatever this planet Mesini was, or at least the area this outpost had been in, it'd likely been a barren, rocky wasteland without much plant life. There was wood present, and even a few very scrappy-looking gray trees, but not much. The houses and buildings were a mix and match of metal plating, clay patchwork, stone walls, and even tar. She wouldn't go as far as to say it was dirty, but the most colorful aspects of the town were orange and yellow paintings found on some of the walls. Otherwise it was very brown and very gray wherever she looked.

Eventually after a few twists and turns, Nora and Azmoth were led into a moderately sized two-story building, the largest one around, and told to wait below while two of the guards jostled up the stairway with bounding steps.

There was a small commotion up at the top as three scantily clad human women covering themselves with blankets clambered down the stairs and rushed out the door with embarrassed flushing to their faces, and a gnome about two-and-a-half-feet tall was quick to jump down each of the stairs one by one moments later.

He landed in a cloud of green dust when his hands smashed two green vials of sparkly powder into the floor, theatrically so, and he waved his small hands around as if it was supposed to be impressive. He had a pointy wizard's hat on and had a tobacco pipe in his mouth that he continued to puff on while the cloud of green powder around him dissipated. "Welcome to Outpost Number 84! I am Warden Zuk of this fine town, wizard extraordinaire! You may prostrate yourselves now!"

Nora gave the incredibly short man a flat look, then shot a glance at the guards, who each shamefully glanced away when her eyes met theirs. Azmoth just scratched the back of his metallic, spiked head with a single claw—but didn't move otherwise as he towered over not only the gnome, but all the human men as well.

"Warden Zuk." The captain of the guards sighed with a shake of his head. "Take it from one drinking buddy to another, but this is not the time to be playing silly games. We have a monster wave induced by Elysium itself on its way about six hours from now and we could all very well die if we don't figure out what exactly is going on, or if there are any rules and obligations about this event that we need to know."

Warden Zuk snorted, lowering his hands and taking the smoking pipe out of his mouth to put it into a spatial sack on his side. "Fine, fine. You there—Gragle, as a fellow gnome, would you say that these people are upstanding citizens-to-be, or should we be wary of them?"

Gragle, for his part, had been trying to escape on the outskirts of the room after the warden's flamboyant entrance. His scarred features scrunched up in irrita-tion and he swore under his breath before sighing and walking back into the room with a defeated glower. "I have no idea."

"Well, that's not very helpful! Were you not taking them on a tour of the town just now?!" The warden raised an eyebrow and tipped his gray wizard's hat to one side.

Gragle put both small hands to either side of his head, began rubbing his temple, and groaned. "It was more than I would have liked to do."

Nora watched the small man glance up at her, and then at Azmoth, amuse-ment edging itself into the back of her mind. She could tell that he was considering talking about Riven and the others, as well as their open talk back in the pub, but she wasn't concerned. Each of these guards was easily below level 50, and she'd be able to kill all of them by herself should the time come.

That of course was opposite of what she wanted to do, given her quest was to save the town from this monster wave. She wouldn't necessarily lose event points if only a few of these people died, but she did know that Riven would. Though they were technically still competitors for Chalgathi's inheritance even if they were both noncultists, Riven had still helped her up those pyramid steps and had likely saved her life. She would not undermine his attempts here.

[**Nora's Quest 1 of the Altars of Despair and Hope: Tag along with any other noncultist to defend their town for the upcoming monster waves. Your job is to successfully assassinate the enemy leader, as well as any enemy cultists who may appear with the monster wave. 30 event points for assassinating the enemy leader. Extra event points (+3 total) for any enemy cultist slain.**]
[**Tagged Quest: Riven's Quest 1 of the Altars of Despair and Hope: Other F-grade participants have been either voluntarily or involuntarily dragged into this event from across the multiverse. Unlike the chosen of this trial, they do not respawn twenty-four hours after death. You have been given the task of defending one of these populations. Your first quest is to travel to the marked quest location and save as many people as you can. Each person who dies subtracts one event point. Successfully defending the town from the monster wave will gain you 30 event points.**
>>> Time until monster wave: six hours, twenty-nine minutes.]

"That's a funny feathered hat you've got there, lass," the gnome warden stated with a finger pointing up to her green-and-black headdress sticking out from the green-and-black Chalgathi cowl that labeled her as a noncultist. "What's a noncultist?"

"You really don't know?" Nora asked curiously, folding her arms. "What exactly were you all told when you got here?"

"Not much. That we were supposed to fight a monster wave and survive, and that we'd be provided more details if we did."

"Huh. I can see why you asked me to come here, then." She looked around, then spotted a plate of pastries set up in a nearby kitchen—and a large smile spread across her face. "Of course I'll have to get going soon to scout out the area, but I can give you a rundown of what's going on if you treat me to that food over there. How's that for a deal?"

"Agreed." Azmoth nodded, surprising many of the people there who hadn't heard the deep, demonic voice of the brutalisk up until now.

"Your hellish ape can talk?!" The gnome wizard gawked—only for the captain of the guard to nearly choke at the unintentional insult while quickly ushering both Azmoth and Nora into the kitchen.

"We'll provide you with whatever food we have . . ." The guard captain glared over his shoulder at the warden. "Please forgive our resident idiot in charge. He means well—he's just thoroughly stupid."

Grakzee's gills flared while water magic cycled through them to moisturize his insides. The silver cowl with blue trimmings with the sigil of a kraken stitched into its top was irritating to wear, but every time he'd tried taking it off, the damn thing would appear back on his head again seconds later. This hadn't been the case earlier when he'd only been in the presence of other cultists at the Altar of Despair, but the notification of "while in the presence of noncultists, you must retain your Chubin cowl at all times" was now plaguing him.

> **[Chubin Cowl (Cultist): This is a soul-bound item only you can wear for the remainder of this event. It gives you no stats or bonuses, but it marks you as a Chubin cultist to friend and enemy alike.]**

At least this would act as a kind of radar to detect nearby enemies, but he didn't know what the radius on this effect was or how many of them there were. As for his side, he'd already met with the other five cultists who'd been assigned to this mission. Two of them were Chubin-affiliated naga cultists like himself, blue-green scales adorning their reptilian bodies with the lower halves of serpents and the upper halves of humanoid lizards. The other three were all Nekra cultists, two being dark elf females who hid whatever equipment they had underneath thick black robes, while the third was a male chaos dwarf barbarian. He was an axe-wielder with Chaos-derived sigils all over his body. This species of dwarf was a rarity to see, and their sigils were supposed to be present at birth rather than created or tattooed, with the story being that once upon a time many millennia ago, one of their ancestors made a pact with some kind of demonic god to acquire such power for his people.

Unfortunately, Grakzee was the only one of the group of six that had a stealth-based class, so he'd been put at the forefront of the scouting mission while the other five were delegated to other things. They chose to either sit and wait, to speak to the monster swarm leader about tactics until it was unchained by the system event, or they were applying buffs to some of the stronger monsters in anticipation of the fight to come.

He just wished he found himself in more swamp or ocean rather than thick forest. He wasn't used to being on dry land, and his Waterspear Ambusher class wasn't as good out of the water.

And why was the system delegating six of the twenty-one cultists to a single quest anyway? Unlike all the other cultists, who had their own individual quests, the six of them had been assigned a group quest for enhanced difficulty. The prize had also been escalated when compared to others he'd talked to or those who'd compared quest logs with him, and he didn't know whether or not he'd been given a gift by the system—or whether this was a cursed quest destined to fail.

[Grakzee's Quest 1 of the Altars of Despair and Hope: Other F-grade participants have been either voluntarily or involuntarily dragged into this event from across the multiverse. Unlike the chosen of this trial, they do not respawn twenty-four hours after death. You have been given the task of attacking one of these populations. Your first quest is to travel to the marked quest location and kill as many people as you can. Each person who dies gains you one event point. Successfully destroying the town alongside the monster wave will result in 30 more event points. This quest is at an enhanced difficulty—killing either of the two noncultists present here, only while during the active quest, will reward you with an additional +280 event points per kill.
>>> Time until monster wave: six hours, nineteen minutes.]

His eyes narrowed on the +280 quest points. Killing these noncultists would result in far more points than the actual quest itself gave. That was quite a lot when compared to any of the other quests the other cultists got, but it didn't take a lot of thought to cycle through possible options for why that would be.

It was just a guess, but as he slithered through the underbrush with his short water-made spears in either hand, Grakzee could only hope that his theory about why six would be pitted against two, and why the system would grant such a large boon for success, was wrong.

Because though the cultists had the numbers, and all of them were in the S rank and Paragon rankings on the Panu power ladder, there was one that stood out above all the rest.

Grakzee could only hope that he wouldn't have to fight that monstrous warlock ranked at the very top, because from what he'd seen of Riven Thane so far on the world forums, he was a walking catastrophe waiting to happen. The pureblooded vampire was also a known Chalgathi chosen after he'd wiped out an entire city to massacre the Chalgathi cultists who'd wronged him. There was at least a chance that Grakzee was about to pit himself against the most powerful man Panu had to offer, and if so, Grakzee would need to devise a scheme that would give him an advantage. He did have the skeleton of a plan so far, but he just hoped he'd not have to use it—because even with his schemes, the odds would not be in his favor.

[Chubin, the Apocalypse Beasts World Quest, Panu, subevent has been INITIATED: The Altars of Despair and Hope.
A temporary pocket world for this event has been created. The chosen finalists of Chalgathi, the Plague Dragon; Chubin, the Glass Kraken; and Nekra, the Skeletal Devourer, have all been sent to this pocket world to compete.

Locations of Chubin's altars have been marked for you. You will be required to visit all four Chubin altar sites and activate each of the shrines as well as acquire ten thousand event points before being allowed to leave this event. Doing so will also give you knowledge of the location of Chubin's sea-bottom lair, where Chalgathi's incubation chamber has been hidden.

There are twenty-one registered cultists.

- Seven Chalgathi cultists, six Chubin cultists, and eight Nekra cultists

There are nine registered noncultists entering this event.

- Three Chalgathi noncultists, four Chubin noncultists, and two Nekra noncultists

You have arrived at the Altar of Despair and are now registered as a cultist. Killing other cultists will result in a decrease in your event points. Each participant will have their own set of unique quests that allow them to gain points and level up; only quests will allow level-ups and XP gains during this event. Other rules will be reviewed again and in more detail after your first quest is completed.]

CHAPTER 36

Nearly three hundred years ago . . .

Sheline sat meditating upon an ocean of blood, her vampiric heritage roaring about her while her ancient, spunky grandmother Nephridi went on and on about how annoying her most recent suitors were.

The beautiful, pale vampire rolled her eyes—but a smirk still played at her lips. "Grandmother, can you just settle down and pick one already? You're going to give yourself another headache. And that's on top of the one you're already giving me!"

Nephridi humphed, scowling down at the woman who would no doubt claim the throne to the Blood Moon Requiem when Nephridi handed the reins to a successor. Her long white robe flowed out around her, a stark contrast to the bloodred-and-black dress her granddaughter had on, but their features and long brown hair that shifted like silk in the wind were one and the same. "Oh, let an old woman gossip, will you?!"

The high queen laughed, sitting down on their chosen cultivation spot and sending ripples across the otherwise perfectly smooth ocean beneath them. Flipping her hair over one shoulder and snorting at her granddaughter's expression, she raised a hand. "Fine! Fine. Let's get on with the plan, then. Are you ready?"

"As ready as I'll ever be," Sheline muttered under her breath, calming her beating heart and clasping her hands tightly before closing her eyes.

She was still young and hadn't fully grasped the concept of forcing her Malignant Prophecy to activate, but she could prod and poke at it until it did something. Whether or not it did what she wanted was something else entirely, but Nephridi had faith in her and Sheline didn't want to disappoint her grandmother.

Plus, Sheline's grandmother was strong enough that she'd be able to fix anything that went wrong.

Sheline searched, tugging at the little filaments of soul particles that swirled around her constructing sin core—with each piece of sin having cost the royal family sums of money beyond imagination. The sin of wrath raged inside her, constantly screaming at her to get up and kill without reason or direction—but she'd already gotten used to the nagging sensation and was well on her way to clamping it down altogether.

That would likely change for the worse when the core finished, though, and that was why they were doing it the safe way.

The world began to turn gray around her, and unlike the thin clouds overhead that stopped in their tracks amid the shifting winds, Sheline found herself staring down at her body from a phantasmal form. She looked right to where her grandmother, also a holder of the gift, stared back at her—waving in the eerie gray.

A black door formed in front of her on the ocean of blood, and despite the time freeze, it slowly began to etch runes of gold into the black backdrop. The symbol of three dragons, each eating the next to form a circle, took form in front of her eyes.

The phantasmal figure of her grandmother came to stand beside her, one of only a handful of people across the cosmos who could enter Sheline's malignant zone. She turned to look at her concentrating granddaughter, smiling in appreciation and approval while the three dragons began to spin faster, and faster, and faster.

"Have I ever told you the legend of the Temple of Three, dear granddaughter?" Nephridi asked with a slight cock of her head.

Sheline grunted while continuing to channel her sin energy into the door, manipulating it and simultaneously forcing Malignant Prophecy to activate outside the bounds of normalcy. "You know you haven't, Grandmother. You always keep that information close. Why? Now that we're finally here, you're going to spill the secrets? Is that it?"

An amused chuckle followed that, and the high queen sagged her shoulders into a more relaxed posture while the golden circle of devouring dragons began to blur—sending sparks of mana across the black door as the barrier between their world and the abyss began to crack. "Well, let me tell it to you now, then. Once, in the age before this one, long before the cycle of nirvana had come to fruition to destroy the old and replace it with the new, three dragons were born. One was imbued with the power to manipulate the past, one was imbued with the power to manipulate the present, and one was imbued with the power to manipulate the future."

There was a long pause as the high queen considered her words, and eventually her granddaughter gave another huff of irritation and glared up at the older woman. "Don't just stop there! Tell me, damn you! You're doing that on purpose!"

"I would never!" High Queen Nephridi said, aghast at the accusation, but she winked, gave another laugh, and clasped her hands behind her back. "So the first of these dragons, that which could control the past, was named Steadfast. For steadfast was the nature of the past—it was set in stone outside the manipulations of this dragon and could not be changed otherwise. The second of these dragons, that which could control the present, was named Balance. For it would balance out the actions between past and present, and manipulations of the past needed to be controlled in order to not let the future run rampant with shifting possibilities. As time spreads out from the past and into the present, the possibilities begin to shift into a spiraling network of more and more futures. Which leads us to the dragon of the future—the last of these dragons. This dragon that could control the future was named Malignancy . . . for it is the nature of the future to be malignant—to have an ever-spiraling growth of possibilities.

"Each of the three dragons grew so powerful that they even surpassed the death of the old multiverse and were birthed here into the new. But they were too weak to continue on their own, and their heritages were split among the most powerful of bloodlines that they deemed worthy."

The golden cracks spreading out from the sigil of the three dragons began to break down, and the door now began to crumble—revealing a never-ending sea of black behind it that opened up into the resting place of the elder gods. The resting place of the birth of creation and chaos.

Sheline's eyes widened at her grandmother's words, and her gaze shifted through the world of gray to stare at the high queen with mouth ajar. A look of understanding crossed over her, and she slowly nodded. "I think . . . I think I'm beginning to understand."

Nephridi chuckled. "Yes. Our bloodline, that of Malignant Prophecy, is that of the dragon of the future. One day, Sheline, your children will embark on a journey into the abyss. And when that day comes, we need to have prepared keys for them to find. That of past, and that of present, and perhaps then—finally, after untold millennia—we will finally be able to claim the ultimate prize."

Sheline's eyes were like saucers now, and the rest of the door faded away as dust in the wind. "My . . . children?" Her smile softened, and a blush overcame her. "What will I name them? Have you seen it? Who will the father be? To think myself a mother . . . it is insanity."

"Telling you such things would only ruin the surprise and potentially change the timeline," Nephridi replied with a ghostly pat on the shoulder. Then she turned to look at the approaching figure and gestured for Sheline to get up. "We have a visitor. Come, child, stand, and meet the Keeper."

The green of the leaves here was turning into autumn colors, reds and oranges that crunched underfoot. The change had been rather abrupt—it had happened over the course of ten minutes, making Riven wonder if weather patterns like this would continue for the next year.

"Cultivation isn't something I've really understood much of whenever I do it," Riven replied, walking alongside Athela through the forest while holding hands. The Unholy tattoos along his body abruptly shifted when the third eye appeared again, focused on a point farther into the woods, and then disappeared with Gluttony's whisper calling out to him.

Riven chuckled underneath his Chalgathi hood, acknowledging the sin's words with a nod in his full plate armor. "I've received visions of inspiration that I glean meaning from, usually in battle, but otherwise have not sat down to truly comprehend the meaning of what it is I am able to do. Nor have I spent time dwelling on where my path leads. Rather, my path has been one of forced brutality . . . action and reaction. It is a flaw I must correct, and trying to forge totems recently has shed light on my misgivings."

Jackal looked up from where it trotted behind them when Riven's free left hand opened palm-up. A flash of light, and his most recent totem in the making appeared to hover there. The icosahedron had twenty triangular faces on the outer surface, each face holding a black or crimson rune, and was about one-by-one-by-one foot, with the outer skeleton being made of metal.

[Partially Constructed Totem of Bloodforged Rift Sparks: Status page is currently on standby. Soul acquired, affinity to Shadow acquired, sigils acquired. Totem soul is currently absorbing the minor sigil of Black Lightning and will reach comprehension sometime within the next hour. Unable to bind at this time.]

"Creating even this half-baked totem made me realize that there's a lot of the intricacies of my magics that I do by instinct rather than by knowledge." Riven gave her a sideways smile and shrugged. "But it is good to identify my weaknesses now rather than never."

Athela eyed the creation with a raised eyebrow, licking her lips after the rather romantic picnic they'd just been on and still gushing while riding the coattails of the date he'd finally provided her. "I think you've come a long way in a short time concerning your totem-making skills! But you definitely have a long way to go. I also agree that you could improve your performance with cultivating your power and upgrading your abilities, but so could I. From what my mother says, cultivation is more important in the E-grade and beyond than it is in the F-grade. So now that you're about to transcend into the E-grade, this is the perfect time to start thinking about such things. That's actually why I brought it up. In order to break into the E-grade, you're going to have to form a soul core lattice. It is the key to transcending into the next state of being, and Gluttony will need to be incorporated into it from what my mother says, because you two have a symbiotic relationship. You're going to be stunted from growing past level 200 until you do so, and when you finally do create your lattice, leveling is going to rely a lot less heavily on just killing things, with a lot more emphasis on actual cultivation."

She squeezed his hand encouragingly. "Anyways, I'm excited to see what your new totem can do when it finishes! Just an hour or less left!"

Riven glanced into the forest, through the falling leaves and into the shade of shrubbery and trees north of here—if north could still be judged by the way the sun was moving in the sky. "I'm sure I'll be able to use it by the time our fight with the monster wave rolls around. By the way, you never did show me your last martial art. I'm thinking maybe now would be a good time?"

"If we're going to do that, then I need to get appropriately dressed! Hold one moment!" Athela began putting on her gear from a small spatial sack she'd recently been gifted. First came a pair of red boots, then red pants, a red vest, a black cloak with a red underside, and her ruby-studded black tiara.

[Tiara of Silent Killing (Blood/Shadow Trinket): After successfully killing a target without being noticed by anyone else, gain a charge of critical strike. Your next unseen attack has a 100% chance to be a two to eight times critical hit, with multiplied damage coming in the form of kinetic burst energy from the strike site. Requires a 26% or higher Blood or Shadow subpillar affinity to wield, and the wearer must be female.]

The clothes fit her perfectly and emphasized her more feminine qualities, with tiny sleeves in the cloak for her arms to go through and holes in the back that her arachnid limbs could also fit into.

She giggled at Riven's simultaneously amused yet intrigued expression while she dressed, then held out her hands in front of her and slammed them into her chest. Drawing out two long katanas from her heart, made completely of red metal aside from parts of the redwood handles with intricate carvings of doves decorating the blades, the weapons began to whisper in ominous tones.

Spinning each of them around in a flurry of motion, she gave Riven an evil smile. "I've been practicing with these ever since I got them as a dungeon prize! Every time I visit Mother!"

[The Twin Red Doves (Awakened Weapons, Dual-Wielding Set. Blood Artifacts. Twin Katanas): 899 average damage on strike with each physical strike on flesh adding a guaranteed stack of the Bleed debuff for damage over time. Hidden strikes that land before an opponent is aware cause additional guaranteed damage of +5%. If the strike is a critical hit, deal an additional two times critical modifier. These items, when bound to a wielder, may be stored in the heart of the wielder and withdrawn at will. These items are nearly indestructible while the bound wielder is still alive. Requires a Blood affinity of over 51% to wield.

- **Whispers of Agony: From time to time, these blades will whisper to you. The stronger your bond, the louder they whisper, and the louder they whisper, the more pain your strikes inflict regardless of damage.**
- **The Red Tide: Unleash stamina, mana, or divinity into these blades via your Blood subpillar to charge ranged sweeping attacks in the form of a red crescent. Damage and range depend on the amount of energy infused.]**

Riven smiled at how excited she was to show it all off, and he gave her a nod of approval and clapped with a laugh. "You look great, as always. Why don't I see Azmoth wearing his antlers or belt? Does he not like them?"

Athela tossed one of the long red katanas up into the air in a spinning flick of the wrist, then caught the twirling blade effortlessly before giving Riven a side-eye. "Riven, you're his first and only master. You're also his friend. Unlike Fay and I, Azmoth doesn't have a family to go back to in the nether realms . . . Hellscape brutalisks are very solitary by nature, or at least they usually are. So your gifts to him have a very deep-set meaning, and he hoards them as sentimental treasures rather than risk breaking them."

Riven didn't know what to say to that, so instead he just put on a warm smile. "I'm glad he feels that way. But you should probably use that ability of yours and take him down before he leaves—we don't know how long he'll stay and I can only pinpoint the general direction through smell."

Athela laughed and closed her eyes. Walking over and pushing his helmet back while grinning wickedly, she kissed Riven's lips with both hands on either cheek. "Blood Art—Mark of the Hunted."

The world around her abruptly changed to various shades of red, and farther in the distance, a single hulking figure lit up along a ledge where it lay hidden and watching.

A naga.

The demoness growled as the mark targeted and highlighted her prey. The whispers of the red katanas in either hand grew into a storming howl. Her eyes grew to twice their normal size and her arachnid limbs tore out of her back as she screamed with a primal and frenzied glee before tearing through the forest with blinding speed that caused trees she passed by to upend themselves with the current of air that followed her.

Grakzee stalked the vampire at a distance under the cover of thick plant life, trying to find an opening for a quick, lethal strike. Two of his skills allowed him to use piercing ranged attacks focused on critical energy if unseen, and he could often strike down enemies at a distance without ever being noticed because of it.

Water-based abilities were, in his opinion, very underrated by the land dwellers.

The naga's gills flared, and his sharp teeth bared into a grin when the sky suddenly went red.

The air around him grew cold.

His heart began to thud in his chest.

And amid it all, he saw two sets of red eyes turned in his direction. A feral scream tore out of the demoness Athela—who was famous across Panu—before she tore through the forest like a tornado of vengeance.

"Oh no . . ."

Grakzee's eyes went wide and he let out a shriek, only barely vaulting out of the way before Athela's red blades tore into the ground with a double-handed slash that sent debris flying.

Grakzee didn't even have time to think, whirling and deflecting three follow-up strikes. His arms acted in reflex, his water-based stamina surged, and within seconds he found himself in a fight for his life against one of the two world-boss enemies in this trial.

He'd somehow completely lost the element of surprise.

The ground tore apart and energetic exchanges of stamina-infused strikes blasted into each other with resounding booms. He activated an agility buff and grew faster, lunging backward and to the side over and over again while being pressed hard into a retreat.

"WATER DANCER'S RAGE!" Grakzee screamed, his body blooming with swirling arcs of streaming water that acted as trailing blades behind the two spears he wielded—clashing them against the red katanas of the cackling she-demon.

He dodged, rolled, and exploded into a cloud of mist before rematerializing, only to find her upon him in an instant with a flurry of jabs, slashes, and cuts that made him curse under his breath. Grakzee was no pushover—he was a Paragon rank himself at number 960 on the power ladder—but this demoness was incredibly agile even when compared to him.

With a roar he sent out illusionary bodies made of water to match his own, narrowly dodging a spray of thousands of red needles that leveled dozens of trees in an explosion of shrapnel while the demoness giggled and lunged for his throat.

"HAVE YOU COME TO PLAY?!" Athela screeched with wide-eyed glee, turning into a puddle of blood to avoid one of Grakzee's counterswipes, only to appear on his other side—crashing the sharp end of one blade through his left elbow.

The limb spun off, and Grakzee screamed in outrage and pain before he exploded yet again in a spray of mist—re-forming his arm a second later while heaving and huffing twenty yards away.

His reptilian eyes narrowed when the demoness turned to look at him with a scowl, and his heartbeat thumped in his chest when he heard the sound of leaves cracking underneath feet directly behind him.

He turned to—

BOOM

The ground shook, and Grakzee's dual spears collided with a black halberd flowing with blood. The naga felt bones in his arms snap under the strain, and he began to panic as he tried to think of a way out.

Grakzee was an assassin, not a duelist. Not a fighter or a tank. With the loss of surprise, he was as good as dead if he didn't make it out of here soon. He needed to get out, he needed to get away, and he needed to do it now.

CHAPTER 37

Riven watched with interest as the naga assassin took another one of his strikes, the earth shattering and erupting under the impact of the sin energy flowing out of his body.

The naga's scream of pain was accompanied by another flash of power when he regenerated and vaulted away in a swirling river of water, only to be intercepted by Athela's own blood form as her river of red crashed into his river of clear blue.

The two entangled figures slammed into the ground, Athela laughing madly while loud shock waves from their blows eradicated nearby trees—while Riven continued to observe the dark fractals coming out from his skin to encase the Gluttony-based armor he now wore.

"Interesting," Riven muttered under his breath, feeling the great maw itself leak out of his soul and into both Messenger and Jackal—empowering them both as black energies flared to life.

Without looking up, Riven stepped to the left in a blur of speed.

BOOM

The ground beside him erupted with a thin, sharp, solid wall of water that cut through the forest for a mile, creating a solid trench in the ground. The naga flashed forward, empowered with another water-based martial art, only for Riven to look up with a flick of his wrist.

A dozen spinning blades of black and red erupted around him and slammed into the naga—splitting him open in multiple spots and then exploding. However, the naga's agility and regenerative properties let him off with only another pained scream—and he teleported back a few dozen feet, gasping out ragged breaths.

Riven went back to inspecting the runes traveling out from his body that were still embedding themselves into his weapon and armor, fusing with it and giving him a more innate sense of control over the items. "Gluttony, what are you doing?"

The great maw only laughed inside his soul, the third eye emerging from his forehead to stare out at the naga with terrorizing hunger pulsing out from it. The very grass beneath their feet shriveled and died under the gaze of the sin, and the sky above them darkened with a malevolent laugh that echoed throughout the landscape.

That was when Riven realized this wasn't a skill at all. Rather, this was actually Gluttony's aura—similar to how Riven's aura of red frost was akin to Crimson Ice but didn't actually involve any skill activation. It was just a pure flex of raw, semidirected power.

The sight of the eye caused the naga to freeze midstride, true fear giving it pause right as Athela caught up to it and impaled the assassin with both of her red blades.

"It's not fun when you stop moving!" Athela hissed over the screech of the cultist, tearing her blades out from his body, headbutting him midscream—and with a blur, she kicked the man in the chest to launch him like a cannonball.

She looked over her shoulder, to the dying plant life that was quickly drying up all around them at exponentially rapid speed, then up to the sky overhead, confused. "What are you doing?"

Energy began ripping from all life around them, feeding into Messenger and Jackal alike. The dark runes pulsed various shades of black, red, and purple, sparking with power, shifting and churning. The ground began to turn gray, and without warning a pulse of sin vaporized the forest all around them for hundreds of meters.

The darkening sky overhead screamed as the figure of the maw appeared to open wide, and Riven reached out a hand as a bolt of sin crashed down onto his position.

Riven felt electrified in both figurative and literal senses, coursing with power as his mana channels rearranged and inserted themselves into the two sin-affiliated items. The eyes of the horned, vampiric pauldrons burned bright and the flowing rivers of blood encompassing Jackal roared to life like an ocean.

He felt his pillars react, and the sin core orbiting his soul core reached out to form a pillar of its own. Now, instead of being disconnected from one another, Gluttony had fused the sin core as a newly born pillar—placing it directly beside his Blood subpillar and tripling the size of his soul core as it pulsed and waned.

Riven let out a shudder, and as the sin pillar solidified, he felt a strong sense of oneness when his mind linked with Gluttony, his Mythic-tier upper-body armor, and his ascended Legendary-tier weapon. The spiked knuckles on his gauntlets crackled, the four plates on his back expanded with torrents of fire as Launch began to activate, and the replica maw of Gluttony along his front began to open.

God, he needed new pants, especially after his Lich-Kin Boots had been destroyed by the blast in Deepnest.

His three eyes fixated on Athela, and he smiled. "Gluttony, Messenger, Jackal, and I were just having a bonding moment is all. Now . . . let him flee for a while. Hopefully he'll lead us to the others so that we can finish this quest ahead of schedule."

Athela stared blankly, then chuckled and turned—flashing forward as she morphed into a stream of blood that crossed the desolate landscape he'd created, further flowing in between the trees to advance out of sight.

With Mark of the Hunted still tracking her fleeing naga friend, Riven was sure she'd be on him soon enough.

Grinning and feeding Messenger a pulse of mana, he forced his armor to explode with power—shooting him skyward in an arc before he disappeared into the clouds.

[Launch: The back of your suit can open up, creating a blast of sin energy that damages enemies and acts as a propulsion method to blast you in a given direction at speeds dependent on how much energy you drain from the stored reservoir of your pauldrons.]

The forest erupted all around him as the crazy she-demon unleashed red crescents from her blades alongside storms of needles that showered the land. It was like watching a hurricane of destruction running after him, and despite being a speed- and agility-based fighter in the Paragon tier, Grakzee was having a very hard time getting away from her.

The naga assassin cursed and swore, dodging more of those red needle threads while they rang out like the bullets of a Gatling gun to mow down animals, plants, and even boulders while the demoness gave chase. He'd nearly died eight times by now, and that was considering the fact that Riven Thane hadn't done more than half-heartedly attack him three times, twice with his spear-staff and once with a relatively small amount of magic at close range.

Time dragged on, and he suffered more and more wounds—but none of them were lethal. He felt like a rat being toyed with by a cat. It seemed like this Athela bitch was playing with him, as if she was intentionally letting him live just to cause him more pain and suffering, and the more he thought about it, the more he realized why.

They wanted him to lead them to the others in his flight.

Looking over his shoulder at the manic grin on Athela's face only twenty yards away, he decided he would be more than happy to oblige.

CRACK

The air thundered and he felt his knee explode as he screamed again, but yet again, the attack wasn't aimed at his vital points.

He vaporized and then reappeared to heal himself, almost drained of a third of his energy now and cursing the ability that was allowing her to keep a perfect target on his back. No matter whether he backpedaled, used stealth skills, or dashed far ahead, it was like she had a radar that homed in on his soul—and he had the odd sensation that the very heavens were watching him as he tried to avoid their unceasing gaze.

He thought about it, groaning inwardly when blood sprayed from his shoulder and he had to re-form the limb amid Athela's cackling, howling laughter. Truthfully, there was no reason why he WOULDN'T lead these two to other hostile cultists. Not only was their monster swarm there and just unable to leave a particular area at this time, but Riven would have received reinforcements from the town if they'd attacked like originally planned. If the vampire was willing to fight without those reinforcements, then all the better. Not only that, but that other unnamed noncultist wasn't here, either . . . and his other minions were also absent. The two elves, the succubus, and the hellscape brutalisk were all eerily gone.

This raised a question: Why? Were they setting up an ambush for the others? But Grakzee wasn't in much of a situation to question things and would take what he could get. He was also pretty sure that Riven could summon his demonic minions to him by using the Unholy pentagrams on his chest that he'd seen in previous videos on the cortex, but he wasn't absolutely sure about it. Regardless, if Riven wanted to do without the other noncultist who was no doubt at bare minimum S-tier, and forgo his reinforcements from the town and the two elves of unknown threat level—that was more than okay with him.

Riven watched Athela's game of cat and mouse from high up in the clouds as his armor kept him aloft, though he was able to use his own mana to do so at a less viable level even if he didn't have Messenger on at this point. It wasn't as pure as air- or storm-based mana, but by fluctuating it and using it to propel him in certain directions he was able to shift his body's placement aboveground without physically moving it. Albeit poorly. He still had a long way to go, so until he perfected the art he'd be sure to only utilize Messenger unless absolute necessity called for other plans.

"Do you feel it?" Gluttony whispered in his mind, focusing on the threads of light only he and Riven could see. Threads that connected them to one another, combining and meshing the shattered pieces of Riven's soul with Gluttony's own— making them almost inseparable.

It was more than just a symbiotic relationship, but the way it felt . . . Riven wasn't just okay with it. He LIKED it, and even better—he was still the one primarily in control. Having Gluttony there and meshing his thoughts with the great maw on this level gave him an understanding of the creature he now shared a vessel with on a deeper level than any other being had ever been able to grasp, and it made him look at Gluttony in a new light.

Gluttony wasn't necessarily evil at all. Rather, he was just a machine—a being bred for war, bred to kill, and bred to devour.

Gluttony was the very essence of genocide itself, put into spiritual and physical form alike. There was no greater truth Gluttony strived for other than to become THE apex predator above all others, devouring his way to the top, and for the first time in a while, Riven felt a sense of meaning integrate and resonate with his own desires.

It was as if Riven had been lost in the ocean, adrift amid the waves and not having true direction. But now—he had been given that direction.

He, too, wanted to become great.

He, too, wanted to reach the apex.

"I do feel it . . ." Riven replied, feeling Gluttony's abilities mesh into his own status page while Gluttony pushed their intertwining souls together—the maw's sigil radiating sin energy across the new pillar he'd acquired. "I feel everything that you are, as you, too, feel me . . ."

Riven's attention turned from the threads of their souls onto other, external connections. He followed one that pulsed the brightest of all to his lover Athela. He could read her thoughts and chuckled to himself at the mirth she felt while chasing the naga far below.

Poor guy.

The other threads varied in size and length and crossed time and space in ways he could not physically see, but following them allowed Riven to peer beyond physical space. He followed one to Fay, who was sitting on a couch—rather upset—in her mother's nether realm while talking to her clan. He felt her swirling emotions that bubbled up from deep inside her mind—thoughts of inadequacy, doubt, fear, and a longing for him.

He reached out through the thread, touching her consciousness with a feeling of warmth, and smiled lovingly as she received the message with a surprised jerk of her head.

The next thread led to Azmoth, who right at this very moment was gorging himself on pastries back in town. The large demon felt his presence immediately, and Riven couldn't help but explode into laughter when he saw Azmoth give him the middle finger. Only a deep sense of playful trust and admiration resonated from that bond, and it was directed solely at Riven. It was the kind of trust one would have with their family, and it made Riven remember that Azmoth was still just a kid. Despite his maturity and size, Azmoth was supposed to be an infant, without any other blood-related family he kept in contact with—though truth be told he didn't know what age range demon infants were considered to be. He'd have to ask Azmoth sometime just how old he really was. After all, Athela was over two hundred years old—and she'd said that was very young for a demon.

Luke Blissfallen, the Stormrazor Battle Priest thrall, had a far weaker link than any of the others. It was still there, and pulling on it found Riven's sight to be . . .

Riven immediately withdrew his vision when he found the old man was visiting a brothel. He'd touch up on that one later, and he couldn't necessarily blame the guy—Luke didn't have anyone special that Riven knew about, and they had a good while until the monster wave actually hit. Maybe it was even a method of stress relief.

Lastly, Genua's thread was the one that fluctuated most. Fixating on it and following it out, Riven found himself viewing the inside of a temple. High marble pillars held up an immaculately carved ceiling depicting creatures and artifacts he did not recognize, alongside vampires and a huge red moon carved from stone at the very back end of the—

His vision changed, and he found himself looking directly out of Genua's eyes into the face of a very old but pretty priestess. The woman wore the same formal clergy robes as Genua, as well as the glowing crimson tattoos littering her skin, and she tsked his way before the vision ended.

Riven let out a snort, coming back into his own body while scratching his neck. "I guess they don't want me looking into the blood god's realm just yet. Gluttony, what's your opinion on the blood god?"

"Neutral," Gluttony immediately replied with a hiss, his black soul clone visage appearing in the air beside Riven. "I have never had many interactions with him in the past, from what memories I do retain. I suggest you decide on how to proceed, and I will support you in whichever way you choose to go about it."

Riven nodded, glancing at the slowly twisting maws that leaked the essence of the abyss itself. "I see. What about the Scythe?"

"I have had minimal interactions with that one. They were overall positive, but we did fight two wars against one another in the past."

"Two wars? And your interactions were positive?"

"Wars breed conflict, conflict breeds ascension. It is creation's will, and we were competing for supreme treasures. I needed to display my dominance."

Riven smiled, then chuckled. "Not so dominant now, eh?"

Gluttony hissed. "If the Scythe had been as powerful as I and the other sins back then, he'd have been banished, too. My banishment and reincarnation are only testaments to the strength I once had, and to the strength that I will one day reclaim. Do not goad me, child."

Riven kept his smirk but didn't push the matter. He could tell by the way their souls were intertwined that Gluttony wasn't actually mad, but he would be respectful to his new playmate nevertheless.

Meanwhile, the connections inside his soul apparatus were only condensing, growing thicker, and being tied together in odd formations and weblike patterns—like a lattice. Two more connections formed shortly after as he watched, one to Messenger and one to Jackal, though these threads looked a little bit different than the ones to his minions did. They were semitranslucent when he focused on them, and Riven could only guess that was due to them being items rather than people.

He was about to ask Gluttony about it after briefly reviewing Athela's progress below when a flash notification appeared ahead of him and his mind briefly turned black. His body went numb and he shuddered as the Mark of the Sinner lit up across his skin, Messenger, and Jackal all at once—with a hungry, gnawing sensation carving itself into his gut. A sensation of hunger that was bottomless, without end, that spurred him onward to feed.

The markings on the black and deep-purple pillar of sin in his soul apparatus finally stopped moving, the new mana channels etching themselves into it and solidifying, and he gasped alongside Gluttony as they exchanged abilities and traits with one another. Just as Gluttony gained access to many of Riven's own inherited skills as their souls intertwined, so, too, did Riven gain access to Gluttony's.

[Congratulations, host and reincarnation of Gluttony. You have acquired the following abilities and traits from Gluttony now that your symbiosis has reached its height:

- Ravenous Beetle Swarm (Sin): Open your mouth to summon a swarm of ravenous beetles. The more biomass they eat, the more your health, mana, stamina, and divinity replenish and the more beetles you can create. Consuming targets with this ability applies toward your Gluttonous trait.

- Farsight Banishment (Sin): Send a pulse of sin that eradicates all ties to the area around you concerning scrying, remote tracking, spying, karmic ties, or long-range visualization abilities. Very long cooldown.

- Soul Clone Projections (Sin): Create projections of your ravenous maw, allowing you to devour and attack enemies with tendrils of sin and sin-afflicted teeth. Attacks with your primary soul clone body cause soul damage, decreasing all mana, stamina, divinity, and health regeneration until the enemy soul has healed. Replicas of your soul clone with additional projections only halve this effect. Consuming targets with this ability applies toward your Gluttonous trait.

- Gluttony's Aspect of Demonic Heritage (Sin) (Tier 3): A martial art that enhances you through the power of your fully formed Mark of the Sinner. Your body merges with your soul clone for one minute, allowing you to take on an ultimate demonic form as an aspect of the great maw. Very long cooldown, which can be reduced by killing and eating others.

- Gluttonous (Trait): You are required to eat at least one enlight-ened being every week, or you will suffer a 1% debuff that stacks on all stats. Feeding on more than ten enlightened beings in a day gives temporary bonus stats that decay over time; the number of bonus stats depends on the power and number of consumed vic-tims. Feeding on more than five thousand enlightened beings in a day temporarily doubles your stats and all the stats of your gear.

- Reincarnation of Gluttony, Original Sin (Trait): You once were a being feared across the cosmos. Reaching the SSS-grade again after your reincarnation will unlock previously unattainable aspects for your Path of Gluttony, allowing you to ascend higher than ever before. If your vessel and host dies, you will be forced to restart on this path once again. You have been labeled as a MYTHIC-tier creature in comparison to others your level across the multiverse.]

Riven's red-and-black eyes widened when focusing on the Gluttonous trait in particular. The abilities were nice to have, but needing to feed on at least one enlightened being every week . . . did that include monsters? Sentient monsters, maybe?

Perhaps he needed to really take that vampiric heritage of his to the next level as he upped his game to feed on more people, though he'd have to find targets that weren't so innocent. He was sure there'd be more than enough to go around.

Beyond all that, though, was a sense of competence and assuredness in himself that flooded through his mind like a tidal wave. It was Gluttony's presence, one that had been around for eons, and despite the loss of much of his knowledge and skills, Gluttony still had a lot of memories pertaining to combat.

Pertaining to the hunt.

Riven's mouth twitched, and he gave an involuntary, malicious sneer that focused on the fleeing form of the naga far below. Hunger built up inside him, and his stomach ached as he began to salivate.

He shuddered, and Gluttony's voice rang clearly beside him to bring Riven back to the present.

"We will feed shortly, my friend . . ." Gluttony stated—disappearing from his soul clone form and reentering Riven's body with a flash of darkness. "But these opponents of ours are some of the best your planet has to offer. It would be a waste to merely eat them outright. Instead, we should use this as an opportunity to find oneness."

Riven's eyes narrowed, still following the naga through the trees before he disappeared into a shimmering wall of illusion in the forest below. Athela followed the cultist through the illusory wall shortly after, and Riven's grip around Jackal tightened as the weapon in his hand howled for blood.

"You want to use them as a whetstone, to test our skills now that we have joined."

"You are correct," Gluttony stated as a matter of fact. "Such opportunities to truly struggle against and fight competent opponents, before leaving your world to travel into the greater multiverse, will not come often. They will respawn here in this trial, it is true, but we can use every opportunity to push ourselves—even by self-imposed restrictions if need be. But for now, I do believe that there are multiple S-grade and Paragon-grade enemies beyond that shimmering wall. Perhaps it is time to join Athela and hone our skills so that you may for the very first time truly pursue the Path of Gluttony, while I pursue the unfamiliar Path of Red and Black you have so recently gifted me. We will be two halves fighting as one, and we will need to know each other thoroughly before we perfect the dance of a dual soul in combat. We will become a single predator, two parts of one beast. Only then will we be able to start our next step into ascending toward the E-grade."

Riven paused, his focus skewed by the building hunger—a hunger that until now, he'd not even known was possible, even when he'd been starved of blood. He let out a gasp, and his red eyes began to burn with power. "Afterward, we will eat them together."

Gluttony seemed to grin internally. "That, my dearest friend, is a certainty. We will gorge on their bodies as they still take breaths, so that they remember what it means to oppose our will and might."

CHAPTER 38

Despite his sister's choice to abandon the blood god as a path to power, Riven wasn't so sure doing so would be a good idea for himself. He was relatively certain that, over the course of his climb so far, the blood god had been the man in his visions under the light of the blood moon, the shrouded man over an ocean of red.

If that was the case, this entity had gone out of its way—or his way—to help Riven without being asked. Shouldn't Riven reciprocate if chance allowed? Riven did know that gods acquired power from the strength and worship of their followers. More followers meant more power, but better quality candidates could make up for dozens, hundreds, or who knew how many less powerful worshippers. Perhaps this was why the entity had been so angry at Allie for leaving? Due to the loss of what she could potentially become? Perhaps this was why Gluttony didn't have a direct conflict of interest with Riven pursuing the goodwill of this blood god? Due to Gluttony not truly being a god—but something else entirely? At least, Gluttony hadn't said anything about it so far. Thus, he would need to talk to Genua when she got back about how to go about fixing whatever damage Allie had caused. Not only was it a likely good path to progression, but it was also probably important in getting the Blood Moon Requiem off Allie's back since she'd probably pissed them off to the nth degree.

The reason he was even thinking about the blood god as he flew toward the forest was because of the last significant vision he'd had concerning the entity.

"Blood, Shadow, and Death. These are the three pillars the vampires were created from," the hooded figure said, turning his red gaze and with it forcing Riven's own toward the piles upon piles of dead far below them. *"You have taken the first step by converging the paths of Shadow and Blood, but you lack the trio in its entirety. Descendant, you show promise . . . otherwise Gluttony would not involve itself so directly in you. But you need to broaden your horizons now, before you hit the E-grade, or you will fall short of what you could otherwise become. Death is a sister component to Blood in more ways than one. Why do you neglect it so?"*

That vision had empowered Riven with the gift of insight pertaining to the Death subpillar and had allowed him to call upon eight skeletal champions of the blood god's realm to temporarily fight for him. The symbols—a scythe, a red tear-drop, and a black sun—even now they reached out to him from their individual subpillars across his soul, but now alongside them the visage of Gluttony's maw joined the trio to make a quartet.

How was he supposed to solidify his foundations with these four pillar ideologies?

What about his Path of Red and Black?

Was the path of Gluttony the same thing as his sin pillar?

Riven was on the cusp of E-grade and needed to figure out how to ascend. Gluttony had given him vague notions of what to do, hinting at it a couple times now—but Riven got the feeling that it wasn't a one-plus-one-plus-one-plus-one-equals-four situation. More than likely, and based on all the context clues he'd received from multiple people on the outside now—it was probably semi unique for each person—at least to a small extent. Or, based on what the blood god had said—*"you will fall short of what you could otherwise become"*—there were likely things Riven could do that would make his ascension into E-grade far better than if he just ascended immediately.

He didn't really know yet. What he DID know was that no one had outright come to tell him, and he hadn't asked—but again, there'd been more than a few subtle hints on what needed to be done. Perhaps he'd have that conversation with the great maw after this little fiasco he was about to participate in.

Because right now, he had some cultists to kill. The air about him screamed as he kicked his mana channeling up to the next notch, and a torrent of roaring power exploded behind him to launch him into the distance toward where Athela had disappeared.

Six cultists in total. Three reptilian naga of the Chubin cult, and three others of the Nekra cult—two dark elf females and a chaos dwarf.

They'd made camp together on the outskirts of their system-given horde, with Grakzee going ahead to scout the area, but just because they were technically on the same team for this specific mission didn't mean they were friends. Nor did it mean they were on the same team at all as soon as this subsection of the world quest ended. No, they were all in it for themselves. Each apocalypse beast could only have one winner, one to claim the egg—or to use it to create an item of supreme power. In the end, the chosen would all be at odds with one another—cultist or not—and that went doubly true for those within their same bracket of apocalypse beasts, who'd have to kill one another in order to get what they wanted.

And thus the uneasy alliance had been formed, with three big reasons keeping them from ripping into one another. First was that every one of the chosen would respawn here in this subevent until they left in a year or so by the system's estimation. They would continue to respawn until they got the necessary points needed to leave, and that could only be done by completing quests or killing noncultists.

Second was that if they DID kill one another, they'd get negative points for it—so an attempt on one another's lives would need to have bigger rewards than repercussions. The third and last reason was that, just as Grakzee had already deduced, it was very likely they were up against a harder obstacle than any of the other cultists here. There were only two noncultists defending this town based on the system quests they'd each gotten, with a much larger potential for points should they kill either one of them. Two hundred and eighty points for a single kill would net them far, far, far more than any of the others got for their noncultist kills. Only three points were being awarded to other people at other quest lines for killing noncultists, but everyone had a pretty damn good idea as to what having ninety-three times the normal points for a kill meant.

It was likely they were up against Riven Thane.

Each of them was a cold-blooded killer, each of them in the S and Paragon rankings on Panu, but that fucking vampire was nearly unkillable and had the equivalent power of a meteor strike. Videos of him wiping out Daskus, fighting the Azag Hive Cluster in Chicago, wiping the floor with Rippenvire invaders in Dawn alongside the Harbingers of Gluttony, and then killing the elites of the Empire of Dying Suns invading force alongside a dungeon boss had circulated numerous times over—along with some other less well-known videos, too.

He might not be as ruthless as his batshit crazy sister, but he was even more dangerous in actual combat. It also didn't help that he had incredibly strong demonic familiars and that he might or might not have somehow ascended by absorbing something related to Gluttony based on system messages and the titles on the ranking ladder for Panu.

So that was the third and final reason they didn't kill one another in their sleep and avoided antagonizing one another. They needed to work together if they wanted to beat him, and in a worst-case scenario, they'd agreed to try and have one of their own sneak around him to destroy the town so they could claim the thirty points bare minimum. To do this, the others would need to distract the vampiric warlock and his demons when the monster wave was unleashed a few hours from now.

Other than Grakzee, who was the only stealth-type fighter their group had, the five remaining cultists were a mix of warrior and caster types. The remaining two aquatic naga, who were lizard-like Chubin cultists, were both mages specializing in the Glacial and Storm subpillars, respectively. Of the three Nekra cultists, the chaos dwarf was an axe-wielding barbarian with a long black beard and Chaos-attuned runes he'd been born with—enabling him to utilize the power of the Chaos subpillar at an astounding affinity of 73 percent. The larger of the two drow or dark elf women was a death knight who wore a large black cloak over her bone armor. She also carried a large bone-made claymore, and her eyes glowed with a neon-teal light. Meanwhile the last of the Nekra cultists, another, smaller drow woman, was an affliction caster who specialized in plagues and debuffs that rapidly rotted, corrupted, and ate away at her enemies over time.

Currently these five cultists sat around a campfire, either looking into the flames contemplating what they would do when the fight finally came—or glancing over their shoulders at the huge swath of roaming monsters nearby. One in particular stood out above all the rest, the monster swarm's boss unit, and it was no less impressive than many of the dungeon bosses any of them had seen up until this point. It was a large level-180 ELITE monster. More specifically, it was a winged tomb cobra, with the largest difference other than size being it had two clawed arms like a dragon. It was so large that it could swallow a small house. Lightning coursed over its golden scales and white feathered wings, and bright-orange eyes surveyed its smaller kin from the center of the swarm. It'd already spoken to them once, after having been dragged from its own world along with its brood to participate in these integration trials—and it was more than excited to be given a town of humanoids to eat for its mission.

"How long will your lizard friend be gone, you think?" Chasindir, the cloaked and armored death knight asked, leaning forward and brushing a long braided lock of white hair from her face. Her helmet rested beside the log she was sitting on, and her neon-teal eyes flickered while souls danced around one of her hands.

Merris scoffed irritably, glaring out from his silver-blue hood—his reptilian features contorting into a sneer as the lightning mage crackled dangerously as if a threat. He pointed a clawed hand at the death knight and rose up slightly from his coiled position with a hiss to his words. "I have told you numerous times, drow. Grakzee is not my friend. You insult me by asking this, as my tribe is far superior to his."

Chasindir grinned slightly underneath her own sandy-brown hood trimmed with teal coloring, that of the Nekra cult, and head-bobbed over to where the large, winged tomb cobra remained coiled like a giant hill among her writhing swarm. "What about your cousin's tribe? How does yours compare to hers?"

"That is of a different species, you ingrate!" Merris snarled, causing his aura to explode—but none of the others bothered getting up from their spots or even acknowledging his tantrum. Merris was by far the easiest to rile up, and Chasindir, the death knight, had been doing so time and time again just out of boredom—and because she thought it was funny.

The chaos dwarf, who was sharpening the large obsidian axe across his lap, just sighed and grumbled something to himself while rolling his eyes at the duo again.

Chasindir snickered, loving that she'd hit a sore spot for the naga and prodded it verbally again with her eyes flaring brightly. "Are you sure you're not of the same species?! You both have scales, you both control lightning, you both have clawed humanoid hands yet have the lower bodies of snakes. If I didn't know any better, I'd think you naga were beasts rather than enlightened creatures like myself. It pains me, actually, to even consider you as more than a fish!"

The naga mage bolted upright with another clap of thunder roaring from overhead, and he quivered with rage. But he dared not strike—despite his temper he knew that infighting was stupid—and he settled back down into a coiled position while the drow woman in bone armor started laughing loudly at his expense.

"You fall for her jabs too easily," the larger Glacial naga mage from farther down the campfire line stated simply, not opening his eyes and remaining in a meditative state. "A weak mind brings about ruin. It would do you well to sharpen yours. If you did not react, she would no longer find it fun to annoy you."

Merris scoffed audibly again, snapping his jaws in Chasindir's direction while the death knight continued to howl in amusement, but he managed to not reply to her next two quips, either. Instead, he began focusing on one of his internal lightning braids—one of multiple soul-space creations he wanted to use in his ascent into the E-grade later.

The unknown plaguebringer and afflictionist remained staring at the flames without speaking a word to anyone despite multiple attempts to get her attention, and with Merris not playing by Chasindir's goading any longer, the camp fell eerily silent minutes later. Only the hissing of the monster swarm and rustling of their wings and scales interrupted the silence, but even they were unusually quiet—considering most of them were the size of a fully grown human or bigger.

"I grow bored of this, and we still have another five hours to wait," Chasindir stated grumpily, putting her bone helmet on and adjusting her hood again. "That Grakzee is taking way too long. Do you think he got lost, with that little pea-size reptilian brain of his? I bet you he did."

Fortunately for Chasindir, none of them had to wait long before things got a lot more exciting.

The illusory wall separating themselves and the horde of monsters from the outer world shimmered and exploded as—off in the distance along a large tree-spotted hill—Grakzee came barreling out of the mirage covered in blood. He was moving fast, far faster than any of the others could due to his agility-based class, and hot on his heels was a cackling demoness who all of them were very familiar with.

It seemed that Athela had arrived at the scene, and without a word, the others sprang into action.

Athela's evil smile widened at the sight of the monster swarm before her. And "swarm" was putting it lightly. There were man-size, winged serpents with golden scales and white feathers, a beast swarm that stretched out for two or three square miles—some of them even having taken to the air.

And at the center was a monster even larger and longer than her drider form.

This was going to be a fun time. Maybe, just maybe, after killing everything in sight she might finally catch up to Riven and join him on his quest to pursue E-grade!

The thought made her giggle, and she stopped playing around with the naga she'd been chasing this entire time. Pulling on Mark of the Hunted, which had lodged itself into the naga's soul, causing him to freeze up only for a moment, her eyes blazed red. Her body exploded into a wave of crimson blood, and like ten thousand tiny rivers of death she crashed into and through the naga in a motion so fast that a sonic boom resounded behind her.

The naga screamed and only barely managed to get away by means she wasn't entirely clear on. She found herself staring at the spot he'd been in only a second later, and he was somehow a hundred feet away.

He turned around, looking at the hole in his chest in astonishment, and then stared back at her with incomprehension in his eyes. "You . . . You took it? How? I didn't . . . didn't see . . ."

The assassin flopped forward onto his face, bleeding out onto the ground, unable to regrow the beating heart that was spasming—impaled—by Athela's two red katanas. She'd cut it out before he'd been able to move away, but she still frowned in dissatisfaction with her own performance after being unable to take his head, too.

"I'm losing my touch," Athela spat with irritation, grumbling to herself about how he'd managed to step away—because if that'd been anyone else with better regenerative properties, such as Riven had, then taking out the heart wouldn't have been all that was needed to kill the man.

CRACK

SNAP

The earth shuddered as lightning ruptured the ground beneath her feet. A storm of wails accompanied it just as she dodged the bus-size lightning bolt, and she narrowly missed an arcing swing of soul fire that ripped out of a bone claymore only a couple feet away.

Her arachnid limbs and red katanas clashed furiously with sparks flying as meticulous footwork created a dance between herself, a death knight's claymore, and a huge obsidian battle-axe.

The ground beneath her feet shattered when the dwarf barbarian smashed a martial art–infused strike into her position—which she managed to deflect to the side in a spray of debris. A storm of ice-made blades roared from high up in the sky and thundered downward by the thousands, and her arachnid blades tore them out from the air with movements that blurred while she kept the two frontline warriors at bay with her katanas.

She had to admit, whoever these cultists were, they were good. Individually she'd have an easy time, but together they were just barely putting her on the back foot—forcing her to play defense rather than offense.

A lightning strike tore into her leg, and she cursed as blood sprayed out of it—only for her body to twirl around and spray lacerating red needles in all directions as she gave a high-pitched laugh. "YOU ARE NOT AS WEAK AS I'D ANTICIPATED. THIS IS GOOD!"

The clang of her blade on a pauldron sent the death knight spinning from the impact, causing the drow woman to smash into a nearby stone and shatter it on impact. The dwarf let out a bellowing roar, lowering himself into a battle stance as the illusory figure of a spirit bull formed behind him. The bull was made from chaos energy, a dark gray that shattered the ground the bull walked upon, and then it charged when it overlapped the dwarf's own body as the two entities tore across the ground.

Athela blocked; axe and horns met with katanas and sharpened spider limbs. The resulting shock wave from her many blades against the charging chaos dwarf and his bull caused the land to explode in a cataclysmic typhoon of expelled energies. It was enough to garner the attention of the nearby swarm, which had mostly stopped to watch the ongoing battle without interfering just yet—but some of them were beginning to inch closer.

Leaning in to be within a few inches of the snarling dwarf, Athela sneered down at the shorter man with true killing intent pumping into the aura around her as the world gained a sanguine hue. "I will enjoy cutting your heart out next!"

But then the dwarf smiled, and the ground underneath her shifted—hands created from gray stone tearing up from the earth to latch onto her feet and legs. Athela felt something odd come crashing down onto her position right after that. It wasn't necessarily forceful, but it was certainly potent. The feeling was akin to drowning in a lake far beneath the surface, being compressed by the pressure around her, rather than being outright crushed instantaneously. She felt her muscles begin to weaken, and pinpricks of pain began to spring up all over her body as a cloud of dark-green energies crackled to life around her.

She looked up, and there in the sky was the floating figure of a drow woman with short white hair in dark robes. Dangling from one hand she carried a severed, rotting head that had necromantic and Unholy runes inscribed onto it—where torrents of energies were cycling through it and being amplified before she cast them down on Athela's position like a judge sentencing one to a slow and painful death.

The drow caster cackled at Athela's grimace while the ice and storm mages got into positions to charge up building attacks on the outskirts of the cloud, and the death knight snapped her shoulder into position with a backward glare before getting up next.

"Finding it hard to move?" The dwarf snickered, his body pulsing with chaos energy that continued to wind up his legs. "And those little rot spots seem to be spreading fast! Overconfidence killed the cat, you know!"

Athela glanced back down at her legs, which were held in position rather solidly at this point while open ulcers began to form across her skin, and she wondered if she should take it up a notch and transform into her drider aspect. The drider wasn't as fast or as agile as her humanoid form, nor was it as stealthy as her tiny arachnid form, but it did have the additional strength, sturdiness, and mana output that would be needed to free herself from this position.

But she felt another wave of oppressive intent bear down on her as another set of runes flashed overhead in the sky, creating an intricate circle of Unholy sigils that expanded into a dome over her position. She felt even weaker and gasped as the curse leeched her strength away while making her arms barely able to hold back the axe from tearing into her.

The dwarf edged forward, the storms of swirling ice and sparking thunderclouds from either naga on both sides grew to extreme proportions while the world shook, and the afflictionist overhead called down to her with a shrill laugh.

"I WONDER WHAT WE WILL GET FOR KILLING A WORLD BOSS!" The drow woman floating in the sky cackled, waving her hands around to perform a Tier-2 spell of some variation while the severed head flailed around with her. "OR PERHAPS IT WON'T COUNT DUE TO RESPAWN AND WE'LL JUST HAVE TO FIND YOU ON THE OUTSIDE TO TRULY GET THE PRIZE! LET'S FIND OUT!"

The woman let out another shrill fit of laughter, her body lit up bright green with curse energy, and the sky above her tore open with a pillar of Unholy flames that—

The caster's laughing fit was abruptly cut off. There was a quick flash-snap of crimson and black, of a projectile that eradicated the woman from existence instantaneously, coming from somewhere far off behind her. The movement was so fast that Athela couldn't even follow it with her eyes, but remnant pieces of the drow's body fell slowly to the ground as the spells she'd been channeling vanished in an instant.

She recognized the ability that killed her as Riven's Blood Lance enhanced with Snipe.

The lightning storm to her right was launched like a cannonball by the storm mage, and the blizzard on her left was launched from the frost mage like an avalanche. They both tore toward her with the sound of a thunderclap, colliding with two thick walls of Crimson Ice that rose up from the ground around Athela, akin to the protective hands of a god. The ground shook, the backlash causing both of the naga casters to dash backward while crystallized red blood shattered on the outer layers of each wall—but the ability held firm enough to deflect each of the elemental storms.

The death knight, who'd been waiting for the exchange to happen so she could rush in for the second kill after Athela's first form was taken care of, gawked at the exchange as another sonic boom echoed out from somewhere high up in the clouds.

Another flash of crimson-black light bore down from above and sent the dwarf spinning end over end, causing the barbarian to lose his grip entirely on his battleaxe while he screamed in pain. He was akin to a smoldering stone being skipped across a lake. However, unlike the afflictionist, who'd been absolutely eradicated by the Snipe, the dwarf warrior was far sturdier and managed to roll to a coughing stop while sealing shut a deep wound that sparked with Black Lightning in his chest.

All four of the remaining cultists—the dwarf barbarian, the drow death knight, and the two naga elemental wizards—turned their eyes upward as a figure descended from the clouds in a swath of black, red, and deep-purple energies. Then the figure abruptly accelerated and crashed into the ground, creating a crater in front of him as the four cultists backpedaled again.

Through the cloud of dust, debris, and swirling energies, Riven Thane stepped out in full plate armor, the flaps underneath his thrusters billowing with the torrent of energy encompassing his form.

The monster swarm roared and charged, and without looking their way, the warlock raised his free hand to summon thousands of spinning storm blades that rushed the oncoming wave of enemies in a series of explosions that lit up the sky in black and red lights.

"Athela," Riven stated calmly, turning to look at his minion who'd picked herself up from out of the barbarian's holding martial art, kicking at the gray stone hands that'd somehow kept her in place. "Take care of the monster swarm. Gluttony and I are wanting to test our mettle with these ones, a little bit of . . . experimentation. Would you mind?"

Athela huffed, glaring daggers at the cultists in turn, but gave Riven's helmet a kiss and began skipping out toward the oncoming horde that was still reeling from Riven's attack. "Fine! I guess being designated to small-fry cleanup is okay this time, but not next time. Got it?! I'm not just your cute little side-piece spider princess who you can use for your carnal desires. I'm an independent woman who needs to level up, too! And I GET THE BOSS MONSTER!"

Riven chuckled, shaking his head and looking her way while she skipped beyond the wall of crimson he'd constructed to block the elemental blizzard. "You can have it. Be safe, dear."

"You, too, honey!" She blew him a kiss before laughing and rushing forward, transforming into her large drider form with a scream and spewing out an army of little frost weavers that entered melee combat a second later.

Riven's black-and-red eyes shifted toward the other four, who were all staring him down with mixed expressions, and the third eye of Gluttony on his head opened up along with a piece in his armor set to let it see. Unlike his others, this one had a more purple hue in the sea of black around it—and the visage of a black maw tore through space behind him as he entered a battle stance.

That maw then began to speak. "Remember . . . do not use any mass-casualty spells. We are using them as a whetstone so we may find errors and places that need fixing in our dual-spirit controls for fighting. No need to eradicate them immediately. We will need to improve our unification if we ever wish to survive the scions of established factions in the greater multiverse. Skill and technique are the focus here, rather than sheer power."

Riven chuckled, and his body erupted into the infernal flames of Hell's Armor while simultaneously sparks and threads of blood from Blessing of the Crow bloomed about him—making him look like the aspect of some lost evil spirit. His weapon Jackal screamed in anticipation of the kills—and he took a deep breath. "Let's see what these new changes from fusing have brought about, then. After that, we eat them. I'm already starving."

CHAPTER 39

The four remaining cultists looked right, to where Riven's carpet-bombing of the swarm had devastated hundreds of flying golden serpents that were in large part still recovering just as Athela and her spiders plowed into them. Abilities from both sides activated, arcs of yellow lightning crashing into the archdemon, while a pillar of sin, ice, and flame shattered the field and began decimating even more of the monsters.

"Did I hear that demonic mouth right?" the drow death knight asked, cracking her neck and turning her teal eyes on Riven's flickering position not far off. "He's not going to use those mass-casualty spells he's so famous for?"

The larger naga, the ice mage, snickered as he held out a large white staff in front of him, creating floating orbs of crystallized water that began orbiting his position. "To use us as training dummies, what arrogance! But it is not something we should take lightly—it gives us more of a fighting chance. RIVEN THANE! I WILL ENJOY COLLECTING THE POINTS ASSOCIATED WITH YOUR DEATH!"

"RAAAAAHHH!!" the dwarf bellowed, his body exploding in size as he tripled his bulk, bones cracking and chaos energy radiating off his being. "I'VE BEEN WAITING FOR A REAL FIGHT SINCE THE INTEGRATION STARTED! BRING ME A GLORIOUS DEATH, OR I'LL BE CARVING THAT PALE FACE OF YOURS OFF TO HANG ON MY WALL!"

With that, the dwarf crafted another apparition of the bull—this time much larger—and blasted forward as he activated a martial art with his battle-axe. The axe began spinning around and around with his muscular body until he spun so fast that he became a tornado of violence, empowered by chaos, and the gap between himself and the vampiric warlock quickly narrowed.

Tendrils of sin wrapped around Riven's soul core, his pillars, and started spreading into his physical body as Gluttony's very being intertwined with Riven's own. Riven's neurons hastened their signals, his mind seemed to expand, and the deep sense of hunger enveloped him as a wide, fanged smile lit up his face.

With a roar of his own, Riven's body burst forward in a torrent of flame, blood, and dark lightning. Space ruptured, and a killing intent tore out of his body in a wave of malice that was so potent it made the very heavens cry. As the world shuddered underneath Riven's lust for violence, a raven with orange eyes drifted down to land on a far-off tree and looked his way.

"DODGE, YOU IDIOT!" the drow death knight screamed, eyes widening in shock at the absolute malice pouring out of Riven in almost physical form.

But the barbarian's spinning swings only continued carrying him forward in his own enraged state.

Riven shot forward, empowering his muscles and body with the physical enhancements he'd given himself and the flood of sin energy roaring across his energized cells. The ground beneath him exploded, and Jackal's blade swung down in a hiss of power.

The earth tore open as the two powerhouses locked weapons, and the dwarf was absolutely flattened—crushed into the ground like an insect along with the visage of the bull behind him, which dispersed instantly.

Riven scoffed at the groaning idiot half buried in the ground, then kicked dirt into his blinking eyes with a shake of his head. "How pathetic . . . but I'll give you another chance. Get up and try again. We're not done yet."

Turning his three eyes to the other cultists, Riven's flickering, mana-charged body exploded with power as he lifted a hand and pointed. "Don't waste my time. All of you at once. Come."

Just like the two naga casters to either side of where she stood, Chasindir gaped at the absolute domination of her compatriot in a physical confrontation. Sure, that brutish dwarf had just charged in swinging with a rather up-front attack—but he was still a berserker. His build was literally made for close combat; the runes and aspect of the bull he used were made to make him stronger. That martial art was one she was familiar with, and with every spin of the axe it built up both momentum and power until it finally made a strike.

And yet, Riven had charged headlong into it—as a warlock, a caster—and completely smashed the dwarf three feet into the ground.

Casters weren't supposed to be physically strong. Even with buffs, they weren't ever supposed to be up to par with physical fighters like herself or the dwarf. Yet with a single blow, Riven had downed one of the strongest melee fighters on Panu.

She shuddered involuntarily, then gritted her teeth and glared daggers at the vampire taunting them. Her hand gripped her bone claymore tightly, and she raised it up to be eye level. If she was to be beaten here, she would at least get a good measure of what he was capable of so that she might try again in the future. Even a single win against him would be the equivalent of dozens of kills that he landed against her during this event. And, perhaps, if he really did stick to his plan of not using any massive area-of-effect spells or swarms of blades like how he'd killed off entire armies and cities in the past, then perhaps she still had a chance.

"Rite of the Soul Weaver." Her soul core screamed as it was dragged out of her inner domain, coating her body in a thick aspect of her pillars and her Dao. Her eyes flared with teal fire, and she lunged forward with a quickstep and a deathly strike—sending arcs of death energy at the vampire as the two naga spread out.

Thunderclouds rumbled overhead, a blizzard began to build around them, the wailing souls of dead victims rose up from the grave to empower her, and the visage of a maw echoed across the shuddering landscape with laughter.

He merely stared at her passively, like a man who thought himself above her.

Her anger only rose, and she screamed in rage while reaching deep into the soul enveloping her for more power.

Her deathly strike shattered against Riven's body like glass on forged steel, and her claymore tore through the air to follow up the wave of death energy like a viper strike. Riven's own blade spun rapidly in the air and intercepted her forward momentum, causing sparks to light up the darkening arena of their own making as their magics blotted out the sun.

In an instant Riven countered, and Chasindir sucked in a quick breath— barely matching his speed as she intercepted two more of his blows before she exploded in a dome of pale light that blew him backward a couple feet.

The storm mage took his opening and uttered a chant, calling lightning from the heavens that surged through the air with a snap of sound that reverberated across the land.

Black lightning tore from Riven's own body and met the charging pillar of yellow electricity, the two colors intertwining hundreds of feet above them as a wall of ice rushed in from the other side.

It was like watching a tidal wave of cold death encroach upon an insect. The surge of ice formed spikes right before it struck Riven's position, only to be met with an opposing tide of red frost that tore through the white ice and snow in an absolute rebuttal.

Chasindir flung two death balls at the man and lunged again, roaring out a battle cry and quickstepping left to swipe at him at the same time as a huge disk of lightning tore through the air and crashed into his side.

To Chasindir's surprise, Riven smashed the lightning disk apart with his fist while simultaneously flipping over her attack in a horizontal, acrobatic motion before landing on two feet.

She tried to engage him the moment he landed and smashed her blade into the ground, opening a rift into the underworld so that souls of the dead began springing up around him and dragging him into the rift, only for the rift to shatter as the visage of a maw came up from underneath the tear in space to snap down on it.

Chasindir spluttered in denial. "THAT'S NOT FAIR!"

Riven caught an ice lance with his free hand, sidestepped another, and flung the one he'd caught directly at her with a force that caused the air to hiss.

The ice lance shattered against her right pauldron, but a searing pain set in as the cold magics caused her shoulder to nearly go numb. She swore violently, rolling and getting back to her feet right before she saw his downward swing.

When she discharged her Reaper Waltz martial art with the sacrifice of two captive souls from her reservoir, time slowed down around her and she vanished from her position.

Three ghostly replicas of Chasindir appeared in different positions around Riven's body with a speed enhancement that sent their blades smashing down into Riven's armor, shattering against it but causing him to stumble right when she reappeared behind him.

Grinning at her first big success of the exchange, she backed off and watched the lightning mage create four hounds from sparks. The mage unleashed the howling dogs, their paws creating thunderclaps as they ran and tore up the ground upon their passing—

The visage of a red jackal snapped out and obliterated the incoming dogs in an instant, and Riven turned to open a black Shadow-made portal on his other side.

The ice drake that the other naga had summoned lunged its open jaws directly into the intercepting portal before it was closed off, and the beast crumbled in an explosion of frost when the black rift snapped shut around its neck.

The decapitated sculpture's jaws landed dozens of yards to her left, crumbling just as the larger body did into a pile of snow that blew away in the roaring winds of the building thunderstorm above.

Chasindir spat at the amused twinkle in Riven's eyes when he turned his gaze upon her, and her body flickered as it absorbed a nearby soul to use as fodder for her next attack. Her free hand made the proper motions and building pressure lit up across the tip of her extended blade. "SPIRITUAL RIFT!"

Her feet lifted off at blinding speed, her body a blur, and a huge cone of necromantic energies surged ahead at the point of her weapon that was lowered at the vampire ahead of her. Twenty yards cleared in less than half a second and a snap-fire flurry of attacks crashed into one another as she entered into melee combat with the warlock in building resentment.

She would not be looked down upon.

Claymore clashed with spear-sword in a storm of bone on metal, death energies smashing against blood energies in rapid, miniature explosions while the two weapons sang promises of pain.

She grunted, wove, dodged, blocked, and hit back as the elusive figure of the fully plated caster ahead of her began to laugh. Her efforts grew more impulsive, more furious, and she began to hit harder as the sparks lit up the darkened landscape. Lightning bolts expertly tore out of the thunderclouds above when gaps in their exchanges allowed for the naga Merris to strike Riven without hitting Chasindir, and spines of frost shot up from the ground or were launched in a myriad of directions and from all angles whenever Riven had his back turned—but the vampire seemed to be growing more and more impossible to hit by the second.

Their first real hit had been when she'd used Reaper Waltz for a trifecta of simultaneous attacks. But it'd only worked once, with the next two attempts at the same attack only having minimal effect as he anticipated her strikes and struck out to deflect one attack while using the space it created to dodge the other two.

"STAY STILL!" Chasindir screamed in frustrated anger, spinning her blade and launching it like a boomerang. Riven raised his spear-staff to strike it down, but she clapped her hands together with a chant and caused the blade of bone to explode instead.

Fragments of the bone claymore flew into him like shrapnel, many of the pieces going out to either side of his flaming, flickering, sparking body—but she tore her hands apart a moment later and re-formed the blade with the will of thought.

The weapon reforged itself on his other side, keeping its momentum and slamming into his lower thigh right where the armor was weakest.

The blade sank in deep, and Chasindir let out an excited squeal of delight and victory when it pierced through his leg entirely in a spray of blood. "YOU'RE NOT SO INVINCIBLE AFTER—"

CRUNCH

The hilt of the blade that'd been lodged in Riven's thigh between the metal plates smashed into her nose, breaking it cleanly and sending her reeling as a spray of blood erupted out of her face. She fell to her knees, crying out in pain and backpedaling, only to feel a swift kick to the back of her armored skull.

She was sent sprawling, flipping end over end until she smashed into a boulder with a dull thud and the snap of bones.

Groaning and feeling her shattered spine beginning to repair itself, Chasindir coughed blood and spat it out before glaring up at the laughing vampire in the distance. His laughter grew louder, climbing over the roar of the lightning strikes and thundering snow as he caught lightning bolts and flung them back, shattered ice lances with the spin of his weapon, crushed summoned elementals with mere fluctuations of Hell's Armor, and redirected entire barrages with summoned shadow rifts.

Then, with a sinking heart, Chasindir realized that during this entire fight, Riven had barely moved from the same spot. He'd simply stayed there, taking them all on as they unleashed powers that would devastate entire armies back on Panu, only for this vampire to mock them now with his uproar of smug amusement.

BOOM
    CRUNCH
    THUD
    SNAP

"AHHHHHHHHHH!!!" the drow death knight screamed in agony as he tore off one of her arms and slapped her across the face with it in a spray of blood.

Still laughing, Riven turned—deflecting a desperate barrage of lightning as his spear-staff blurred to meet the incoming projectiles. Gluttony whispered in his mind, sharing his movements and empowering his reaction time to meet the energized magics as he swatted one lightning bolt after another down from the sky like they were bugs. The barrage ended just as a cage of ice sprang up around his position, and a wave of oppressive energy bore down on him when the glacial mage erected a domain.

The bars of absolute cold formed a dome and began to fill in, compressing on his position in an attempt to kill him—and potentially sacrificing the flailing death knight behind Riven—but with a mere flex of his own aura, the domain of the naga caster shattered as the ice was converted from white to a bright crimson red.

Taking charge of the mana in a forced conversion, Riven twisted his hand and shot a stream of red ice back down upon the glacial mage.

A wall of white came to meet Riven's attack as the naga deflected Riven's attack, and Riven winced at the backlash of having forcibly converted his enemy's attack so quickly.

"Probably not a good idea to do that again unless absolutely necessary . . ." Riven muttered to himself, getting an internal confirmation from Gluttony that he was spot-on. Riven had only done it on a whim after feeling the connection there, similar to his own Crimson Ice control, but it was from another source entirely and a foreign aspect at that. His lingering headache was testament that maybe just creating new Crimson Ice instead of converting actual elemental ice would be a better way to go about it in most circumstances.

His flaming, spiked gauntlet shot forward, fist smashing into the battle-axe of the dwarf, who'd peeled himself out of the hole in the ground to attack Riven once again.

It was like watching a home run, where the bat was Riven's fist encased in Messenger—while the battle-axe was the baseball.

The weapon tore out of the dwarf berserker's hand in a spray of shrapnel as the weapon was obliterated, and the roaring dwarf's right arm snapped out of its socket as he was flung back around.

Riven's eyes narrowed on the man beneath him, the pathetic, disgusting excuse of a warrior on the ground. Fangs sliding out and his smile stretching beyond what should be normal for any human, Riven peeled back his helmet as a rumble from his stomach began to drive him forward.

He slapped the death knight warrior into the next time zone, sending her flying when she went in for another strike—and retaliated against another thunderclap of electric power with a strike of his own Black Lightning. Again the two spells canceled each other out in an instant, and his foot crashed into the back of the dwarf who was just about to pick himself up again.

Once again, the dwarf found himself embedded into the ground like a bug under Riven's heel.

Riven cocked his head to the side, staring down at the man squirming underneath him, and sneered. "You've been deemed inadequate for training. Perhaps you'll find a way to weasel into the graces of your apocalypse beast, to claim it as your own by a stroke of sheer dumb luck despite the lack of thought on your approach. Perhaps you will by a lottery's chance be the one who causes the civilizations of Panu to fall, as your own quest dictates. But for now, I think not. Because for now, you'll need to go through me. And you cannot brute force your way through this one, buddy. This is my trial to claim, and you unlucky fuckheads are all trapped in here with me for the next year! How great is that?!"

He knelt, and Riven's abnormally wide smile unhinged with another cackling laugh, making him look monstrous as his jaws snapped down onto the struggling dwarf's neck.

The dwarf screamed as he felt himself being drained, and then began to flail in a panic under Riven's hold as meat was stripped from bones to be swallowed whole. Clawed gauntlets tore muscles off in wrenching motions, blood was drained by the bucket between large chomps of flesh, and gluttonous beetles began to climb out of the corner of Riven's mouth—helping him devour the man even faster as they swarmed across the horrified dwarf's body.

> **[Invitation to the Blood God's Temple: Your weekly session of worship, combat training, and scripture has come about. Please access the clergy system and teleport in so that we may start. We would also like to discuss recent events involving a certain angel on your planet and hope that you can discuss the things we show you with Riven after the fact.]**

The inside of the blood god's temple was vast, with sculptures of monsters and vampires in abundance all along the walls and pillars that held up the high ceilings of many interconnected rooms. Crimson creatures of nightmares the size of skyscrapers loomed in these halls, and their many eyes often centered themselves on her in passing curiosity before settling on other clergy—relatively ant-sized to their massive figures.

Genua knelt at an altar underneath the sculpture of a giant blood moon, in front of an indoor lake of blood, surrounded by other priestesses wearing similar red metal headdresses and formfitting black silk robes. Crimson tattoos littered all their bodies in the places that the clergy outfits didn't cover, and all of them were women.

She had seen actual priests before, gathered in long flowing robes that only differed slightly from her own, but it appeared that men were in the minority here. Why that was, Genua was unsure.

"That is enough scripture for now," the elder priestess stated, snapping her small black book shut and letting it flicker away into wisps of red that vanished in front of her face.

Genua did the same, though she stored her own in a small bag on her hip rather than some fancy-schmancy miracle work. "Very well. Is it time for combat training? I am rather intrigued about what it is you have to show me, Priestess Lithania."

The beautiful but rather old priestess scowled deeply—emphasizing her wrinkles by doing so. The other women around Genua in a semicircle all turned to look at the lead priestess of their group—ignoring the other clergy bathing in the lake or walking between rooms akin to entire landscapes given the size of it all.

"You will have your combat training in time, but I wish to speak to you about both Riven and Allie first."

Genua didn't frown back—she'd been expecting this, but she couldn't say she was looking forward to this conversation, either. "Very well. Please let me know what I can answer for you or assist you with."

Priestess Lithania nodded solemnly, then stood up—being lifted up by tendrils of blood mana instead of actually using her muscles—until she smoothly came to a graceful stance ahead of the rest. "Follow me, Genua. The rest of you are dismissed."

The older woman gestured for Genua to come stand beside her, and the other women all got up to leave before heading off to wherever the hell it was these clergy lived. Though Genua knew some of them were like her and had vampiric masters in the mortal realms, most of the blood god's clergy actually lived here permanently for reasons she could not fathom.

Stepping in line with the old woman, Genua and Priestess Lithania began to walk along the lake's edge in a slow but steady gait.

"Tell me . . ." the old woman eventually said, turning a red gaze upon Genua's slender figure. "What is your opinion of Riven?"

Genua raised a questioning eyebrow. "I had thought this conversation was to be about his sister, Allie."

Lithania didn't miss a step, nor did she blink. Instead, she turned her gaze ahead of them—watching the path underneath their feet glide by with purple grasses on their right and the lake on their left. "It primarily will be. However, I'd still like to know—as it is still relevant. What is your opinion on Riven?"

Genua pursed her lips at this, eyes flicking between the old woman and her own feet as she walked. "I suppose he has been kind to me, and to Len, over past months. However, I still cannot fully forgive him for what he did to my eldest daughter and husband."

"Do you blame him?" Lithania asked with a flat expression, not bothering to look over at the other priestess as they went. "I'm surprised you still feel animosity toward the man after becoming his thrall. Usually those feelings go away rather quickly as the thrall contract imbues you with other, more positive emotions."

Genua scoffed. "Perhaps in the beginning that was true, but not recently. Not since the pregnancy, anyways. Regardless, I do not hate him, nor do I blame him, but I still cannot forgive him. I look back at that time as my own family's fault, as my clan's fault, for initiating the violence and betraying him for a reason that wasn't just. However, a mother's love knows no bounds—and Ethel will always be my little girl."

Lithania nodded. "The pregnancy is certainly an oddity. It is not often that a thrall can become impregnated by a vampire. Thralls can, in time, become vampires if the master wishes it—but until then it is supposed to be an impossibility. For you, however, that seems not to be the case . . . Why that is, we are unsure."

"We?"

"Myself, and the others watching over you. Those assigned by the blood god to monitor Riven and Allie Wraithtide."

"Are they truly important enough to warrant a god's interest to this amount?"

"They are. The malignant bloodline is a priceless treasure, kept sacred by one of the blood god's most devoted followings in the form of the Blood Moon Requiem. Should that bloodline escape from our grasp and fall into another sect of the multiverse—such as the Reapers, or the Phantom Legions, who now have their sights set upon Allie as a recruitment candidate—it would be an unacceptable outcome. That cannot be allowed to pass. And yet we are unsure of what to do."

She paused in both step and sound. "Even the great one, the blood god himself, is unsure of what to do now that Gluttony has chosen Riven as its candidate for reincarnation. The risk of offending Gluttony is not out of the question, but if we can come to an agreement of some sort . . . perhaps we'd be willing to look the other way concerning his sister."

The priestess turned her head to make sure Genua understood.

Genua nodded. "I am more than certain Riven is hoping for a similar outcome."

"Are you sure about this? That he would compromise? Gluttony is not known for such things, and although he is weak, he will not remain weak for long."

"I am certain, Lithania. Riven is not Gluttony; they are merely partners. Riven does want to follow the path of blood and hopes that you will overlook his sister's transgressions if he can somehow appease our church. Are you not able to see this?"

Lithania's smile grew wide, and she nodded in approval. "Our god was banished from viewing Panu for some time, along with many other gods, by Gluttony when he and his demonic servants came back from the abyss. The effect is wearing off, but antiscrying measures—if done properly—are easily made and hard to deter. Even weak mages may block the scrying of high-tier beings if the technique is right, but that is neither here nor there. Tell me, what exactly is he willing to negotiate with?"

The old woman's slender hand lifted, pointing to Genua's barely protruding stomach. Lithania held eye contact for quite some time, and her smile grew wider. "Perhaps, just maybe, he would give us the child of one blessed with the sight of Malignant Prophecy, who also retains a true inheritance from the great maw itself. What do you think he would say, should we ask? Our god is quite interested, and we'd be very certain to forgive Allie of all her misgivings immediately should Riven agree to our terms."

Genua's eyes widened in alarm, and she took an involuntary step back while clutching at her stomach. "My child? You want my child? You cannot be serious."

"YOUR child?!" Lithania laughed, throwing her head back in genuine amusement before lowering her wicked gaze upon Genua once more. "No, Genua. It is

Riven's child, Gluttony's child, though neither of you knew it when Gluttony had already begun to settle into Riven's soul at the time of conception. It is not your decision to make. Rather, it is Riven's, and it is Gluttony's, and it is a bartering piece that we would settle for in order to turn a blind eye to Allie's transgressions. You'd, of course, still be able to see the child here in the temple as it grew up . . . after all, you are one of our clergy, too. It wouldn't be like you're completely giving the child away, you'd just be allowing it to . . . develop differently, living here under our teachings and training."

CHAPTER 40

Azmoth's roars joined the fray as he clashed with the swarm of winged electrical serpents in the field of death beyond Riven's fight. It was a good opportunity for the demon to level and catch up, and as Athela beat the living shit out of the matriarchal boss monster, a huge golden tomb cobra that was getting tossed around the battlefield like a child's plaything, she made sure to keep tabs on whenever Azmoth was in a bad spot.

Not that he was by any means weak; he could take on many of the gnashing tomb cobras and their lightning strikes at once, but he'd slightly fallen behind Athela and Riven's own climb to power. Fay had done so even more, but Riven had plans for all of them to reach the E-grade and level 200-plus by the time this event was up.

"STOP IGNORING US!" the death knight howled, smashing her claymore against Riven's blocking gauntlet with a shower of sparks.

Riven frowned, throwing off the death knight with another sonic-speed backhanded slap and swinging himself left to dodge another lightning strike with a disappointed look. The glacial mage was already panting heavily, covered in shallow cuts that each could have been deadly strikes if Riven hadn't pulled them back to continue the fight a while longer. The lightning mage was missing an arm and had cauterized it with his own lightning, dripping blood down his reptilian face while he coughed occasionally. Meanwhile, the drow woman's bone armor was shattered in a couple places and she was growing quite tired.

Spitting out two teeth, wheezing, and pushing herself up to her feet to stumble forward with a snarl—she let out a high-pitched scream of frustration. "GODS DAMN IT!"

Gluttony snickered inside Riven's mind, even getting Riven to grin slightly at the sin's amusement.

He looked at the three worn-out cultists and then to the body of the dwarf he'd consumed not long ago. "I must say, I'm not very impressed. How are people like you six supposed to bring about a world-ending apocalypse? I was expecting better."

His hand blurred and his staff swung with it, smashing down another spike of ice the size of his torso that shot from the ground. It shattered as he literally caught a lightning bolt in one ivory-covered hand, crushing the storm mana between his fingers and not even bothering to stop the claymore's swing as it made contact with his horned skull pauldron.

The claymore shattered, the lunging death knight widened her eyes, and he abruptly smashed his armored head forward to shatter her nose even further.

The drow's face sprayed blood, and she stumbled back before Riven's spear-staff slammed through her armored gut and out the back of her spine.

Her teal eyes widened, and she coughed up bile as her fingers clenched around Riven's black weapon in astonishment. "H-how are you t-this strong?"

She coughed up more blood, spitting it onto Riven's face as he stared back unblinking.

Lifting her up over his head slowly, he channeled blood mana into the weapon as she began to scream. Ribbons of red that usually kept to the weapon rushed forward in a roaring tide of power as it began devouring her alive, her body being torn apart and absorbed until the remnant energies of her mana channels made contact with Riven's invading magic. Her body then exploded, sending shrapnel of armor and body parts all over the battlefield.

The two naga just gawked before both of them started to run.

"Oh, don't be like that!" Riven laughed, walking forward. "You'll respawn soon enough. Come and fight me!"

Riven stomped a foot into the dirt and a wave of red ice combed across the ground, coating corpses, trees, and boulders in a mad rush that overtook the two injured naga in seconds.

The lightning mage screamed in horror as the red magic began to encase his body, freezing solid before being ripped apart by Riven's will. The glacial mage, on the other hand, desperately resisted the freeze effect and managed to tear himself out of the red ice one, two, then three times before five abrupt spikes of red tore from the ground to pierce his heart and lungs at different angles.

Gasping, then convulsing, the naga died only ten seconds later with a last, shuddering breath. His impaled body then went limp.

"You could have saved at least one of them for me," Nora said with a disappointed sigh after landing with a soft thud, sweeping a pair of dual rapiers low to the ground before coming to a stop beside him. "I didn't get here fast enough."

"We may be friends, but we're still competing." Riven winked her way. "I can't just LET you take the Chalgathi egg, now can I?"

Nora snorted, watching the beast swarms of Athela's spiders, Azmoth, and the archdemoness herself go at it in a frenzy. "At least I'll get the main quest points. Are you going to help clean that up?"

Riven shook his head, planting his spear-staff into the ground and watching the fireworks go off amid the clash of claws and teeth. "Nah. This is their opportunity to level up. I'm at max level for F-grade and can't grow more until I pass into the E-grade, so killing won't do me much good. There are still a couple hours before the beast tide is actually unleashed, and I'm sure they can finish it off by then. Want to go grab a drink back in town?"

There was a pause.

"Are you asking a lady out?" Nora grinned slowly and winked his way.

Riven merely chuckled. "I'm afraid it isn't the way you're thinking. Athela and Fay would be rather mad."

"Oh? I'd been under the assumption you were rather free of spirit after learning from Azmoth that you'd impregnated the elf."

"That was a one-night stand. I'm dating Fay and Athela."

"So who's to say you can't have another one-night stand, then, Mr. Vampire Prince?" She waggled her eyebrows at him, then laughed at the look of discomfort and waved at him while turning around. "I'm just kidding. I'm into girls anyways."

"Really?"

"You betcha. Kind of jealous, not going to lie. Athela's smoking hot. Let's grab a drink and talk about how I'm going to steal your girlfriend."

Riven rolled his eyes with a laugh. "Sounds good, but I'll have to find that gnome before we do. I have a lot of questions pertaining to those abilities he was using, as I think it'll give me some insights for totem-making. In fact, I have a project I want to show him as soon as we get back."

The cavern before her eclipsed most underground lairs Lillith had seen throughout her long years of existence, coming close to but not quite breaking the top ten in terms of both style and size. B-plus material, if she had to give it a grade. It was so large that it fit an entire jungle inside; it was akin to entering another world in the underdark, and she could barely make out the distant figures of ruined buildings beyond the more obvious pyramid ahead of her.

She licked fresh blood off one of her black claws with a hum of delight, taking in all the sights, sounds, and fragrances that permeated her senses while a flock of colorful birds flew by. She watched them go without moving from her position, relishing in the feeling of being alive again.

She'd been a prisoner with her comrades and master for far too long. If she'd been given the choice between relinquishing her power to escape the void where her soul had been imprisoned, and taking this rebirth as a way out—she'd have made that sacrifice every single time. The chances of putting the shards of sin back together outside the purview of Elysium were just too slim, and the wait had gone on far too long. Eons had passed in that dreadful hole, and at a few times during her stay she'd thought she might actually lose her mind if it went on any more.

Thankfully that wasn't a worry anymore. Instead, she was free to explore all the little things she'd once taken for granted.

She could fly if she needed to, and she could teleport to an extent, but she'd rather walk and take in the scenery. To feel alive again. The signature of Allie's soul given to her by Gluttony still pulsed strong. It was inside that temple and hadn't moved for well over three days now, which made Lillith wonder why that was. Alive, but absolutely unmoving for three days straight?

Strange, but she'd figure it out soon enough. Thankfully Lillith was a born tracker, and two of her perks in combination made it almost impossible for other people of her own level and grade to avoid detection if she wanted to find them.

Taking her time, Lillith jumped off the cliff that showed recent signs of battle—exiting the underdark's tunnel and allowing her body to float down into the jungle's canopy.

The earth shuddered underneath her figure as her bare feet touched the dirt, and all the sounds of animal life abruptly stopped when she breathed in the fresh air. The corpses of those blue-skinned vampire precursors littered this place, having no doubt picked a fight with Allie's group on the way in. Monsters of various species that were native to this place stopped feasting on their corpses to scurry away with their tails tucked between their legs as the lithe, athletic demoness wreathed in shadow—features mostly obscured—walked elegantly through the underbrush with silent steps.

Though her aura was not oppressive at the current moment, her mere presence sent waves of power through the ground she trod upon. She was a Mythic-grade being, an Elysium ranking that very few across the entire multiverse ever acquired, and any who tried to identify her saw the purple flames of her obscured information as reason enough to run away very quickly.

"How I have missed these sensations . . ." she said with a sigh, but then abruptly stopped. Her pale white eyes turned downward to a rather odd soul signature in a nearby plant, and her brows furrowed with curiosity. She bent down, flickering void-black toes digging into the mud beneath a small tree where a yellow flower was struggling to grow.

"You're a rather odd find, aren't you, little one? You're not just a normal flower despite your looks."

It was partially wilted and would likely die on its own, but when she plucked it, she took pity on the struggling flower. The smell it gave off was still amazing, and with a thought she imbued her own energy into the tiny yellow petals with a smile.

The wilting flower immediately bloomed, taking on streaks of black down the center of each petal as it grew three times the size it'd been, and she willed it to grow roots.

The flower did as asked after consuming more of her mana, and she let it wrap its small, fragile roots around one of her seven black horns to feed off her while she continued on toward the pyramid.

"I think I'll name you . . . if you ever gain consciousness. Do well, little flower, and perhaps we will become friends."

Lillith giggled at the idea of being friends with a sentient flower, should it actually happen. Her close comrades in Gluttony's order would no doubt make fun of her, but she didn't care. She would not be swayed!

Yes, she would be sure to nurture it to full health and would see what happened. If anything, it would be an interesting experiment. At best, she'd gain a new pet.

An odd radiating pulse of energy reached her, originating at the top of the pyramid and snapping her out of her daydreams. The archdemon raised one of her eyebrows, then began skipping toward the large structure in the distance at a doubled pace. Whatever was going on inside, it was sure to be interesting—and Lillith was rather excited to meet this newly born angel of death. More importantly, Lillith was excited to meet the sister of Gluttony's reincarnation.

She could only hope that they would get along. Perhaps, just perhaps, they could even be friends.

The sight inside the pyramid was rather bloody, without a living thing in sight. She could sense souls up above her in chambers not far off, but powerful wards of an ancient nature she recognized as pre-system blood script wouldn't allow her to peer any deeper than at surface level.

Nevertheless, she skipped and hummed across the mutilated corpses—avoiding traps and giggling to herself whenever one of those silly mechanisms tried to slice her in half or attack her with various forms of poisonous blood mists and explosive shrapnel. The blood energy here was different than what she was used to, though, tinged blue, reminding her of the days before the so-called blood god had wiped out his rival pantheons to claim the top spot of power in the Blood subpillar's domain. These traps had blood energies that were . . . hmm. What was the word?

Primitive?

No, that wasn't right. Their means of blood magic were just as viable, they were just . . . for lack of better words, different.

It was a long-forgotten path of blood arts that had been declared heresy and taboo by the current blood god.

Why might one want to claim a path as taboo?

Many reasons. But Lillith could only guess as to why the current blood god would do so. Perhaps because he'd not chosen this route, as he'd have less control over a specialty such as this? Perhaps if people didn't choose his route as the prime path through the Blood subpillar, it'd weaken his following and potential for prayer and worship? Or maybe he was just spiteful after having potentially been locked out of this path by one of the enemy gods he'd slaughtered—though this was of course just one of many guesses.

She really hadn't paid much attention to him back then, as he hadn't been a big deal when Gluttony was at his prime. He'd just been one of many gods vying for the top. While being locked away in the abyss, which was the lowest and deepest level of the void that even beings like her couldn't easily get out of, she'd not had the opportunity to observe the ongoings of the multiverse, either.

She ducked, wove, and hopped through another series of explosive traps. She repeated this one floor at a time, avoiding the seemingly alive pyramid's defenses as it tried desperately to kill her, all the while laughing jovially as she made her way to her destination.

More bodies, more blood, more recent signs of battle. Vampires and precursors alike, along with other types of undead, were now present, and she eventually made it to a point where she was standing in front of a large metal door that showed signs of claw marks and bloody handprints on the thick metal.

Allie's soul signature was just beyond this door.

The demoness gave a slight push on the cold steel, and when it wouldn't budge, she crashed one hand deep into the sturdy metal. Claws ripped into it like a knife through butter, and she absentmindedly watched the ancient defensive enchantments across its surface flicker in protest and die before tearing the entire thing off its hinges and casually tossing it aside with a loud crash.

Making sure her new pet flower was okay, she dusted off one shoulder and stepped inside.

What she saw next was somewhat surprising.

"Oh my . . . am I interrupting something?" Lillith cooed, mouth crooked with amusement as she brought a hand up to her lips. "Is this, perhaps, a bad time?"

The room was a large dome in the center of the pyramid, with spikes on the walls impaling well over fifty individuals who were still living—but only barely—and they were all in an unconscious state. They were all vampires or other forms of undead, with energy from their bodies being sucked into a large coffin in the center of the room in swirls of light. The coffin was intricate beyond measure, carvings upon carvings upon carvings that intertwined and radiated that same pulsing energy Lillith had felt earlier in the jungle. It was ancient, powerful, and ominous—but so was she.

Unlike most beings who would look upon a coffin like this, Lillith was not intimidated. The dread that most would have felt only excited her, and she wondered just what kind of power she'd gain if she ate whatever it was that dwelled inside.

Immediately over that coffin was another object—an orb constructed from mana that glowed a dull gray. Blue and red runes clung to the orb, corroding it away time after time before the orb would repair itself seconds later, and inside that gray orb was the hovering form of an angel of death that had defensively wrapped herself in her wings. A magnificent sword in the angel's wings continued to power her barrier, and her halo continued to burn with figments of true death, but she was deep in a meditative state as the spirit of something sinister crouched just outside the sphere.

It was a massive wraithlike abomination, hooded and cloaked with six clawed hands and no legs. It was far larger than either Lillith or the angel, and its dark-blue, partially translucent claws cracked and shattered as it attempted to grab at the barrier with an irritated growl. Its four eyes were black slits in its noseless face that narrowed and turned to watch the approaching demoness with curiosity, letting its claws that were just destroyed rebuild themselves in front of their eyes.

"Transgressor . . ." The wispy voice of the odd wraith echoed through the chamber, filled with power as it looked down on Lillith's form. "You blaspheme by coming here. Do you know where it is you tread?"

Lillith ignored the giant wraith, glancing around at the intricate carvings that even by her standards were of a time long past. "Fascinating work you've done here . . . I think I'd like to study it. Even though blood isn't necessarily my area of expertise, I'm sure my master will make use of it, as his new host is a vampire."

She walked over to where a particularly familiar rune with twin overlapping pentagrams was etched into the wall, blood from one of the staked vampires leaking into it and powering it up over time. "Hmm. This rune is wrong. It's a rather ingenious method of soul transference, but your work with the Unholy sigils is a bit off."

Sensing the wraith shift within a half second to appear behind her, she casually looked up over her shoulder at the hulking undead creature who glared down at her with all six clawed hands out to its sides as if to embrace her.

"I do not know who you are, little one . . ." the dark-blue wraith hissed with its black eyes narrowed, ethereal robes shifting in a nonexistent breeze. "But you made a mistake by coming here."

The attack was so fast that space itself tore apart and the void briefly opened up, claws stretching and cleaving through reality that sent shudders of power through the entire pyramid.

The wraith paused, looking down in shock when it realized it hadn't even touched the demoness in front of it. It tried again, this time harder and faster, and it reeled back in an agonizing, shrill scream when Lillith finally allowed it to touch her. The claws tore off and burned with black flame, sending ripples of her power up across its arms that rejected its attack entirely, before the wraith regained its composure to stare in bewilderment.

"How?" the wraith asked, dumbfounded. "No creature on this planet should be able to compare to one as majestic as I!"

Lillith smiled slyly as she felt the Elite-tier level-199 wraith try to identify her, wagging a finger back and forth at the large creature overhead as its eyes went wide in horror. She literally felt its fear climb to new heights as it realized the gravity of its mistake in attacking her, and the amused smile she wore grew abruptly sinister. "No, no, no . . . That simply will not do."

The room flashed with black light, and in an instant the wraith was thrown across the room with a scream. Pieces of its body shattered and decayed instantly, and it crashed into a barrier on the outer wall of the dome with a howl.

Lillith was there in an instant, seemingly having appeared from nowhere, her mouth widening in rows of sharp white teeth as she began to suck in the air around her.

The undead ghost screamed in terror, desperately trying to get away and leaving huge claw marks in the stone and barrier encasing the room underneath before it was abruptly torn up and into the air. Like being sucked into a black hole, the wraith's body compressed and flattened—vanishing in an instant into the belly of the grinning demoness.

Lillith burped, patted her stomach, and watched her levels climb again with a malicious giggle. "Now, now . . . Let's see just what is going on here with this odd little contraption. I wonder . . ."

Using a finger to pat her lips three times over, she flicked her white eyes from rune to rune—trying to decipher what she could understand and piece together clues from what she couldn't. Then, trotting over to the intricate coffin, she let down a clawed hand and lifted up the lid.

A foul stench came out from the coffin, and seeing what was inside—she abruptly slammed the lid back down with a gagging sound—sticking out her tongue in disgust. "Even GLUTTONY wouldn't eat that thing! How utterly disgusting! Just what kind of foul magic is festering in there?! Gross!"

Putting a hand back over her horns in dismay, she shook her head in disappointment. "And to think that I'd become excited at the prospect. I'd never stoop so low, not ever. That will have to wait for Riven or Allie, if Allie can even absorb it now that she's not a vampire anymore. Now, let's see about waking this little darling up . . ."

She turned around and used her knuckles to knock on the orb, frowning when Allie didn't move, and becoming irritated at the large gaps of knowledge she had after her bid for a second chance at life. With a tsking sound, she growled and grumbled to herself. "To think that I've been reduced to being flustered by an F-grade curse complex . . . My ancient enemies would be laughing themselves to death if they saw this. Curse that damnable Elysium, but I'm just glad I was able to retain some of what I know—or this would be a lot harder."

Lillith was going over her next moves when she suddenly hesitated, focusing on a very familiar sin-powered sigil on Allie's right hand that shouldn't have been there. The sigil of the lion in the middle of a pentagram burned dark purple, and as Lillith stared—the sigil flashed and disappeared into Allie's body. Perhaps it was meant to be a message? Or perhaps the sigil was just preparation for what was to come Allie's way. That . . . that was surprising, and though she knew what the sigil meant—it wasn't Lillith's place to get involved.

Cracking her knuckles and getting into a cross-legged position in front of the orb that was still being attacked by various blue and red runes emanating from the coffin beneath, she began meditating as she entered a transcendent state of thought. Before long the room had turned pitch-black, then the pyramid came after that, and the jungle outside came next. Before long, the entire cavern was bathed in darkness.

CHAPTER 41

Pride, Greed, Wrath, Envy, Lust, Gluttony, and Sloth.

Of all the original sins, Greed and Gluttony were at odds most.

For Greed wanted to claim all, and Gluttony wanted to consume all, and thus these two sins crossed paths time and time again—or so the saying went. No one truly knows exactly what happened between these two in the early dawn of creation that elicited such a rift, but it is known that when followers of Greed cross paths with those of Gluttony, blood will follow, as can be seen by the histories of the hells, written in the blood of the forefathers, in a time when Elysium had yet to be.

—A passage from the journal of Trasindir Ironclaw, lord of the Fifth Legion of Howl's Forge, seventh level of hell.

[Twenty-six billion current participants have been analyzed. The ranking categories are as follows: Apex rank (top 10), Paragon rank (top 1,000), S rank (top 0.0001%), A rank (top 1%), B rank (top 15%), C rank (top 30%), D rank (top 50%), E rank (bottom 50%)]

[Current Top 10 Native Participants:

1. Riven Thane, Level 200 Pureblooded Vampire, Apex rank, Warlock Devastator, Incarnation of Gluttony
2. Allie Thane, Level 162 Angel of Death, Apex rank, primary class in transitory state, Hero of Death
3. Judith Marcina, Level 181 Divine Human, Apex rank, Angelic Fallcaller, Light's Beacon
4. Aren Hrall, Level 169 Snow Giant, Apex rank, Frostmage Berserker
5. Retesh Vorath, Level 200 Corpse Lord, Apex rank, Elder Lich
6. Netithi Bluskish, Level 139 Naga, Apex rank, Champion of the Kraken
7. Chitter Teh-Sneaker, Level 137 Rat Man, Apex rank, Dark-Blade Assassin, Poison Master, Sneaky Sneak Sneaker
8. Nithkik Brutishvase, Level 142 Dark Elf, Apex rank, Depthdweller

  9.   **Sinthil Tuk'tuk, Level 169 Lizardian, Apex rank, Wind Storm**
  10. **Thorman Bame, Level 158 Human, Apex rank, Hammer of the Mountain]**

Netithi Bluskish was an old naga, with a dorsal fin down his head that was marked with holes and rips from his years of battle in the trenches of the sea against enemies of his now-butchered tribe. Numerous scars covered his body where the scales were marred in crisscross patterns, and one eye had been replaced by an enchanted prosthetic, a purple gem that stood out starkly against his otherwise blue scales. His magnificent spear, handcrafted by people long dead and passed down through generations of his lost tribe, was made of a great sea serpent's bones and had notches all along its shaft and spearhead—but the spirit residing in it was that of the dead serpent itself and lent a menacing aura to the weapon's wielder.

Coiled up and meditating in a slouched position, Netithi blinked his eyelids open. From underneath his silver hood with blue trimmings—inscribed with the sigil of Chubin, the glass kraken—his prosthetic scanned the area in front of him.

A small, burned city lay flooded and in ruins, swirling vortexes of water carrying bodies of the dead and pieces of buildings above him in a river of his own power. The screams of his victims had died out long ago, the strongest of their people had only been F-grade human warriors at a maximum level of seventy-eight, so they hadn't lasted long. How this quest was supposed to test his skill was beyond him; he should be tested against bigger and greater things than this. This was just mindless slaughter, and he wondered whether or not the other cultists were experiencing the same thing.

His mind drifted back to when he'd met the other cultists and how he'd overheard a group of them and their combined quest to take on what was likely the biggest obstacle in this event. He frowned at the idea that they'd been able to fight that crazed vampire while he was stuck here instead. He'd gained a handful of levels for finishing the quest, but oddly enough he hadn't gotten any XP for massacring the populace—reminding him that killing these wouldn't actually gain him any XP in this strange event. Quests, on the other hand, would.

Stranger still, he'd seen some of his summoned elementals get killed while simultaneously giving the defenders XP and levels for doing so. This meant that, if he was correct, only the individual cultists and noncultists were stopped from actually growing levels by mindlessly killing things during this event. Why that was, he wasn't sure—but it was likely another initiative to complete quests, if he had to guess. Or perhaps it would stop other cultists from randomly massacring people and towns for no reason.

Regardless, his power did not lie in levels. He was already halfway done cultivating his E-grade soul lattice, and had been doing so for quite a while now. He'd have no problem getting to level 200 by just mindlessly killing things, but the lattice was another story entirely.

Because without it, one could not ascend to the next stage. It was an absolute, a requirement, to pass into the next realm of cultivation. And when you finally did get to the E-grade, merely killing things was not enough to level up. If your lattice was not perfect, if it did not hold the potential to take you far, it would cripple you indefinitely as you attempted to climb to the top.

Chubin itself had told him this, after naming Netithi its champion.

Netithi cackled wickedly to himself, wondering if any of the other cultists in his group had taken the hint by his title. It was pasted right there, in the open for everyone to see, on the world leaderboard next to his number-six Apex ranking. He was destined for greatness, he was destined to set the glass kraken free, and together they would rise up past the ruins of this world into the cosmos as partnered souls.

The sky above him shuddered as his excitement caused the swirling vortex of water to move quicker, with rivers coming and going in an ever-changing web of his water mana.

But that was not all he had.

Opening his palm, he willed a glass shard to form over his hand. His unique pillar activated, forming the abnormal glass into a mirror in front of him—allowing him to stare right into the figure that stood behind him in a silent, trancelike state.

"Are you just going to stand there, stranger?" Netithi asked, his serpentine tongue hissing while he slowly rose to a towering height over the strange, alien figure twenty yards away, yanking the bone spear out of his rubble pile as he did. "Or did you not come for a reason?"

In the shadows of an overturned stone building, casting the creature in darkness, a quick, sharp laugh rose out into the daylight. Stepping out from the overhang, a pale-skinned man lacking ears or any facial features other than a circular, puckered mouth entered Netithi's sight. He wore only a ragged robe but gave off a presence of power.

Netithi involuntarily shrank back in disgust while viewing the monster, and his eyes widened involuntarily as the creature grew to reach his height even at an elevated position.

Swarming leeches and worms roiled and churned in the pale man's body, ripping and tearing at his skin to re-form his limbs one at a time. Brittle fingers became sluglike tails, the clothes he wore ripped and fell off entirely, and the feet and legs buckled under a new weight as the body bulged and groaned.

In the end, Netithi found himself staring at a monster three times his size—some kind of swarm beast, a demon made of slugs, worms, and leeches with two humanoid arms coming out of a blob-like mass. Over a dozen bloodshot green eyes snapped open from within the grotesque creature's body, directly over its maw that had three circular layers of spinelike teeth, and it gave Netithi another cackle when it'd finished morphing.

Then it began to speak. "Netithi Bluskish, level 139 naga, Apex rank, champion of the kraken. How pretentious . . ."

The amusement in its deep, burbling voice caused Netithi's mood to sour as its laugh rang higher.

"Tell me, slug creature, hive mind, what it is you're here for," Netithi stated slowly, causing his spear to light up with power as he failed to identify to creature.

"What are you, and what have you come for? You've been watching me for nearly an hour without making a move, and I am growing tired of waiting for your approach."

"Slug creature?" the giant repeated, still amused. "'Hive mind' is a more accurate statement than calling me a slug, but I will forgive your transgression just once. Any more than that, and you will be . . . punished."

The creature flared with black and deep-purple light, crushing the aura Netithi set up for himself in an instant.

Netithi gasped as he felt his bones crunch under the ominous pressure; his vortex of water crashed downward onto the ruins from overhead, and he fell to the ground heaving and vomiting blood. Then the aura of the monster abruptly vanished, allowing the naga to lift his head once more and breathe through his gills again.

He came face-to-face with the smiling visage of the beast.

"I have been watching your progress, concerning your soul lattice. Without any guidance, you have figured out what you need to ascend into the next grade . . . We are . . . impressed."

We?

Netithi straightened himself, giving the large monster a healthy amount of respect after it crushed his own aura so easily. Even his prosthetic, purple gem eye could not decipher what this creature was, and the feeling of inferiority was gradually creeping in while he stared at the numerous green eyes glaring down at him.

"Who is we?" Netithi asked, somewhat impatiently despite his grudging respect for the beast.

The monster blinked, then scoffed and reeled its head backward. It looked around, holding up the disgusting, crawling swarm that made up either arm. "Who is we, he asks? There was once a time that everyone knew who we were, who I was, where the heavens trembled upon our passage and the hells would sing our praise. There was a time when even some of the greatest civilizations of the multiverse would sacrifice their offspring once a year to satisfy my needs, or the needs of my master, and would shower us with the greatest of treasures that we so desperately desire . . . I am the equivalent of what Lillith is to Gluttony, but I serve another master."

It leaned forward again, shifting position around his hill of rubble effortlessly despite its great size. "Do you know of the great maw, little naga? Do you know of the one called Lillith? Do you know of the vampire scum that now sits atop this world's power hierarchy, that even now will attempt to sabotage your own rise to the top?"

Netithi's eyes narrowed, following the swarm beast as it circled him—turning his head from time to time to watch its transition. "I do not know of Lillith, but the great maw and the vampire prince I know of. The reincarnation of Gluttony, Riven Thane, prince of the Blood Moon Requiem is here as a noncultist. But he is a Chalgathi follower and will not contradict my path."

"FOOL!" the creature roared, flaring with that strange black and dark-purple energy that crashed down into Netithi once again, causing the very earth to rumble under the monster's rage while Netithi gasped. "OF COURSE IT CONTRADICTS YOUR PATH, YOU SMALL-MINDED NEWT!"

The monster's rage quickly subsided, and it took a deep sigh to calm itself as Netithi shuddered—wide-eyed and struggling to regain his hold on reality.

"I realize that you have the brain of a reptile, and that it may be quite small, and that you only have one, as opposed to my many thousands," the creature eventually said when Netithi shakily propped himself up on his spear. "Regardless, you are able to think ahead. Use that small brain of yours to tell me—what do you think will happen when the three apocalypse beast quests are finished? Let us say that you complete Chubin's trials, that you do all that you set out to do and unleash the glass kraken from its prison in the sea . . . Do you think that will be the end of your quest?"

Netithi did not answer, not even daring to, in case he was wrong and incurred the wrath of the monster again. Even now he felt his internal organs were damaged, and it was painful to keep himself erect or even breathe.

"Let me answer for you, then," the monster stated flatly. "It will not be the end. I have seen this scenario play out on many other worlds before in times long past, back before I was banished into the deepest realms of the abyss. The end of this quest leaves only one apocalypse beast at the pinnacle. If the noncultists win, they either acquire an item of power or are able to take the egg of a juvenile apocalypse beast to raise as their own. If the cultists win their trials, they gain a fully grown beast and rampage across the planet, but there are two important things that will happen when this comes to pass. First is that all noncultists who obtain the item or the egg will be given a massive damage bonus perk that can put heavy afflictions on any living apocalypse beast they ever find."

The creature raised two sluglike, writhing fingers. "Second is that in order to leave Panu, you will need to kill all other living fully grown apocalypse beasts that are claimed by another of the cults should it come to that scenario. However, seeing that Riven is a likely contender for his own beast, he will likely gain the egg or the item—along with an affliction bonus toward your glass kraken when the time finally arrives. He will be given a quest to slay it, and you will be put into direct contention with one another for the final prize."

Netithi coughed, furrowing his brows, and scratched at some of the numerous scars across his scaled body. "Why are you telling me this?"

The monster snarled. "Because I want you to win, and you need the help."

Netithi blinked, caught off guard, and he slowly tilted his head to reevaluate this monster and his situation. "You want me to . . . win? Why? Who are you and what stake do you have in this gamble?"

There was a pause, and the creature's smile grew wider.

"I want you to win because, if you kill the vampire, Gluttony will have to reset and find a new bonded companion for his reincarnation. He'll have to start over with a chosen one who will no doubt be far, far less valuable and less compatible than this freak he's been able to claim by a massive stroke of luck. Gluttony cannot be allowed to maintain a reincarnated bond of this magnitude. I want Riven Thane dead so that Gluttony's rise back to power is hampered by a lesser creature he must fuse to. You see, Gluttony and my master go very far back. The original sins as well as the commandments are now heavily dependent on whatever or whoever they can bind to in their new ascent into the infinite beyond." The creature lowered its head in a mocking bow, swinging both fleshy, wiggling arms out to the sides as it did. "May I present myself . . . I am the Gambler, but you can just call me Gambler. I am a servant of the original sin of Greed, and I have come here to help you kill Gluttony, to help you kill the one you will come to know as Lillith, and to make you the number one power on this planet so that we may see it burn along with all of Gluttony's legions. If you do as I say, if you allow me to augment your body and participate in our plan as a willing servant, the Church of Greed will be more than happy to assist you in your rise far past this world in the cosmos beyond."

A small, hesitant smile crossed Netithi's lips, and as the creature rose to its full height, the old naga's smile widened. "I do not know what the Church of Greed is, and I know little of the original sins. I will need proof that you are able to help me forge this path to become number one in this world. Think of it as a show of faith so that I believe the words you speak."

The monster's green eyes brightened, and it lifted a hand to hover over the naga as if to bless him. "More will be given to you in time, after you burn through quests here for power leveling. But I suppose I can part with a small gift now, a core of sin and the power of Greed, to show you what potential you'll truly have if you choose to follow our path."

There was a ticking noise that echoed across the land, and the sky split apart overhead in a dark aura of sin energy. The naga screamed as his body ruptured from numerous scars. Giving off a sickly dark light, the monster laughed, and black-purple energy erupted from inside Netithi's soul aperture as a new black core began to build itself inside.

[Riven's Quest 1 of the Altars of Despair and Hope has been completed. Outpost Number 84 has been saved, the enemy cultists have all been killed, and the monster wave has been eradicated without losing a single resident of the town. This quest has been completed one hour early as well, adding bonus event points. Congratulations! You have been granted XP. All XP has been funneled to your minions, due to your grade cap hindering you from leveling further until you reach enlightenment and enter the E-grade. You have gained thirty-nine event points. Quest 2 will be dispensed tomorrow.]

Versions of that same notification had appeared in front of everyone in Outpost Number 84 at the same exact moment Azmoth had killed the last of the flying serpents, with Athela giving Riven a confirmatory message via their telepathy link. The instant that'd happened, the entire town had their own system messages ping his location while he was taking a drink back at the pub he'd originally visited with Nora, and he'd been mobbed with people thanking him, yelling out his name, and offering to buy him booze while sighs of relief were in abundance. Word had already spread about his minions, and watch parties had seen the explosions of battle in the forest miles off, and with their hoods labeling Nora and Riven as non-cultists it didn't take much to piece together that they were part of this integration quest even before the mass notification.

"OUT! OUT! EVERYONE OUT!" Warden Zuk, the odd wizard-gnome leader of this outpost, had his town guards shove and push people out of the rowdy pub into the streets to celebrate elsewhere, at Riven's request. "My god! I could barely hear myself think in here with all those ruffians! Good riddance!"

Gragle, who'd been dragged here by the warden himself at Riven's request, fidgeted nervously while looking between the vampire sipping ale and the Asian woman who was repeatedly sighing at the extra points she'd missed by not assassinating a single one of the enemy cultists—nor had she finished off the monster swarm leader.

"Don't look so glum!" Riven cackled, shoving another glass across the bar to take a fifth mug from the bartender, who'd warmed up to him a lot more since their first encounter, especially after the notification had lit up the town. "You could have killed that flying tomb cobra if you'd wanted to for the thirty-point bonus! You just chose not to."

Nora gave him a flat look. "Did you see the thousands of swarming electrical lizards around it? There was zero chance I was heading into that rat's nest. I'm far more fragile than either of those two monsters you sent in to clean up."

She took a drink, choking on the strong taste of the alcohol and ignoring the little gnome wizard who plopped in a seat beside her.

Riven grinned. "Yeah, you can just go ahead and say it, my summons are pretty awesome. Speaking of which . . ."

A shimmering blue-purple portal lit up in the middle of the bar, and all eyes turned to the portal as Fay stepped out. She looked amazing, getting a lot of hoots and murmurs from the crowd as they ogled her beautiful figure, but many of them were hushed by their comrades or slapped by their partners when they realized whose contracted familiar she was.

The gorgeous succubus wore an unusually exquisite gold-trimmed black dress that hugged her breasts and hips and came down to her shins. It also split down the middle in a way that allowed her to walk without tripping—with her slender black tail coiling on the floor behind her and wings outspread. Her ponytail was done up in golden decorative pins and she wore large golden hoop earrings that dangled from her bowed head as she took a knee and prostrated herself before Riven on the floor.

"Master, I . . . I . . ." She almost stuttered and choked on her words, trembling slightly as Riven raised an eyebrow her way. "I greet the great maw's reincarnation!"

Riven finished sipping on a drink, pulled the shaking succubus up gently by one arm, and stood up. Smiling kindly down into her wide black eyes, he leaned in and pressed his lips against hers before resting his head against her small horns. "Stop that, and come have a drink with me. Nothing has changed between us. Okay? Also, you look absolutely stunning."

He gave her a wink and saw just a tiny bit of the tension in her face melt away. Just a tiny bit.

The last time she'd seen him was when Deepnest had exploded and she'd been flung into the nether realm. Obviously a lot had transpired in the last twenty-four hours, to the point that she'd now presented to him while undergoing some kind of panic attack, and based on what Athela had told him about Gluttony, he could guess why.

She began to protest, but Riven put a finger up to her lips as Gluttony's third eye opened on his forehead. Seeing the eye caused her to immediately shut up and go rigid, and she began to focus on the Unholy scripts of ancient tattoos that littered Riven's body now that he wasn't wearing Messenger but instead a basic sleeveless shirt and some pants, which emphasized his toned body as he led her to a seat and pulled the chair out for her.

"Nothing has changed," Riven repeated softly, pushing her chair in and chuckling at the way she blushed furiously at his lightest touch. "Put your wings away so I can sit next to you and we can talk."

Without being told twice, Fay retracted her wings and her tail back into her body, staring at the bar in front of her as Riven gestured for another mug of alcohol.

"Ale, beer, or harder stuff?" the bartender asked, trying hard not to stare at the beautiful woman. His gaze turned to Riven instead, outwardly forcing himself to remain locked on the man instead of the beauty. "What do you think, Mr. Scary?"

Riven smiled at the nickname. "Mr. Scary? I like it. Let's go with the harder stuff. I think my girlfriend here is going to need it."

Fay blushed even more furiously at the title of girlfriend, and she put two hands over her face as he began to laugh.

The middle-aged man wearing an apron behind the counter raised his eyebrows with a confused smile. "I'd thought the other demoness was your lover. The one with night-black skin."

"Athela? She is. I'm dating both of them. Or, more accurately, we three are dating each other—Athela, myself, and Fay here."

"You're dating both of them?!" The bartender sputtered a laugh, rolled his eyes, and took out a bottle of some kind of rum-like substance that he poured into a tall glass. He passed it to Fay, who took it wordlessly. "Some people have all the luck. Count me jealous, vampire. But considering you and yours somehow saved our town from a monster swarm, likely avoiding many deaths, I'll try to ignore that side of myself for the night. What about the blood priestess? Are you dating her, too?"

"No, I'm not."

"And this fine lass here?" the bartender asked, winking at Nora, who was still actively sighing.

"I'm afraid not. She's into girls, apparently."

The bartender's eyebrows rose, then gestured to Fay, who was sipping on her drink—implying a couple things about Nora, Fay, and most likely Athela with a series of hand gestures most men would certainly be able to make out.

Riven smirked and shook his head but didn't reply as the festivities inside and outside began to climb to new heights with cheers and laughter all around. Instead, as his succubus companion began to sip on her drink to calm her nerves, he leaned in and kissed Fay on the cheek before calling out to Gragle a few seats down. "So, my short, stout friend, I was hoping we could chat about those things you called graphics earlier today."

The scarred gnome coughed halfway through taking a swig, then set his mug down to glare up at the smirking vampire with an irritated huff. The silence was telling, but eventually the gnome mustered the courage to reply—with a little bit of help from the alcohol. "You seem good-natured enough now that I have some booze in me, but are you really related to Gluttony somehow?"

The vampire prince blinked. Had he been too drunk to notice Fay's comments on the great maw? Apparently so.

"Nope."

"What about being a prince of the requiem?"

"Nuh-uh."

"Are you sure?"

"Positive," Riven lied with a raised eyebrow. "All that talk was just us being stupid and fucking around with you natives."

Gragle eyed him skeptically, then nodded slowly. "Fine, fine. You'd be a really scary fucker if that multiverse-wide system notification was about you, but I'd think Gluttony would choose someone of a higher level if he had to reincarnate, so I suppose that makes sense you'd be lyin'. I just wouldn't want to wake up being eaten alive tomorrow night, ya know?"

Gluttony's amusement rose inside, and Riven had to beat back a grin of his own. "Yes, yes. Of course. Who'd want that? Now, are you going to talk to me about these so-called graphics or not? That was really unique magic you had there, and I was hoping to implement it in my own totems."

"You make totems?" the gnome asked abruptly, suddenly becoming interested in the conversation as he turned his entire body to stare around Fay's timid figure between the two men. "Seriously? You?"

Riven held out his tattooed arms to either side with a shrug. "What?! Didn't I mention that earlier? You were probably just too scared shitless to hear me right. Is that so unbelievable?"

"Yes, it is. Do you have any recent works?"

Riven smiled, then nodded. Reaching into his spatial sack, he drew out the prized possession he'd been working on since visiting Hakim's place a little while back. It'd finally absorbed the minor sigil of Black Lightning, and had evolved from partially constructed into a fully blown totem. His previous totems couldn't level up, so it was very interesting to see that this one could. He'd had the option to negate this effect in favor of having a static damage output when creating the totem, and that would have increased the power it had significantly in the beginning—but it would have stagnated its growth in turn.

So he'd allowed the soul to grow and gain levels, starting out at a weaker point rather than stretching the soul out and limiting its potential for the future.

> **[Totem of Bloodforged Rift Sparks: The Path of Red and Black has been imbued into this totem, along with three different ability sigils, allowing it to create combination abilities from the following: Black Lightning, Rift, and Crimson Ice. Due to having a high-grade soul imbued into this totem, it is able to move around autonomously and will follow your will to fight or defend. Elite Tier, level-1 totem. Requirements: 90 Willpower, Blood subpillar, Shadow subpillar. Bound to Riven Thane.]**

Gragle's eyes widened with interest, and he hesitantly put forth a hand before asking if he could see it. "It's a beautiful piece. These enchantments are very high quality, even if the materials could do better. May I?"

"You absolutely may," Riven replied, enjoying the eager look the gnome was giving his creation while picking up the totem with one hand and setting it gently in the smaller hands of the other man. "Just don't blow it up. I have high hopes for that totem, and it's the first real one I've ever completed now that I have the Death subpillar. So it's kind of special to me, and I was hoping that it could potentially get an upgrade if you have any thoughts on what might work."

CHAPTER 42

Retesh Vorath's unnatural, fleshy organs randomly curled and uncurled across his bones as the undead lich called a black mist from the ocean around him and flung the cloud at his pursuers.

Judith Marcina's golden wings pulsed with energy, encompassing her in a shield of white light that let her rip through the cloud of necrotic gases to tear her flaming sword through Retesh's mount—cleaving a wing off the large drake in a single go.

The two other undead drakes on either side of Retesh screamed in rage as their brother let out a cry of pain and started spiraling down toward the sea below, where an even more violent battle between the merpeople and his fleet of black ships was taking place. Explosions of water and death, ice and storm, plague and rot all ripped and tore across the waves far below while giant sea creatures—both living and dead—ripped and bit at one another frantically.

Retesh cursed as Judith's high-pitched laughter rang clear through the clouds, and the two drakes on either side of him diverted their attention to attack the angelic bitch as he summoned dark tendrils of death mana to his bony fingers.

"Artun Regles Unimor!" he hissed while performing the needed hand gestures, still spinning out of control and barely able to manage the spell.

The tendrils tore out of his hands and grasped at the severed wing of the skeletal beast he rode on. Reeling it back in, the wing was forcefully reattached and the drake quickly reoriented itself about a hundred yards up.

The eyes of a giant kraken pet of the merpeople glared up at him from the frothing sea underneath him, promising a quick demise if he let himself climb too low, and the explosion of another black galley made him wince. Winged Nephilim in the sky battled undead gargoyles of his making, one of the drakes he'd raised into undeath exploded in an echo of celestial power to fall past him, and his hands trembled at the realization that he might actually die here.

These undead were monsters to the merpeople, and to Judith's forces. To them, the undead were creatures to be purged. But to Retesh, these undead were just as eager to pursue a fulfilling life as any of those who would want to purge his kind.

They were his brothers and sisters, his sons and daughters, and they were being slaughtered for merely existing. Just like on his last world, the living would never understand him or his people—and thus he would make them pay in the end.

If he survived this fight.

He screamed out in rage and pulled a medium-length stone staff off his back, causing it to light up with bright-teal lights before turning back around at the vengeful incoming presences behind him.

Three high-level Nephilim decked out in Valkyrie attire were gaining speed alongside Judith, swords and wings aflame, and Retesh spat before holding his weapon aloft.

"YOU MAY HAVE WON THIS BATTLE, BUT IT IS I WHO WILL BE LAUGHING IN THE END WHEN I USE YOUR CORPSES AS SOLDIERS IN MY ARMY!"

Judith summoned spears of white lightning that pulsed and snapped across the sky, only to meet an orb of death mana that deflected the blow. The explosion caused a cloud of conflicting energies to roil up into a blinding cloud, and Retesh used that moment to shatter the stone staff in his hand.

He flung the shattered remnants of the object behind him in the path of his pursuers while using his own life force to infuse more power into the mount he rode on. The drake underneath him doubled its speed in an instant, then pulsed into even faster speeds with a sonic boom, and the sky illuminated with a blinding flash of teal behind him.

Using a series of hand gestures to camouflage his escape, and keeping his course straight for Brightsville across the ocean, the guilt he felt for leaving his soldiers behind began to build.

"I am sorry," Retesh whispered, enraged—perhaps hypocritically—at the culling of his people, but he kept his head down and his mind set. "Brethren, you will be avenged."

[System Message from the Elysium Administrator:

Integrating planet Panu has been deemed lopsided during its integration phase. Key outliers noted times five. Stagnation of participants is highly likely. Parameters have been changed to encourage growth. Changes are as follows:

The original sin of Greed has been allowed to send a single agent to Panu in direct opposition to Gluttony.

World Quest total time limits have been expedited. Time limit is now set to three years total before integration ends. All time limits concerning quests and subquests related to the World Quests of Panu have been reduced and expedited as well.

Expeditionary forces are now allowed and granted and will be paid for by myself. Invitations for expeditionary forces have been granted to numerous empires across the multiverse, with different restrictions on given armies. Each major faction across the planet, including invaders, will be granted a certain number of tokens to allow for intergalactic troop movements based on the algorithm that would most encourage ascension.

You have been identified as a potential candidate to help put together one of these expeditionary forces. To whom your forces will serve, should you accept: Allie Thane and Riven Thane of Panu.

Concerning where this comes into play for you, General Viku of the Blood Moon Requiem, it means that you have seven days to put together an army. A requirement for all chosen soldiers will be that they not have ill intent directed toward Allie Thane despite her choice to shun the Blood God, and they will be vetted by myself to make sure the proper balance is maintained. Your goal is to help finish the World Quests within the three-year time limit for your side, and then to conquer Panu afterward.

Should you accept these conditions, you will be granted forty thousand tokens for Sarak slave soldiers from your controlled planet of Vartesh, fifteen thousand soldiers from the ranks of House Wraithtide, and ten thousand soldiers from the greater empire of the Blood Moon Requiem, all F-grade. One additional low-E-grade participant may be selected as well. No advanced weaponry in the form of ships or weapons of mass destruction will be allowed. Your specific restrictions will be as follows: Your expeditionary force will be restricted to the continent of Umbra for the first year before being allowed access to the rest of the world. You will be allied with the forces of Negrada, a minor hellscape dungeon that has already accepted these conditions. Upon victory conditions being met, the Blood Moon Requiem will receive one Elite S-grade treasure, one Supreme A-grade treasure, two Legendary B-grade treasures, three Elite C-grade treasures, and the potential for warp gate access to Panu should the native faction decide to allow it.

You have one day to decide whether you will take up this offer.]

The Wraithtide fleet filled the sky—sleek daggerlike spacecrafts of black, red, and dark gray—and elites from all over the empire were flying in as the communication lines were abuzz with activity. General Viku of House Wraithtide watched from a balcony with the other members of his house, alongside High Queen Nephridi, as the forces of the younger generation scrambled to organize themselves at such short notice. Below them, thousands of soldiers were being geared up for battle.

This was a perfect chance to bring the queen's great-grandchildren into the fold, establishing a link between the empire and Panu and even creating an outpost in an entirely separate part of the multiverse for the requiem to expand from.

The council, for their part, had been either absolutely enraged at the activity of the two Wraithtide children, or had applauded them outwardly, with mixed emotions from many after realizing what Riven had become. What Allie had done by defying the patron of their kind, the creator of the vampire, the blood god himself, was blasphemous—but having Gluttony's reincarnation on their side was something else entirely. When Lillith herself, a figure of myth and legend, stepped out to dispel the ritual that would have stripped Allie of her prophecy, it made Gluttony's stance on the girl very clear.

To the secret pleasure of High Queen Nephridi, she'd been especially pleased when Elder Thune's possessed thrall had been slapped into a bloody oblivion by the archdemon, cackling all the way back home and for many days beyond that.

"Are you smiling again about how Elder Thune reacted to the notice?" General Viku asked with a sideways grin, seeing the high queen giggling to herself for the third time that day. "I don't think I've seen you in this good of a mood since your granddaughter was still around."

Nephridi's shoulders shook with continued giggling, her long brown hair swaying under the dark clouds that were ever present on the Wraithtide home-world of Vartesh. "Yes, things have turned out quite nicely. The blood god's clergy have sent emissaries to speak to us about this matter and should be here soon, and though I am not certain of what they will say, I have it on good faith from my own bishop that they'll likely forgive my great-grandchild for her transgressions. It will be an absolute order, should I be right, for I believe that he who created our kind also wishes to bring Riven into the fold. Having the reincarnation of Gluttony as a member of our empire would far outweigh any potential insult Allie's actions have caused, and the council even voted to keep her status as princess intact after seeing the event transpire."

General Viku nodded thoughtfully, his shiny bald head having been waxed twice in the last hour out of nervousness—but he kept his cool. "Out of respect: Rippenvire sends word that they have withdrawn their bid from the planet entirely, when realizing the Blood Moon Requiem is becoming fully involved with these matters. They were able to pay Elysium a tax to retrieve what remained of their forces and are now completely absent from the planet as of an hour ago."

"I suspected they'd do so, yes," Queen Nephridi stated with a sly grin. "They are merely a vassal of one of our more competitive allies, but they could never hope to muster the kinds of forces to compete with our own youth. The blood that runs through our lineages is far purer than that of Rippenvire, our affinities are greater, our training is better—and they know it. In the beginning they'd hoped to secure the prince and princess as a way of saving face, and potentially gaining access to a royal bloodline through the right of vampiric conquest, but those aspirations are now over."

Looking over his shoulder, General Viku caught a glimpse of the purple Sarak man Jeltuna. The one Riven had appointed as the voice of the Sarak—to the dis-appointment and disgust of many of House Wraithtide. Still, the slave held his head high, and he was proud to be here. Nervous, but proud, for this was the first time a Sarak had ever been allowed in the presence of nobility and royalty at this magnitude. Usually he'd have been executed just for looking at the queen, but due to Riven's proclamation, she'd even made her way over to talk to him—which had stunned everybody. Even General Viku.

Lady Riska, Count Amestrius, Count Jaricock, and Baron Orimus were just some of the many faces in the small crowd of Wraithtide nobles—lesser and greater—and they all wore expressions of excitement, as the Wraithtide name was on the rise. With Riven's ascent to his current position and the possibilities unfolding astronomically, with even many of the reclusive high-grade demonic forces already having sent emissaries to the Blood Moon Requiem for a chance to speak to Riven, the prestige of their house was unlike anything it'd seen in its history.

But the hushed whispers of other House Wraithtide elites came to a quick close when the sounds of the doors behind them caused the general and queen to turn.

Walking out and bowing before the high queen, two of the younger generation led the way.

First was Kathrine Vonsilla Crushada the Ninth, eldest daughter to the duke and duchess of House Crushada, 107th in line for the vampiric throne. Her usual black-and-red dress was replaced by thin, formfitting armor of the highest quality for her grade—decorated with their house emblem of a rose. Her pale, beautiful features remained steadfast while she knelt, but beads of sweat were accumulating across her forehead. Her mother and father stood proudly in the background with beaming smiles.

Beside Kathrine was the single E-grade they were allowed to send: a military genius and a combat veteran of the frontier wars, Crendir No-Name, an orphan of low blood born to no family who had made a man out of himself even in the eyes of the proudest nobles. He was an undisputed choice for the lead of this expedition and would be serving directly under Kathrine in the public eye. In private, he would be the true hand that guided the armies of the Blood Moon Requiem on this conquest of Panu for the sake of both Allie and Riven. He had multiple scars along his otherwise pale face, and through the slits in his helmet, his eyes were a dimmer red than the many purebloods here, but he still kept his back straight and proud when the queen bade them rise.

"Hello, children." High Queen Nephridi then gave the Crushada parents a warm smile. "Hello, Lord and Lady Crushada, as always, a pleasure."

They both bowed silently and returned her smile.

She gestured to the two younglings and allowed them to join her at the railing where she and General Viku were watching the marching columns of soldiers. She snorted when she saw the untrained thousands of Sarak being herded onto the fields, where vampiric commanders were—for the very first time—going to allow them to pick up weapons for training and soon become the first true soldiers the Sarak had seen since this world had been conquered.

"As leaders of this expedition, you must realize that you may not return to the empire—even if you win," High Queen Nephridi stated solemnly, glancing at both Crendir and Kathrine with a sigh. "We can only hope that Gluttony and my great-grandson will decide to incorporate themselves into the empire through a show of goodwill, despite what we nearly did to Allie not long ago. It will be your job to maintain as good a connection with the Wraithtide siblings as possible, to convince Riven to establish the gate when the fight is over, and—without question—to eliminate all other outside forces during the integration. Help them complete the world quests and dominate the planet. But above all, gaining Riven's approval and convincing him to join the Blood Moon Requiem is of utmost importance."

Kathrine, who'd kept her lips pursed this entire time, gave a hesitant frown. "I was under the impression he was already a prince of the empire?"

The queen chuckled. "He is. Again, we nearly stripped his sister of her prophetic abilities . . . I just want to be especially careful around this situation now, and to maintain our expectations of him—rather than lose him entirely. Usually if an heir of royal blood who has the gift of Malignant Prophecy strayed, we'd just capture them. Or kill them, to keep the bloodline in our hands. However, now that he is the reincarnation of Gluttony, it drastically complicates things. In the worst-case scenario that I'd never wish upon any of the heirs, capturing or killing him wouldn't be a viable option unless we wanted to make enemies of numerous demonic factions that would no doubt see that as a declaration of war. With the rise of the commandments and the other sins soon to follow, and the eternal war between celestials and demons coming to our doorstep in the next century, we are going to be very sure not to put ourselves in the middle of it."

A new, older male's voice called out from the doorway where Kathrine and Crendir had just entered. "Not to mention, it is the will of the founder himself that we try to bring Gluttony's bonded partner into the flock."

An aura of power settled down on the balcony as the voice spoke, making everyone there excluding the queen and the general feel as if they were swimming in a thick, viscous pool. It wasn't oppressive or directed at them, thankfully, but most of the onlookers widened their eyes and bowed or even knelt as two esteemed bishops from the blood god's domain walked slowly toward High Queen Nephridi to pay their respects.

Each was shirtless, bearing the crimson tattoos of his order and wearing long, flowing skirt-pants and large, circular, flat-brimmed hats that had red drapes covering their faces. They both bowed low, and the high queen returned their bow before all three lifted themselves into straighter positions seconds later.

"It is an honor to host such figures as yourselves, gentlemen," High Queen Nephridi stated with a pleasant smile. "To grace our trading hub of Vartesh is an honor to all of us. What brings you out of your esteemed halls and to our humble planet, if I may ask?"

One of the priests turned to the other, and the second man chuckled from underneath his red veil. "Come now, Queen Nephridi. Let us not play games. You know why we are here—your own bishop no doubt told you of our passage and what we expect to talk about."

Nephridi raised an eyebrow and gave them an innocent, taken-aback look. "I must say I am unsure about what you speak of."

The bishops stared at her wordlessly.

She sighed. "Fine, you're correct. But I must ask since you're here, as it is the most pressing question I have . . . Will my great-granddaughter be forgiven for her transgressions? Or will she still be labeled as . . ."

Her voice trailed off.

"As an apostate?" the first bishop asked, filling the word in for her. "No, she is forgiven. Speaking of which, one of our priestesses recently tried to leverage Riven's child, Gluttony's child, as a token piece to acquire our forgiveness, without our knowledge. I thought you should know."

"Genua's child? The elf thrall?" Nephridi's eyes went wide in shock, then her face contorted into a horrified expression. "Did . . . did Gluttony take offense?"

The second priest scoffed. "We intervened, apologized, and executed the priestess in front of Genua to make it very clear on our stance, the blood god's stance, concerning Gluttony's progeny. The traitor's head will be sent back to Riven as an apology, and the founder has decided on forgiveness concerning Allie's status as an apostate. She will be granted leniency, as long as Riven remains a loyal servant of the true path. It is not ideal to let such offenses go, but the benefits outweigh the downsides. I hear that you've already assigned our battle priests to the expedition?"

Nephridi nodded. "We have a single unit of battle priests, without masters, from your order in our ranks. Over one hundred strong."

The bishop nodded in approval. "Good. It will be a good opportunity to spread our religion to the frontier, a rare opportunity of expansion indeed. Under your banner, of course."

The man bowed low again. "I must say that I am rather hungry, and was hoping that I could try some Sarak blood while I'm here. I heard it was quite a delicacy. Is that true?"

He shot Jeltuna a glance, and the Sarak man stiffened.

Queen Nephridi smiled. "Of course! But please keep in mind that this is Riven's birth planet, and he has forbidden the slaughter of his slaves in favor of wanting to improve their lives. Ridiculous! I know! But we still wish to honor his wishes, especially now that he has become a reincarnation of an original sin."

CHAPTER 43

KABLAM

An explosion lit up the small workshop Gragle and Riven were working in, for the third time that day, and Riven blinked away dust with a cough to the laughter of his two girlfriends.

Wiping soot off his face and spitting out dirt, then spitting onto the ground, Riven playfully glared over his shoulder at the two demon women, who cackled even louder at the absolute mess his attempt at creating graphics had caused.

"Laugh it up, you two," Riven said with an eye roll as Athela laughed so hard she fell out of her seat, rolling on the floor while Fay wiped away tears.

He didn't think it was THAT funny, but at least the two women he had fallen for were having a good time.

Azmoth, who'd been holding the new totem they'd been working on together, was entirely unaffected by the blast and just sighed with a shake of his head. "Sad, sad, sad. Good thing you powerful mage, because you bad at this."

"I've got to agree with the big guy," Gragle the gnome said from behind a blast shield a few feet away, looking down skeptically at the smoldering remains of Riven's latest attempt, where hellfire still ate away at pieces of wood on the reinforced metal table. "You're really quite terrible at this."

"Well, that's not very nice!" Riven said with a dramatic humph, folding his arms grumpily in large part to put on a show for the two girls. "I take offense to that! Let's try again. I'll get it next time."

Nora, who'd been out to grab some more alcohol, knocked on the door of Gragle's estate and then walked in. Snapping a look to the still-cackling women, and then to Riven's blackened, soot-covered face, she couldn't help but grin in amusement as well. "I see things aren't progressing too fast. Oh, and Gragle—there are some men out there looking for you. They asked me to have you come out."

The scarred gnome's face paled. "Who? Don't tell me it's those damnable mafia guys again."

"The guy's name was Ronnie? I think he was the same one from the bar. He said you had an order to fill for him," Nora replied with a shrug, setting down the jugs of wine she'd procured with a snort. "He didn't seem too intent on coming in here, though."

Gragle's scowl became more prominent, and with a sigh he hopped down off his stool. "Of course he doesn't want to come in here with the savior of our town around . . . Gods damn it, I'll—"

"I'll take it from here, li'l bro." Riven got up, dusted himself off, and started to walk out the door. "Just to confirm what Nora said—Ronnie was that guy who was bullying you back at the bar, right?"

Gragle blinked, rubbed a hand through his short black beard, then slowly nodded. "Y-yes . . . I owe him a lot of gold due to interest. And I'm lucrative, so he's going to be resistant to letting me go. I make graphics for him to imbue into items for rare or higher-tier enchantments and sigil skeletons while I pay my debt off."

"You owe him gold? For what?" Riven asked curiously with a head tilt.

Gragle opened his mouth to reply, then thought about it. "I suppose it's for protection?"

"Protection from who?" Riven asked, brows furrowed.

Gragle paused again. "From . . . himself? And other gangs here in the outpost."

With a click of his tongue, Riven nodded and gave Fay a kiss before playfully jabbing Athela in the side to make her squeal with laughter. "All right, well, I'm going to go talk to him, see if I can knock some sense into him."

Before Gragle could object, Riven pushed through the door to immediately come face-to-face with a man in full steel-plate armor, trimmed in red. It was the same knight-looking motherfucker from the bar, just as Riven had expected, but the man's posture straightened when it was Riven who came out instead of the gnome. He had with him four other thickly built men dressed in similar attire, each with short swords and round shields imbued with various enchantments—all of them wearing the same strange sigil of what Gragle called the Scrags mafia.

Apparently this guy was more invested in Gragle than Riven had thought.

"Honored savior," Ronnie, the central figure, said from underneath his helm. No doubt he was talking about Riven saving the town. When he bowed in respect for just a moment, the other four men undertook the same gesture. "I apologize. I didn't realize you were the one who was keeping our employee company. Perhaps this is a bad time?"

Riven put on a fake smile, looking left and right down the alleyway behind Gragle's house. "I'm afraid Gragle is preoccupied. He says he owes you money? I was hoping that I could buy out his debt, because I'll be utilizing his skills for a good amount of time while I'm here."

They stared at each other after that. Birds chirping overhead broke the silence, and Ronnie eventually cleared his throat while standing up straighter. "Gragle is employed by us out of choice, not necessity. He does owe me quite a sum of Elysium coins, but that is neither here nor there—and I don't think you'd be able to afford to buy his debt out."

Riven raised an eyebrow, taking note of a scrawny human man who turned the corner, saw Ronnie, and quickly scrambled away. He let out a tired sigh. Picking through his spatial sack and pulling out a hundred gold pieces from the mountain of gold he'd collected off bodies after the monster swarm, he threw them to the ground with a jingling of coins. "I'm not giving you a choice on the matter. Leave with the money, or your guts are going to be plastered along the alley walls here in the next thirty seconds."

Three quick flashes of red light illuminated the alleyway, as seen from inside Gragle's workshop just a minute after Riven had left through the back door, and within seconds, the vampire returned with a wide smile on his blood-flecked face. He held up both hands to Gragle and chuckled ruthlessly. "Problem solved, buddy! I . . . Oh, hi, Genua. When did you get here?"

He turned his head to where Genua had just sat down at another table off to the side. She'd joined Athela, Fay, and Nora while they poured glasses of wine and gave him looks tinged with different but positive emotions. Fay especially had come a long way since her arrival earlier that day, and had settled into a far calmer and more normal way of thinking about things after being in Riven's presence— seeing that he had in fact NOT changed much in terms of how he treated her.

Despite having Gluttony as a symbiote.

"Hello, Master," Genua said with a small smile, standing up to bow in respect. "I just arrived back from the blood god's realm. I apologize if I am coming at a bad time."

"No, no, of course not," Riven said with a grin—waving her back down to her seat and joining Azmoth and Gragle at the thicker metal worktable in the center of the room. "How was it? Good, I hope? Did they teach you how to fight? You've been gone hours."

Genua looked like she had something to say, but thought better of it and shook her head. "Um . . . Well . . . it was all right. Interesting, certainly, but they didn't teach me how to fight just yet. It was full of lore on the religion, going over my duties as a priestess, and some other . . . interesting topics were brought up."

"Such as?" Riven asked, curious.

"Um . . ." Genua scratched the back of her neck with a sheepish smile. "I'd rather tell you in a more private setting. Also, it's been . . . a while. I was hoping to relieve some stress as I talk about it . . . Perhaps later tonight, I can visit you to talk more? Perhaps with Fay and Athela as well?"

There were a brief few moments when absolute silence enveloped the room.

Fay glanced over at the elf thrall with a raised eyebrow and a curious frown but didn't say anything. Athela also looked rather surprised, as Genua wasn't usually so forward, but shrugged while she continued drinking and laughing with Nora about something they'd seen earlier today in the market.

Riven gave her the same expression Fay had, raising a single eyebrow, then nodded slowly. "Sure . . . that would be . . ."

He glanced at Fay, who shrugged, and then Athela, who waved him off.

He raised his gaze back to Genua. "Should be fine?"

Not sure how to take the odd shift in Genua's demeanor, he turned his attention back to the table where Gragle had set out another set of already partially completed graphics for Riven to take a shot at.

Concentrating, and not yet getting the totem pieces in line until he had the graphics down again, Riven closed his eyes and began to focus on the three-dimensional skeletons of runic infernal mana hovering in the air ahead of him.

The thing about these graphics that Gragle was trying to conceptualize for Riven was that they were both far more basic and far more intricate than normal enchantments or inscriptions, by a long shot. As contradictory as that was at first glance, it made sense when Riven got the feel for just what it was he was looking at.

Graphics were a way to formulate the magic of thought into physical concepts by utilizing the basic code of the system. So, in a way, he was building up basic enchantments or spells, much in the same way computer codes back on Earth could have been put together by numerical ones and zeroes. So it was basic in the aspect that he wasn't dealing in anything very complex on a conceptual level, but it was far more intricate because he could make minute and specific changes to the "code" based on an incredibly small tweak to the source code of the spell.

Instead of ones and zeroes, however, Gragle had told him there were five concepts to be aware of when constructing a graphic. Three of the concepts were Re, Vo, and Tin, which acted like an axis to travel along when inputting source code. Based on mathematics from Riven's home planet, they could be conceptualized the same way X, Y, and Z axes were made when describing a three-dimensional space. Then there were the concepts of Nun and Zika, with Nun representing orientation and affinity of a power source such as a pillar orientation—and Zika representing the power of intent.

Re, Vo, Tin, Nun, and Zika.

Riven was having a hard time putting it all together, but then again this was his very first day, and despite all the laughs his two drunk girlfriends were having at his expense, he was pretty proud of himself for grasping what he had.

"He's missing a concept, but I can't remember what it is," Gluttony whispered in the back of Riven's mind, causing him to frown in wonder at what that could be—but after further probing on the subject, it was apparent that this particular bit of knowledge had been stripped from the sin by Elysium's purge.

"Regardless," Gluttony continued inside Riven's head while he started working on a new source code based on the start-up Gragle had already created for him. "This is good practice for us both. I'm rusty. Perhaps I'll remember it if I gain some insight and inspiration while working."

"One can only hope . . ." Riven muttered under his breath with an appreciative internal nod to Gluttony, before going back at it with the Infernal burning graphics hovering ahead of him over the table.

Adjusting Ro, Vo, and Tin—he was able to shift the three-dimensional structure of the source code and thus change the burning markings in the air. It was all based around a central point of intent, which was marked by Zika, but it appeared Zika was also far more complex than just being a starting point, so to speak. Riven could feel his intent on Zika from the already started graphic phase and change whenever he shifted from the concept of "explosion" to the concept of "solid wall" or "create weapon." Each of these conceptual changes also changed the runic markings themselves, altering Ro, Vo, and Tin slightly as they did—whereas Ro, Vo, and Tin didn't directly influence Zika in the reverse direction.

Which was slightly puzzling.

Changing Nun, in turn, caused even more dramatic changes, because it changed the pillar or power source the graphic was based on. This further influenced the other four concepts, but again did not work in the reverse. Changing Nun caused Zika, Ro, Vo, and Tin to change. Changing Zika caused Ro, Vo, and Tin to change—without changing Nun. Changing Ro, Vo, and Tin had no effect on anything but themselves.

Riven shifted between Death, Infernal, Blood, Unholy, and Shadow pillars as orientations for Nun that would cause the entire graphic to change in ways he didn't necessarily grasp just yet. Experimenting at the urging of Gragle, who said that self-exploration was the best way to go about it and that he was only there to start the process and answer base questions, Riven found that infusing Nun with different levels of his affinities also caused changes to the overall structure of the graphic. He could infuse Nun affinities of 10 percent, 29 percent, 84 percent, 93 percent, or whatever he chose to do all the way up to the maximum affinity he had on a given pillar. This in turn made it so that people with higher affinities in a given pillar or subpillar would be able to have the most leeway for change in a graphic based on how high they infused the graphic.

Changing from Infernal to Shadow, Shadow to Unholy, Unholy to Blood, and Blood to Death, Riven quickly found out that his Blood infusions were not only quicker than all the others, but that he had a far more precise control of the Ro, Vo, and Tin changes.

The runes flickered, changed colors, reorganized themselves, and spluttered or died in the air in front of him over and over again. And over and over again, Gragle would restart the process and scurry back behind his blast wall. It was rather helpful, because the hardest part of utilizing graphics was actually starting them in the first place—which was why Gragle's particular set of unique abilities concerning graphics was so highly valued.

Or so the gnome said.

But as Riven got to work, he quickly came to the realization that the gnome probably wasn't lying—as despite Riven's high affinities, he had an incredibly hard time manifesting these graphics at all. Thankfully, they were easier to manipulate whenever they actually appeared after their initial summons.

"Hand me that board, Azmoth." Riven motioned over to a pile of supplies.

Azmoth did as asked. He was the voluntary experiment buster—activating the runes and graphics Riven created and taking much of the blow with his armored body hardly getting scratched. Due to this being a training session anyway, Riven hadn't really infused much mana into these things—rather, he just wanted to get the basic concepts down so he could create REALLY deadly totems later on.

Hours rolled on by, and, immersed in his work, he only got up to give Athela and Fay a warm set of hugs before they went off to Gragle's guest bed. The gnome and Azmoth stayed up with him as they got to work fusing pieces and odds and ends of various totems together while infusing graphics into the objects and then utilizing them to create new and intricate runes.

"I can't say I've had this much fun creating graphics in quite a while!" Gragle mused, looking up at Riven's charred eyebrows that sizzled from another recent explosion. "Though I do wish you wouldn't be so destructive in your attempts. I'm running out of hardware, you know."

Azmoth snickered, and Riven glanced over at the pile of scraps from his many failures.

"Yes, well, I'll pay you back," Riven muttered under his breath, getting to work on the next project. "And thanks for all the help with teaching me. I appreciate it, and I won't forget it. Azmoth, hammer, please."

Later that night, Genua's tales of the changes on the outside of this event disturbed Riven. Why had he not heard of the expedited changes to the World Quests? The news of Greed's interference, a passage in the system notification passed on through the grapevine, so to speak, particularly caused Gluttony to become irritable. Though the sin didn't seem like he wanted to talk about it right now, so Riven didn't push.

And to be certain, he hadn't been the only one out of the loop—none of his minions knew anything about it, either. This meant that only a select few knew about the change in the expedited world quests, as well as the incoming armies that would array themselves for different factions across the planet.

Perhaps news of the world quests being reduced from five to three years would come to the rest of Panu later—when the armies selected by Elysium actually arrived?

Wasn't there enough killing already?

Apparently not, according to Elysium. For whatever reason, Riven and his sister—along with three others on the planet if the "times five" remark on its notification was accurate—had become prime candidates for Elysium's intended "ascension."

Whatever the fuck that meant. Though Genua said it had to deal with an abstract concept, rather than actually ascending into something one could see on a status page.

What was even more irritating was that Riven had been relatively certain of his ability to wipe the floor with anything and everything on Panu prior until now, but if Elysium was actively going out of its way to make things challenging for him so that he and the others would be pushed to their limits . . .

He sighed. For all he knew, he wasn't going to be the one who came out of this. Because although the stakes had been raised, his failed opportunity for ascension—should that come to pass—would be another's achievement. From what Genua told him, in the words of the bishops she'd spoken with, his death would grant boons of fate to the killers. They would essentially be stealing the power of his fate for themselves.

It was all a bit irritating to think about, considering he still didn't understand what fate even was, as this was the first time he'd been hearing about it as a real concept that influenced the things around him. Or perhaps they'd just been babbling nonsense.

"You're worrying far too much about things that don't matter," Gluttony whispered into Riven's head. "Whatever it is that comes against us, we will prevail. We will devour all who oppose our path."

Riven absentmindedly stroked Fay's long white hair while she snored lightly in the crook of his arm, her warm, bare body pushing up against his on the opposite side of where Athela lay mumbling in her sleep in a sprawled facedown position.

He looked over at the Arshakai, chuckling to himself while Athela drooled into a pillow. She always liked to cuddle while she was awake or dozing off, but nearly every time she ended up being a bed hog after falling asleep, taking up half the goddamned mattress while unknowingly pushing him and Fay off to the side.

Fay, on the other hand, was far more clingy as she slept, but not in a bad way. Whenever he'd rearrange himself, he'd find that she almost gravitated to him. She'd even wake up if she didn't feel his touch, using him as a body pillow the majority of the nights they slept together.

"I wonder what the purpose of all this is . . ." Riven wondered absentmindedly, his gaze drifting down to where Genua was sitting nearby. "This system . . . Elysium . . . Why would it care whether or not people grow in power? What's the point? What does it get out of it? And why does it prioritize some people and not others?"

Genua stopped sipping on her tea, looked out the window, and sighed. "I'm not one for philosophy, so I'm afraid that those questions will have to be answered on your own, Riven. Anyways, I'm going to bed. Good night. And thanks for the chat."

CHAPTER 44

Riven was pushing another spoonful of rich-tasting, brothy soup into his mouth after having Luke and Genua sprinkle some of their blood into it. Both his thralls were up far earlier than his demons, and the three of them were sitting around a small table over breakfast.

"So where were you all this time?"

The old elf was examining the recent wound on his wrist, which was already healing. Riven waited curiously for the answer.

The elf thrall paused in thought, then grinned and gestured out the window of their booth down the road toward a large flat, one-story building where a bouncer could be seen outside. "Spending my hard-earned money at a whorehouse."

"That entire time?" Riven asked, taking a sip of water. He let out a relieved sigh due to the refreshing sensation it let off. "That's a bit impressive. You missed out on a lot of the experience, though. I can't grow levels here unless I complete quests, but you all still can."

"Bah!" Luke waved his hand dismissively at the idea of the fight, setting it onto some cheese and crackers that'd been supplied by the bar next to Gragle's home. "This old man is tired of fighting. I'll leave it to the young'uns like you and the pretty lady sitting next to us."

He gave Genua a smile, and she hesitantly returned it before taking a bite of her own soup.

Riven ignored some of the stares he and his two thrall minions were getting, seeing that Luke wanted to say more by the hesitant way he glanced up at Riven from time to time. The old man's body language was also a bit off. Sighing, Riven set his spoon down into the bowl and steepled his fingers while other patrons of the pub began to settle in. "Come on, Luke, you and I are friends. There's no reason to hide anything. What is it that you're thinking about?"

Pausing halfway from bringing up another set of cheese and crackers, Luke put the food back down on his plate with a sigh of his own. Fidgeting somewhat, he leaned back in his chair and stretched his arms before resting his head back on his hands. "You know that many of the blood priests and priestesses, or other higher-ranking clergy members of the blood god, are thralls without masters. Right?"

Riven raised an eyebrow. "Yes, I'm aware."

The old man's eyes fell back down from the ceiling where he'd been staring and met Riven's gaze. "I hold no ill will toward you, but I was hoping you'd let me go. To let me be masterless. There's something that I need to do."

There was a long pause, and Genua looked over at the old man curiously without saying a word as the two men stared at one another.

"It's about my grandson, Ren," Luke eventually said, eyes falling to the table when Riven didn't immediately reply. "I was going to go looking for him, and if you let me go I think Elysium will kick me out of the event and send me back to Panu, based on what the locals tell me—and they know more about system events than we do. He's the last family I had before the integration began, and if I don't go now it may never happen—or I might be too late. I'm not even sure he's alive, but he's a talented young man. I have to have faith. I have to find him before the rest of Panu devolves even more into war—and I'm sure those announcements concerning the updated world quest timelines will come any time now. If what Genua found out from the other clergy of the blood god's temple is true, where Greed itself is making a move to intervene against you and there will be more outsiders brought onto the planet, that only decreases the chances of me finding him should he be swept up in the escalating violence."

Another pause.

Riven's eyes fell, and he pushed his bowl away to rest his elbows on the table. He nodded slowly. "It makes me sad to hear, but I understand. Of course I'll let you go. Do you have a plan for finding him?"

Genua's eyes widened in shock, and Luke's face fell into an expression of relief.

The old man nodded. "I have already put out notices in the old elvish kingdom of Tereen, and I've made requests for information on the Panu cortex, but haven't heard anything yet. Missing-people requests come up all the time on those boards, and riffling through them is like trying to find a needle in a haystack. I was hoping to cross the sea, to start looking for him there. I also know he was a skilled mage in his own right and did a lot of work with construction companies before the integration. I was going to start looking at those. Perhaps he went back to it."

Riven paused, then pulled out a large sack of coins that he set on the table. Using paper and a pen from his dimensional sack, he started scribbling on a note— then folded the parchment before handing it over to the elf along with the sack. "Take this to the necropolis and talk to Dr. Brass. He'll outfit you with whatever supplies you need, will help you charter a ride to whatever continent you want to go to, and the gold will allow you to buy whatever you want within reason from the Elysium altar or other merchants. Perhaps you could even hire some mercenaries—I know there are a lot of adventurers looking for work."

Blinking in surprise at the gifts, eyes widening when he saw what Riven had written on the parchment, Luke's eyes began to water. Wiping tears away, sniffling, and then glancing back up at Riven, he gave the younger man a bright smile. "Thank you, Riven. I'll be sure to bring my grandson back if I find him."

Riven grinned. "You'll always have a place back here with us if you want it. Do you want to say goodbye to anyone else before you leave?"

Luke hesitated, then clutched at the note and the bag of gold with a shake of his head. "No, I think I'm anxious to get going. I wasn't too close to any of your other minions, anyways."

Riven's smile faltered slightly, putting on a tinge of sadness. "All right, then. Now, assuming the locals are right about what I'm about to do, I suppose you should probably get going, my friend. Find him soon, so that we can spar again at the manor like we used to do when time wasn't so tight."

Reaching over and putting a firm hand on Luke's shoulder, Riven nodded once before accessing his status page.

"Tell Len that I love and miss her before you leave the city," Genua said somberly, giving a half-hearted smile to the old elf, who nodded in turn. "And that I'll be back as soon as I can."

Luke attempted to reply, but then shut his mouth and merely gave her a shaky smile. He nodded to her, and then to Riven, before a set of notifications appeared for both the men. The next instant, Luke was gone—leaving only Genua and Riven sitting at the tableside, with the cheese and crackers Luke had been eating left behind.

[You have dismissed a thrall minion, Luke Blissfallen, from your service. You gain all Willpower attributed to controlling that thrall back as free points to use on other minions. Luke Blissfallen has been banished from this World Quest event now that he is no longer affiliated with you.]

Picking up some of the cheese and popping it into his mouth, Riven slowly waved to the spot where Luke had been not long ago. "Wish you luck, buddy."

Genua slowly moved her gaze to her master, who was sitting across from her. "I'm surprised you let him go so easily. Don't you need thralls to maintain a blood source?"

"Well, I have you, don't I?" Riven asked, a bit downtrodden, looking up to meet her eyes. "Unless you were wanting to leave, too."

She blinked once, then twice, then sighed and put on a warm smile with a slight sideways bob to her head. Her eyes squinted in amusement, and it was the first time he'd seen in a long time that she'd looked genuinely happy. "The fact that you'd even give me a choice now makes me feel good. Appreciated, even. But no. Even if it is the effects of being your thrall, I think that we've come a long way over the past couple months—don't you?"

Riven's lips quirked at the edges, thinking about the previous night, and he nodded. "Yes. I think we have—"

Riven's words were cut off as the pub ruptured down the middle in a flare of cutting water blades and crackling sin energy, the form of a sea serpent created from liquid and bathed in deep-purple lightning tearing through Genua's abdomen in a flash of power.

Riven's eyes went wide as he watched his thrall get cut in two, blood spraying out her side as she let out a surprised and horrified scream. Other people in the pub, along with floorboards, pieces of the walls and ceiling, and furniture were all obliterated along with her midsection—but due to Riven's own reflexes he was able to react just in time to stop the torrent of winding, watery death from crashing directly into him, too.

The water around him dissipated as his rage soared, an aura of Blood and Shadow roaring to the heavens as the land shook. Black lightning flashed around him and, focusing fire back into the direction the attack had come from, he blindly let loose a resounding blast of energy high up into the air.

What remained of the ceiling evaporated in an instant in a storm of red and black, but he didn't take time to see whether or not he'd hit the ambusher before encasing himself and Genua in a dome of red crystallized ice.

She gasped, shaking violently as her upper body let intestines and her spine dangle from where her waist had once been. Her legs were nowhere to be seen, swept up in the flood that'd killed nearly everyone else there, and her fingers clawed in wide-eyed panic against his chest in a silent scream.

"You're going to be fine!" Riven hissed, reinforcing his dome of ice as another, more direct hit slammed into his position. The earth underneath him shook violently and the barrier cracked, but it held as Riven activated his Voodoo Doll spell with a quick series of hand gestures.

[Voodoo Doll (Blood) (Tier 2): Scan your target to map out their vessels and infuse your mana into their bloodstream. You then gain the ability to replicate their bloodstream regardless of whether they have extensive wounds—enabling you to keep them alive as long as their brain remains intact. You may also use this ability on hostiles to form painful blood clots. Heart attacks caused by this ability do critical strike damage. Dependent on both Intelligence (90%) and Willpower (10%) stats. Medium cooldown. This is a channeling ability and will not work if interrupted by using other spells.]

Redirecting the blood that was pouring out of Genua's upper body like a spurting fire hydrant, he stopped her from completely going into shock and made sure her blood remained oxygenated as he fed it right back into her brain.

Gripping one of her bloody hands, he looked up into her eyes, where tears were flowing down her cheeks, and frantically snapped in front of her face to get her attention. "Genua, I don't know where your lower half is so you're going to have that Body Fusion miracle that came with your class! Do you understand?"

She only continued to gasp, looking blankly at him while continuing to shudder—her hand clasped in his own as yet another resounding boom tore layers off his red dome.

"GENUA!" Riven screamed, looking up and seeing a swirling storm of sin and water condensing overhead. "I CAN'T KEEP YOU ALIVE AND FIGHT WHOEVER THAT IS AT THE SAME TIME! FUCKING ACTIVATE THE—"

Azmoth's flaming figure blurred through the sky and slammed into whatever or whoever was attacking Riven's position, and Athela's loud cackles were audible as she screamed, "I SHOULD PLAY BASEBALL!"

They'd likely been woken up from the blast, since they'd been only a few houses over, still asleep at Gragle's place.

Calming slightly and grinning at what had likely been Athela throwing Azmoth like a pitcher would, he began snapping his fingers in front of Genua's pale face again. "GENUA! Pay attention; get a hold of yourself! I know it hurts, but I'm keeping you alive. Okay? Just concentrate on fusing with me, can you do that?"

Genua rapidly blinked the tears out of her eyes, holding on to Riven's hands for dear life, and shuddered with a nod. "It . . . it hurts so badly!"

"I know it does!" Riven hissed. "But the pain will likely go away if you use your Body Fusion technique. Can you do that? Have you done it before?"

Genua hesitated. "I haven't t-tried it before, but I . . ."

Her eyes went wide, and she gasped. "OUR CHILD!"

Netithi Bluskish, the Apex-ranker naga at number six on the power boards, cursed and swatted the large demon back to the ground in an explosion of water before taking higher to the skies again. A large, searing set of claw marks still burned his scaled side with hellfire, but it was rapidly healing due to his body's natural regenerative properties. He couldn't keep this flying ability up for very long and needed to expel tremendous amounts of water mana to do it, using the pressure it provided as a form of propulsion, but at the very least he'd be able to make it to the next river before being caught, even if Riven did give chase.

Looking back down at the archdemon who was attempting to pursue him as it scrambled out of the town borders, and then glancing beyond that to where the pub had once been, he chuckled to himself while his eye prosthetic scanned the building.

It'd been a direct hit, and he wasn't entirely certain if he'd actually killed the child in her womb—but at the very least it'd been a decent attempt. Worst-case scenario, she and Gluttony's child would likely be severely injured and the message would have been sent. Best-case scenario, both child and the mother would die.

Greed's demonic envoy, the one who called himself the Gambler, would be pleased either way.

"We will see if all those rumors of your power are truth or bluster, vampire prince. Come and find me, or better yet—I'll be finding you again soon enough."

He let out a husky laugh. With a snap of power, large tentacles akin to the kraken spread out all around him, and Netithi Bluskish rapidly accelerated into the distance through the clouds, creating a trail through the sky with a shock wave of sin.

An enormous bridge of dark-gray stone with rolling hills of bloodied corpses marked the entrance into Negrada's demon city of Herenwa. On one side were the defending forces, mostly made up of demons and some of the stray groups of mercenaries from Brightsville that'd been overly eager to get there early, illuminated by the fires of the trench under the bridge and the torches along the high city buildings, while the other side contained a swarming army of undead that had been repelled seven times over now. In the sky, battles between harpies, gargoyles, phantoms, and other winged creatures clashed as corpses fell like rain.

Tre'Zix of the Purple Claw, archdemon of the Klinac'Tal clan and officer in Gluttony's legions, stood tall over his comrades in the lesser hellscapes of Negrada. His large, pointed legs dug into the mountain of undead bodies over a large bridge entering one of the key locations in Negrada's defenses, facing off against the hordes of undead that were regrouping after the latest bloody rebuke. Other archdemons of his clan, also devout followers of Gluttony, were with him and jeering or laughing loudly at the pathetic attempts of their enemies while flaring their insectoid wings out to either side with a demonic, Unholy touch to their textured chitin carapaces.

"COME, DUNGEON TARUS! DO NOT FALTER NOW!" Tre'Zix crowed with a mocking laugh that echoed across the rivers of hellfire to either side of the bridge, with an army of friendly forces at his back made from gargoyles, apelike red Jabob demons, satyrs, minotaurs, imps, and other breeds of lesser demons. They all stood far behind where he and his seven brothers and sisters were, though, as they would only get in the way of the Klinac'Tal clan's slaughterfest.

And Tre'Zix would not be kept from his glorious victories in Gluttony's name. If the forces of Negrada got in his way to try and steal his kills, he would simply throw them off the bridge and into the depths on either side of the choke point where he and the other archdemons now stood.

"COME!" he roared again, with the clacking of his comrades on either side— their mandibles gnashing, wings flaring, and blood-bathed scythes glinting in the light of the hellfire rivers. "OR IS THAT FEAR I SENSE?! I CHALLENGE ALL OF YOUR BROOD, ALL OF YOUR LEGIONS, ALL OF YOUR ARMIES TO MEET THE EIGHT OF US HERE ON THIS BRIDGE SO THAT WE MAY SHOW YOU THE MANY GLORIES AND HORRORS OF WAR!!!"

His seven clan mates screamed their approval, all eight of the archdemons flaring with power that boomed in a shock wave of challenge—out across the hordes of mulling undead that had invaded Dungeon Negrada from another subsection of hell. Dungeon Tarus had pushed far into Dungeon Negrada's second level by now, wiping the first levels entirely clean, but they'd come to an abrupt stop when Gluttony's forces had arrived to wreak havoc in their old stomping grounds.

But Tre'Zix, along with some of his clan, were only a few of the groups now manifesting to power level under the banner of Gluttony. Seventeen more defensive points had been selected, with telepathic communication keeping their officers in contact in case reinforcements needed to arrive, and forces from Brightsville—in the form of other FRIENDLY undead—had bolstered the battlefront in an absolute rebuke of this invasion. Tre'Zix was personally responsible for one such regiment, which was currently marching here after Negrada had been mass-hiring them as mercenaries through the guild systems, though it was more of a babysitting job for Tre'Zix than anything else. Tre'Zix wasn't necessarily commanding Brightsville's regiment—that was the duty of the officers General Bruner had selected—but the archdemons felt it was their duty to oversee these battles so that Gluttony's new forces would be able to grow at a faster and safer rate.

As long as they didn't deprive him of his choke-point kills, that was. They could fire spells and projectiles from behind his position. After all, he needed to power level, and he was in many ways doing them a favor by saving their sorry hides from dying this day.

"DEMON SCUM!" a voice boomed out from the roiling hordes of undead. Between ruined buildings and the wreckage of the city beyond, a huge explosion of death mana rocked the ground and shattered the ruins around the point of detonation in sprays of debris. Hundreds of undead were annihilated in an instant, with more falling just afterward, as a large humanoid figure stepped out with power roaring about his figure.

It was a death knight with two skulled heads, each one glaring out at Tre'Zix with balls of neon-teal flame for eyes. A huge claymore wreathed with the trapped bodies of ghosts screamed, echoing power as the spirits tried to escape and giving the large blade a ghostly gray coloring that shifted and writhed around it. A single intentionally shattered pentagram was laid out across the huge black chest plate of the death knight's plate armor, with the image of a scythe crossing it at a diagonal overlaid on top.

The horde of undead creatures of varying species reeled back from the skeletal champion as he stomped forward to the edge of the bridge with a hiss and cackle from his two respective heads. Lifting his enormous weapon and causing the air to shake with another fluctuation of his mighty aura, the being called out to Tre'Zix with malice oozing off his words. "DEMON ABOMINATION! IT IS KNOWN THAT WE WHO WALK THE PATH OF DEATH ARE ABOVE YOUR KIND, THOSE WHO CLING TO YOUR NETHER REALMS TO CODDLE YOUR YOUNG LIKE WEAK COWARDS! THIS CLEANSING OF NEGRADA CANNOT BE STOPPED, IT CANNOT BE CHANGED, AND DUNGEON TARUS ALONG WITH HIS COALITION OF ALLIED DUNGEONS WILL SEE TO IT THAT ALL OF YOUR CORPSES END UP ON OUR DINNER PLATES THIS NIGHT!"

The death knight shot his left arm out, and a massive tower shield rushed from a pocket dimension to his calling—slamming into the bridge and causing it to shudder under the strike. "I CHALLENGE YOU, BUG DEMON OF NEGRADA, SO THAT I MAY HAVE YOUR DECAPITATED HEAD AS A CUP TO DRINK FROM AFTER THIS WAR IS WON! FACE ME IN ONE-ON-ONE COMBAT AND WE WILL SEE WHO IS SUPERIOR HERE IN THE DEPTHS OF HELL!"

The cheers and roars of the undead horde echoed like a tidal wave from the opposite side of the bridge, while Negrada's forces stoically watched to see what Tre'Zix would do. This particular death knight commander had already slain many of Negrada's champions in this same exact duel setting, and though it wasn't something one had to accept, the death knight was an even bigger menace on the larger battlefield. There he could utilize recent kills of his own make to strengthen his sword by absorbing their souls.

Despite the confidence of the enemy and the wariness of his allies, Tre'Zix began to laugh alongside the others of his clan. Their laughter heightened and continued to rise until he had reached a hysterical state.

The demon called out above the ruckus. "YES!!! THIS IS WHAT I CAME FOR!"

Wiping one arm over his face to get rid of a tear, Tre'Zix brandished his two scythe-like blades and jumped off the mountain of bodies to slam farther onto the huge bridge. Just like when the death knight had slammed his tower shield into the thick metal, so, too, did Tre'Zix's landing cause the bridge to shudder under his impact. Flaring his wings out to either side and opening his mandibles wide to reveal three writhing, pronged tongues each the size of a human arm, he began circling the death knight while his clan members continued to laugh.

"It has been some time since I've had anyone brave enough to challenge me in a one-on-one duel! Aside from Lillith, that is!" Tre'Zix called out while the two-headed death knight got into a defensive stance. "It appears that my brood and I, and perhaps even most of the others of our order, have been forgotten due to the passage of time. So much so that a babe in the eyes of the multiverse such as yourself would so confidently rush to his death!"

He cocked his head to the side with an amused chuckle when the death knight flashed forward in a blazing ball of black and teal flames. "PERHAPS IT IS TIME TO REMIND EVERYONE OF JUST WHO I AM!"

Tre'Zix slammed his two scythes directly into the bridge in front of him, and fissures split through the deep metal with waves of kinetic force that reached the sky. They blurred ahead and shattered the death knight's armor, taking off both arms of the commander only a split second before Tre'Zix moved to flank the undead.

Before the death knight even had time to stumble forward, armless, Tre'Zix's pronged tongues crashed into the skulls of his enemy—drawing him back into the mandibles with a resounding crunch as his scythe arms crisscrossed so fast that the very air around them was sucked into a billowing cyclone.

The duel was over before it even started.

Bone, metal, and what little flesh the death knight had left all crashed into the floor as Tre'Zix screamed in victory to the roars of his comrades. Then, turning to the hordes beyond, his yellow eyes began to glow. Afterimages of his form tore out of his position as he collided with the nearest clump of skeletons, liches, and ghouls, and like a frenzied storm of sharp steel he began to tear apart the enemy army.

CHAPTER 45

"Into a bloody oblivion," Gluttony stated sourly, watching as their mana tugged Genua's lower and upper halves together while both Fay and the blood priestess herself cast healing abilities in the forms of Dark Pact and Transfusion Zone. "That is where the child would have gone if I'd let your careless, carefree attitude take it from us. You may be strong in the eyes of these lesser beings, Riven, but you are nowhere near the point of infallibility. Not even with me. I truly hope that Elysium's attempts to increase the difficulty of these trials even more is true, so that you may learn a lesson in humility. And I hope that lesson comes before it is too late."

Swirling auras of red, black, and green, manifestations from the area-of-effect zones from Riven's two contracted minions, flashed around them. At the epicenter of it all, Gluttony's maw produced a bloody womb from the depths of the abyss—holding it out to place it back inside Genua's body as the flesh knitted back together.

Riven stood silently, meeting the invisible gaze of Gluttony upon him while taking the criticism in stride. His fists clenched, and his eyes became downcast as the healing powers ended. "I apologize."

"Do not apologize to me, Riven. Apologize to Genua's child. To our child. The child who bears not only your blood, but my own now that we are one being." Gluttony's vertical maw gritted its teeth in apparent agitation. "This has highlighted a problem that I was already meaning to speak to you about. Far too often you are caught off guard by way of stealth. Throughout your battles, over and over again, it is assassins and acts of subterfuge that pose the greatest threat. We do not know if that mage was truly an assassin or not, but the fact still remains that you are rather pathetic in the face of hidden knives and attacks—despite your tremendous potential for mana control. You are an unbalanced scale, one that needs fixing."

Riven failed to meet the eyes of his minions, with Athela and Azmoth having just returned to remain silent on the outskirts of the devastated building. Fay was keeping her head bowed low in reverence to the visage of the maw, and Genua was still recovering on the floor after having her body put back together.

There was a long silence, and Riven could feel his bonded sin's irritation subside.

"You have potential; you merely need to focus on reaching it. I will let you dwell on your shortcomings so that you may think of your own methods to fix this problem of yours," Gluttony eventually said with a growl. "Perhaps making you think about it will give you better insight on the ideas that I myself have. Regardless of what you come up with, remember that my chastisement is meant to make you grow. Perhaps this next quest Elysium has in store for us will shed light on how you are not the height of power, either. We will see."

The rip in space shattered, and the visage of Gluttony's maw vanished with it in a split second. The shroud of mana that'd hidden Gluttony's presence from onlookers also crumbled.

Behind Gluttony's point of exit, another system message was left in the maw's wake.

[Riven's Quest 2 of the Altars of Despair and Hope:
A piece of the multiverse, taken out of the Narwali sector of Universe 16, has been transported to this territory. Inside it you will find one of a few portals here in these Chalgathi trials that lead into the Abyssal Descent, and three ticket holders who are waiting to enter. Kill a ticket holder, or barter for it, before the portal opens fully in three hours.

The Abyssal Descent, a monumental event that only happens every three hundred years, is being hosted starting today. It is meant to help forge the lattice meant to transcend into E-grade, and helps give insight into the way of ascension.

Young elites of numerous factions across the multiverse still within the F-grade will be able to participate, as long as they hold true to any pillars associated with the Unholy foundation. Use your status page to find the option to teleport in. You will be escorted via Elysium's own power into this trial within a trial where only those touched by Unholy power may be found. Death in this trial will not result in permanent death despite being hosted on an outer world, but will disallow any reentering of the descent at any time. Successfully completing the Abyssal Descent will result in fifty event points. Completing in the top one hundred contenders will result in three hundred event points. Completing this event in the top five contenders will result in one thousand event points. Finishing first will result in three thousand event points. Any other cultists of Unholy affiliation who enter this trial within a trial will also have a 1,000% damage boost increase when attacking you or your minions.

Unlike other participants in this outer trial, you will be able to come and go between the Abyssal Descent and the Altars of Despair and

Hope at will via your status page.
Total event points already accumulated: 39]

It took a while for Genua to calm down, with Athela and Fay doing most of the consoling as she sobbed in the back corner of the room in Gragle's small house. The shock of being ripped in half, and then nearly having lost their child, was weighing heavily on her. Meanwhile, Riven was contemplating Gluttony's words. The lecture wasn't meant to be malicious, but rather insightful, and the more Riven thought about it, the more he realized that Gluttony was right.

Had he done anything wrong?

Not necessarily, when you looked at it from a two-dimensional perspective. But Gluttony had hit it right on the mark when he'd scrutinized Riven's actions more closely. Riven had become complacent in his own power as of late, having wiped the floor with numerous high-powered individuals on Panu and even having cleaned up with two off-world invading forces and the Azag Hive Cluster to boot. Yet here he was, nearly having lost his unborn child if Gluttony hadn't stepped in.

Even the anger he felt toward the unknown assailant was on the back burner, taking a second seat to the anger that was directed inward instead.

He would improve.

He would learn from this.

He would figure out a way to make up for his weaknesses, would fix his lack-adaisical attitude and his superiority complex that'd so recently developed, and he would sharpen his senses. A spark of insight triggered in his mind, but then the flashing ping of a location marker burned into his head across the span of many miles at his left.

Setting a recall marker here in Outpost Number 84 on his status page for whenever he wanted to return to this plane from whatever hell he was about to find himself in next, he motioned to his minions. "I apologize for the callousness, but we need to leave now."

His eyes met Genua's, where she was being held by Fay, and she sniffled with a nod while Athela finished up her patchwork repair of the blood god's clergy outfit.

"Riven." A feminine voice turned him around, and he saw Nora Lang in black leathers with dual-wielding blades on either hip. She folded her arms and displayed a notification screen of her own that matched his. "I don't mean to be nosy, but if you're traveling to that beacon out east—would you mind taking me along? It appears that Elysium may be pairing us up again, and I was hoping that we could enter the Abyssal Descent together."

Riven nodded, ignoring the stares of many of the townsfolk who'd gathered around nearby to watch or work on repairs. Some of them even glared his way, after having lost family members in the attack on the pub, but no one said anything or accused him of fault. Not that he'd necessarily blame them—he'd be upset, too, but he hadn't been the one to strike them down, either.

"Fine," Riven said nonchalantly, reaching out a hand to place on her shoulder. "We'll leave in a few minutes. Gragle?"

The scarred gnome, who'd been standing on the outskirts of the onlookers, came forward with a wary side-eye. "Yes?"

Riven held out his hand. "I expect you can continue to improve that totem for me while I'm gone? I'll pay well."

The gnome's eyes lit up with a gleeful expression, and he hastily nodded, grasping Riven's hand. "Of course! Of course. How long will you be gone?"

Riven shrugged, letting go of the gnome and folding his arms. "I don't know. I'll probably check in from time to time, because Elysium allowed me to set a recall point here in town, so probably not too long. Have you ever heard of the Abyssal Descent? That's where we're headed."

Immediately the eyes of numerous onlookers shot back to him, some gaping and others trying to mask ill-concealed jealousy.

Gragle just gawked. "You have an opportunity to acquire a ticket into the Abyssal Descent? Are you sure? Here? How is that even possible, while you're already inside another system event?"

Riven and Nora shared glances. "I don't really know . . . ? Elysium has taken pieces of all sorts from different areas across the multiverse to place here in this Apocalypse Beasts quest line, and I get the feeling there will likely be opportunities like this one scattered around from time to time. Why? Is it good?"

"Is it GOOD, he says?!" Gragle said, slack-jawed. He glared at the demonic minions and pointed a grubby finger at them in a hastily made gesture. "Have you not asked them?! Of COURSE it is a good opportunity! It is a road map for any F-grade being on the Unholy path to create a high-quality E-grade soul lattice! A soul lattice is required to ascend from F-grade into the E-grade and will determine your future potential growth! Doing it wrong means you grow slower, while creating a good one means you can progress through the E-grade far faster! I cannot believe you got such an opportunity in an integration phase such as this!"

Gragle sighed, shaking his head and rubbing his temples. "To think . . . Usually events such as this cost even the wealthiest of families tremendous amounts of money to acquire tickets from Elysium. Did the system at least make you BUY the tickets?"

Riven frowned more deeply. "No. I have to travel to a certain location to kill the ticket holders, or I have to barter for the tickets to acquire access when the portal opens in three hours. Same goes for Nora."

"THREE HOURS?!" The gnome gasped. "THEN WHAT ARE YOU WAITING FOR?! Riven, I don't know who or what you are to get such an opportunity, but despite who you may have to kill, you need to acquire those tickets! The path of cultivation is a long and hard one, and you cannot let an opportunity like this pass you by! Go, and go now! I will see you when you get back. And one more thing!"

Gragle held up a hand to stop Riven's departure, and he put on a silly grin. "Will you pay extra for duplicates of the upgraded totem you have provided for me?"

Riven raised an eyebrow from underneath his hood, red eyes glinting. "If you manage to duplicate that totem and make them better than what they are now, then yes. I'll pay very well for them."

"How much?" Gragle asked, grin growing wider. He stepped forward, eyes flicking about to make sure none of the onlookers could hear him while diving his voice into a whisper. "The materials alone will cost me quite a sum, and I'll have to substitute for things that aren't available here at an increased cost from the shops in town. No doubt they'll become even more expensive as scavengers realize this new landscape doesn't have the same types of materials available, and until our identifiers are able to make out what new materials are actually usable in totem-crafting. Perhaps a small fee of one hundred thousand F-grade Elysium coins per totem?"

Riven lifted an eyebrow.

"For labor as well, including my integration of graphics to each!" Gragle pressed more hesitantly. "I know it seems like a lot, but you won't find almost anyone on any given planet capable of producing graphics like I can!"

Catching Athela's nod, Riven let out a sigh and looked into his spatial sack to see just what the current number was at after all his battles and looting over the past nine months. All the monsters he and his minions had slain, the dungeons raided, the enemies killed—all the coins he'd collected during that time.

It amounted to a staggering twenty-two million.

His eyes lifted, and after mentally selecting three hundred thousand coins, to his surprise, the sum came up as a small disc rather than a pile of money, with the number etched into the platinum surface.

That was odd.

Gragle's eyes bulged and he quickly took the disc, stuffing it into his own spatial sack like a mantis strike while rubbing his hands together eagerly. "This will do! I'll have three prepared for you within a few weeks. Come back then, and we can talk more business!"

Riven gave him a thumbs-up, then turned to Genua. "We're leaving. Genua, use Body Fusion to merge with Fay so the flight there isn't inhibited by needing to carry you. We'll talk more after we arrive."

A mile-wide platform of black metal floated far above the ground, just over the peak of a mountain, where three individuals stood around a system-made warp gate that was just now beginning to light up with energy. The circular structure was made of Unholy mana rather that anything physical, but the runes inscribed into its perimeter were a dark-green color rather than the darker backdrop.

Gentry's guard was up, his face just as sour as the rest of the ticket holders' while they waited for the portal to open. There was only twenty minutes left before the portal into the Abyssal Descent opened, and given Elysium's updates, they'd be able to go back home to the Narwali sector if none of these integration-stage idiots showed up.

He could only hope they didn't come. His family, despite being a major noble house of his kingdom, had used up their entire savings and political favors to garner one of these tickets—an investment in his future as the heir of their estate. He was confident in his abilities to fight, but then again, so was any potential candidate who entered the descent. You had to be, or you were a fool for even trying, and not one single candidate who was given an opportunity to descend was a pushover.

Lacing a hand through his long white hair and letting out a long breath he didn't know he'd been holding in, his drow features scrunched up when he caught sight of something bursting through the clouds on the horizon. His hand came down to rest on the intricate jade scimitar on his hip—while his gold-trimmed, dark-blue cultivator's robes swirled around him amid a surge of chaos energy.

His counterparts, two other drow men of even higher standing than himself, drew out their own blades and summoned protective jade armors to await the arrival of whatever was coming.

And as the clouds distorted like ripples on a pond, the sky split with a crack of power as a figure flashed forward with a burst of momentum.

The black platform rocked underneath the impact, sending up a cloud of metal shrapnel that left a trench behind the man until he came to a stop. Gentry's purple eyes widened slightly as he took the man in, and his grip around the scimitar at his waist only grew more firm.

This man was still supposed to be in F-grade if he wanted to enter the descent, so why was there so much energy fluctuating around him? This kind of power was only supposed to be felt well into the E-grade, and yet . . .

Gentry absentmindedly gulped and took a step back. "Just what kind of integration-phase planet has a participant like this?"

Ahead of him, the man blazing with the power of hellfire tore himself out of the self-made crater. Writhing ribbons of blood and shadow interrupted the outpouring of flames as well, with a vertical maw splitting the chest plating of his armor and two large horned pauldrons on either shoulder. Red-and-black eyes peered back at the three men near the portal one at a time, before a third vertical eye of purple light ripped open across his forehead to glare out with even greater intensity.

The two other drow didn't even give the newcomer time to speak before they dashed ahead, blurring forward with tremendous speed as they activated protective sigils along their intricate jade armors and utilized speed-enhancing abilities to clear the distance.

A jade claymore sparking with chaos swung down from the left, and a jade spear encased in blood rippled through the air with a sonic boom toward the newcomer's throat.

Gentry watched, and his eyes went wider when the man's body vanished only to appear ten steps ahead of him through a rip in space. With speed that defied the laws of physics, his own spear-staff lunged forward to take the spear-wielder in the chest.

The man's jade armor cracked and he was sent sprawling across the platform in a tumble of curses before the other drow scion flashed forward again with the visage of a towering demon at his back. Hellfire engulfed his body and he swung his sword down, the visage of the winged demon following his motion with a roar as magma and flame were sent out in a vertical wave that caused the air to hiss due to the heat.

The wave smashed against a wall of crimson ice, then crashed through it only to meet the snapping jaws of a red jackal that crashed down onto the attack in an instant. The spell was dispersed, and through the shock wave the three-eyed man burst forward with his rippling black weapon pointed at the drow warrior.

Three consecutive strikes quickly connected between spear-staff and claymore as the drow scion batted the attacks aside, only for hundreds of spinning blades made from black-red energies to bloom in the air around him. In an instant, they crashed into the jade armor protecting his body in a cacophony of tearing, lurching attacks that sent sprays of blood in all directions.

It was akin to watching an animal go through a meat grinder, and the splattered remnants of the drow warrior hit the floor as the burning man turned to Gentry with narrowed eyes.

They stared at each other wordlessly, Gentry's hand gripping the handle of his scimitar as he took even, steady breaths despite the building fear he felt, and he let out a sigh of relief when the other man turned around to retrieve a flashing, glowing tablet that hovered over the other scion's body.

"So this is the ticket . . ." the armored man said from underneath his hooded helmet, casually turning it around in his hand. He turned back to Gentry, and then to the other remaining scion, who had a deep gash in the chest plate of his jade armor. "I'll be needing one more."

Farther up in the clouds, two more figures slowly descended toward the platform above the mountain's peak. One was a woman who wore the same style and make of hood as the first man, clad in dark leathers and wielding two thin blades in either hand as she was set down by the third figure. This third figure in turn was some kind of demon, probably a succubus—and she was carrying the other woman down on their descent.

Blue skin was splattered with patches of tanned white, like the spots of a cow, with eyes that had two sets of irises—one black and one red in each eyeball set side by side. Circlets of swirling blood divinity encased her ankles, wrists, and neck, while two black horns sprouted out of her head near pointed ears. A long, slender black tail was also present, alongside a pair of demonic black wings, with flowing white and blond hair that was mixed and matched like she'd dyed it to be that way. Otherwise she wore a purple witch's hat, along with feathered boots and a purple skirt that showed off her thighs.

And when the demonic woman spoke, her voice sounded like it was overlaid by two voices speaking at once. "This form is rather nice. We may stay this way for some time—it would help in our own insights while here. Two minds working together are better than one."

Pulling out a book that flared with abnormally potent Unholy energies, the woman started flipping through the pages—and Gentry palmed a family artifact in his pocket that worked the same way an identifier's class would to a lesser extent. His breath caught in his chest when he began to identify it out of curiosity's sake.

[Viper Grimoire of Curses and Schemes (Unholy Specialization Grimoire, Unique): +129% mana regeneration when held. +9% damage to all curses when held. By binding this grimoire and adding a single one of your curses to its pages, you will decrease the cooldown time on your chosen curse by 10% while simultaneously allowing for spontaneous evolution options of that curse with insights drawn from the Unholy Foundational Pillar and its related subpillars. Spontaneous evolutions will occur as the grimoire actively writes out different variations of the curse across its pages with random trial and error experiments in an internal, limited plane. Evolution options will occur in the form of insights once a breakthrough is made.]

Gentry blinked away his growing greed and surprise, then began to identify each of them in turn. What he saw made him very curious and simultaneously stumped. He didn't know whether to laugh or to be afraid. Should he attack and take the grimoire for himself? Finding such a treasure was a boon that he shouldn't pass up, and he had no doubt after giving a sideways glance that the other drow scion was no doubt thinking the exact same thing.

[???, Level 56 Succubus–High Elf Chimera, Thrall Priestess of the Blood God.]
[Nora Lang, Level 113, Shadow Blade Duelist. ??? Elite]

Levels 56 and 113? What in Elysium's name were these two doing—attempting to get into the descent? They'd be destroyed mercilessly! The thought was actually laughable!

A wide smirk set upon his face, and relief swept over him. But when he finally took time to identify the flaming man who'd demanded another ticket, Gentry's plans of potentially taking the grimoire by force quickly died in his guts. His hands began to shake, and he visibly paled—stepping back involuntarily as his breaths became quick and short.

[???, Level 200 ???, ???, Pureblooded Vampire, ???. MYTHIC. ???.]

The burning purple flames of the man's MYTHIC status made Gentry want to vomit, and he literally began to feel sick. Nearly everyone entering the descent was considered at least ELITE by the system. It was even expected. Occasionally some of the greatest scions of the multiverse would send LEGENDARY-tier offspring into the descent as well, but most often they had artifacts or Dao treasures to hide their LEGENDARY tag and affiliated red flames entirely so they weren't targeted or mobbed by groups that worked together to secure higher footholds on the descent's progress ladder. However, Gentry had only heard of the MYTHIC tag in old stories. He hadn't even thought it to be real, much less to see one in person here, and now coming from an integration world, of all places. If it HAD been real, he'd have expected it to come from one of the ruling clans of the multiverse rather than see it here.

Just what kind of monster was he looking at, to have acquired the kind of raw power and potential for such a label by Elysium?

Fortunately for Gentry, though, the other drow either didn't have an identifying artifact of high enough quality that could identify this man as a MYTHIC-tagged individual—or he hadn't bothered to do so after seeing the quality of the grimoire the succubus hybrid had in hand. Greed took hold of the young scion as he vanished entirely, only to have afterimages numbering in the dozens rush the vampire as his true body appeared right next to the demon.

Gentry could only watch in awe as a giant black maw full of teeth opened up behind the jade-covered drow, pulling the screaming man in with tendrils of sin before snapping shut and crunching down on the man's midsection in a spray of blood.

ABOUT THE AUTHOR

Ranyhin1 is the pen name of Trent Boehm, author of Elysium's Multiverse, an apocalypse LitRPG he originally released on Royal Road. A lifelong lover of fantasy, Boehm is also a science nerd, Dallas Cowboys fan, and wannabe gym rat. He hopes one day to pursue writing full-time.

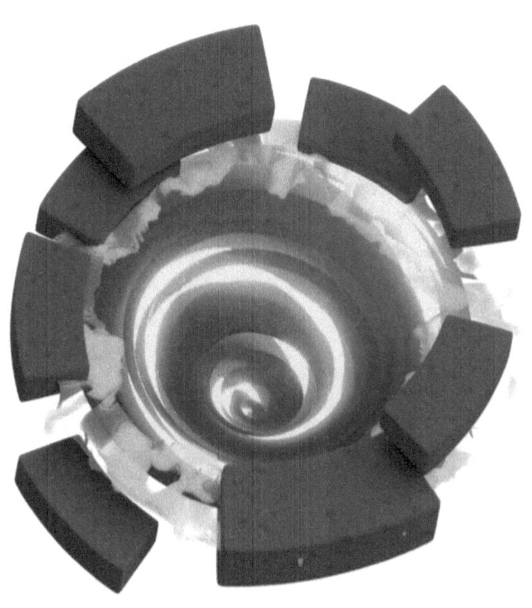

RESPAWN YOUR CURIOSITY

follow us on our socials

 podiumentertainment.com

 @podiumentertainment

 /podiumentertainment

 @podium_ent

 @podiumentertainment